A
Season
of
Harvest

Books by Lauraine Snelling

LEAH'S GARDEN

The Seeds of Change
A Time to Bloom
Fields of Bounty
A Season of Harvest

UNDER NORTHERN SKIES

The Promise of Dawn
A Breath of Hope
A Season of Grace
A Song of Joy

SONG OF BLESSING

To Everything a Season
A Harvest of Hope
Streams of Mercy
From This Day Forward

RED RIVER OF THE NORTH

An Untamed Land
A New Day Rising
A Land to Call Home
The Reapers' Song
Tender Mercies
Blessing in Disguise

RETURN TO RED RIVER

A Dream to Follow
Believing the Dream
More Than a Dream

DAUGHTERS OF BLESSING

A Promise for Ellie
Sophie's Dilemma
A Touch of Grace
Rebecca's Reward

HOME TO BLESSING

A Measure of Mercy
No Distance Too Far
A Heart for Home

WILD WEST WIND

Valley of Dreams
Whispers in the Wind
A Place to Belong

DAKOTAH TREASURES

Ruby • Pearl
Opal • Amethyst

SECRET REFUGE

Daughter of Twin Oaks
Sisters of the Confederacy
The Long Way Home

A Blessing to Cherish
An Untamed Heart

A
Season
of
Harvest

LAURAINE
SNELLING

with **Kiersti Giron**

BETHANYHOUSE

a division of Baker Publishing Group
Minneapolis, Minnesota

Published by Bethany House Publishers
Minneapolis, Minnesota
www.bethanyhouse.com

Bethany House Publishers is a division of
Baker Publishing Group, Grand Rapids, Michigan

Printed in the United States of America

Library of Congress Cataloging-in-Publication Data
Names: Snelling, Lauraine, author.
Title: A season of harvest / Lauraine Snelling.
Description: Minneapolis, Minnesota : Bethany House, a division of Baker Publishing
    Group, 2024. | Series: Leah's Garden ; 4
Identifiers: LCCN 2023033540 | ISBN 9780764235788 (paper) | ISBN 9780764235795
    (cloth) | ISBN 9780764235801 (large print) | ISBN 9781493443635 (ebook)
Subjects: LCGFT: Christian fiction. | Novels.
Classification: LCC PS3569.N39 S35 2024 | DDC 813/.54—dc23/eng/20230724
LC record available at https://lccn.loc.gov/2023033540

Scripture quotations are from the King James Version of the Bible.

This is a work of historical reconstruction; the appearances of certain historical figures are therefore inevitable. All other characters, however, are products of the author's imagination, and any resemblance to actual persons, living or dead, is coincidental.

Cover design by Dan Thornberg, Design Source Creative Services

Published in association with Books & Such Literary Management, www.booksandsuch .com

Baker Publishing Group publications use paper produced from sustainable forestry practices and post-consumer waste whenever possible.

24 25 26 27 28 29 30   7 6 5 4 3 2 1

To Wendy Lawton.

Wendy is one of the most creative
people I know, in so many ways.
Her marvelous business sense is put
to good use as an agent,
where she blesses us all through
her skills and encouragement.
The LEAH'S GARDEN series would not be
what it is without Wendy.

Larkspur

The name larkspur first appeared in a sixteenth-century book of plants, and it references the flower's resemblance to the claw of a lark. A relative of delphinium, larkspur adds grace to summer gardens with its airy blue spires.

Larkspur attracts hummingbirds and butterflies and is a hardy, self-seeding annual. Traditionally, larkspur symbolizes an open heart, a positive spirit, and strong bonds of love.

1

Make sure you send me a telegram when you get to Linksburg."

"Larkspur Grace Neilsen, what has come over you?" Lilac stared, or, more accurately, glared, at her sister. "You're not usually such a fussy mother hen."

"I've not sent my baby sister off on a train alone before." Lark forced a smile that used her mouth but didn't make it to her eyes. With a half shrug, she added, "Not that this is an everyday occurrence. You have your basket of food?"

Lilac nodded and looked toward the train engine when the whistle blew.

"Ah'll watch out for her, Miss Lark. Don' you go worryin' 'bout her," Arthur Palmer, a conductor who had been with the railroad ever since it came through Salton, reassured her. Jonah, their younger brother, often swapped stories with him.

"Thank you, Mr. Palmer. Jonah said you were the best part of his last trip and that you have more stories than a library."

"Thank 'ee, ma'am." He held out his hand to help Lilac aboard. "Don' want to get left at the station."

Lark hugged her sister one more time and stepped back,

7

waving as soon as she saw Lilac seating herself by a window. Palmer swung the iron steps back up on the train and stepped aboard. He leaned out the open door and waved to the engineer that all was well.

Sniffing and failing at blinking the tears back, Lark waved until the train disappeared over the horizon and she was the only one still on the platform.

Prince, her favorite of the team, snorted from the hitching rail.

Lark walked back to him and patted his gray neck. "Getting impatient, eh? Sorry."

She unsnapped the lead line from the railing and climbed up in the trap. "You can have a drink at Sythia's."

In her mind, she ran through her list of things to do today till they pulled up at the Brownsville house. At the water tank near the windmill, Prince drank until he heard Robbie calling. He raised his head, letting water drip from his lips back into the tank. Laughing, Lark turned him around to the hitching rail.

"I thought you forgot me!" Robbie, who seemed to grow an inch between the times Lark saw him, stroked Prince's nose and discreetly slipped him a cookie. The crunching was a noisy giveaway.

"What would your ma say?"

Robbie rolled his eyes. "Uh, have another cookie?" He patted Prince as he flipped the lead over the rail.

Half giggling, Lark climbed down in time to be broadsided by a hug. "I said I would be back after Lilac left on the train."

"I know. I have my things all ready. Do I really get to stay until Saturday?"

"Or maybe Sunday so we don't have to make another trip to town." She lifted a basket of eggs from behind the seat on the trap. "Where's Sofie?"

"Taking a nap. Ma said she was being a grump." Together they climbed the steps to the back door.

Robbie put his forefinger to his lips. "Shhh, don't want to wake Grump."

"And Mikael?"

"Napping, and Ma is feeding Nils Peter."

Lark set the basket of eggs on the table and followed Robbie into the parlor, where her sister Forsythia was just buttoning up her bodice with the baby now lying sound asleep on the sofa beside her. She and Robbie each carried in a chair to use as a barrier so Nils didn't fall off.

"He sure is growing fast." Lark gazed down at the infant sleeping with one little fist against his cheek.

"He should be. I have to be careful not to call him a little pig because Sofie keeps reminding me he is not a pig but a baby. Even if he eats and grows as fast as a piglet. He even snorts when he nurses." Forsythia stretched her arms over her head and yawned. "You have time for coffee?"

Lark glanced at Robbie, whose happy face had sunk into unhappy. "I would love some, but I hear the hoes calling our names. Del is probably already out hoeing. I warned her to be careful, but you know how little good that does. Think she knows she's due to have a baby soon?"

"Perhaps she's related to someone else we know." Forsythia's eyebrows arched. She reached down and hugged her eldest son. "Now, I know you'll be so busy you have no time to think of home, but we shall miss you and see you on Sunday."

"I could stay longer," he offered. "They really need help at the farm."

"I know they do, but you are needed here too. Sofie and Mikael both depend on you."

He huffed a sigh and picked up his bag, giving Lark a plaintive *please let's go* look. "I'll put this in the trap."

"He's right, you know, about us needing help at the farm," Lark said. "Have you found someone to help you here?"

"Tilda, though I sent her over to help Climie for a while.

Robbie's been over hoeing the boardinghouse garden too. He and Klaus really hit it off and have been helping together when his mother brings him along. Why do you suppose it is always more fun to help others than do the same work at home?"

"Human child trait? Right now our garden is in pretty good shape."

The sisters hugged, and Lark waved good-bye as she joined Robbie at the trap. "We have supplies to pick up at the mercantile, then Del will have dinner ready for us."

Robbie climbed in with a sigh. When they stopped at the shaded side of the store, he knotted the lead over the hitching bar.

"Thank you." Lark ruffled his hair. This boy sure was growing up.

Lark had left a list on her way to the train station, so they had all her supplies ready and loaded in no time. They both climbed into the trap, and Lark turned Prince toward home.

"Lilac left on the train, huh? Were you scared?" Robbie asked.

Lark thought a moment. He was mighty perceptive for so young a boy. "No, not scared, more sad, I think. I miss her already."

"Me too. But I can do most of her chores."

Ah, Robbie, if you only knew. His coming out to the farm was indeed a godsend. She would not be all alone. She'd been dreading that when Lilac was getting ready to marry Rev. Pritchard last spring. She was ashamed she'd felt such relief when her sister broke off the engagement. But after helping their older brother, Anders, reopen the family mercantile back in Ohio, Lilac would be returning in a few weeks. Their younger brother, Jonah, with her.

"Look, Scamp is coming to meet us." Robbie pointed ahead with a grin. "Did you tell him I was coming?"

"I might have. We'll take the supplies to the barn and the house and you can let Prince out in the field."

Scamp jumped up into the trap and onto Robbie's lap before he could get down, making the boy giggle and Lark shake her head. She retrieved the supplies for the house and motioned Robbie to lead the horse down to the barn. With the trap emptied, she lifted off the harness, and Robbie took Prince to the pasture gate. Starbright and Rose waited at the fence, the mare whuffling her welcome to her favorite boy. He dug two cookies out of his pocket and gave one to each.

"Watch your fingers. Rose forgets to be careful at times."

Robbie nodded and scratched Starbright's nose and ears.

Scamp woofed when they heard the clang of Del's triangle, letting them know dinner was ready.

"Race you." Robbie tore off past the house and on to Del's, Scamp yipping around his feet.

Lark laughed as she followed them. Robbie had healed so much since he became part of their family. To God be the glory, that was for sure.

Del grinned at Lark while hugging Robbie, the bulk of her belly between them. "I was beginning to think you forgot the way home."

"No chance, Robbie would have taken over." She set her straw hat on the hat rack and washed her hands at the sink. "Oh my, but it smells good in here. What are you making?"

"Rabbit stew thanks to Lilac's trapping skills."

Robbie pushed his chair closer to the table. "I can check them for you tomorrow. Tante Lilac taught me how to trap too."

"Aren't you kinda young for that?" Del stared at him as she set his plate down.

Robbie shrugged. "Tante Lilac said I could do so. Scamp'll go with me."

The two sisters swapped looks and bowed their heads.

"Thank you, Jesus for food, for fun, and help me 'n' Scamp trap rabbits. Amen. Oh, and, Lord, please make Sofie not such a grump." Robbie opened his eyes and grinned. "Tante Del, you made fried bread. That's my favorite."

"I know." She took the basket from the warming oven and set it on the table.

"And you made syrup for dunking." He took a piece from the basket and started to dunk it in the syrup but stopped. "All together." Laughing, they all dunked and popped the treats into their mouths. Robbie's chortling was contagious.

As soon as they were done eating, Robbie slid off his chair, thanking Del as he set his plate in the dishpan on the reservoir. "Are the hoes in the garden?"

"Hooked over the fence," Del said. "You can start where I stopped there in the carrots."

"I will" trailed over his shoulder as he charged out the door.

Lark shrugged. "He takes gardening seriously."

"What about him out trapping? Could you go with him just to ease my mind?"

"I will."

Del soused her plate in the soapy hot water. "I'll take care of this, you go on outside. I'll join you soon."

A couple of hours of weeding later, Lark sent Del inside to lie down for a while, and she and Robbie sat down in the shade with a swizzle. "I hope we don't run out of vinegar to make this." She hoisted her glass. "So refreshing."

Robbie held up a cookie. "These too."

"You can go play with Rose and the new calf while I water the garden. Be careful to lock the gate. Starbright has figured out how to open it."

"Thank you." Robbie slapped his thigh, and Scamp raced him to the farmhouse.

A few moments later, Starbright nickered a welcome, and Lark figured Robbie went to the barn and brought back oats in the can kept for scooping grain out of the bin. She hooked the hoe on the rail fence and, after pulling up a stem of grass to chew on, ambled down the path. She pumped water in the bucket at the windmill, which was silent with no wind.

"Come on, Rosie-Posie," Robbie called, his special name for the filly. Lark watched as he ran out into the pasture. Starbright trotted after him, tossing her head and snorting, Rose by her side. Scamp ran circles around them, as if he were herding. He managed the flock of sheep, driving them back to the corral every evening as the sun slid toward the horizon.

The next day, after a morning of picking strawberries, Lark sent Robbie over to help Del wash and stem them at her house. She had a bigger kitchen, and it made a good excuse to get her sister to sit down for a while.

Meanwhile, Lark gathered nails, wire, and tools, then pulled on the men's work gloves she'd ordered from the mercantile and strode out to the pasture. One corner of the fence had needed attention for a while. Examining the spot, she let out a whistle. The sheep must have been rubbing against it, several damaged boards had nearly come loose. Good thing she'd thought to do the mending now, or they'd have had escaped livestock to wrangle.

And how would I manage that without Lilac or Jonah? Del can't chase sheep in her condition. Lark chuckled at the image that popped into her head. Now, that would be a picture Lilac would love to draw.

Lark found a few extra planks in the machine shed and settled to her task, falling into the rhythm of the familiar labor. She stripped away the rotten boards, assessed what could still be used, and cut the new planks to fit. After some time, she lifted her head at the sound of footsteps. Had RJ come home early?

No, that was Isaac McTavish's rugged silhouette, ragged army uniform and all. Did the man intend to wear those clothes till they fell apart at the seams?

Lark stood to be seen above the tall grasses about her. "Hello, stranger."

"Stranger is it, Miss Larkspur?" Isaac slipped off his cap, his movements as easy as the mountain cadence on his tongue. "Reckoned we'd got past that by now."

"Well, one never quite knows whether you're here for good or will be off on the next train." Lark bit her tongue at the tease she heard in her own voice. Was she flirting with Isaac? Her neck heated at the thought.

But his face sobered. "Reckon I deserve that. But I aim to set a stop on my driftin' ways. Start puttin' down roots, as it were."

"Really? Is some of your family still moving to Salton?" He'd said something about that last winter, but so much had happened since then.

He hesitated, turned his worn army cap in his hands, then met her gaze. "Among other things."

Lark's heart started pit-a-patting oddly, as if trying to beat its way up her throat. "What brings you out this way today?"

"Saw RJ in town. He said might be you could use some help out on the farm today with most of your family away."

Was RJ trying to play matchmaker? Or did he just think she couldn't handle things on her own? Lark frowned, oddly nettled, and bent back to the fence. "I'm fine."

Isaac chuckled and hooked his hat over a sturdy post of the fence. "Easy now. Weren't no one meanin' you can't handle this here farm on your own. Can't abide any offers of help, is that it? Or only from me?"

He'd matched her thoughts so nearly, Lark stared at him a moment, then shook her head and half laughed at herself. "Sorry. You can hold this rail for me while I fasten it back in place."

"At your service, ma'am." Isaac gave a courtly bow, sweeping low his mane of shoulder-length hair, the same sandy brown as his beard.

A smile tugging at her cheeks, Lark held the peg steady with gloved fingers and hammered the railing firm. Isaac moved down the fence with her, replacing a board here and tightening a connection there. He said little, yet seemed able to anticipate her steps without being in the way. A trait her siblings could do to imitate, at times.

"There." The fence secure at last, Lark arched her back against a kink from bending over so long. "That should hold. Thanks for the help."

"Anythin' else that could use seein' to while I'm here?" Isaac scanned the fields around them, then glanced at Lark with quirked brow. "Not that you need my help, mind."

"Can't think of anything right now. Will you stay for supper?"

"Climie's expectin' me back at the boardin' house, told her I'd see about settin' a loose chair leg to rights. But thank you kindly. Maybe another time?" He held her gaze a moment, gray eyes steady and questioning.

"Of course." Lark tried to smile naturally—after all, Isaac had supped at their table many a time these last several years. Yet lately something felt different. . . .

"Then I'll be seein' you." He dipped his head, then clapped his army cap back on. He ambled off across the prairie, heading back toward Salton.

So many times she'd seen Isaac leave . . . and come back. Then leave again. They'd accepted his intermittent presence as a part of their lives in Nebraska and never asked or expected much of him, though when around he always lent a hand to all.

Yet just now, working alongside him with barely a word needed between them, she'd known a grounding in his presence, an easy rhythm that drew her . . . and scared her.

2

Lilac peered out the train window again, marveling at the speed of the flashing landscape. After a full day's travel yesterday, she'd finally gotten used to the constant rattle of the train car but not the wonder of it.

"How're you likin' your first time on the railroad, young lady?" Mr. Palmer paused by her seat with a fatherly wink.

"It's . . . wonderful." Lilac shook her head. "When I think how many weeks it took us to travel this distance by wagon just a few years ago, I can hardly believe it."

"Me neither, and I ride these rails ever' day." He chuckled and touched the visor of his conductor's cap with a finger. "You let me know if you need anythin', now."

"I will."

Mr. Palmer moved on down the aisle between the seats, his legs as sure with their rolling gait as any sailor riding the seas.

Lilac's stomach rumbled, and she dug through the basket on the seat beside her, packed full by Del so she wouldn't have to spend much on food at the train stops. Fare available there could be dubious, not to mention expensive. She pulled out a cheese sandwich and a handful of cherries for her lunch, bowed her head for grace, then popped a bright cherry into her mouth.

Lilac closed her eyes at the explosion of sweetness. Though warm from the train ride, the juicy fruit still refreshed. It was always a treat to have fresh fruit again after the last wrinkly winter apples had been eaten, and cherries were among the first to ripen in Nebraska. The Jorgensens had several trees, and they were gracious to share and barter, even selling basketsful in their mercantile.

Stuffy heat built inside the train car, and Lilac pushed up her window, though the hot, sooty wind wasn't much better. Hard to believe that tomorrow she'd be back in Ohio. Back in the town where she'd spent her whole life, up until three years ago. Had it only been three years? So much had happened . . . building a homestead, starting their Leah's Garden seed business in honor of their mother, not to mention a boardinghouse. Forsythia and Del getting married—and Lilac herself almost getting married. She didn't doubt she was right to break off the engagement, but what did the future hold for her now?

Perhaps this visit back to Ohio would ground her a bit. And Anders should have at least one of his sisters there to support him and Josephine in the grand reopening of the rebuilt store.

The next morning, she stepped off the train, her traveling dress heavy with cinders and perspiration. She squeezed Mr. Palmer's hand after he helped her down.

"Thank you so much. You made my first train trip a memorable one."

"Always happy to oblige." He handed over her carpetbag. "You got everythin'?"

Lilac nodded, taking her carpetbag in one hand and basket in the other. "I'm only staying a few weeks."

"Lilac!"

She turned at the call to see Anders hurrying toward her, a grin splitting his face. She ran to meet him faster than was ladylike, then dropped her baggage to throw her arms around her big brother.

"I can't believe I'm really here."

"Well, we're sure glad you are." Anders stepped back and nodded to his approaching wife, one little girl clinging to her hand and a younger toddler in her arms. "Come meet your nieces."

Lilac crouched to the two-year-old's level. "Hello, Marcella. I'm your Tante Lilac."

The blond-curled little one studied her, a finger in her mouth.

"Say hello." Josephine gave her daughter a gentle nudge.

Marcella tugged the finger out and waggled her hand.

"We'll have lots of time to get to know each other." Lilac smiled at her niece and stood. "Josephine, so good to see you." She embraced her sister-in-law, then ran her hand over the darker curls of the child in her arms. "And this must be Greta."

The toddler bounced on her mother's hip and grinned at Lilac.

Josephine laughed. "We think she resembles you—both in looks and personality."

"Well, I take that as a high compliment." Lilac drew a long breath and scanned the bustling, treelined streets, so familiar yet foreign. She shook her head. "It feels so strange being back."

"Well, let's get you home." Anders grabbed her bag. "Mr. Holt is joining us for supper tonight."

"Mr. Holt?" Lilac's heart gave a glad leap. "What a treat to see him right off. But where's Jonah?" She glanced around, memories stealing her joy. All the times her younger brother had run off in the years before they moved to Nebraska tripped through her mind. The saloon, the gambling table . . .

"He stayed working at the store while we came to get you." Anders tipped his head for her to follow. "Don't worry, we'll stop by there on our way home. He's as eager to see you as we were."

"Oh good." Lilac's heart settled back. Of course he was. Jonah had turned over a new leaf these last couple of years, as they'd seen when he came to work on their homestead for some months last fall. Being here just brought back all the memories, good and bad.

That evening felt nearly like being back home before everything had happened. They sat around their parents' beloved old dining room table again, Anders at the head, with the children's babble, Mr. Holt's gentle good humor, and Jonah's droll imitations of various customers making them all laugh near to tears.

Lilac finished her last bite of mashed potatoes and glanced at the papered walls, as familiar as her mother's woven napkin in her lap. "Almost feels like I never left. I keep expecting to hear Lark's voice coming in from outside. Or Ma and Pa's." Her throat tightened. It had been a long time since she'd missed them this much.

Josephine reached under the table to squeeze her hand. "We're so glad you're here."

Lilac smiled at her sister-in-law. "Me too." She looked to Mr. Holt. "Hard to believe it's been three years since you hid Lark at your place in the wee hours of the morning." This good man had stepped in to help them after witnessing Lark's besting of a crack gambler in a game of poker, all in trying to save Jonah from a sticky situation. Deacon Wiesel had shown up long before dawn that same night, making drunken threats. A chill ran down her arms at the memory.

Mr. Holt shook his head and wiped his gray mustache with his napkin. "And now the deacon has gone on to his just reward, and that Ringwald feller doesn't seem to be doing too good either, lost a lot of weight. Folks say he's got some sort of illness eatin' him alive."

"Ringwald is *here*?" Lilac nearly dropped her buttered roll. The gambler's threats against Lark had combined with those of the deacon to send them packing for Nebraska in the first place. But they'd thought he left town.

Anders glanced between Mr. Holt and Josephine. "We've heard he's back in town, but I haven't seen him yet."

Jonah stared at his empty plate.

"As Mr. Holt said, it sounds like he is unwell. So I doubt he'll cause much trouble." Josephine wiped Greta's face and rose. "Dessert, anyone?"

Lilac shook her head, the news still pounding in her temples. Slate Ringwald was back in Linksburg just as she reappeared from Nebraska—after they'd fought so hard to conceal any traces of where the Nielsen sisters had gone.

Maybe she shouldn't have come at all.

"What can I do to help with the grand reopening?" Lilac stepped into the kitchen Monday morning and breathed in the smell of the biscuits Josephine was taking out of the oven. After attending church with her family yesterday in the old familiar building, she felt a bit steadier and ready to dive in—though she was glad they'd left church before too many familiar faces started asking questions.

At the kitchen table, Marcella was eating a biscuit in tiny bites, while Greta, in her high chair, seemed more interested in strewing crumbs as far as she could.

"Anders is already over at the new building." Josephine popped the hot biscuits into a basket with quick fingers. "You could go over after breakfast and see what he needs. One thing we could definitely use is some nice signs. Anders and Jonah were going to do it, but I'm afraid they haven't an artistic bone between them."

Lilac laughed. "I'd be glad to make signs. What should I use to make them?"

"I think we've got some old signs stored up in the attic. You could check up there, then just sand them down and repaint, if you don't mind. Anders should have plenty of paint over at the store." Josephine lifted the lids off two pans on the stove. "There's bacon and fried potatoes to go with the biscuits and coffee. Mind helping yourself? I need to see to the girls."

"Of course. Sounds like a feast." Lilac fetched a plate from the cupboard and filled it, then sat down with her nieces and sister-in-law. She bowed her head for grace, a fresh wind of gratitude lifting her heart. *Thank you, Father, for this new day, for family and good food, and for how faithful you have been every day of our lives. Forgive me for my fears.*

After breakfast, she headed upstairs to the attic before the day's heat set in. Pausing at the top of the narrow stairs, she breathed in the familiar scent of dust, dried lavender, and time. A smile tugged as she spied their old rocking horse in the corner, dusty but carefully preserved. She stepped over boxes to pat the horse's dappled gray neck. "Soon Marcella and Greta will be big enough to ride you, old fellow." So many memories.

She found the signs Josephine had spoken of, seasonal ones they'd once used to advertise spring planting sales or summer produce at the store. Lilac tucked them by the stairs, then moseyed around the attic a bit more, not ready to leave. She found one of their mother's old hatboxes and lifted the lid, brushing her fingers over the faded green silk poke bonnet. "Ma," she whispered, tears softening her tongue. "I miss you so much." And there—the trunk where their mother had kept some of her old finery from when she lived back east before she came to Ohio to marry Pa. Lilac and her sisters spent many a happy rainy day in the attic playing dress-up in the old gowns and gloves.

She knelt in a burst of nostalgia and opened the trunk. There lay that same old purple velvet spencer jacket and lace fan she'd loved to wear to their imaginary balls. And the yellow silk slippers Forsythia had favored.

Some old books had been tucked in among the clothes now too. She lifted a simple brown leather volume from beneath a pair of lace gloves. Could this be something of Ma's? She didn't recognize it.

She opened the cover gingerly, the aged leather flaking beneath her fingers, and turned the fragile pages. She stopped at the first entry, penned lines so faint now she had to peer close to read them.

Juli 1825

Lilac sat up straight. That was *July* in Norwegian, if she remembered correctly. And 1825? Over forty years ago. This wasn't one of her parents' diaries. They'd been small children then. And if it was written in Norwegian, which a glance at the page below the date told her it was . . . She turned to the flyleaf of the little book: *Cornelius Nielsen*.

Her grandfather, who had died too soon for Lilac to even remember him. A thrill ran down her arms. Was this his diary from journeying to America? She thought back to what she knew of the dates. It could be. How had they never found it before? And how had it ended up in Ma's trunk?

She turned the delicate pages, wishing she could read them. Neither she nor her siblings could read Norwegian well. Who could they ask to decipher the stories held in the leatherbound volume?

She halted at another page, which held not words but a drawing. A skillful sketch of a small sloop on the sea, sails filled. The ship slanted bravely into the wind, courage in each line and mast.

Hadn't her father said she got her artistic talent from her grandfather? Lilac's skin prickled again. She'd never seen any of his work before.

She kept turning pages, finding more drawings. A welcoming harbor, families standing hopeful at the railing of a ship, a log cabin half built. Children playing in a garden—her father and his siblings?

"Lilac?"

Josephine's call up the stairs made her jump.

"Did you find the signs?"

Lilac closed the journal and trunk and stood. "I did." She grabbed the signs from by the stairs, the journal tucked safely under her arm. She lifted her skirts and stepped carefully back down the narrow stairs. "And you'll never guess what else I found."

After showing the journal to Josephine, Lilac headed down the street toward the new store, rebuilt on the same site of their father's original mercantile before it burned to the ground last fall. She couldn't wait to tell her brothers.

She mounted the steps of the broad wooden porch, still smelling of new-cut wood and fresh paint, and poked her head inside the open door. "Anders?"

"Back here" came his call, apparently from the storage room behind the counter. A similar layout to the original store, that helped.

Lilac made her way through the store, glancing along walls and shelves ready to fill with goods. Some barrels and boxes of tools and supplies already lined the aisles. She headed behind the counter and into the storage room, a larger space than in the old building. "There you are."

Both her brothers looked up from stacking crates of supplies.

"Just got the big shipment we've been waiting for." Jonah hefted another crate. "Now we can really start to stock the store."

"That's wonderful." Lilac peeked into an open box of button shoes. "You'll have to put a lock on the door now." Her middle jumped from wanting to spill her news. Maybe they wouldn't be as excited about the journal as she was, but it was still quite a find.

"Planning on it." Anders knelt to pry a crate open. "I thought I heard a clink in here, want to make sure no jars are broken."

"Well, I came to be put to work. Josephine said you could use some signs for the grand reopening. But first, look what I found in the attic." She pulled out the journal from her handbag.

"What is that?" Jonah cocked his head.

"I think it's our grandfather's journal."

"Farfar Nielsen?" Anders raised his brows.

"Ja." Lilac smiled. "I don't know why we never found it before—it was tucked into Ma's old trunk."

"Josephine moved some things around up there when we needed more storage after the fire. Maybe she stuck it in there and didn't realize what it was—or that we hadn't seen it before." Anders brushed off his hands and came to stand by her. "Isn't that something. May I?"

She handed the journal over.

Anders flipped through the first pages. His lips moved, trying to decipher the writing.

"Can you understand any of it?" Anders had learned a little Norwegian, more than any of the other siblings.

"Not much. But I see the word *Restaurasjonen*—that was the name of the ship they came over in, I think. The 'Restoration.'"

"They were mostly religious dissenters, Quakers, isn't that what Pa said?"

"That's what I remember. Though not all of them—our grandfather wasn't a Quaker, I don't believe."

"Well, I just wanted to show you." Lilac accepted the little book back from him. "There are even some drawings he did inside. Maybe we can look more together later."

"That would be good." Turning back to his work, Anders shook his head at the cracked glass canning jars Jonah held up from the crate. "Just get rid of those. At least the rest look all right."

Jonah nodded and carried them out the back door.

Lilac tucked the precious journal into her handbag. More careful examination would have to come later. "I brought the old signs I found in the attic. Where would you like me to work on them?

"I've got some extra paint out on the porch. I'll show you."

She followed her brother. "How does it feel to be this close to opening shop again?"

"Well, you know we've done our best to keep business going in the barn since the fire. But it will be good to be in a real store building again." He stepped out onto the porch and blew out a breath. "It's been a long nine months."

For the first time, Lilac saw the new lines around her older brother's eyes, the weight he'd lost with the burden of this past year. She touched his shoulder. "I'm sorry it's been so hard."

He cast her a Nielsen grin. "We're all right. The Lord has been faithful, and the town rallied around us. I think we'll be able to pay back our loan quicker once we get fully up and running again." He sobered. "I'll never forget that night, though."

Her chest tightened, imagining their beloved family mercantile engulfed in flames. "Who sounded the alarm?"

"The Gubberuds, who live next door—you remember, we went to school with their son. They woke up smelling smoke, and Mrs. Gubberud came running to us screaming the news. Her husband was organizing a bucket brigade before I even got here." Anders shook his head. "I just thank the Lord their house was spared."

"And how did you figure out it was Deacon Wiesel's fault?"

Anders grimaced. "When we found what was left of him next to evidence of a candle melted into the charred floorboards, it seemed pretty evident."

Lilac shivered. "Do you think he could have done it on purpose?" The thought had poked at her for months. "He was so angry at our family for supposedly taking Climie away from him." He and Ringwald had each threatened to come after them years ago, Ringwald even claiming that Jonah, in one of his old drunken slips, had said something about his sisters being bound for the west. But none of them had heard anything of the gambler for years. . . . Surely he'd given up his vendetta by now.

"Of course I wondered, but I don't think so. The deacon really did seem changed last fall—broken, you might say. Though I'm not sure how much was true repentance and how much just giving up. But if he wanted to get back at us, surely he wouldn't have burned himself up in the process. I'm still trying to forgive myself for letting him sleep in the store, but I thought I was doing the right thing." Anders shrugged as if letting the weight of the unknowns roll off his shoulders. "How is Climie, by the way? Since the wedding?"

"Happy. She and Jesse . . . they fit together like two sides of a broken painting made whole. Sometimes seeing such joy on her face almost makes me cry."

"I guess the Lord does bring beauty from ashes." Anders's mouth tipped. "Sometimes quite literally."

Anders hauled over a couple of half-used cans of paint, and Lilac propped the old signs against the porch railing.

"One should say 'Grand Reopening,' I imagine?" she asked.

"Let's have two of those, one for the front and one for the side. And maybe a smaller one saying 'free samples' or 'lemonade' or something like that." Anders scratched the faint stubble on his cheek.

"Well, what are you going to have? Free samples or lemonade?"

"Both. We'll have lemonade for everyone, and the refreshments will be free samples of items we carry in the store. Plus Josephine and her mother are planning sandwiches and a baking spree."

"I'll make a sign for each, then."

"Thanks. You sure it's not too much?"

Lilac leveled a look at her big brother. "Four signs? I came out here to help, remember? And you better give me another job once this is finished."

"Fair enough."

Anders headed back inside with a chuckle, and Lilac found herself a stool to perch on while she sanded and painted. It felt good to have a brush in her hand, even if it was a big one, not at all like the delicate instrument used for watercolors. She needed to try painting again. She'd been so focused on her drawings for the series at the *New York Weekly* this past year, she hadn't picked up a brush in far too long. And she itched to study her grandfather's drawings more. What if she could copy one and enlarge it, maybe make one big enough to frame for their family home? The thought sent a swell of excitement through her.

Focus, Lilac. She finished the big signs first, *Grand Reopening* in bold but elegant letters and a few flourishes for effect. She set them side by side against the storefront wall to dry and stepped back, cocking her head and then nodding. That would do. Now for the smaller signs.

"Want some dinner?" Jonah poked his head out of the store some time later.

"Is it that time already?" Lilac squinted up at the sun through the leafy branches stretching over the front porch. Thankfully, the lovely shade trees had been only minimally damaged in the fire. Even so, her curls clung to her neck and collar, damp with the muggy heat.

"Josephine sent some sandwiches with us. You're welcome to share, unless you want to go back to the house."

"I'll stay. I still want to finish this last sign, then I can help you with unpacking or whatever else."

They lunched in the relative cool of the store's interior, then after finishing the lemonade sign with an added tracing of a lemon wedge that made Lilac's artist heart happy, she spent the rest of the afternoon stocking bags of flour, sacks of coffee, cans of beans, bolts of fabric, and coils of rope.

"Feels like we could supply the whole county." Anders swiped his sleeve across his forehead. "I hope we haven't overstocked."

"You've never had to stock a whole new store before, not counting what you had in the barn." Lilac sat back on her heels after lining boots on a bottom shelf, her lower back aching. "This uses different muscles than farmwork."

"Lark must be missing your help with the summer work."

Lilac nibbled her lip. "I'm sure she is. But at least the planting is done. And I'll be back before Del's baby is born. And before haying, I hope."

"Wish we could come meet that little one. And Nils Peter."

"Someday." Lilac hoisted herself to her feet. "Now what?"

"I want to go over my inventory lists. Feel free to head on home if you like." He turned. "Jonah?"

"I have an errand to run. See you at supper." Their towering little brother shrugged on his brown jacket and headed out the door.

Lilac rolled her tired shoulders. "I think I'll take the long way going back and walk through town a bit. I'd like to see all the familiar old places."

She donned her straw hat and headed down the street, grateful the lengthening shadows eased the heat a bit, even if the sun was hours away from setting. She passed the blacksmith—making her think of the Hoffman family back in Nebraska—and the haberdashery, then the school she and all her siblings had attended. The brick church, full of mixed memories. There they'd grown up and been nurtured in the faith, but also there Lark had enraged the deacon by jumping up in church to try to aid Climie when she fainted during a "sermon" spouted by her abusive husband. He'd flat out forbidden her interference, sending Lark marching out of the service. Lilac hadn't been back inside its walls till yesterday, but she'd been glad to see it led now by a true minister of the gospel, not a hypocrite. Still, it felt far different from their beloved little church in Salton.

She kept walking, awash in memories. The bank, the post office, the livery stable . . .

A burst of raucous music announced she was nearly at the saloon. In a long habit returned, she headed across the street to avoid it. How their lives had changed because of that awful saloon. She shuddered to think of Lark stepping inside that fateful night. Bent on getting Jonah out of one more scrape, she had ended up beating Slate Ringwald like he'd never been beaten—and his ensuing vile threats had sent them all packing.

She couldn't resist a glance back over her shoulder. And stopped cold in the street as the saloon doors swung shut behind a tall, blond-haired young man wearing a brown jacket.

Jonah?

"Hey, miss, some of us are tryin' to drive here!"

Lilac jumped aside as a buggy sped past her, dust swirling her skirts. Had that been her brother heading back into that saloon, whose swinging doors he'd solemnly sworn never to enter again? Was *that* the errand he'd had to run in town? Surely not. But . . .

She marched across the dusty street, pausing only an instant to suck in a breath before pushing through the swinging doors. She nearly gagged on the swirling odors of tobacco smoke, liquor, and sweat. Stepping near the closest end of the bar, Lilac blinked hard in the dim interior, searching through the haze of smoke for her brother.

"You one of the Nielsen girls?"

Lilac turned to see the hostess, a buxom woman with a tired face, scrutinizing her.

"Bonnie Belle?" Lark had talked about the kind woman from that night.

A smile broke out on Bonnie Belle's face. "What are you, Miss Larkspur's little sister?"

"Yes. I'm just looking for my broth—" The young man in a brown jacket stepped up to the bar and gave an order. He had broader shoulders than Jonah and a beard.

Lilac's knees went weak with relief. So silly of her to chase the man all the way in here. "I'm sorry, I thought I saw someone enter here, but I was mistaken."

Bonnie Belle poured the man's drink. "Land sakes, I heard tell you all picked up years ago and moved some place out west after—" The woman looked over Lilac's shoulder, and her face stiffened. She dropped her gaze to the counter, muttering, "You better go."

Lilac glanced behind her. And froze.

Slate Ringwald. She knew him by description, though she'd never seen him before. The large frame, if somewhat shrunken now. The heavy dark brows. The gold pocket watch and chain, and manicured nails of a hand that tapped unceasingly on the table. The expensive suit, now having seen better days. And a knowing, deep in her gut.

For an instant his eyes flicked over Lilac, then away. Then back again. Or did she imagine it?

Lilac jerked her head around. "Sorry to have troubled you," she mumbled and fled toward the door as fast as she could without attracting more attention than she already had. Why on earth had she gone in here? She charged out the doors and down the wooden sidewalk, head down as if she could still keep Ringwald from seeing her. From overhearing what Bonnie Belle had—

She crashed into someone and nearly fell into the street.

"Whoa, whoa." Strong arms caught her. "Where are you flying to, sis?"

She looked up. "Jonah." She clutched his arms. "I-I thought I saw you go into the saloon. So I . . . followed."

"You did what?" His brows drew together. "I told you I'd never darken that door again."

"I know, I know. But, Jonah, I think Slate Ringwald saw me."

3

How am I ever going to manage all this by myself?

Lark sat outside at the table under the roof and stared across the fields, the morning mist rising along with the sun. Soon they'd need to start haying—and what if Lilac or Jonah weren't back in time to help? But she shouldn't worry. She wasn't alone. She had RJ and Del, and Forsythia and Adam in town. Even Robbie had come to visit again this week—he truly did help, even if his questions kept her busy too. Her little nephew still slept since the rooster had not crowed to awaken him. Scamp sat beside her, waiting for her to stroke his head like she usually did. "What do you think, boy? What are we going to do today?"

He did a quick lick of her hand along with a slight whimper. "Shhhh, let him sleep a bit longer." Robbie had said he wanted to do the milking, so she was waiting. Starbright, head hanging over the fence, nickered and her filly, Rose, tossed her head. The sheep bleated in their pen, and Buttercup lowed from outside the barn, asking for the bar to be dropped so she could go inside. A typical morning, well, typical with Lilac not home yet. Hopefully only a couple more weeks till she and Jonah would come back on the train.

Lark stared across the pastures and over to the hayfields, the grass dancing in the slight breeze that called up the sun. The sun's glow caught the tops of the trees, and the rooster's crow heralded the new day. Time for the day to begin.

Lark drained the last of her coffee and tossed the dregs onto the roots of the yellow rosebush, the first thing they had planted the year they arrived. Thankfully, the rose start was well rooted and had survived the trip west in the wagon. Forsythia had insisted they bring starts of fruit trees, along with garden seeds and flowering shrubs. The cottonwood sapling was now big enough to shelter the soddy. They all figured that any of the plants that lived through both the tornado and the grasshopper plague were indeed miraculous.

Robbie appeared in the doorway rubbing his eyes. "Did you milk already?"

Lark shook her head. "You said you wanted to, but you can change your mind if you want."

"How about I milk Buttercup and you do Clover? She likes to put her foot in the bucket."

"She's teasing you, plus it's only her first year being milked. You have to plant your head firmly in her flank and be ready to snatch the bucket away."

It didn't take long for Robbie to pull on his shirt and trousers that had been cut off at the knees where the holes had been.

He fetched the buckets out of the well house and ran ahead to slide back the bar for the cows to come in. They each stepped into their own stanchion and stared toward the grain bin, where Robbie dished up their oats. Within moments, the zing of milk in a bucket joined the fragrance of warm milk fresh from the cow.

Lark stripped Clover dry with nary a shifting of feet. She swung the bucket off to the side and stood from the three-legged stool in one smooth motion.

There was something almost reverent about milking cows.

The stillness of the barn, the fragrance of milk, and the warmth of keeping one's head in a cow's flank. She'd learned milking was a great place to think, even dream, but was always reminded that while her mind was roaming somewhere else, her hands better be paying attention. Sometimes she thought cows could read a milker's mind and knew just when to try to step in the bucket.

"You nearly done?" she asked.

"I think so. When is Buttercup due to calve again?"

"Not for a while. Next spring sometime." They'd only recently taken her to a bull to be bred, but Robbie didn't need to know those details yet.

Robbie swung the pail off to the side and stood up with a sigh. While Lark picked up his pail, he patted both cows and opened their stanchions. Both backed up and turned to head outside. "What if she has a bull calf?"

"We'll either sell him to someone who wants a bull or raise him to butcher."

"Like last year?" The two of them carried their milk pails to the well house, and while Lark poured the milk through a strainer into a cream can and set it in the tank to cool, Robbie grabbed a basket and headed for the chicken coop. He scattered oats and opened the door to let the chickens out to free range. Next, he let the sheep out, waving Scamp to move them out to a pasture that hadn't been grazed.

"You about ready for breakfast?" Lark called on her way back toward the house.

"Coming." Robbie put two fingers in his mouth and whistled, something RJ had recently taught him to do. Scamp tore across the field, slid under the rails, and trotted beside Robbie, tongue lolling out the side of his muzzle. "Good boy." Robbie giggled as the dog nuzzled his dangling hand. "You ready for breakfast too?"

"That was some whistle." Lark handed him a bowl of oatmeal and nodded to the pitcher on the outside table.

"I had to practice a whole lot. RJ said all boys should learn how to whistle." He paused and looked at Lark. "How come not girls?"

"My ma said, 'whistling girls and crowing hens always come to some bad ends.'"

"Hens can't crow."

"I know."

"Can you?"

Lark pursed her lips and answered his question, making him giggle at the same time.

"Did your ma know you could do that?"

"Oh, I probably never mentioned it to her."

"Do Tante Del and Tante Lilac know you can whistle?"

"You'll have to ask them."

"Can my ma whistle?" He set his bowl and spoon on the table and climbed over the bench.

Lark set a basket of biscuits, along with butter and jam, between them and sat down. "Please say grace."

Robbie bowed his head. "Dear God, good morning and thank you for all our animals and our homes and Ma and Pa and Mikael and Sofie and Nils and this food."

Lark had a hard time holding back a chuckle. As Robbie's prayers went, this one was short. "Amen."

"Oh, I forgot." He closed his eyes again. "And bless Tante Del, Onkel RJ, and Tante Lilac too. Amen." He looked up. "When is Tante Lilac coming home? I sure miss her."

Not soon enough, Lark thought. "I think another week or two. They have the grand reopening of the store tomorrow, I believe."

"Do they have licorice at the store?"

"You'll have to ask Lilac when she comes home." She pushed the basket closer to him, watching as he carefully applied butter and jam. With the first bite, he closed his eyes and savored. "Our rhubarb jam sure is good."

"I agree, and remember, you helped pick and cut up the stalks."

"And Tante Del made rhubarb cobbler."

Scamp leaped to his feet and tore around the corner of the soddy.

Robbie grinned. "You think Onkel RJ would like a biscuit?"

Lark nodded and smiled at the horse and rider who stopped at the end of the table.

"You want a biscuit?" Robbie held up a biscuit half dripping with jam.

"Thanks, but I already ate." RJ nodded to Lark. "Good morning, you need anything from town?"

Robbie mumbled around a mouth full of biscuit.

"Not that I can think of, but thank you for asking. Oh, wait." She pushed to her feet. "I have a letter to mail."

"Did you hear the coyotes singing last night?" Robbie asked. He broke another biscuit in half and brought it to Captain. "You like biscuits, huh, big fella?"

"I did. And you spoil him."

"I know. He likes cookies too." The boy reached up and stroked the horse's soft nose, earning himself a snort that was part biscuit.

"Ewwww."

Lark came out the door and handed the envelope up. "Hope you have a good day. What are you working on?"

"Trying to finish up those hospital rooms Adam wanted added to his new office on Main Street."

"That was a surprising idea but a good one."

"Agreed. Gives ill and injured folks a place to stay nearby if Adam needs to keep watch over them without having people coming and going from their home." RJ reined Captain around and, with a wave, cantered down the lane.

They finished their meal, put the bowls in the heating pan on the stove and, after doing the dishes, headed for the garden, where Del was already hoeing the rows between the potato plants and mounding the dirt into hills to protect the tiny potatoes.

"Where do you want me to start?" Robbie asked with a hoe over his shoulder.

"Good morning to you too." Del paused to arch and knead her back.

"You shouldn't be out here." Lark shook her head. Surely her sister wrote the book on stubborn.

"Why not? Can't get down to weed much anymore, but I can still wield a hoe." She smiled at Robbie. "How about the corn? If we'd get a good rain, our corn might make knee-high by the Fourth of July."

"That rhymes."

"I know. I like rhymes." She shifted her weight and rubbed her back again. "Though I, for one, don't plan on going to the celebration in town for the Fourth."

"Del," Lark began.

"I'm fine. This little one is just mighty busy this morning."

"Why don't you go sit in the shade and—"

"Because this takes my mind off it." She looked toward Robbie hoeing the corn. "He sure is a hard worker for such a young lad."

"He said he wanted to do all Lilac's chores." Lark leaned over and brushed the leaves of the bean plant. "No blossoms yet, but it won't be long."

"Even the thought of a mess of fresh beans makes my mouth water."

"Mine too."

By the time the sun hit midmorning, the piles of weeds had grown between the rows, and Lark sent Robbie for the wheelbarrow to haul the piles over to the fence and throw in the pasture for the cattle to eat. A cooling breeze announced clouds coming in from the west. *Please, Lord, let there be rain in the clouds.* Sure looked possible. As the clouds rolled nearer, they leaned their hoes on the split-rail fence. Jagged lightning danced against the darkness.

"Come on, we better get inside before it hits." Del headed for her house. Robbie whistled for the dog and followed.

Thunder rolled and lightening stabbed.

Robbie giggled as the first drops chased him after the women. They stood together under the porch roof, and Lark inhaled. Nothing smelled as wonderful as a summer rain. Rain hammered on the roof and ran over the eaves, sloshing into the rain barrel.

Lark and Del sat down in the rockers with coffee cups in hand, and Robbie brought out a plate of cookies, along with a glass of milk, and sat down on the steps.

"These gardens are going to grow like crazy," Lark observed.

"So will the weeds." Robbie handed Scamp a bit of cookie and stuffed the rest in his mouth.

"Rain just when we needed it, thank you, Lord." Del reached for a cookie.

"Did it rain like this when you were little?" Robbie asked, this time dunking his cookie in the glass of milk.

"Sure did. One year the creek swelled over its banks and almost flooded the town."

"And into the store?"

"Could have. We were all praying for God to protect us."

Lark glanced over to see Del shifting in her chair, trying to get comfortable. This close to the baby being due, she was so large they sometimes wondered if she would have twins.

"How can I help you?" Lark turned to Robbie. "Would you please go in and bring out that padded footstool and a pillow for Tante Del?"

"Sure." He jumped up the three steps and ran into the house. In a blink, he set the stool down for Del and handed her the pillow.

"Stuff that behind her back," Lark told him, "and thank you."

"Ah, that helps a lot." Del leaned back and closed her eyes. "Remember when us girls would go out and wash our hair in the rain? That always felt so heavenly."

"We could still do that, you know."

"I know, but the rain barrel is a good alternative."

That night, Lark had a hard time falling asleep. The coyotes sent their chorus to the nearly full moon. She listened to Scamp whimpering in his sleep and Robbie turning over in his bed, the ropes squeaking. It was so sweet to hear his little-boy breathing and have his company through the day. But tomorrow he'd go back home to his own family, as rightly he should.

Heavenly Father, why does there seem to be no man for me? She would never experience carrying her own child to birth if she weren't married, and that was looking slimmer by the season. Isaac strode into her mind. But he seemed more interested in locating any family he had left and bringing them to Salton. Other times he just disappeared, going off and finding a job somewhere else, and then he would return to Salton and go back to working for RJ's construction company. Ofttimes he'd help with haying or harvest, and he always enjoyed the music the sisters played. Perhaps they needed to have another social before haying started. *Hmm. A celebration for when Lilac and Jonah arrive home?* She nodded against her pillow and drifted off to sleep.

Lark jerked awake again. She heard snarling, sheep bleating, and Starbright slamming her hooves against the wood walls. *Coyotes!*

Scamp growled as he shot out the door. Lark's feet hit the floor, and she grabbed the rifle she kept above the door. "Robbie, clang the gong. I'm going after Scamp."

Please, Lord, protect our sheep pounded in her head as her bare feet slapped against the hard-packed dirt. Scamp barked and an animal yipped. The sheep gave a panicked cry. Lark reached the fence and swung open the gate of the corral. Firing into the air, she saw silver shadows as the coyotes tore out under the fence toward the open pasture. She set the rifle to her shoulder, sighted on one silver wraith still in the corral, and pulled the trigger. The animal dropped to the ground right next to a sheep struggling to get back on his feet, bleating the entire time.

"Where's Scamp?" Robbie stood beside her.

"Chasing the coyotes." She entered the sheep pen, where the flock was packed in the corner against the barn wall. Prodding the dead coyote with the tip of the rifle, she knelt beside the injured sheep, a young wether. "Go call Scamp before the pack turns on him, then check the others to see if there is any blood."

Robbie charged off to do as she said.

RJ dropped to the ground beside her. "How bad?"

"Hoping that tendon in the hind leg isn't severed. But you know sheep, they can die from fright. Hold him while I check."

RJ locked his arm around the black head and, murmuring gentle words, forced the panting sheep to lie down by wrapping his legs around him.

Lark felt up the back leg. The hide was ripped but the muscles felt intact, as was the tendon. Breathing a sigh of relief, she rose to her feet. "Let's lay him on the table by the soddy. I'll clean this and see if any stitching is needed." RJ gathered the young wether in his arms and stood.

"His heart is racing." RJ kept pace with Lark as they strode to the soddy.

"Better than too slow."

Robbie caught up with them. "Is he going to make it?"

"We'll do all we can."

"How come sheep can die from fright?"

Oh, Lord, how do I answer this one? Her mother's frequent answer when she'd tired of Lark's incessant questions popped into her mind. "God made it so, and so it is." She also remembered thinking, *But that's still no answer.* "Get a lamp and another lantern so we can see better." Though the dawn was lighting the eastern sky, the outside table was on the west side of the house.

RJ laid the sheep on its side and held it there.

Robbie brought out the lamps.

"Please get my sewing basket too. It's under my bed."

She heard banging in the soddy and looked to RJ.

"I figured Del would be right behind me."

Lark shook her head and rolled her lips together. "Of course she is."

Robbie returned with the sewing basket and stroked the wether's face, crooning his own special language for his sheep.

Del set another lamp on the table, along with a bottle of whiskey and a basin of hot water. "Should be hotter, but that is from the reservoir. You want me to thread your needle?" She raised one hand, palm out. "Don't bother yelling at me. Breakfast will be ready when you are."

"Robbie, can you hold up the lantern?" Lark washed the wound to remove all the dirt, then she poured the whiskey over it, lifted the needle from the dish of whiskey Del had set up, and stitched the flap of wooly skin back in place.

"Ba-a-a-a."

"Perhaps we should have given him a sip of whiskey," RJ said with a grin.

Lark wrapped the leg in strips of cloth and tied them in place. "Robbie, is the box stall clean?"

"No one has used it. I can throw straw in there. And put grain in the low box and water in the bucket."

"You go get started, and we'll bring him down." The sun had lifted above the horizon when RJ picked up the sheep again and carried him back to the barn. "What if you brought another in to stay with him?"

"Oh, I have a feeling Robbie won't leave that stall once we settle the sheep in place. That boy knows each of his flock. Like Jesus said, 'I am the good shepherd; my sheep know my voice.'"

RJ laid the sheep down in the straw, and Robbie took his place, crooning and stroking the sheep's face and neck so it didn't try to get up.

RJ and Lark closed the door to the stall and watched for a bit before leaving. "I'll bring your breakfast out here," Lark said.

Robbie smiled up at her. "Thank you. He can get up after a while, right?"

Lark nodded. "He should be able to walk on that leg."

Back at the soddy, RJ sat down at the outside table that Del had scrubbed off.

Lark stepped into the kitchen, and Del handed her a basket of rolls. They carried the three bowls of cornmeal mush out to the table, where the cream pitcher and maple syrup already waited.

"You sit down, and I'll get the coffee," Lark ordered her sister, who wiggled her eyebrows at the order. "Uff da," Lark muttered, while hiding a smile. She returned with the coffeepot, filled the cups, and sat down, blowing out a sigh as she took her place on the bench seat. She nodded to RJ to say grace.

"What a way to start the day," RJ said after he finished the prayer. He poured the cream and syrup over his mush. "I know the crew are wondering where I am, but O'Rourke will get them all started."

"For Robbie's sake, I hope that wether doesn't give up and die." Lark shook her head. *Please, Lord.*

4

I now declare the Nielsen Mercantile officially open." Anders's grin outshone the weariness on his face. "Again!"

Lilac clapped with all her heart as cheers and applause swelled from the crowd around the store. With Greta on her hip, Josephine cut the ribbon Anders had tied across the front door. Marcella, clinging to her mother's skirts, burst into tears at the sudden explosion of noise. Sympathetic laughter rippled through the crowd.

Customers and well-wishers began to stream up the porch and through the door. Lilac hurried inside to help. Anders and Jonah manned the counter, while Lilac helped Josephine greet newcomers and answer questions, as well as direct people to the trays of samples on the counter and on tables out on the porch. Josephine's mother took the little girls to a quiet spot in the shade outside, freeing her daughter to tend to customers.

As the crowd inside thinned a bit, Lilac stationed herself at the lemonade table under the tree outside, where she could catch an occasional breeze on her face.

"Lilac? It's so good to see you!"

Lilac looked up from pouring another cup of lemonade. A smiling young woman stood before her. It took her a moment to recognize the freckled nose and reddish curls, now pinned primly up.

"Gertie?" She rounded the lemonade table to throw her arms around her childhood friend. "Goodness, it's good to see you too."

"It seems an absolute age since you and your sisters left." Gertie held Lilac out by the shoulders to look at her. "When Anders said you were coming for the reopening, I started counting the days. You left in such a hurry, we never even got to say good-bye."

"I know." Lilac swallowed. And with circumstances being as they'd been, she'd hardly written to anyone, save her brothers, just to be safe. "I'm sorry I haven't kept in better touch."

"Well, you can make up for it now." Gertie raised her brows. "Catch me up on everything out in the Wild West."

"It isn't so very wild. Well, except for the grasshopper plague. And the tornado." And the conniving gambler out to get them, whom she might have put on their trail again . . . Lilac snapped her mind shut against that thought. "But how are you? Your parents, your sisters and brothers?" Gertie had been the eldest of eight, a contrast to Lilac's baby sister status.

"They're all fine. And I, well . . ." Gertie's freckled cheeks pinked, and she held up her left hand with a simple wedding band.

Lilac grabbed her friend's fingers. "You got married."

"Last fall. To Wesley Ashton." Gertie nodded to a pleasant-faced young man chatting with Jonah on the store porch. She lowered her voice with a dimpled smile. "We're expectin' a little one, too, come December."

"I'm so happy for you." Lilac noted the new fullness of her friend's figure.

"What about you? Are there as many eligible bachelors out west as they say?" Gertie nudged her.

Lilac laughed. "I don't know about that."

"Truly? No one has caught your eye?"

"Well." She hesitated. "I was engaged this last year, actually. To our town preacher."

"How wonderful! Wait—you *were* engaged?"

"I broke it off." Lilac nibbled her lip.

"Oh—I see." Gertie's face said she didn't see at all.

How could Lilac explain everything that had happened—with Ethan, in Salton, in her family? This friend, with whom she used to share so much, knew nothing of her new life. Lilac sidestepped by asking after their old schoolmates, and Gertie obliged, dishing all the ins and outs of who'd married whom, who'd had twins, and who'd run off and eloped with as much gusto as she used to give schoolyard gossip when she and Lilac pooled their dinner pails.

At last, Gertie's husband called her away. Lilac bid her good-bye with a genuine embrace yet breathed a sigh of relief when she was gone. It had been good to see her friend, but Lilac didn't fit in this world anymore.

She fit in Salton now. Yet what would her future be there? Watching Gertie walk away with her hand securely in the crook of her husband's elbow, her waistline blooming with child, Lilac felt a wistful pang.

She shook it off and headed to help Anders organize the raffle for a new mechanical apple peeler. Afterward, at her brother's request, she stood on the porch awhile with a borrowed violin to provide cheery background tunes as the celebration went on.

Different waves of people came and went throughout the day, though the crowds dwindled with the afternoon heat. Another smaller rush came toward early evening, and Lilac helped Josephine bring over a fresh batch of sandwiches and cookies from the house for the newcomers.

Lilac blew a sweaty curl from her face and bent over one table to arrange a fresh basket of early peaches from Ma's old

LAURAINE SNELLING

trees. The sweet scent tickled her nose, and she picked one up and bit into the fuzzy pink fruit, juice spurting into her mouth.

At a sudden clatter behind her, she turned midbite to see what had happened. A young man bent to the grassy ground, where his plate had fallen and scattered sandwich, cookies, and fruit.

"Let me help." Lilac reached under the table for a stray cookie.

"Thank you." Embarrassment tinged the voice. And familiarity.

Lilac glanced up as she handed over the cookie. Tall, wheat-blond hair, trimmed mustache, and neat suit and vest. He didn't *look* familiar.

But he cocked his head. "Lilac Nielsen?" And a grin she knew shone from beneath the mustache. "Been a long time since I dunked your braids in ink."

"Sam Gubberud?" Her mouth fell open. "A long time indeed."

"I've been . . . gone a good while." He set his plate on the nearby table and awkwardly re-piled sandwiches and apricots, then took the cookie she still held out. "Thank you."

Lilac tried to think back. "You joined your father in the livery business, didn't you? After you left school?" Sam had been in Anders's class at school, so some seven years ahead of Lilac.

"I did. Until the war."

Of course. Always a leader, Sam had been one of the first in their town to join up. "Sorry I didn't recognize you at first. You seem . . . different."

"Well, I'm still awfully clumsy at times with this." His ears reddening, he shrugged his left shoulder.

Only then did she see the empty sleeve pinned shut at the elbow. "Oh." Her throat squeezed. How could she have spoken so carelessly? "I'm so sorry, I didn't mean—"

He shook his head. "Don't be. You'd think I'd be used to it after over four years." He chuckled, but Lilac noted creases around his eyes.

"All I meant was you've grown up." She bit her tongue, cheeks

45

heating. Why couldn't she say anything right? "I mean, you hardly seem the type anymore to get sent to the corner three times in a school morning." She waggled her eyebrows, hoping to lighten the moment.

Sam laughed, the hearty sound easing the air between them. "Poor Mr. Muller. I must have given him early gray hairs."

"Samuel *Jakob* Gubberud." Lilac mimicked their former schoolmaster's nasally tone. "Is that what you call proper conduct for a gentleman?"

"You have quite the memory. You couldn't have been more than six or seven when I was getting in my worst scrapes."

"I'm an artist. Observing life is what I do." So why hadn't she noticed his missing arm right away? Had she been too caught by the intensity in his hazel eyes? Lilac shoved the thought away.

"An artist?" Sam picked up his plate and moved out of the way of others returning to the fresh spread of food. "I remember you were always scribbling away."

"Well, I never stopped." Since no one was coming for lemonade just now, Lilac followed Sam to some of the scattered chairs in the shade. "I 'scribbled' all through our journey west, and I've had a running column of sketches in the *New York Weekly* for the last year."

Sam's eyes widened as he balanced his plate on one knee. "'Prairie Sketches'? That's *you*?"

"You've seen it?" Despite the steady payments from her publisher, Lilac still felt a dizzy pleasure at the reminder her work was actually seen out in the wide world.

"Of course. It's a section I look forward to each issue, or rather every other with that feature being bimonthly." He nodded. "You truly have a gift."

Ethan had said something similar, yet she'd always felt his thoughts were elsewhere—on the next thing he needed to do in ministry and how she should support him in it. The sincerity in her old schoolmate's words crept into Lilac's heart and nestled there. "Thank you." She glanced around the gathering, making sure her help wasn't needed anywhere at the moment. "So what branch did you serve in again? During the war."

"I was with the First Cavalry of Ohio." Sam shifted in his chair.

Of course. He'd always loved horses. "And when did—" She glanced at his arm.

"Not till three years in, when my period of enlistment was almost up, in fact." He gave a wry grin. "I'd risen to an officer by that time. My mother thought that meant I'd be safer, but minié balls don't discriminate by rank."

Lilac winced. Del had lost her first fiancé to a minié ball. And from what she'd heard from Adam, they were far more deadly than a regular musket ball—tended to shatter any bone they struck.

"But enough about me. What have the Nielsen sisters been up to out west? I ran into Anders a few weeks ago, and he told me a little." Sam took a bite.

"Oh my, it's been quite the three years. I don't even know how to summarize it all." Yet as they sat and visited, the words came, and she told him about the trip west and finding their homestead—though still being careful to avoid details of their specific location. She trusted Sam, yet after seeing Ringwald . . . But she told him about Adam and RJ and the children, Jesse and Climie, and the ups and downs of farming, from losing much of their garden to grasshoppers to harvesting wheat by hand before they got the mower last year. Even, to her own surprise, a little about all that had happened with Ethan.

Josephine's call from the store porch started Lilac to her feet. "Goodness, it's nearly sundown. I'm sorry I talked your ear off."

"Nonsense." Sam rose also. "This is the most interesting conversation I've had in a long while." His mouth quirked in some semblance of the teasing grin she remembered. "And I did owe you for all those tugs on your pigtails."

She laughed. "We never minded too much, you know. You were always kindhearted and stood up for us little ones against any real bullies. I distinctly remember you giving me a piggy-back ride around the schoolyard once—I believe I was Joan of Arc and you my trusty steed."

He chuckled. "I've no memory of that at all. Well, I'm glad it wasn't all troublemaking. Seems poetic justice I'm to be a teacher now, with all the torment I gave schoolmasters in my young days."

"Really? A teacher?"

"I went to school for it after the war." He rolled the shoulder of his amputated arm. "Something I can do, you know."

"I'm sure you'll be good at it. You can relate to the students well, I think. Have you found a position yet?"

"Not yet. I just started applying. I'm thinking of looking into positions out west, as a matter of fact."

"Well, perhaps there will be a place for you near us someday. You'd certainly be welcome."

"It does sound like a welcoming place from what you describe. But I should let you go." He nodded to the porch, where Anders had lit a lamp, and he and Jonah were taking down Lilac's refreshments signs.

Lilac took his empty plate and turned away, then back. "Oh, I wanted to thank you, or rather your parents. I understand they're the ones who sounded the alarm on the fire at the store."

"I'll pass it on." Sam shook his head. "I was away, taking some teachers' examinations, but I heard the story. Such a terrible thing."

"It was. Though we're grateful the fire didn't spread farther." She hesitated. "It was good seeing you again, Sam."

"And you, Lilac." He put on his hat with a nod, waved to her brothers, and stepped away into the dusk.

"Sorry I got distracted." Lilac stacked the used dishes and

carried them to a crate on the porch to lug back to the house for washing. "What can I do?"

"Quite a talk you had with Sam Gubberud." Anders gestured for her to help him carry one of the small tables back inside. "I was sorry to learn he lost his arm."

"Me too. He's going to be a teacher now. At least he won't need two arms for that." They set the table inside the darkening store. "The reopening went well?"

"Very. We're back up and running, thank the Lord." Anders rubbed the back of his neck. "And I'm plumb wore out, as Mr. Holt would say. Josephine already took the girls home. I think we can leave the rest for tomorrow. Jonah?"

"Just want to finish taking down the signs." His voice came from the porch.

"I'll wait and walk back with him." Lilac watched from the doorway as Anders headed down the twilit lane toward home, his steps glad but weary. She stepped onto the porch and looked up at Jonah, who stood on the railing using the back of a hammer to wrench out the nails holding a *Grand Reopening* sign on one side of the roof.

"You don't want to leave it up a week or so? At least a few days?"

"Folks know we're open now. I'll leave the front one up a bit longer." Another yank, and he bent to set the nail in a tin can on the railing.

Lilac nibbled her lip and rubbed her arms, then came to stand closer. "I know you're still mad at me."

Wrench, ping. This time the nail flew out and landed somewhere in the grass.

Jonah muttered something under his breath and jumped down onto the porch, the sign in his arms. He set it against the wall and jogged down the steps to hunt for the nail in the grass.

Lilac lifted the lantern off a hook by the door and headed down after him. "Wouldn't some light help?"

"Can't have some child step on it barefoot." Jonah ignored the light she held out.

Lilac bit the inside of her cheek. "You know I only went in that saloon because I was worried about you."

"And I told you I would never go back in there." The words exploded from him, and Jonah jerked upright. His eyes bored into hers in the lanternlight, flecked with fire. "I gave my word, and I've kept my word. You put yourself in danger by going in there. Maybe all of you out in Salton."

Lilac swallowed. He was right. She knew he was right. But had he forgotten he started all this trouble in the first place? "Have you heard anything? About Ringwald?"

Jonah puffed out a breath and bent back to his searching. "Couple of fellas today said he's been talking. They think it's just bluster."

"About what?"

"Ah, you know."

"No, I don't."

"That he's still going to find that Nielsen girl, get even before he dies."

A shiver started at Lilac's scalp and ran down her spine. "Did they say he saw me?"

"No one said anything about that."

The knot in her belly eased a little. "So you really think it's just talk?"

He shrugged. "Kind of shape he's in, he probably couldn't make it out to Nebraska anyway. Even if he knew where you were." Jonah plucked the nail from the grass and reached to plunk it in the can on the porch railing. "There."

Please, Lord, let it be so. How she wanted to believe him. But if Jonah was so convinced, why was he still upset? Maybe he still thought she didn't trust him.

"Jonah." Lilac touched her brother's sleeve. "Forgive me?"

He sighed, then hugged her to his side. "Fine. But no more

stunts like that. I know I was your wayward baby brother for a long time, but I'm not anymore. Promise to try and believe me?"

She raised a brow. "Rather a switch for you to be the one demanding the promises instead of making them. But I promise." She drew a long breath. "About time for me to think about heading back anyway, now that the grand reopening is past."

"So soon?"

"I'll stay another week or so till I know all is running smoothly. But I don't belong here anymore." Today had reminded her of that. "And Del's baby will be due soon. You still want to come out too?"

"Of course. I said I'd help with the summer farmwork, and I'll keep my word." Meaning edged his voice.

Lilac nodded and squeezed his arm. How long would it be till he believed that she trusted him again?

5

*L*ilac and Jonah will be home today.

The thought hit Lark even before she opened her eyes. A grin stretching her face, she stretched her arms, too, then rolled out of bed in the tiny soddy bedroom.

That had been the last night she'd be alone in here. At least for a while.

She found herself whistling as she buttoned up her work dress, twisted back her long dark hair, and grabbed the milk pails to head outside for chores. Birds twittered a hallelujah chorus from the cottonwood sapling and prairie grasses, the air already warming as the sky lightened with summer sun. A meadowlark soared overhead.

Buttercup and Clover greeted her with low bellows in the barn.

"And good morning to you too, ladies." Lark tossed hay to the stock and poured grain for the cows, then let the horses and sheep out to pasture. She set down the milking stool beside Buttercup and wiped her bulging udder with a clean rag. "Look at all that milk you've got today. We're going to need to make cheese soon. Good thing we'll have more folks to help. I can't keep up with everything around here."

Her tongue caught on the words, and Lark bit her lip as she started milking, the milk from swollen teats spurting into the pail. She *had* kept up on everything around here, hadn't she? And would again, if need be. And she'd still had help from RJ and Del and Robbie . . . and Isaac, that day he showed up when she was mending fences and a couple of other times when he'd stopped by too. He'd even brought a brace of prairie chickens one day, saying he guessed they missed Lilac's hunting.

Buttercup shifted her back leg, bumping the pail. "Sorry, girl." Lark picked up the speed of her milking again. With the cow's udder flabby at last, she set the full pail aside and grabbed the empty one for Clover, Buttercup's daughter.

"Your turn now, young lady." Clover was producing well so far in her first year, if not yet as much as her mother. Her heifer from this spring gamboled out in the pasture with Rose, Starbright's filly, now almost a yearling.

Lark finished the milking and carried the pails to the well house to keep cool, then watered the animals and headed to check on the sheep. Thankfully, that young wether's leg had healed nicely—he barely even limped anymore. After feeding the chickens, she took the eggs into the soddy, washed up, and fixed herself a simple breakfast. She glanced at the clock over her bowl of mush and fresh milk, her stomach jumping at the time. She'd barely have time to stop at Del's on the way to the train station.

"How are you doing, sister mine?" Lark poked her head in the door at Del and RJ's a short while later. With Del this close to her time, she didn't let a morning go by without checking on her, even though she knew RJ would let them know at any sign of the baby.

Del turned from the sink and leaned her hands on her hips to stretch her back with a groan. "Waddling like a duck, no other change. I thought this baby might be here by now."

"Maybe he or she has been waiting for Lilac and Jonah."

"I hope so." Del fanned her face with her hand. "Being big as a barn in this heat is worse than I realized it would be."

Lark stepped into the kitchen to hug her, the awkward bulk of her belly bumping between them. "It won't be much longer. Do you need anything from town?"

"I've been craving lemonade, but I doubt Jorgensens' has any lemons. And it's too expensive anyway."

"Not for you. I'll check." Lark kissed her cheek, noting the hair straggling from her sister's usually neat snood. "You put your feet up once it gets real hot, hear me?"

"I usually collapse by afternoon anyway these days." Del ran a hand over her protruding abdomen and blew out a breath. "Bring Lilac and Jonah by on your way back?"

"Of course." Lark gave another glance at the time and flew out the door. She urged the team forward, jostling the wagon across the prairie. She'd have brought the faster trap, except her siblings were bringing fruit tree starts from Ohio, so they'd need the extra room.

She reached the station just as the train was puffing in and saw her younger sister and brother waving through the sooty window of one of the cars. Moments later Lilac fell into her arms.

"It's good to have you back." Lark held her tightly, something in her chest easing. She'd never been away from her baby sister like this.

"Good to be back." Lilac hugged her hard, then released her for Jonah to have his turn.

"Hey, you." Jonah's embrace lifted Lark off her feet.

"Goodness, did you grow again?" Lark shook her head at him but couldn't help a grin.

They headed to the baggage car to collect the seedlings sent from Anders.

"Cherry, another apple, and peach." Jonah hefted the burlap-wrapped starts into the wagon bed.

"Such richness." Lark shook her head, mouth watering at the thought. "Think of the bounty we could have in a few summers."

They collected Jonah's satchel and Lilac's basket and carpetbag, then stopped at the mercantile, where Mr. Jorgensen did indeed have some lemons fresh in from the train. They bought two before stopping at the Brownsvilles' so Jonah and Lilac could hug their nieces and nephews. Promising Forsythia they'd come for a family dinner on Sunday, they headed back across the prairie toward home.

"So how was your trip?" Lark asked, the reins easy in her hands.

"The train trip or the whole time in Ohio?" Lilac pressed her boots against the dash.

"Both."

"It was . . . good." Lilac glanced back at Jonah, sitting in the wagon bed with the saplings. "It was wonderful being with Anders and Josephine, seeing their girls. It was strange seeing all the old places, though. I expected things to be the same—and they were, but they weren't, you know?" She snuck a look back at Jonah again.

Their little brother had fallen oddly silent back there. Lark eyed her siblings. "Something going on between you two?"

"No." They both spoke together.

"Uh-huh." Lark raised her brows. "You still think you can fool your big sister after all these years?"

Jonah sighed and turned on his knees to stick his head between his sisters on the wagon seat. "Might as well tell her, Lilac. She'd going to dig it out one way or another."

Lilac scrunched up her face, then sighed.

Lark tightened her grip on the reins. "What happened?"

Lilac worried her lower lip between her teeth. "I saw Slate Ringwald."

"What?" Lark froze, though the horses kept plodding ahead. "Where? How?"

"In the saloon."

"You went in the saloon?" Lark's voice rose with the pounding in her head.

"Well, so did you once upon a time." But Lilac flinched. "I know, I know, it was foolish. I thought I saw Jonah go in there, and—"

"Did you?" Lark swiveled to glare at her brother.

"No!" His voice a growl, Jonah slapped his hands on the wagon sides.

"He didn't. It was someone else," Lilac hurried on. "And I didn't know Ringwald would be there, though Mr. Holt had said he was back in town."

"So you went into the saloon, knowing that low-down snake was back in town, and—" Lark clamped down on the words that wanted to boil forth. "Did he see you?"

"I didn't think so. I don't think so. Jonah says . . . he's heard some talk."

"And?" Lark speared her brother with her look next.

Jonah shifted on his knees. "Just heard some men say Ringwald was still saying he wanted to get even. They didn't say he'd seen Lilac, and apparently he's dying of some sort of cancer. So hopefully it's nothing to worry about."

Odd for Jonah to be the one trying to reassure everyone, even if he sounded as if he were trying to convince himself too. Lark blew out a long breath.

"Lark, I'm sorry." Lilac's voice came small.

"I know you are."

They rode in silence for some time, hardly the joyous sibling reunion Lark had looked forward to. Memories flashed through her mind, more vivid than in years—that smoky room, the hours ticking toward midnight, the cards in their hands. The glint of Ringwald's gold watch and a calculating sneer on his face. A chill made Lark shudder. She'd beaten the man soundly, caught him cheating by her keen observations and quick mind, and humiliated him in front of all gathered. But would he really hold a grudge this long?

"I've been mad at Lilac, but I know this is still all my fault to begin with." Jonah sat back in the wagon bed. "If only I hadn't been such a fool and gotten mixed up with Ringwald in the first place."

"And if only I hadn't rushed into that poker game to try and bail you out. And if only Lilac had waited to talk to you instead of dashing into the saloon without thinking. We could go on and on with if-onlys." Lark ran her tongue over her teeth and sighed. "We will just have to pray it is indeed just talk. And keep a vigilant eye on our farm, just in case." Tamping down the worry that fought to clamp her throat, she turned the wagon into the lane toward Del's.

"Lilac found something interesting in the attic back home, though," Jonah volunteered.

Lilac let out a breath. "I did. I'll show you when we're at Del's. I think it could be quite a special find."

"Sounds intriguing." Lark pulled up by Del and RJ's house and wrapped the reins around the wagon post. She gave each of her siblings a long look. "Let's not worry Del with all this just now, shall we?"

They both nodded. "Agreed."

Their moods lifted with Del's exclamations of delight at seeing them all, and with opening the baby gifts Anders and Josephine had sent. Lark smiled to see Del's face light up as she sat in the rocking chair RJ had made, her feet up as ordered and a glass of lemonade by her side, poring over the tiny crocheted cap and embroidered baby gown in her lap.

"They wish they could come and meet the baby." Lilac reached to touch the hem of the long gown. "And Nils Peter too, of course. It's a pity Marcella and Greta can't grow up with their little cousins. They'd have such fun with Sofie."

"Maybe someday." Del folded the dress with careful hands.

"I still dream of Anders moving his family out here. Do you think they ever might?"

"They've invested so much in rebuilding the store, I doubt it. If they were ever going to, it probably would have been after the fire."

Jonah nodded. "I might end up staying out here someday, though. We'll see. I like the fresh air, open spaces. Room to breathe. Might even think about claiming my own homestead."

"There's a thought. I believe there's still plenty of land to be had, even if you have to go a little farther west. But what is this discovery of yours?" Lark nudged Lilac's foot with her boot toe. "You found something in Ma and Pa's attic?"

Lilac's face brightened, and she dug in her handbag, pulling out a small leather book. "This. It seems to be an old journal of Farfar Nielsen's."

"Our grandfather?" Lark reached to take the slender volume in her hands. She opened it and examined the fragile pages. "It's in Norwegian."

"I know. I'm hoping we might find someone who can translate it for us."

"I think Lars Olsen, on RJ's crew, speaks Norwegian. Though I'm not as certain he can read it, or read at all, frankly." Del craned her neck to see, and Lark held the book closer for her. "What a find, indeed."

"There are drawings inside too." Lilac took the book back, seeming a little protective. "I want to show everyone when we get together."

"Forsythia invited us all to come to dinner Sunday." Lark glanced at Del. "All right with you?"

"That sounds good. As long as this baby hasn't decided to come by then, I'd just as soon not have to cook anyway." Del winced and shifted in her chair. "Ow."

"What's wrong?" Lark and Lilac spoke together.

She chuckled. "Settle down there, mother hens. This baby just likes to play the drums on my ribs sometimes."

"Maybe it's another boy to keep Nils company." Jonah grinned.

"Or a very lively little girl. So who else did you see back in Ohio, Lilac?"

"Gertie Thompson—well, Gertie Ashton now. She married Wesley from school, remember him? Oh, and I talked to Sam Gubberud."

"Samuel *Jakob* Gubberud?" Del raised a brow.

Her siblings all chuckled at her mimicking of their old schoolmaster.

Lark settled back in her chair. "What is he up to these days? He joined up early in the war, as I recall. I'm glad he made it through."

"He did, not without loss, though. He's missing an arm."

Lark rolled her lips together. She hadn't thought of their energetic schoolmate in years, but the toll of the war on so many lives still took her breath away sometimes. She thought of Anders, RJ, and Isaac and the wounds they still bore, seen and unseen. "I'm so sorry."

"How did you end up talking with him?" Del asked.

"He was at the grand reopening. Actually, his parents were the ones to sound the alarm for the fire. They still live near the store. Sam is going to be a schoolteacher now. He went back to study for it after he lost his arm. He's even looking for possible positions out west."

"Really." Lark nibbled her lip. "That reminds me, I hear Reverend Pritchard and Sylvia Linden are getting married. I wouldn't be surprised if they announce their engagement this Sunday."

"Oh, I'm glad." Lilac's face lit up. "They'll be so good for each other."

"You don't mind at all?" Del pushed her foot on the stool to rock her chair slightly, hand caressing her belly as if already rocking her baby. "It's only been a few months since Ethan was engaged to you. Seems a bit fast to me."

Lilac shrugged. "If they know, they know. Sometimes what's right does happen quickly—look at us moving to Nebraska. And I never felt right being engaged to Ethan. It wouldn't have mattered how long we had waited."

"It will leave us without a schoolteacher again. I wonder how soon they'll be moving to Lincoln." Lark shook her head. "This town sure does go through schoolteachers in a hurry."

"Maybe we should write to Sam Gubberud, let him know about the position," Lilac suggested. "Wouldn't it be wonderful if he could find a place right here in Salton?"

Wonderful, was it? Lark studied her little sister's face, then exchanged a glance with Del. Any special reason Lilac was so taken with the idea of Sam Gubberud coming to Salton?

Jonah drove them back to the soddy, the late morning sun beating hot overhead. Grasshoppers whirred in the high grass around them, evoking memories of the plague two summers before. Lord willing that scourge wouldn't come again this year, or any other for that matter.

"We'll need to start haying soon." Lark scanned the fields with a practiced eye. "Glad you two are back in time to help with that."

"How are things on the farm?" Lilac squeezed her hand. "Did you get along all right?"

Lark's tongue poised to tell her the truth about her lack of sleep and how some days she'd been so tired from weeding and hoeing and tending the fields, garden, and livestock all by herself that by evening her limbs shook.

But then she thought of the light in Lilac's eyes as she spoke of Sam Gubberud. Even if nothing came of that, she had no guarantee of how long Lilac would be around to help. Her little sister was winsome and enchanting—some man was sure to snatch her up someday. And then Lark would have to go it alone again, and probably for the rest of her life, with only occasional help from her siblings along the way. It seemed God's path for her. Even if she had to swallow hard at the thought of it.

She put on a smile. "Everything was fine."

Because Del and RJ were here to help you when the coyotes attacked. Lark pushed the thought away. They had their own growing family to think of, and she certainly couldn't count on Isaac McTavish showing up, not with how he'd come and gone from their lives these last three years as changeably as the prairie wind.

She could count on God and her own strong back. That was all.

6

"Before we close, I have something I'd like to share with all of you."

At Rev. Pritchard's words, Lilac looked up, adjusting five-month-old Nils Peter in her arms. She'd been jiggling him on her lap through the church service so Forsythia could relax and enjoy the sermon.

Their preacher beamed out over the gathering, then nodded to the front row, where Lilac could see the auburn bun and slender shoulders of Miss Sylvia Linden, Salton's schoolteacher.

"I have the honor of sharing with you all that Miss Linden, our beloved schoolteacher, has graciously agreed to become my wife."

Spontaneous applause broke out from the congregation. Lilac propped Nils against her shoulder so she could join in, clapping till her palms tingled. *Thank you, Lord. This is so right.*

Rev. Pritchard grinned, holding up his hand. "Thank you. We are so grateful you share our joy. However, this news also means much change for all of us. I just heard from my mission board last week, and I have been officially assigned to a new church starting in our nearby capital of Lincoln. They wish me to begin ministry work there right away, so Sylvia and I have decided to have a quiet wedding and move within a fortnight. Next Sunday will be my last in Salton."

A stunned hush fell over the congregation. Even Ethan's smile dimmed a bit.

"I realize this may cause some challenges for this congregation, but I am confident you will meet them with grace and wisdom, as you have so many others. And now . . ." He held up his hands. "May the Lord bless and keep you. May He make His face shine upon you and be gracious to you."

Lilac bowed her head, her eyes pricking with unexpected tears. So many times she'd heard Rev. Pritchard give this blessing . . . and so many times last year, when his path had been fraught with trials, she had been by his side.

"May the Lord lift up His countenance toward you and give you peace."

Now he and Sylvia would be gone, on to the new adventures God had for them.

Did He also have new adventures for her?

After the service, Lilac handed her little nephew back to Forsythia and joined Lark in a cluster of women in the churchyard, bonnets close together and talking hard.

"Not that I begrudge the pastor his happiness to be sure," Mrs. Jorgensen said, "but it seems a poor way to manage things, leaving our congregation in the lurch like this. Now what are we supposed to do? It can take months to find a new minister, not to mention one willing to come all the way out west."

"Haven't we known for a bit that the reverend might be movin' on to Lincoln?" Bridget O'Rourke put in gently. "'Tisn't like it's a complete shock."

"No doubt it's to be expected from such a young man." Mrs. Dwyer sniffed. "Off to greener pastures, can't stay in one place. Of course, after the scandal of this last year, who can blame him."

Lilac's scalp felt hot. Had the woman never heard of Christian charity?

"A scandal of which Reverend Pritchard was fully cleared, Ellen," Mrs. Caldwell put in, her voice firm. "Let's not forget that."

Mrs. Dwyer squared her bony shoulders. "All I'm sayin' is, we might do well to seek a more mature pastor this time. Perhaps an older man with a family. Not one who bounces from one engagement to another."

"I'd hardly call that fair." Lark's voice cut as crisp as a paring knife.

Lilac stepped back from the group, her ears burning. Drawing a breath to quiet the pounding in her chest, she looked around for her other sisters. She spied Forsythia under a cottonwood tree, where a quilt had been spread for mothers and babies, and headed over.

Forsythia's brows drew together when she saw Lilac's face. "Everything all right?"

Lilac plunked down beside her with a sigh. "I'm afraid Reverend Pritchard's announcement has got feminine tongues wagging more than I could stand any longer."

"Oh dear." Forsythia adjusted a blanket over Nils, who was nursing. "I'm sorry to hear that."

Lilac smoothed her skirt over her knees. "Why do people always have to be difficult?"

Rachel Armstead chuckled and snagged her nine-month-old daughter from crawling off the quilt. "The question of the ages."

"I wish everyone could just be happy for them. And forget about . . . well, everything this past year." *And my part in it.* "I just hope Reverend Pritchard and Sylvia don't hear too much ugliness." She scanned the churchyard and found the pastor and his fiancée standing near the church door, talking with a few of the town leaders. Mr. Young, the owner of the bank, looked a bit ruffled. Lilac chewed the inside of her cheek.

Forsythia reached to squeeze her hand. "It isn't your job to fix this. You know that, right? Let God work on it. As He already is."

"Thanks." Lilac squeezed back. "You're right as usual."

"We should give some sort of going-away party for them," Rachel said. "After all, Reverend Pritchard has been with us for some time."

"What a wonderful idea." Forsythia nodded. "Food, music, dancing—lift everyone's spirits and send them off properly to their new life."

"I like that." Lilac's heart lightened. "I'll talk to Lark about it."

RJ approached. "All right if we head on over to your place, Forsythia? Del needs to get off her feet." He nodded to his very pregnant wife, standing by the wagon with her hands supporting her lower back.

"Of course." Forsythia expertly buttoned her bodice under the blanket, then drew the covering off and propped a sleeping Nils on her shoulder as she rose. "About time for us to leave, too, but go ahead. I need to gather the children."

"I'll get them." Lilac pushed to her feet and headed across the churchyard. "Robbie," she called after her oldest nephew as he streaked by her in a game of tag. "Your ma says time to go."

"Okay." Robbie sped to tag the boy ahead of him, then charged toward the Brownsville gathering, feet churning up dust.

Lilac shook her head. Where did he get that energy? She found Sofie and Mikael playing house with a collection of leaves and sticks by the church steps, along with two of the Weber children.

"Time to go." Lilac crouched beside them and gave one of Sofie's blond braids a tweak.

"No, Tante Lilac. Still playing." Mikael shook his head with three-year-old emphasis.

"I know. But you don't want to miss Sunday dinner, do you?" Lilac waggled her eyebrows. "Why don't you choose one stick to bring home with you? You just have to be careful not to poke anybody with it."

Mikael eyed her, then nodded and wrapped his chubby fingers

around a crooked twig. "Dis my wood-making tool yike Cousin Jesse. See?" He rubbed it along the side of the steps as if smoothing the wood.

"I see. Very nice." Lilac straightened and took his hand. "Come along now."

A child's scream cut across the churchyard. Lilac scooped up Mikael, stick and all, and ran around the corner of the building, Sofie dashing ahead.

They found Adam bending over little Klaus Hoffman under the tree on the other side of the yard.

"What happened?" Rev. Pritchard hurried up, Sylvia close behind him.

"The branch broke, and he fell on his arm." Adam gently felt the sobbing boy's forearm. "Klaus, I think you may have broken your arm. I'm going to need to take you back to my office so I can fix it, all right?"

"Mama," Klaus whimpered, tears streaking the grime on his face.

"I'm right here, *liebling*." Charlotte Hoffman knelt beside her son and stroked his hair. "My poor boy. Shall I have George bring our wagon over, Doctor?"

"I'll do it." Caleb, the eldest Hoffman son, spun and headed for their wagon at a run.

"We'll go to our home, the rooms on Main Street aren't quite ready yet. I'll help you move him. Gently now." Adam rose, the child in his arms, while Charlotte supported Klaus's feet.

Rev. Pritchard and Sylvia stepped back while Lilac shepherded Sofie and Mikael out of the way. Robbie stood sober faced, watching his friend be carried to the wagon.

"Well, that's an unfortunate ending to today's gathering." Rev. Pritchard pulled off his hat and ran his hand through his hair. "Poor little fellow."

"I've warned them time and again about climbing so high in these trees." Sylvia sighed.

"Now maybe you'll understand why I tell you to be careful, young man." Forsythia approached, baby in arms, and took Mikael's hand. "Lilac, Jonah is going to drive our wagon to the house since Adam is going with the Hoffmans. See you and Lark there?"

"Of course." Lilac drew a long breath and turned back to the reverend and Sylvia. "Despite all this, I wanted to tell you both congratulations. I'm so happy for you."

"Thank you." Sylvia smiled. "Though I'm afraid not everyone in the congregation seems particularly thrilled just now."

"They're only upset I'm leaving so suddenly." Rev. Pritchard puffed a sigh. "Seems I can't do right in everyone's eyes any which way this year."

Sylvia slipped her hand through his arm with a quiet squeeze.

"They'll get over it." Lilac shook her head. "Goodness, you were telling us way back at Climie's wedding you'd be moving on to Lincoln. Folks just don't like change and take any excuse to air their opinions."

Sylvia laughed. "As a schoolmarm, I can certainly attest that is true."

"Do you know where you'll live? And where you will have your wedding?" It still felt a bit odd to ask such questions with only a few months since Lilac and Rev. Pritchard had been discussing *their* wedding. Relief sprang again that she had finally realized that it wouldn't be right for either of them. This was so much better.

"They've already built a small parsonage by the church where we'll be serving." Rev. Pritchard looked down at Sylvia. "Reverend Douglas will marry us. Just a quiet ceremony with two witnesses. We've asked the Caldwells."

"They'll be perfect. Your family won't be able to come, though?" They had planned to come out at Easter for Lilac's wedding-that-wasn't-to-be.

"Sadly, no." Rev. Pritchard glanced at her as if remembering too, then down again at Sylvia, the light returning to his eyes. "It's all happened too fast, and my sister has a new baby and has been needing a good deal of help from my mother. But we're hoping for a trip to Pennsylvania in the fall."

"Well, we're planning some sort of send-off for you, just so you know." Lilac smiled. "Can't let you go without knowing how much we appreciate you both." She looked back over her shoulder at Lark's call and lifted her hand to tell her sister she was coming. "I'm being summoned. But I'll be praying for you both with all these changes."

"Thank you." Sylvia pressed Lilac's outstretched hand, her smile genuine. "We need it."

"Have a good visit with Reverend Pritchard and his wife-to-be?" Lark asked as they drove the short distance to the Brownsvilles'.

"I think so." Lilac pressed her hands between her knees. "Sometimes I'm still not quite sure how to feel or how to act around Ethan—I mean, the reverend. But it was good to talk to them. I really like Sylvia, and they seem a much better match than we were. They fit together, somehow. We never did, not really."

"I think it's just as well in many ways that they're moving to Lincoln," Del put in. "Give everyone a fresh start."

"Sythia and Rachel and I talked about planning some sort of celebration before they go. We can discuss it later." Lilac pulled her sunbonnet forward against the July sun, brightening toward midday. Del's words circled through her mind. Surely God had a fresh start for her too. But what would it look like?

At the Brownsvilles', Robbie threw open the door before they even climbed out of the wagon. "Ma's in the kitchen, Pa is still setting Klaus's arm in his office, his pa's helping. I heard Klaus holler once. I hope they're almost done." His eyes shone round.

Lilac met him on the porch and squeezed her nephew to her side in a hug. "I'm afraid bone setting is never a pleasant process, Robbie boy. But your pa knows just how to do it. And you youngsters heal fast, so don't worry. Klaus will be good as new before long."

"I hope so." Heading inside, Robbie cast a glance at the closed door of his father's office, then led the way to the kitchen. "Ma told me to keep Sofie and Mikael playing in the sandbox out back, that way they wouldn't hear anything."

"What a good brother you are. Why don't you go tell them we're here?"

Robbie dashed off, and Forsythia greeted them with a tired smile. "Sorry, between the accident and having to settle Nils again, I'm running a bit behind with dinner. I think he might be teething."

"What can we do?" Lark reached for an apron. "We brought biscuits and jam."

"Wonderful, just set them out and cut that cold roast, if you would. I've got new potatoes about ready. Lilac, would you get some lettuce from the garden for salad?"

"How about me?" Del asked.

Forsythia pointed to a chair with her wooden spoon. "You can put your feet up."

Del groaned but obeyed. "Did we boss you this much before you had Nils?"

"Oh, far more."

Soon they all gathered around the large dining table, RJ and Jonah arranging the chairs and benches for everyone. As they settled the children in their places, they could hear the Hoffmans leaving through the front door and the reassuring murmur of Adam's voice. A moment later, he appeared in the dining room doorway.

"You're just in time for grace. Is all well?" Forsythia asked.

"It's a minor break, should mend quickly, and I gave him a little laudanum for the pain." Adam heaved a sigh and sank into his chair. "If only we all healed like children." He reached out his hands to his wife and Sofie on either side of him. "Shall we pray?"

All bowed their heads.

"Father, thank you for this bountiful spread, and that we can gather as family. Thank you for bringing Lilac and Jonah safely back to join us. Thank you that Klaus's injury isn't worse, and we ask your healing for him and grace for his whole family. Bless Del and RJ and their coming little one, and continue to lead us all as we follow your path for us. In your Son's name we pray, amen."

Everyone joined in the "amen" and began passing plates.

"So, Lilac and Jonah, a rather eventful Sunday for your first week back." RJ helped himself from the bowl of potatoes.

"I guess so. I take it Reverend Pritchard's leaving is unexpected?" Jonah speared a bite of roast.

"Not unexpected, but we didn't know the transition would be so sudden." Adam shook his head. "I'm afraid there are more than a few ruffled feathers over what we're going to do now for a pastor. With him ministering in both Salton and Antelope Creek, those are some big shoes to fill."

"And now we're left without a schoolteacher once again too," put in Forsythia. "I confess that has me more worried than the other."

Sofie bounced on her seat, singsonging, "I want to go to school with Robbie."

"Not quite yet, sweet girl. Maybe next year, when you're six."

"Oh, that reminds me." Lilac put down her fork. "Adam, I ran into an old schoolmate back in Ohio who's looking for a teaching position out west. Who do you think will be in charge of the new hiring process?"

"Probably the usual town leaders: Young, Caldwell, myself. We really should organize an official school board. What's her name?"

"Actually, it's a he." Lilac's ears warmed, though she didn't know why they should. "Samuel Gubberud is his name."

"You saw Sam Gubberud?" Forsythia exclaimed. "Goodness, that name brings back memories. How is he? I always liked him, despite his schooldays shenanigans."

"We all did. He's well but lost an arm in the war. He went back to school to become a teacher and is looking to start over, I think."

"I'm sorry to hear that. But he could be a wonderful possibility for a teacher. I'd be glad to have our children taught by someone we know." Forsythia nudged her husband's arm. "Adam, you should have them write to him."

"I certainly will. Do you have his address, Lilac?"

"He's still living with his parents, right by the new store. I'll write Anders right away and ask him to speak to Sam." The thought of Sam coming out to Salton gave Lilac a pleasant tingle she wasn't ready to analyze quite yet. But surely it would be a good thing all around if he came. Good for the town and good for Sam to have a place to start fresh and yet have people he knew. They could help him get settled at the school, invite him out to supper at the farm . . .

"Lilac." Del tapped her elbow. "Where are you, dreaming up a new drawing? I was telling Sythia about the journal you found. Do you have it with you?"

"Oh yes." Lilac jumped up to grab her satchel. She pulled out the journal and stepped around the table to hand it to Forsythia. "I think it must be Grandfather Nielsen's. It's in Norwegian."

"Land sakes." Her sister turned the faded pages. "How did we never happen upon this before?"

"I'm not sure. Things were always a bit of a jumble in the attic. Apparently Josephine unearthed it when she was making room for more storage after the fire, but she didn't realize it wasn't something we knew about. She tucked it in that old trunk we used to raid for dress-up, remember? I saw your old favorite yellow slippers."

"Goodness, what memories that brings." Forsythia traced

the penned words with a gentle finger. "Now I wish more than ever I'd really learned Norwegian."

Having finished her plate, Del leaned back in her chair, resting her hand on the bulge of belly. "RJ, we were trying to think of someone who could translate the writing for us. Do you think Lars Olsen could?"

"Not sure. I can ask."

Lilac bent her head near Forsythia's blond one and turned a few pages to one of the sketches. "Look, he was an artist too. I remember Pa saying that, but I never saw any of his work before. The drawings are beautiful, so detailed and finely done." Lilac straightened. "Actually, there's something else I wanted to show you all." She reached back in the satchel and withdrew the paper she'd begun working on. "I've started enlarging one of his drawings. See?"

With murmurs and exclamations, her family gathered around. Lark took the paper carefully in her hands, studying the sketch of the children playing in the garden.

"I think that little boy might be Pa and his siblings." Lilac swallowed around the sudden lump in her throat. "By the first cabin his father built. Working on this has made Pa seem closer again. I want to finish it so it can be framed for the house back home."

Lark blinked hard. "Lilac, this is beautiful. In fact"—she smiled, though her eyes shone teary—"I'm going to commission you to make another one, maybe of a different picture, for our homestead here."

"Oh, what a wonderful idea." Forsythia clasped her hands. "I want one too!"

Del waggled a finger. "Don't think you're going to leave me out."

Lilac laughed, her throat tight with tears and joy. Well, she had her work cut out for her with Christmas gifts for this year. What a sweet serendipity the discovery of this journal had been already.

7

Standing in front of the newly rebuilt Nielsen Mercantile, Sam Gubberud fingered the sealed envelope he'd just picked up from the post office. Would this be the answer he was waiting for? Should he open it now or wait till he got home? Home would be the logical choice, but with Mor ever present to hover at his elbow . . . He grimaced and made a decision.

Stepping to the side so as to be out of the way of entering and exiting customers, he leaned against the store's porch railing and sliced open the envelope with his pocket knife, holding the envelope under his arm against his chest as he did so to secure it. Just one of many ways he'd learned to manage such simple tasks with only one hand.

He withdrew the sheet of paper. *Lord, thy will be done.* Sam unfolded the letter and began to read.

Dear Mr. Gubberud,

It is our pleasure to offer you the position of school-master in the town of Salton, should you choose to accept it. We have reviewed your application and impeccable references, and your education and interest in inspiring young lives seem an excellent answer to our town's

*need for a schoolmaster. As our fall term generally begins
by mid-August, we request a response at your earli-
est convenience. Accommodations for room and board
will be readily available at the Nielsen House, our town
boardinghouse, until you should wish to secure more permanent quarters. We eagerly await your reply.*

> *Respectfully,
> Henry Caldwell, Esq., Hiram
> Young, and Dr. Adam
> Brownsville*

Sam blew out the breath he'd been holding, then felt a grin tugging his cheeks. They wanted him to come. He, Samuel Jakob Gubberud, had his first official offer of a teaching position. A real, respectable job, and one where he need not be hampered by his injury.

Stuffing the letter inside his jacket, he headed into the store with a spring in his step. He still had a shopping list to fill.

"Morning, Sam." Anders greeted him from behind the counter. "You look mighty chipper today."

"I am, as a matter of fact." Sam pulled out the letter again. "Just got a reply from—uh, out where your sisters have settled." He cast a quick glance round the store. Anders had explained their continuing caution about sharing the specific location. "I surely do appreciate you helping make that connection. They want me to come."

"Well, how about that." Anders grinned. "That little town just keeps sucking away my old friends. First RJ, now you. You're planning to go?"

"I think so." He was more than ready for a fresh start some-where. Almost anywhere. "I just hope my parents will accept my going so far away." More specifically, his mother. Sam held back a wince at the thought of telling them tonight at the dinner table.

"Maybe it will help that you already know folks there. I know my sisters will do their best to help you get settled in any way they can. And you could stay at the boardinghouse till you get your bearings."

"That's what the letter suggests." He couldn't deny that Lilac Nielsen's presence there lent an extra appeal to Salton's invitation. Seeing her at the grand reopening had been a surprise, no less how she'd bloomed into womanhood from the lively little girl he remembered. He'd thought of their visit that day too many times to admit. The way she'd listened to him—really listened—the sparkle in her brown eyes, the way her dark curls had sprung about her face in the heat . . .

Anders was staring at him, an odd look on his face.

"I, uh." His ears burning, Sam fumbled to put the letter back in his jacket. "Sorry, what did you say?"

"Can I see your mother's list?"

"Yes." He drew a breath and forced his pulse to slow. "I'll go look for the buttons she wanted if you don't mind gathering the rest."

He kicked himself as he headed to the corner with ladies' dry goods. If merely thinking about Lilac turned him into an absentminded fool, he needed to get his head on straight before he headed west, if indeed he did. No matter what attraction the youngest Nielsen daughter might hold, he'd no business presuming anything would come of that. She no doubt still thought of him as the bothersome boy who'd pulled her pigtails. And now a man missing an arm at that. He flinched inwardly. Would any respectable woman ever want him, maimed as he was?

Sam pulled out a drawer of buttons and forced himself to focus on his mother's instructions. One dozen pearl buttons—not too white, no more than a quarter inch across. He fingered a card. These ought to do. Being his mother's only child had taught him some competency when it came to notions and things. Sometimes he wondered if he'd gone so hard into football, leadership, and mischief to help remind her—and himself—that he really could be an independent young man.

He shut the drawer and headed for the counter. Now he had only to stand his ground when he faced her tonight.

Sam inhaled deeply as he stepped inside the door of his parents' home that evening, the familiar aroma of his mother's Norwegian leek soup setting his stomach growling. He hung his hat in the entry, made sure to wipe his feet, and set his purchases on the sideboard to remove his summer jacket.

"Mor, I'm home."

"Goodness, I wondered what had happened." His mother instantly appeared in the hallway, her crown of barely graying blond hair pinned in the usual perfect swirls. "Here, let me help you." She reached to tug his jacket sleeve off his good arm, then folded the garment neatly, the pinned half sleeve on the inside, and handed it back to him. "There you are."

He'd nearly had it off himself. Sam bit the inside of his cheek. "Thank you, Mor."

"You got everything from the store? I never dreamt it would take you so long." His mother bustled over to the sideboard to inspect the packages. "I hope it all wasn't too much for you to carry."

"Everything should be there. And I had other errands to run first." Like the trip to the post office. The letter seemed to smolder in the inner pocket of his jacket, the one his mother had just folded and handed to him. Good thing she hadn't noticed the envelope, he wouldn't have put it past her to pounce on it then and there.

"Well, supper's nearly on the table. Come wash up and say hello to your far."

Sam obeyed, brushing water through his hat-mussed hair at the washbasin, then headed into the dining room where his father already sat, reading a newspaper. A quiet, round little man with a blond mustache thicker than Sam's own, his far looked up with a placid nod of greeting. Sam smiled back, grateful as always that his father rarely demanded talk.

His mother, God love her, more than made up for it.

Sam sat and glanced around the familiar dining room, the rosemaled plates displayed on shelves on the walls, their hand-painted florals proclaiming his family's heritage. While a few other families in town hailed from Norway, like the Nielsens, the majority hadn't held to the traditions as tightly as his. Mostly thanks to his mother, though his father had ensured Sam could not only speak but also read and write the language of their heritage.

"Here we are." His mother sailed into the room with the tureen of soup. "Now just to bring the fowl and the salad. It's such a hot day, I thought roast chicken would be lovely."

"Let me help you." Sam pushed back his chair and stood.

"No, no, I'll get it." She flapped her hand at him.

"It's silly for you to carry it all. I'll get the chicken."

"No need to risk you dropping it on the floor. I can get it."

"Nora," his father remonstrated, emerging from his newspaper.

"Oh, honestly." Fluttering her hands by her shoulders, his mother disappeared back into the kitchen.

Sam hesitated on his feet a moment longer, then sank into his chair in defeat. He glanced at his father, who sighed and shook his head.

"She means well, son."

"I know." But meaning well didn't make someone easy to live with, however loved. He lifted his good hand to massage the tension in the back of his neck.

"All right, then." His mother bustled back in with the chicken, smile in place. "Jakob, do set that newspaper aside before you get newsprint on my clean tablecloth." She seated herself and extended her hands for the blessing. "Now, let us pray."

Sam had a sudden urge to ignore his mother's hand reaching across the table. She'd specifically rearranged their family seating after he lost his arm, ensuring she could still hold Sam's hand, though that meant he couldn't hold his father's. As if their mother-son bond mattered more than anything. It had always irked him, but he'd never said anything, except a quiet word to his father, who told him not to mention it.

"You've no idea how hard it hit your mother when she heard you'd been wounded, son." Far had shaken his head. "Took to her bed for weeks till they finally sent you home—I nearly thought it'd kill her."

What about the fact it had nearly killed him? Sam shut his mind against the memories of lying on the battlefield with a mangled arm, of the amputation tent, of lying in the hospital surrounded by the moans of fellow soldiers. He was one of the lucky ones. He knew that. So did his mother . . . and she seemed determined never to let him far from her side again.

"Samuel?" She held out her hand, eyes expectant.

Sam tightened his jaw and took her hand, bowing his head so as not to see the tenderness in her gaze. Guilt clamped his middle. What an ungrateful wretch he was . . . yet sometimes, he felt far too much like an overgrown bird whose mother kept trying to force him back under her wing.

"*I Jesu navn* . . ." His father intoned the opening words of the traditional Norwegian table prayer.

Samuel joined in with his mother, the familiar words soothing his heart and easing the tension in his stomach.

After the amen, his father carved the chicken, serving small enough slices onto Sam's plate that his mother wouldn't offer to cut it for him—a kindness of Far's that Sam never failed to appreciate.

"So who did you see in town today?" Mor dipped a spoon into her soup.

Sam swallowed a spoonful of his own, the leeks, potatoes,

and carrots savory on his tongue. Try him though she might, he would dearly miss his mother's cooking if he headed west. "Anders, of course. At the store." Perhaps this might be an opportunity to bring up the letter from Salton.

"I do like that new building. The old one was always too dark inside. Not that I'm glad it burned down, of course. But there's always a silver lining."

"I know the Nielsens deeply appreciate you sounding the alarm that night. Anders, Jonah, and Lilac all mentioned their thanks, and for how you started the bucket brigade, Far."

"What are neighbors for?" His father rubbed his mustache and shrugged.

"I never did see Lilac when she was in town. She must be a grown woman now."

"She is." And a lovely one at that. "We had a nice visit reminiscing about old schooldays."

"The Nielsen girls were always a bit unconventional. The way they set off west without a word to anyone—well, it's never what I'd think of for proper young ladies. But their parents were fine people, and I've nothing against them, and of course, as you say, you all went through school together." His mother dabbed her lips with her napkin. "Which reminds me, I inquired about whether there'd be an opening for you at the local school, Sam. The headmaster said they may be looking for an instructor for the upper grades."

Sam's jaw tightened again. "Mor, I told you I'd rather not teach here in Linksburg."

"Nonsense, you already know everyone, and they know you."

"Which isn't necessarily an advantage for a schoolmaster."

"And you can live right here at home."

Another disadvantage, in his mind. But he wouldn't break her heart by saying so. *Just by moving several states away?* Sam flinched at the thought.

"At any rate, I told the headmaster you'd be in touch."

"Mother." Sam set his fork down with a sharp rap. "You'd no business doing that."

"I beg your pardon?" The sharpness in his mother's voice matched his.

His father looked from one to the other and cleared his throat. "Nora, it really wasn't your place."

"What, a mother can't look out for her only boy?"

"Ja, but let him do the talking, next time."

"Well, all I said was—"

"Listen, both of you. Please." Sam spread his hand on the table and drew a breath. "Mor, I'm sorry I spoke sharply."

Her sniff either spoke acceptance or nursed resentment, he couldn't tell.

"But there's something I need to tell you. I have a job offer out west."

His mother stared. So did his father.

"What?" Mor's voice came as fragile as blown glass.

"It's in Nebraska, a town near where the Nielsen sisters have settled—though I'll have to ask you to keep that information to yourselves for now, I'll explain later. But they're in need of a schoolteacher. I applied, and they've asked me to come."

Silence. The evening breeze lifted the curtains of the open dining room window.

"How long have you been planning this, son?" His father pushed his chair back and folded his arms.

"I've been looking into positions out west for some time, but I only got the letter this afternoon."

"You're not . . ." His mother seemed struggling for breath. "You're surely not going to take it?"

"I am still praying about it." Sam inhaled through his nose. "But, yes, at this point I plan to. And I need to let them know as soon as I can."

"But we can take care of you here!" Her clasped hands strangled each other. "How are you going to manage out there on the frontier? No modern conveniences, no family to help you? I've heard what it's like out there, blizzards and outhouses and outlaws—"

"Whoa there, Nora." His father half chuckled. "He's only going to teach school, not ride the trails."

"And you both act as if it's settled. I suppose it doesn't matter a particle what I think." She leaned her head on her hand and covered her eyes.

Sam narrowly refrained from rolling his own eyes. He glanced at his father. Far met his gaze a moment, then the lines around his mouth softened. He gave Sam a slow, firm nod.

Something relaxed in his chest. *Thank you*, he mouthed. Then he rose and rounded the table to lay his hand on his mother's shoulder.

"Mor, of course I care what you think." He swallowed, the next words catching in his throat. But he needed to say them. "You've been caring for me for years—and I appreciate it, never think I do not. But I need to learn how to be a man on my own. Find my own life . . . if I can. And learn to stand on my own two feet." His mouth quirked. "At least I've still got two of those."

His mother lowered her hand and heaved a sigh. "I simply don't see why you need to go so far away. If you refuse to teach here in Linksburg, why not try somewhere else close by? There must be plenty of schools in Ohio who would welcome your expertise."

"But maybe not my lack of experience. I've yet to actually teach a class, after all." Salton's desperation for a teacher had no doubt worked in his favor, though he hoped their choice of him came based on more than that. "And as much as I love you both, I do feel the need for something new, something different. A fresh start."

They all sat a moment, the breeze from the window blowing its cooling breath over them. His mother absently stroked his hand on her shoulder. His only hand.

Then his father stood, leaning on the table. "Well then, son. If this is where you sense the Lord leading, then you have our blessing." He glanced hard at his wife. "Doesn't he, Nora?"

She released a shuddering breath. "Clearly I don't have much choice in the matter." She pulled Sam's head down to her level and laid her hands on either side of his mustached face. "You will always have a home here with us. You understand me?"

"Ja." Sam covered her hand with his own, then leaned forward to kiss her forehead.

That night in his room, he stood long by the window, lifting the single dumbbell he used to strengthen his good arm in various exercises each evening. He had also devised various calisthenics to build his shoulder and back muscles overall, not wanting his injury to let him grow slack, even if he couldn't achieve the athletic prowess he'd once known.

At last setting the weight aside with a long breath, he stepped closer to the window, letting the evening air cool the perspiration from his face and ease the strain of the day. So many years he'd watched from this window—as a child, watching other kids in the street and wishing for brothers and sisters who never came. His mother had some complication after Sam's birth . . . he wasn't privy to the details, but it had meant no more children for his parents, no doubt an extra reason she cherished Sam so. Then as an older boy, he'd climbed from this window many a time to reach the spreading branches of the oak growing beside, sneaking from the house for one adventure or another when he was supposed to be studying. Sam winced and chuckled, remembering the time he'd fallen and broken his wrist. Disobedience had brought its own punishment that time for sure.

He touched the healed stump at his left elbow. He no longer had that wrist.

He closed his eyes. *What now, Lord? Are my days of calling this window, this room, my own coming to an end? Is Salton where you would have me go? I want to . . . I do want to. But more than that, I want your will.* A fragment of Scripture whispered through his mind: *"he that openeth, and no man shutteth."* Well, God had opened the door, hadn't He? Perhaps now it came for him to walk through it. By faith.

Sam lifted his head and grinned, a stirring in his chest. He had a telegram to send tomorrow.

8

So meet at Del's tomorrow to can peas?" Lilac asked after church.

"And make raspberry jam," Lark added. "Forsythia, are you sure you can come?"

"I asked Tilda to come along and take care of the little ones, or she can stay here with them."

"Perhaps that would be better. You want Robbie back?" He'd been at the farm more this summer than at home in town. Lark had come to depend on her nephew's help since he'd kept on doing many of Lilac's chores even though she had returned home from Linksburg, freeing her to work on her drawings for the newspaper.

"Is he a big help out there?"

"Far more than I ever dreamed he would be. The three of us will start picking peas as soon as chores are done. Del will be getting the jars ready and sitting down shelling peas."

The next morning, peas were picked, and they sat down to shell by midmorning.

Robbie popped a full pod open and threw the peas in his mouth. "Wish we could eat them this way all the time." The others copied him.

"Sofie, well, the others too, sure have missed you this summer." Forsythia closed her eyes in delight at the sweetness of the peas. "She could be here shelling peas too, but she entertains Mikael, and Tilda brought her little brother so her mother can work at the boardinghouse."

Del came out and sat down with an "oof."

"Are you all right?" Forsythia asked.

"I know this baby can come any day, and as far as I'm concerned, the sooner the better." Del struggled to put a bowl to catch the peas on her lap and looked up to see Robbie trying to hide a giggle behind his hands. Del winked at him and set her bowl on the small table Lark moved in front of her. When they filled one bucket with empty peapods, Robbie brought out another.

"While you're up, how about fetching that plate of cookies on the table." Del shifted and grimaced. Robbie grinned at her, returning almost instantly to hold the cookie plate out for the others before setting it on the table and grabbing two.

"I know you don't want to go lie down, but perhaps even a bit will help." Forsythia and Lark swapped concerned looks.

"Let's get these peas shelled, and then I'll lie down while you put dinner on the table. I have a pot of soup simmering, and I baked bread yesterday." Del shifted again.

By the time all the peas were shelled, a second bucket of empty pods was almost full. "You want me to throw the pods over the fence?" Robbie paused. "Do horses and cows like pea pods?"

Lark shrugged. "Toss them over and find out. If they don't, we'll put the next buckets on the compost heap."

"The chickens will like them. Chickens like everything." Robbie whistled for Scamp, and the two headed for the pasture fence.

Forsythia smiled to her sisters and waggled her eyebrows. "He is growing up so fast."

Del struggled to push herself upright, so Lark and Lilac each grabbed an arm and helped pull her up. "Uff da." Del kneaded her lower back. "I think I will lie down."

When they had dinner dished up, Del joined them at the table. "Thanks, that did feel good." As soon as they finished eating, they began pouring peas into the jars on the counter.

Robbie filled the woodbox and dusted off his hands. "Now what?"

"Uh-oh." Del looked to Forsythia, her eyes wide. "Robbie, how about you and Scamp go check on the sheep?"

"Sure." He stuffed the final two cookies in his pockets and out the door he went, whistling for Scamp again.

"Del, what's wrong?" Lark stepped closer.

"I think my water just broke." She pointed to a puddle on the floor.

Forsythia grinned. "It sure did. Probably what you've been feeling all morning were beginning labor pains."

"So now what?"

"Now you start walking."

"Let's get the canning finished first." She doubled over. "Ow!"

"Wouldn't you know, Adam left early this morning on a call," Forsythia said.

"You want to send Robbie out to find him? He could ride Starbright," Lilac asked. She fetched a rag to wipe up the floor. "That would keep him busy."

"Good idea." Lark nodded. "But there's no rush. Sythia has helped bring plenty of babies into this world. We're all right."

"And a first baby usually takes longer." Forsythia wrapped her arm around Del. "Come on, let's walk."

Lilac left to get Starbright saddled and tell Robbie to go find his pa.

Lark poured boiling water over the peas in the jars, then placed a set of jars in the big soup kettle of boiling water. She stoked the stove and set the kettle on the hottest part. Stepping out on the porch, she waved at Robbie as he set off for town. Whistling for Scamp to stay home, she lifted her face to the breeze. "Lord God, thank you the peas are now getting canned, and what a perfect time for Del to go into labor, with the peas done and all of us here together." Jonah had gone over to Jorgensens' farm today to help the storekeeper set up his own new mowing machine—also good timing.

Back in the house, she found Del mixing up something in the kitchen. "I thought you were walking."

"Might as well keep busy. I'll walk too."

"What are you making?"

"Sourdough biscuits—rolls, buns—whatever you want to call them." She scrunched her face and waited out a contraction before dumping her dough out on a floured board. Inhaling a deep breath, she started kneading. Forsythia and Lark swapped shrugs.

"Think I'll go out in the garden." Lilac snagged her broad-brimmed straw hat off the peg by the door. "Call me if I can do anything."

"We'll have fresh buns for supper, and if Robbie comes back, I'll make some fried bread."

Lilac paused in the doorway. "He's not the only one who enjoys fried bread."

Del shrugged. "Fine. It should be ready to fry in about an hour if I set it in the window."

As she set the dough in a bowl a short while later, her body tightened up again, and she braced her arms on the counter. "That was a harder one." She looked to Forsythia. "Wasn't that one closer?"

Sythia nodded. "Come walk with me." With the covered bowl on the west window sill, Del gave in to her sister's extended hand.

"Do we have to stay in the house?"

Sythia shrugged, and she and Lark both held their sister's arms as they stepped down to the porch. "You want a wet cloth to tie around your head?"

"No, thanks. It's not that bad out here. Let's go find Lilac." Del stopped talking and instead bent over to wait for the spasm to pass. She straightened back up. "Uff da."

"You all right?" Lilac called from the garden.

"Ja!" Del answered. "I think they are getting worse."

"You are progressing well." Forsythia rubbed her shoulder.

"Glad you think so." Del mopped her face with her apron. "Any idea how much longer?"

"You never know with a first baby. Some firsts take twelve, twenty-four hours, who knows how long."

Del shook her head. "You are so encouraging."

Sythia shrugged. "Now, now, no sarcasm allowed." But her grin took any sting from her words. "That can come later when you are closer to delivery."

"How come the cows and sheep seem to have calves and lambs so much easier than we do?"

"Good question. Want to go back inside?"

"I'd rather scrub the porch steps."

"That's fine too."

As soon as another wave passed, Del began scrubbing the porch steps on her hands and knees, and Lark went inside to put another set of jars in the kettle to boil.

While she waited for the peas, Lark started mashing raspberries for jam. She glanced at the clock. The afternoon was ticking right along. Had Robbie found Adam or RJ? *Thank you, Father, for giving us peace regardless.* Such a wondrous thing to have a baby right here in the midst of daily life. She switched jars, then headed out to check on her sisters.

Del was sweeping the area around the table in the shade. "Are the pains getting further apart?"

"They are. Sorry." Forsythia wiped the table with a rag, working around Lilac, who had brought her drawing tablet over.

Just then, another contraction left Del leaning on the broom and panting. "Uff da, that . . ." She put the broom away and started walking again. She paused to look over Lilac's shoulder. "Ha, do I really look that bad?"

"No, this is more of a caricature." Lilac grinned at her sister.

"Thought I'd frame it for RJ." At her sister's intake of breath, Lilac shook her head. "No, I wouldn't."

With a sigh of relief, Del returned to her walking. She waddled, and Sythia stayed right beside her. "I'm hankering for some swizzle."

Lark followed along. "You want me to fix some?"

"No, I will." On her way back to the house, Del grabbed Sythia's arm and clenched her teeth as she nearly doubled over.

"Good one."

"The thought of hours more of this makes me want to puke—or scream."

"Go ahead and scream. No one else is around to hear. And there is no clean up."

She pulled herself up the steps by the railing RJ had built. "Might a beached whale feel about like I do?"

"No idea, never been a whale. I'll get the ingredients out for swizzle." Lark led them into the kitchen.

"The raspberry juice is in the well house."

"I'll send Lilac to get that."

"You don't have to stay right with me," Del said as Lark came back in.

"For our peace of mind, we do. If you had your way, you'd go find a dark room and curl up like a cat would do."

Del wasn't listening, her arms rigid, braced against the counter. She blew out a breath, just as Lilac came into the house.

"Another one, huh?"

Sythia stirred the raspberry mix and poured it into their glasses, which Lark set on the tray and carried outside.

"There are cookies in the tin in the pantry." Del started toward the pantry but doubled over instead. "Am I allowed to lie down for a while?"

"If you'd like," Sythia said. "Swizzles first? The breeze is lovely outside."

Del nodded. "I'll get a pillow to sit on."

"I will. Lark, will you move the rocking chair outside?"

"Of course, then I think I'll take over in the garden for a while."

They quickly had Del sitting in the rocker with a pillow behind her and a hassock at her feet. "This feels really good. Thank you."

"You're welcome." Lilac handed her sister one of the glasses. "I was teasing you about the picture."

"I know." Del held the cool glass up to her forehead and blew out a breath. After a sip, she sighed. "You know what I'm grateful for?"

The others shook their heads.

"The breeze, the canned peas now sitting on the counter, and that this isn't one of those horribly hot muggy days."

They raised their glasses. "Hear, hear."

Lark drained her swizzle, then headed down the steps. "Call me when you need me. I'll be in the garden."

A groan turned her around at the gate to see Del doubled over on the porch, Forsythia catching the glass from her hand.

Lark chuckled and headed back up. *Or maybe not.*

When she could breathe again, Del panted, "Robbie sure has been gone awhile."

"Lilac told him there was no rush." Forsythia eased her back up. "But if you get in trouble, we'll send Scamp for him."

"Um, I know this is part of the birthing, but I feel a lot of pressure."

Forsythia nodded. "Let's get you lying down so I can check to see how you are doing." They helped Del get up out of the chair and into the bedroom, where the bed was all ready for her, the covers folded over the quilt stand in the corner, extra sheets folded over a chair. She breathed a sigh of relief when she laid down. Sythia checked her and smiled. "You are doing very well. Keep on like this, and we might have a baby pretty soon."

Del gritted her teeth and arched her back. "Can't be too soon for me."

"All right, let's all lay our hands on her belly and pray."

Lark lightly rubbed her sister's belly. "Lord God, thank you for such a perfect day for having a baby, us all together, a breeze, birds singing outside, and you right here with us. Thank you that you are in charge, and we trust you to bring this baby into our world without undue pain and problems. Amen." Another contraction made Del groan and puff afterward.

After both of the others prayed Del through another contraction, Sythia said softly, "Del, hang on to my hands. Lark, you prop yourself against the headboard and spread your legs wide so Del can lean against you. Lilac, please bring in a basin of cool water. The hard part is just about here."

Lark kissed her sister's head. "You're doing well, Del. Keep it up." She found herself pushing against the headboard behind her as Del pushed against her. *Oh, Lord, keep this baby and my dear sister safe.* All her thoughts seemed to be prayers. "Do you all feel the Lord's presence here? It is so calm and peaceful." The others nodded, and Del pushed.

"Go ahead and scream, Del. It's just us and God here." Forsythia blinked and sniffed. "I can see the baby's head. Here we go, Del, push when that contraction comes."

Three more screams, and a baby slid right into Forsythia's waiting hands. "Del, you have a baby girl." She laid the squalling baby on Del's chest. "And far as I can tell, she is perfect but not real happy about this whole thing."

Del smoothed a hand over her daughter's head. "I think she's an opinionated one. Hey, little one, you are indeed unhappy. We'll fix that."

While Del flinched through another contraction, Forsythia tied off the now flaccid cord and cut it with scissors that had been boiling on the stove, along with needle and thread if needed. "How about Lilac gives her a bath while you and I work through getting the afterbirth delivered, and then you can have her back?"

"Any idea what you are going to name her?" Lilac asked as she picked up the baby.

"No, we have several names in mind for a boy and haven't agreed on a name for a girl yet." Del clenched her teeth.

"Well, we'll find one."

Sythia massaged her sister's belly. "Come on, let's get the afterbirth delivered so you can take a nap. Surely Robbie will be back with either Adam or RJ soon."

"First thing he always says is 'What's for supper?'" Del winced and arched her back against Lark. "Ow."

"Good one, sister mine," Sythia encouraged, "now we can finish cleaning up."

"Did you plan something for supper?" Lark asked, stroking her sister's hair.

"Have a rabbit cooling in the tank, thought I'd fry that. . . . We forgot the fried bread." She stretched and raised her arms for Sythia to drop a clean nightdress over them. Lark slipped out from her place, and Lilac laid the now clean and swaddled baby in Del's arms.

"See if you can get her to nurse," Sythia whispered.

A meadowlark sang from the meadow, and the cooling breeze lifted the curtains. Mother and baby drifted off to much-needed sleep.

Lark fried rabbit in the kitchen while Forsythia dug under the potato plants in search of new potatoes to go with the leftover peas. Lilac was out picking lettuce leaves for salad when they heard Scamp charge down the lane to greet the two horses and riders. RJ on Captain and Robbie astride Starbright stopped at the hitching rail.

"They're sleeping," Lark called.

"They? Already?" RJ flipped the reins over the rail and charged into the house. Lark nodded toward the bedroom.

"You have a daughter and all is well."

"I wish Robbie'd found me sooner."

"He was off searching for his pa first. Short of Scamp, who could we send? Our job was right here."

RJ tiptoed into the bedroom. Lark followed, stopping in the doorway as RJ knelt by the bed and stroked Del's hair. Her eyes fluttered open.

"Meet your daughter." Del shifted to unwrap the babe in the crook of her arm.

"Oh, Del, she's beautiful. No hair?"

"Just a faint fuzz. All us were born towheads so I guess it carries on."

RJ stroked a gentle finger over his daughter's head. "She came fast."

"Didn't feel like it to me, but I didn't know she'd come today when you left for work."

RJ turned to see Robbie standing with Lark in the doorway. He motioned to the boy. "Come see our new baby."

Robbie stood beside him, hand on his uncle's shoulder. "Mikael was little like that. Does she have a name yet?" Both RJ and Del shook their heads. "She needs a name."

"Yes, she does," said RJ. "Any suggestions?"

Robbie shrugged, then his face lit up. "Well, her ma and aunts are all named after flowers, so how about Lily Belle?"

Del and RJ looked at each other and smiles spread across their faces. "Lily Belle Hope Easton." Del held her hand out to Robbie. "Perfect. We'll tell her Cousin Robbie came up with her name."

"I named the cows and the sheep, so why not a new baby?"

RJ shook his hand. "Well done. Let's go put away the horses and do the evening chores."

Lark blew out a long breath. Chores marched on regardless of the hard work and miracles on any day. *Thank you, Lord God, for a safe and healthy mother and baby girl.* Yet a sudden longing pierced amid the joy.

Would she ever get to be a mother someday?

9

"Look, a letter from Anders." Lilac flapped the envelope in her hand at Lark and Jonah as she hurried into the soddy a few days later, back from mailing a set of drawings in town.

"Oh good." Lark turned away from stirring supper on the stove and reached for the letter. "Want to read it now?"

"Might as well." Lilac glanced at Jonah, her middle tensing. Their younger brother sat down by the table, arms folded across his chest, his shirt showing sweat stains and stray bits of hay from mowing all day. Would Anders say anything about Ringwald?

Lark cocked a brow at the two of them, then slit the envelope with Pa's letter opener, kept nearby on a kitchen shelf. She unfolded the letter—only a single page, written on one side—and read.

Dear family,

We are well, and business is booming. Despite my weariness each night, I am so thankful the Lord has enabled us to come back from such a disaster, seemingly stronger than before. We are hopeful we may be able to pay off

*our loan by the end of next year, which would be such a
weight off my mind.*

*I chiefly wanted to write to let you know some news
about Slate Ringwald. Last week, I heard he has set off for
the east, presumably to die there, so I hope that relieves
your minds on that score.*

*I hope Jonah is earning his keep and not eating you out
of house and home. Josephine sends her love, as do the
girls. Tell Lilac that Marcella and Greta asked for their
'Tante Lila' many times a day after she left.*

More soon. Love to all.

*Your brother,
Anders*

Lark blew out a breath and handed the letter to Lilac. "Well.
There's something to thank the Lord for."

"Sure is." Lilac rubbed her thumb over the penned lines, tears
pricking her eyes. "I've been trying to trust Him with this, but
sometimes I lie awake at night imagining Ringwald coming out
here on the train or—"

"You know what Ma would say about those thoughts."

"That they're fear talking, I know. And we know where fear
comes from." Still, she felt she could breathe more freely. "You
want to see it, Jonah?"

Their brother took the letter, silently scanned it, then nodded.
"That's good." He stood and handed the letter back to Lark. "Did
you still want to look at the mower after supper?"

Lilac and Lark shrugged at each other. Who knew what went
on in their brother's mind.

"Yes, we need to make sure it's still in good shape after these
first days of mowing." Lark pulled out a loaf of bread to slice.
"Be nice to have our fields done before we head to the celebration tomorrow night if we can, since the other farmers in our

mowing rotation will be expecting us to start next week." It sure helped having Jonah here—they never would have made such fast progress with haying already otherwise.

"I'm so looking forward to the party." Her feet now light as a spring lamb's, Lilac set plates on the table. "About time we had another town gathering, even if it's mostly to send off Ethan and Sylvia. Jonah, all the girls will be glad for another young man to dance with."

He shrugged and glanced out at the falling dusk. "If you say so."

Lilac bit her lip. Was he still thinking about Ringwald? Surely they could finally put all that behind them.

Off to a dance. The thought sent a happy tingle through Lark's middle as she hupped the horses the following Saturday.

Lilac sat beside her on the wagon seat, Jonah in the back—he'd let them have the seat so as not to muss their party dresses. Del had elected to stay home, not yet ready for a night out with a newborn, even to honor Rev. Pritchard and Sylvia at tonight's festivities. RJ stayed with her and Lily, of course.

And they'd meet Forsythia and Adam there. Would she see Isaac? The thought snuck in, but Lark batted it away.

The setting sun cast gold-edged shadows across the prairie by the time they arrived at the train station, which had become a town gathering place for celebrations thanks to the ample building size and large outdoor platform for dancing. Musicians already stood tuning their instruments at one end of the platform, where Lark and Lilac would soon join them. Lark set the wagon brake, Jonah helped them climb down, and they carried their platters of food into the train station, where long tables already bore hams and chickens, salads and preserves, pickles and baked goods. Jesse, setting up a barrel of lemonade, waved at them with a grin.

"This is so fun." Lilac clasped her hands and beamed at the families gathering, the laughter and chatter. "I'm so glad everyone finally put aside their petty differences."

"They may just be saving them for the congregational meeting tomorrow." But Lark smiled and straightened one of the lilac-hued ribbons adorning her sister's dark curls. "You look so pretty."

Lilac gave a little twirl, her lavender lawn skirt swirling about her. "So do you."

Lark lifted a hand to her lace collar, fastened tonight with Ma's pearl brooch. She rarely wore it, but tonight seemed a fitting occasion, and it set off her blue church dress nicely. She'd even worn her hoop under the full skirt, something she rarely did these days. She still found the bell shape awkward to walk in, but tonight . . . she'd wanted to look her best.

As if reading her thoughts, she caught a glance from Isaac McTavish across the platform and had to swallow, her eyes darting away. Why did her heart insist on pattering lately at the sight of that man? *Be sensible, Lark.*

The twang of a concertina lassoed her focus. "We better get our instruments." They'd promised to play tonight, as usual, though she'd make sure Lilac got a chance to dance and hoped to get in at least a reel or two herself. With whom was a question she refused to contemplate.

Lark fingered the familiar strings of her guitar in the musicians' corner while Lilac tuned her violin. George Hoffman drew his washtub near, with Anthony Armstead on concertina.

Mr. Caldwell stepped forward and beamed at the gathering. "Welcome, all. What a joy it is to celebrate together tonight— even if mingled with sadness at bidding our beloved minister good-bye. Yet we rejoice also in the new future the Lord has for him and his lovely new bride. Reverend and Mrs. Pritchard, won't you come forward?"

Rev. Pritchard stepped to the center of the platform, Sylvia on his arm, a rare pink in her cheeks. They'd already moved to their new home in Lincoln and were just back tonight for the festivities. By the settled happiness on the young pastor's face, married life agreed with him nicely. Lark glanced at Lilac and smiled to herself. At least now that he was with the right bride.

"We're here to celebrate tonight, to make merry, dance hard, and eat well. But first, we want to ask the Lord's blessing over you, Reverend." Mr. Caldwell extended his hand to his wife, and Beatrice joined him. Together, they laid their hands on the shoulders of the young couple.

"Father God, as Reverend and Mrs. Pritchard have so served and blessed our community, we now ask that you bless them. Bless them with grace as they learn a new place, with strength and wisdom as they begin a new ministry and life together. Bless them with joy in their marriage, with love and patience when they encounter trials. Most of all, bless them with the continual awareness of thy presence with them at all times—as you also are with us. In the name of Jesus Christ we pray, amen."

"Amens" resounded from all sides. Lark noticed the reverend had to lower his glasses to swipe at his eyes.

"And now"—Mr. Caldwell cleared his throat, clapping the preacher on the back—"before we all end up in tears, remember these two just had a wedding. Let's celebrate!"

Cheers and applause. Lark lifted her brows at the musicians and nodded. Lilac struck the pitch on her fiddle, and they all launched into "Soldier's Joy" as couples formed into squares on the dance floor, Rev. Pritchard and Sylvia leading off the closest set.

Laughter and music swirled around them, paced by the sashay of skirts and stamp of feet as the sky faded from sunset gold and rose to deep blue and violet.

Lark's fingers flew, hardly needing to pay attention to chords she knew so well. She smiled to see Mr. and Mrs. Jorgensen dancing, the mercantile proprietress wearing a uncommon beam on her careworn face. And was that Jonah promenading with Tilda Hoffman? Quite a light in the young woman's dark eyes as she looked up at their younger brother. *Hmm.* Lark glanced at Lilac to see if she'd noticed, but Lilac had her eyes closed as she fiddled with all her heart.

At last everyone took a break to eat. Lark set down her guitar and wiggled her fingers to get the feeling back, then followed the line snaking into the train station and out with laden plates. She could do with a glass of lemonade—the early August evening was warm, even if she hadn't been dancing.

She lost track of her sisters in the crowd and emerged from the building alone, plate in hand. She searched for Jesse's lemonade barrel and headed toward it.

"May I?" Appearing at her side, Isaac McTavish held out a tin cup.

"Oh, I can get it." Lark bit her tongue. She hadn't meant to sound rude, but where had he suddenly come from? "I mean, thank you. That would be very kind."

One corner of his mouth tipped, but Isaac said nothing as he filled her cup and handed it over.

"Thank you," she said again, the metal of the cup cool against her palm. She glanced about, her stomach flipping. "Did you eat already?"

"Left my plate over yonder." He nodded to some lumber stacked by the edge of the train platform. "Just thought you could use a hand."

So he had deliberately come over to offer his assistance. Lark's neck warmed beneath her high collar.

Isaac tipped his head. "Care to join me?"

Unable to think of a reason not to, Lark nodded.

"Afraid this ain't quite proper seatin' for a lady." Isaac attempted to brush sawdust from the boards with his old army cap. "Shall we find us another spot?"

"I'm not exactly a fine lady." The tangle in her middle easing,

Lark grinned and sat herself down on the lumber, lifting her hoop with one hand from behind to let her skirt flounce properly over the boards. "Even if I might look it tonight." She arched a brow at him.

"You surely do." Isaac chuckled and perched beside her. "Well, here we are, then."

"Are you enjoying the evening?" Lark bit into a bite of crisply fried chicken and closed her eyes at the flavor. Must be Beatrice Caldwell's.

"Mighty nice." Isaac surveyed the gathering. "Always good to be among these folks."

"Any word yet from your family who were coming out? Your uncle, wasn't it?"

His brow furrowed. "My uncle passed on toward the end of winter, sudden-like. Pneumonia, they said. Guess all the worry with those outlaws had took a toll on him more than we knew."

"Oh, I'm so sorry." Lark lowered her fork. How had she not known that?

"Well, he'd lived a good life, as they say. And his son, my cousin Ambrose, he's still fixin' to come, 'long with his wife and children." Isaac cast her a quick grin. "So looks like I'll have kin of my own around here soon after all. Been a mighty long time."

"You know we see you as practically family ourselves." Lark bit the inside of her cheek—would that seem forward? "I mean, you know you're always welcome at the Nielsens'."

"I do." He held her gaze.

"Lark, they're getting ready to start up the music again." Lilac stopped in front of them. "Do you want to dance now?"

She did, but Lark kept herself from glancing at Isaac, who sat silently. "I can wait. You go ahead and dance a couple of rounds. I'll come play." She snatched another bite of corn bread and nodded her thanks to Isaac, who took her plate. "Thank you."

"Thank you kindly for joinin' me." He dipped his head in that courtly way of his.

Lark shook her head to clear the swirls from it as she headed back to the musicians. What was up with that man? Seeming to seek out her company, but did he give any hint of asking her to dance, even at a good opportunity like that? No.

She played several more dances, then stopped for a dipper of water. Lilac hurried up, rosy-cheeked and breathless. "All right, your turn."

"I don't know . . ." If no one were to ask her, perhaps she'd rather just play.

Lilac nodded to behind Lark. "You've got a partner waiting."

Lark's heart leaped. She spun to see Adam smiling and holding out his hand. "Care to dance, sister Lark?"

Working hard to keep her plunging disappointment from her face, she smiled and laid her hand in her brother-in-law's. "Thank you. I suppose I would."

"Did Forsythia put you up to this?" she asked as Adam led her into place in a forming set.

"Now, why would you think that?" The doctor winked.

"Because I know my sister." Lark chuckled, but her chest felt hollow. At twenty-six, was she now merely the old spinster sister, her younger sisters having to nudge their husbands to provide her with dance partners? She pressed her lips against the thought.

Her feet weighted clumsily on the first few steps, but soon the music took over, her spirits lifting with the flying of her feet as she sashayed and circled, swinging from one to another as the sets moved in and out.

Forward and back with Adam, circling around the Hoffmans, then on to dance with the next couple.

And she found herself face-to-face with Isaac McTavish.

"Well, hello again. Enjoying yourself?" He smiled beneath his beard and reached for her hands, circling her around once.

"Hello." Lark barely had time to smile before he sent her back to Adam again.

Another couple of brief clasps of Isaac's hand in the right-hand chain, and then off they spun to dance with another set. Yet Lark kept glancing for him around the floor, keenly aware of his tattered army coat and sandy hair in and out among the dancers.

She and Adam had nearly circled back to dancing again with Isaac and his partner, Lizzy Wells, when the music came to an end in a burst of applause and laughter.

Lark joined in the clapping, pushing down a silly pang. What did it matter? If Isaac wanted to dance with her, he would. That was all there was to it.

"Thank you kindly for the dance." Adam bowed.

"And thank you." Lark curtseyed back, hoping her smile held the gratitude she did feel. How blessed she was with such loving family—she had more than enough to be grateful for.

She sighed as she glanced about her, couples forming for the next dance. *More than enough.*

"Care for another turn on the floor?"

Lark's breath caught in her throat for a second, then she turned and smiled into those perplexing gray eyes. "Why? Do you, Mr. McTavish?"

"'T'weren't quite satisfactory, bein' merely ships passin' out there." Isaac held out his hand. "Shall we?"

Lark laid her hand in his, her fingers slipping into place right and easy, despite the flutter in her middle. "Thank you."

He drew her into a circle of four as the musicians struck up the plaintive strains of the next dance.

Isaac cocked his head. "'Irish Lamentation,' I do believe. An old one, but 'twas a favorite of my ma's."

"It's a lovely one. I haven't heard it in a while." Lilac showed no trouble following the tune, her fiddle clear and true carrying the melody.

Lark's feet fell into the lilting rhythm of the dance, balancing in and out, circling round the other dancers in their set. Weaving through a chain of rights and lefts. And finally, back to Isaac for a gentle waltz round to join the next set. His hand steady at the small of her back, strong hand guiding her around. So near she could hear his breathing, see the rise and fall of his chest. Gray eyes holding her own.

She barely saw the faces of any other dancers, the rest of the floor a blur around her. There was only Isaac, till the musicians sounded the final strain, and everyone dipped in curtseys and bows.

Lark drew a long breath, steadying herself as she joined in the applause. "Thank you." She smiled at Isaac, hoping her voice sounded natural. She'd danced with him before, at the Valentine's dance the previous winter. But this . . . this had been different.

"And thank you." He still looked at her, face a serious blend of—what? She couldn't read him. She, Larkspur Nielsen, who noticed every detail and could read most everyone. Was that what alternately drew and frustrated her about this man? That she never quite knew what he was about?

He reached for her hand once more as if to shake it, then suddenly bent and kissed her knuckles. And just as quickly, slipped away into the crowd.

Lark expelled a short breath and shook her head. And there he went, off again. No wonder she could never make him out.

"Mighty fine couple you two made out on the dance floor." A feminine hand slipped into Lark's and squeezed it.

She twisted her head to stare at Climie's knowing eyes and gentle smile.

Her friend cocked her head. "Didn't you see the way he looked at you?"

Unable to form a response, Lark slipped away from her friend and hurried back to join the musicians. At least there she knew what was happening and what she was supposed to do.

Even if, all the rest of the night, her heart kept beating time with the lingering rhythm of their dance in her head.

10

What was he to do about Larkspur Nielsen?

Isaac McTavish sat in a back pew of Salton's little church, trying his hardest to focus his mind on the congregational meeting—even if the gathering of congregants near the front reminded him of nothing so much as a flock of bickering chickens. Already what was supposed to be a simple Sunday afternoon meeting was stretching toward evening.

And here he'd hoped to get a chance to talk to Miss Larkspur again afterward. Now she'd be in a powerful hurry to get home to chores, more than likely.

Rev. Pritchard's up and leaving sure had thrown the town into a tizzy. Isaac hadn't seen this much debate even when the pastor had been accused of unseemly conduct last year. The charitable mood at the celebration last night seemed a far piece behind them now.

"Everyone, please. One at a time." Mr. Caldwell raised his hands at the front, his usually level voice strained. "If everyone keeps talking over everyone else, we'll never get anywhere."

The clamor settled to a murmur. Mr. Caldwell leaned one hand on his cane to ease his war-injured leg and sighed. "Hiram, you had something to say?"

Banker Young rose to his feet and hooked his thumbs in his expansive vest. "All I'm sayin' is, we should stop hashing back and forth and just take action. Write to the American Home Missionary Society, where Reverend Pritchard came from, and tell them what we need. The sooner we put our request in, the sooner they'll make it a priority to find us a replacement. We took steps for a schoolteacher, and we've already got a man coming."

"I agree," Mr. Jorgensen offered. "Be nice if church life could move forward with as little disruption as can be."

"Having a preacher don't mean no disruption. Look at last year," Ephraim Dwyer scoffed. "I say this time we better be mighty careful who we call."

The murmuring rose again.

"Don't want no more scandals. That's for sure."

"We all know that wasn't Reverend Pritchard's fault," George Hoffman spoke up with a firm nod. "No matter who we get, there's no guarantee against all trouble."

"I agree." Dr. Brownsville stood. "It seems we'd do well to devote ourselves to some prayer over this. If we're divided among ourselves, how can we be listening for the Lord's guidance? And isn't that what we all want?"

"Prayer is all fine and dandy, but what are we supposed to do in the meantime?" Mr. Young jutted his chin. "Even once we do write a letter to the mission board, it may take months to hear back."

"I say we start right now, draw up a list of requirements in what we're looking for."

That at least seemed to bring some agreement, and Caldwell pulled out his notepad and asked for general suggestions.

Isaac saw Larkspur Nielsen lean over to whisper something to her sisters. His mouth tipped. He'd wager she would have had more than a thing or two to say today, were women's opinions invited. As well they should be. Trying to push thoughts of their dance last night from his mind, Isaac glanced out the window, dimming with twilight, then along his own pew at William Thacker perched at the other end. The young man bent forward with his elbows on his knees, listening. He had an insightful head on his shoulders . . . too bad his opinion wasn't likely to be asked either, even if most folks in Salton had tacitly accepted him by now.

Isaac leaned to the side. "You ever hear tell of such a church kerfuffle before?"

William shrugged and gave a half grin. "My church back east usually had bigger problems to worry about."

"I bet y'all did." Isaac studied William's face. "Helpin' with the freedmen and such?"

"Once the war was over. Before that, we was a stop on the Underground Railroad."

Isaac shook his head, feeling his respect for this quiet young man rise once again. "Any news on your little brother?"

William rubbed his hands on his thighs. "Nothin' yet. I wrote to the Freedmen's Bureau again a few weeks ago, but they're still a mite overwhelmed. And no way of knowin' if anyone has record of Ben anyhow, or where he mighta been sold."

"I'm sorry," Isaac said. His chest tightened—he knew the pain of loss, but at least he didn't have to wonder whether any of his family members had died while enslaved or were out trying to survive in an unkind world. Even if he didn't know where his own sisters were since the war.

"Thanks for askin'." William managed a smile. "Most folks don't think to." He massaged the back of his neck with a dark brown hand and nodded toward the front. "Looks like things are heatin' up again."

Isaac glanced forward to see Liam O'Rourke and Ephraim Dwyer in a near-shouting match. With a shake of his head, he sat back in his seat and crossed his arms.

"What do ye mean, someone born in this country?" O'Rourke's

red-bearded face flushed. "Are ye sayin' immigrants like meself are na' welcome in this town?"

"Just think our preacher should be an American, not some imported fellow like that Scot they've got in Lincoln. I heard tell folks can barely understand the man."

A sudden stomp, and Larkspur Nielsen shot to her feet ahead of him.

Isaac sat up straight, his pulse quickening.

"Honestly." Lark set her hands on her hips and glared at the gathering. "I've always thought our church to be overall a charitable body, one that thought kindness and character, not to mention solid doctrine, most important in a minister of the gospel. But if you men can't agree on a simple list of requirements, perhaps you'd better let the women take a stab at it." Her voice carried clear to the back of the church. "And if you won't allow that, as I strongly suspect, then I don't see much purpose to us being present for this meeting at all." She spun on her heel and headed down the aisle toward the door.

"Lark." Lilac got to her feet and hurried after her sister. Forsythia half rose, baby in arms.

Isaac stood and stepped into the aisle to intercept her before the door. "Miss Larkspur, wait."

She stopped and glared at him, fire in her eyes.

"Hold up just a moment. Please, ma'am?" He touched her arm, the faintest brush of her calico sleeve. Even if he dearly wanted to take her hand, as he had at the dance. *Their dance.*

The fire eased only a mite, but she pursed her lips and nodded.

Isaac stepped forward to the center of the aisle. "Folks, I've got a morsel of an idea, if you'd be willin' to listen."

Rows of faces stared back at him, causing a pang of doubt.

Mr. Young cleared his throat. "No offense, Mr. McTavish, but you haven't exactly been, well, a consistent citizen of Salton."

Isaac dipped his head. "I know I'm still somethin' of an outsider here—though I call Salton the closest to a hometown I've known since the war. But I've got a cousin set to move here this year, him and his family bein' the nearest kin I've got left. Seems about time for me to be puttin' down roots." For more reasons than one. He kept himself from glancing at Lark.

"If you've got an idea, Isaac, let's hear it," RJ said.

He turned his worn army cap in his hands and scanned the congregation. "Back when I was knee-high to a grasshopper in Appalachia, we didn't always have a pastor for our little mountain church. Just a circuit-ridin' preacher that stopped by every now and again. But that didn't mean we couldn't worship together all the same. We had members of our community take turns sharin' on different Sundays, stories from their own lives where they'd seen the Lord show up and do mighty things, or sometimes just readin' passages of Scripture so we could all talk it over. I don't see why we couldn't do the same here. Or are we gettin' so big for our britches we think only some big-city preacher can bring us the Word of God?" He stopped for breath, hoping he hadn't offended half the citizens and wouldn't be ridden out of town on a rail.

Silence fell, then a solitary person began to clap. Isaac glanced to the side. It was William. The young man met his gaze, nodding hard.

The clapping picked up at the front of the church. RJ stood, slapping his hands together. "Let's do it."

A swell of agreement rose, far different from the discordant mumbling earlier. Isaac let out a breath he didn't realize he'd been holding. Why he should care what this town thought of what he said, he didn't rightly know—as Mr. Young had implied, he'd hardly become fullly one of them—yet right now, he did.

"That's all very well," intoned Mr. Dwyer's nasal voice again. "But fillin' our services in the meantime with folks from town still don't answer for the long term. We need a preacher."

"Agreed." Mr. Caldwell made a note. "But this idea certainly gives us something to look forward to each Sunday while we give our pastoral search the time, thought, and prayer that it deserves. I think we should form an official committee to devote themselves to this task. If you'd be interested in serving or have a suggestion of someone to do so, please come and talk to me. Beyond that, Dr. Brownsville, would you be willing to start us off by sharing with the congregation this coming Sunday?"

"I—I suppose so." A rare look of uncertainty crossed Adam's face. He rubbed his neat brown beard and looked back at Isaac. "Something from the Scriptures or my own life, you say?"

He nodded. "I'd say whatever the Lord puts on your heart, Doctor."

Adam nodded. "I'll pray about it."

"Well then." Mr. Caldwell removed his spectacles. "I think we can officially bring this meeting to a close."

The gathering began to disperse, people moving about and chatting. Isaac saw Jesse and Climie Brownsville coming toward him and moved to greet them.

"How are you folks keepin' these days?" He grasped Jesse's hand and gave Climie a little bow.

"We're doin' fine, just fine." Climie smiled and looked up at her husband. "Jesse and William have nearly finished that addition on the boardinghouse they've been building for us. We'll have our own place real soon, not just my bedroom off the kitchen."

"As well you should."

"I liked your idea in the m-meetin'." Jesse put his arm around his wife. "Was about time somebody said s-something with some g-good sense."

"My mama always told me, 'Speech is silver, silence is gold.'" Isaac chuckled. "But I figured the Good Book also says there's a time to be silent and a time to speak. I was rather surprised they took to it, tell the truth. We'll see what happens."

He bid them and William good-bye and looked around for Larkspur, but she and Lilac had disappeared, along with Jonah.

Disappointment kicked him in the chest. He'd wanted to talk to her, see if she were all right. He knew Miss Larkspur didn't hide her opinions on matters, but he'd yet to see her as riled up as she'd been tonight.

Truth be told, he always wanted to talk to her. And since last evening . . . well, he'd tried and failed all night to get her off his mind.

More and more, he was of an intention to court that woman. And do it proper.

But would she let him?

Driving the wagon home across the prairie, Lark breathed deeply, grateful for the surrounding silence of darkness and stars.

She was glad Isaac had stopped her. After all, it wasn't the first church she'd walked out of. Or, in this case, nearly.

Lilac and Jonah sat quietly for most of the ride as the wagon jounced along. Finally Lilac nudged her knee from the seat beside her. "You all right?"

Lark inched her shoulders toward her ears, then dropped them. "I guess. Just hoping I didn't set too many tongues to wagging today."

"And when have the Nielsen sisters let that bother us before?"

Lark slanted a look at her, though in the darkness its effect might be lost.

"You were thinking of that time back in Linksburg, weren't you?" Lilac's tone sobered. "With Deacon Wiesel."

"More like trying not to." But the memories kept poking up their persistent heads. Even now, thinking of that hateful man spewing condemnation from the pulpit and his then-wife, Climie, cowering on the pew below till she'd actually dropped in a dead faint set Lark's scalp on fire.

Lilac patted her arm. "I think Isaac's suggestion took the

focus off you a bit. I wouldn't worry. And goodness, someone needed to intervene."

"I can't stand it when folks start bickering over things that don't even matter. Or, worse, start acting like bigoted hypocrites." Lark's chest heated again, remembering Mr. Dwyer's comments. "I'd hoped we were better than that in this town."

"I love Salton, but it's no paradise. Remember how many people got hot under the collar when we let William stay in our boardinghouse at first?" Lilac's voice tightened.

"That's true." Lark had noticed Isaac sitting in the back with William. She hoped William didn't sit there because he thought people in town would object if he sat closer to the front. But regardless, Isaac seemed to gravitate toward those on the margins. Quiet though that man was, he could also speak up. And shift the entire tone of a meeting when he did, apparently.

She should have stayed longer tonight, at least long enough to thank Isaac. For saying what he had, for stopping her from burning any more bridges she'd regret. But after the party last night . . . she didn't know what to make of the thumping in her heart when he came near. So she'd skedaddled.

Lark blew out a breath. "Jonah, you have the mower ready to go again tomorrow?"

"Oiled, sharpened, and clean as a whistle."

"Good." The familiar talk of farmwork steadied the tangle in her middle. "I talked to Mr. Jorgensen before the meeting, and he said thanks to you, his mower is ready too. So now that we've got our fields done, we'll have two machines to split the labor of mowing for other people."

"Anyone you know of who'd let us use their teams to spell ours tomorrow?"

"The O'Rourkes, of course, they already helped with our fields. And the Webers. We can start with them, then expand from there like last year. I believe the Jorgensens are working with the Youngs and the Kinsleys to begin with."

"How long do you think you'll stay out here, Jonah?" Lilac craned her neck.

"Through harvest, if I can. Unless Anders needs me back sooner."

It wasn't till she sat milking Clover in the barn, after her bellowing mother had her turn first and Lilac and Jonah had hurried through feeding the animals and the rest of the belated chores, that Lark leaned her head against the cow's warm side and let herself actually think. Isaac McTavish, with his Appalachian drawl and enigmatic gray eyes and the feel of his work-roughened palm against hers, kept circling the edges of her brain like Scamp around the sheep, keeping her awake long into the wee hours after they returned from the celebration last night.

Then this evening, his stepping out to stop her, the brief touch of his hand on her sleeve . . .

Lark squeezed the cow's teats and let her eyes shut. *Lord, what is happening here? I thought I'd resigned myself to running the farm and being the maiden aunt . . . at least mostly. So why all these feelings all of a sudden?* And Isaac . . . he'd never said anything to indicate more than friendship. And even if he did, what could that lead to? She'd heard him claim to want to put down roots before—only to vanish again, sometimes for months at a time, riding the rails or working at ranches farther west.

She shouldn't get her hopes up. She knew better, surely.

"Didn't you see the way he looked at you?" Climie's words trailed a gentle tease through her brain.

That was the problem. She had.

11

Mor, you've got to let me go."

Sam glanced back at the train puffing smoke behind him, his shoulders tightening as time pressed. Yet still his mother clung to him.

"It's so far. How do I know when I'll see you again?"

Sam dug deep for patience and patted his mor's shoulder as she wept into the front of his coat. Despite her supposed blessing on his decision, the last two weeks had been filled with fears and tears.

"It's only a few days' train ride now, nothing like it used to be. I'll come home for Christmas if I can, or at least next summer."

The train whistled again. Sam cast his father a pleading glance.

Far cleared his throat and stepped forward to touch his wife's arm. "Nora, it's time. Let him go."

She stepped back at last, dabbing her handkerchief at her eyes and shaking her bonneted head. "But who will take care of you all the way out there?"

Sam bit his tongue to keep from bursting out that he could take care of himself, that he had been taking care of himself for years, however much she tried to interfere. That indeed a chance to be left alone would be welcome. Shame burned his ears for the thought.

"God will." His voice firmer now, Far tucked Mor's arm through his and reached to clasp Sam's hand. "And may He be with you, son."

"And also with you." Sam gripped his father's hand hard, then bent to kiss his mother's damp cheek once more.

"All aboard!"

Sam drew a breath, grasped his satchel—his trunk was already loaded—and headed for the train car. His feet hitched briefly at the steps. He couldn't grasp the handle to pull himself up while holding the satchel, not with only one hand. *Lord, please don't let me prove my mother's fears true right here in front of her.*

"All aboard!" The conductor bellowed again, almost in Sam's face. With one smooth motion the man reached down, grabbed Sam's satchel, and tossed it up the steps, then nodded for him to climb on. Face burning with gratitude, Sam hauled himself aboard. He grabbed his bag and made his way down the narrow aisle of the passenger car, ears full of the screech of metal on metal and chatter of passengers. Finding a seat by a window, he sank into it, tucked his satchel beside him, then turned for a last glance out the window.

There his parents stood, Far with his arm around Mor, his mother pressing her handkerchief to her nose. The train lurched forward, engine chuffing. Sam braced himself with his feet and lifted his right hand in a wave. His mother flapped her handkerchief, a flag of surrender. His chest tight, Sam kept his eyes on that fluttering scrap of white till the train chugged around a bend, and she was gone.

Sam leaned back in his seat, a burning in his nose. He was thankful for the empty seat across from him, lest his eyes betray the sudden threat of tears. This was the right decision—at least he'd thought it to be. But . . . would his mother survive it? He closed his eyes, the familiar pinch of guilt in his gut. Mor's life had been wrapped up in him, in being his mother, for, well, all his life, and over half of hers. What would she do now with him simply not there?

He remembered a friend of his from the cavalry, who shared how an aunt of his simply stopped living after her son was killed in the war. Pulled away from family and friends, refused food. And died herself only a few months later. Sam shook off the morbid thought with a shudder. Mor wouldn't do that, his father wouldn't let her. And Sam wasn't dead, for pity's sake, merely moving a few states away. He could visit—and so could they.

Still, his mother's handkerchief fluttered in his dreams that night, a relentless undercurrent to the rattling rock and sway of the train.

Between fighting spasms of guilt, Sam spent much of the train trip reading. *Ray's Arithmetic*, *The Columbian Orator*, *The Art of Reading*. He trusted the school would have books of geography, American history, and penmanship. He'd had a good education, but sometimes the sheer scope of knowledge he'd be expected to impart to the young minds of Salton made his head spin, his breath squeezing past strictures. He closed his eyes after reading five chapters of complicated mathematics and leaned his head against the seat back. He laid the book on the seat beside him to free his hand to rub at the headache building behind his eye sockets. Or was it just from the ever-present soot and smoke in the air?

Soon he'd know whether he could actually put all this book learning, not to mention his time at teaching school, into real-life practice. Flesh-and-blood students in the classroom would be a far cry from students in theory, and no doubt infinitely more challenging—as he ought to know.

Would they find it hard to respect a teacher with a missing arm?

Sam lifted his head and glanced out the window. Dusk was falling over the landscape, the rolling hills of Ohio having given way to the farmland of Indiana and Illinois, and now the corn-fields of Iowa.

"Next stop, half an hour." The conductor stopped beside his seat. "Fine place to get off and get some supper."

"Thank you." Sam's stomach rumbled at the thought. Though his mother had stuffed as many eatables in his satchel as he'd allow, the idea of a hot meal made his mouth water. "Tomorrow we'll cross the river at Council Bluffs, is that right?"

"Sure is." The conductor shifted a toothpick from one corner of his mouth to the other. "Load up passengers and railcars alike on them big steam ferries and tote us right across the Missouri."

Sam shook his head in wonder. Whole train cars being ferried across the river. "I can hardly picture it."

"'Course, this is just till they finally get that railway bridge built, once folks can agree on the location. Whole thing's been a passel of trouble, not to mention Council Bluffs and Omaha always arguin' over who's the real beginning of the Union Pacific rails. But President Lincoln named Council Bluffs the terminus, so I figure so it shall be. Even if the UP tracks proper don't yet begin till the other side."

"What a world we live in these modern days."

"Ain't that the truth." The conductor chuckled and swayed on down the aisle to the rumble and screech of the locomotive's song.

The next morning, Sam leaned his head out his open window to stare in amazement as the train cars were rolled onto special tracks on the huge steam ferries, then slowly towed across the rolling water of the Missouri. He breathed deeply of the river's tangy air, a precious change from soot and smoke, then looked ahead to the other side—Nebraska. Might this be his own Jordan River crossing, of sorts? A passage to a new land . . . a new life.

The thought of Lilac Nielsen worked its way into his mind again. Could she be part of that new life? Shaking his head, he pushed away the thought. He wasn't about to take advantage of her family's kindness in helping him get this job by throwing himself at their youngest daughter. Not to mention not being a whole man himself . . . No, he'd best devote himself to learning to teach and teach well. To stand on his own as a man, navigate life in this new world while missing a limb before he took any thought toward matrimony. Lilac's dark curls, dancing eyes, and compassionate listening ear notwithstanding.

They reached the other side, then rolled back onto the tracks through Omaha before heading south toward Lincoln . . . toward Salton. Grassland and salt marsh stretched around him, the prairie so open he could scarcely spot a tree on the horizon. So different from the woods and hills of home, yet welcome. And a great open sky stretching above, blue as his mother's favorite mixing bowl.

Perhaps here he might finally breathe freely.

Lilac breathed in the scent of fresh earth, newly turned beneath her hoe. Nothing like working in a garden—especially now that the August mornings were starting to turn cooler. Though the rising sun warmed her shoulders, a faint nip in the air heralded autumn not far away.

She knelt between the rows of purple coneflowers, gently pulling the weeds by hand lest she uproot any of the precious plants. Around her were black-eyed Susans, salvia, asters, catmint, and anemone, late summer blooms still filling Leah's Garden with splashes of rose, violet, and gold. The spring and summer flowers were now going to seed—they'd need to start collecting and saving those soon. Between this year and what they still had left from last year, they should have enough seeds to start filling mail orders by next spring. Lilac flung the weeds onto the pile and rubbed the rich soil from her fingers with a smile as she stood. Finally, their mother's dream of a flower seed business was nearing full bloom.

The clanking of metal came from the machine shed, where Lark and Jonah worked on the mower. Lilac stretched to ease the kinks from her back, then set to whacking at the stubborn weeds between the rows with her hoe. It seemed that as summer waned, the weeds only gained strength. After this, she needed to harvest more green beans—the bushes hung heavy with them again. In the nearby cornfield, Del walked the rows picking early corn, little Lily Belle wound snug against her mother's chest in a fabric sling. Lilac smiled at the sight, remembering Del wearing tiny Mikael that same way on the wagon trip west, after they'd found Sofie and Mikael's mother dying along the trail from a fever. Was that truly only three years ago?

Lilac could have been expecting a baby herself by now if she'd gone ahead with her wedding to Ethan Pritchard. She leaned the hoe into the ground and pushed a stray curl back inside her sunbonnet. She was glad she'd made the decision she did, but she still hoped God had wifehood and motherhood planned for her someday. But with whom?

"Did you want to go to town with me, Lilac?"

Lilac looked up at Jonah's question, the midmorning sun now beating down harder. "You need a part for the mower?"

"Ja, and I'm supposed to meet Sam Gubberud at the train, remember? Anders asked if we would."

That's right, how had she forgotten that was today? Lilac's brain scrambled. "I, uh, I do need to mail a new set of drawings. Maybe I should come." Jonah could mail them, but she liked to send them off herself. And the thought of meeting Sam did hold appeal. But there was so much to do here. . . .

"I can take over the weeding." Lark approached, seeming to read her mind. "If you want to go."

"The flower garden's almost finished, but I was going to pick beans next." Lilac still hesitated, not used to feeling so indecisive. "Maybe I should stay." There was really no need for her to go—except she wanted to. Which was precisely the problem. Why did she want so badly to meet Sam at the train? Was she imagining feelings for him? If so, all the more reason to be careful—she'd had feelings for Rev. Pritchard, and look how that turned out.

"Oh for pity's sake, just go or you'll miss the train." Lark took the hoe from her. "And wash your face, Lilac, you've got dirt smudges on your chin."

Glad for once to have the decision made for her, Lilac rushed into the soddy and splashed her face and hands, then removed her apron and joined her brother in the wagon, where Jonah sat tapping his foot.

"Gotta hurry if we want to be there when the train arrives."

Lilac squeezed her hands together in her lap as Jonah clucked Prince forward. *Calm down, Lilac Nielsen. You're merely going to welcome an old school chum. And you'd better not think of him as anything else, or the possibility of anything else, which you have precisely no right to do.*

And yet . . . there *had* been something between them at the store reopening. Surely she hadn't imagined it. She'd never talked that long or freely to a young man, not even when she was engaged to Ethan.

Well, all she could do was wait and see.

They reached the train station right on time, but the train was late. While they waited, Lilac headed into the station to give her packet of drawings for the *New York Weekly* to Mr. Owens, the telegraph operator who also handled mail. She thanked him, then at the whistle of the train hurried back out onto the platform. She and Jonah both covered their mouths and noses against the billows of smoke and soot that rolled in with the engine.

A few passengers stepped off the train right away, but no Sam. Had they misunderstood the time?

"There he is." Jonah nodded to the exit of the second passenger car, where a tall young man stepped slowly down, gripping the train car handle with his one good hand, then reached back up for his satchel once he had landed on the ground.

Jonah shook his head. "Gotta be tough, going through life with only one arm." He spoke low, though no one else would hear over the hiss of brakes and chuffing of the locomotive's idle engine.

"Hush," Lilac whispered anyway, waving for Sam to see them.

He glanced about, then spied them and hurried forward, carrying his carpetbag.

"Must say you two are a sight for sore eyes." Sam wore a weary grin. "Jonah, Miss Nielsen, thanks for coming to meet me. You didn't have to."

"Of course we did." Jonah thumped his shoulder. "Welcome to Salton. Got a trunk?"

"In the baggage car. Thank you."

Lilac followed the two young men, unusually tongue-tied. Though she'd seen Sam glance her way, he'd given her little eye contact. And what was with the "Miss Nielsen"? He'd called her Lilac before, hadn't he?

Had she offended him somehow? She'd thought they shared a connection at the mercantile reopening, a renewed friendship at least. Perhaps she'd overblown the memory in her mind. But she was being silly—just now Sam's focus was on his arrival to a completely new place and life, as well it should be.

"We'll take you over to Nielsen House, the boardinghouse my sisters started." Jonah hefted Sam's trunk into the back of the wagon.

"Their ingenuity seems to know no bounds." Sam cast Lilac a quick smile.

Heartened, she smiled back. "How was your trip?" At least that question came easily enough.

"Hot and sooty." He chuckled. "Though honestly, the time

passed more quickly than I expected. Incredible how fast one can travel hundreds of miles these days."

"That's just what I thought when I traveled back to Ohio this summer. When I think how long it took us by wagon . . ." Lilac spread her hands. "The speed of this age never ceases to amaze me."

"Exactly. Did you know they have steamboats to ferry the train right across the Missouri River so that tracks can keep on going?" Sam shook his head and chuckled. "Forgive me, of course you do. It just still boggles my mind."

Jonah, waiting by the wagon seat, cocked his head. "Ready?"

Lilac felt her face heat. She hadn't meant to delay them. But at least words had started flowing between her and Sam again.

Sam glanced from the wagon to her and hesitated. Was he wondering if he should offer to help her in?

Jonah settled the matter. "Up you go, sis." He helped Lilac into the back of the wagon by the trunk, then looked to Sam. "Do you, uh, need a hand?"

Lilac bit her lip.

"Thanks, I already have one." Sam smiled and held up his remaining hand, then used it to grasp the wagon seat and haul himself up.

They all chuckled, the momentary tension easing. Jonah climbed up and took the reins. "Sorry, if I shouldn't have—"

"Don't be." Sam flexed his hand. "It's hard for everyone to get used to at first, me included."

Jonah clucked the team and turned toward Main Street. "I need to pick up a new part for our mowing machine, but we can drop you at the boardinghouse first."

"No matter. I'd welcome the chance to see more of this little town I'm to call home." Sam examined the street with interest.

Lilac followed his gaze. What would he think of their town? The wooden sidewalks that didn't even stretch the length of the street, the rustic storefronts. Blacksmith, mercantile, bank.

Mr. Caldwell's simple law office. Compared to Salton, even Linksburg was an upscale town.

"There's the church." Jonah nodded. "And the schoolhouse."

Sam craned his neck to see. "Guess that will be familiar to me soon." He shifted on his seat. "I certainly do thank you folks for helping me get this position. Truly seemed like the Lord's provision just now."

"I didn't do anything." Jonah shrugged. "That was all Anders and Lilac." He thumbed back toward his sister.

"And I thank you, Miss Nielsen." Sam shot a polite smile back, then faced forward again.

Lilac sat back between his trunk and the side of the wagon bed, something deflating in her chest.

But what on earth had she expected, that Sam would ride into town and sweep her off her feet?

She'd let herself start to float after foolish dreams. Again.

12

"Hold still, fella. Won't take but a minute."

Isaac cradled the stallion's massive hoof between his knees, then took careful aim and with quick, precise taps drove the nails into the horseshoe. The horse barely twitched, though Hiram Young had warned him the stallion could be skittish.

"Well, I'll be." The banker shook his head. "Never saw him stand so quiet-like for a shoeing. You must have a way with animals, Mr. McTavish."

Isaac lowered the horse's hoof to the ground and gave the massive shoulder a pat. "Reckon they just want to be understood. Like people."

The clang and clatter of the blacksmith's forge surrounded them. George Hoffman bent over the anvil, hammer swinging with a steady rhythm, while Caleb pumped the bellows, perspiration streaking his young face.

"Well, thank you kindly. I'll just tell George to put the shoeing on my tab." Mr. Young took the bridle to lead his horse away.

Isaac nodded and stepped back. He was used to others getting paid for work that he did, then receiving his portion in due time. Such had been his life since the war—working on other folks' farms and ranches, on the railroad, on construction gangs, both in other towns and on RJ's crew right here in Salton. As long as he had work to keep his hands busy and food in his belly, it had been enough.

Funny it wasn't seemin' so anymore.

He tossed the worn horseshoes onto the pile of scrap metal for reworking. These days thoughts kept circling of a hearth and home of his own, even his own land and farm. Farmin' was what he knew backward and forward, deep in his soul. And if a certain woman he'd had his eye on for nigh on three years now might actually be persuaded to share it with him . . . Had he caught Miss Larkspur looking at him differently a time or two lately? Especially since the reverend's send-off. Or was it purely his imagination?

Isaac headed to stoke the fire in the forge, as it now burned low and Caleb had stepped outside.

"Thanks." George swiped a hairy arm across his forehead. "You always seem to know what's needed." He craned his neck toward the door. "Where is that boy? He was just supposed to fetch some more water to refill the quench barrel. I've got Jorgensen waitin' on this batch of nails." The blacksmith flung down his tongs and headed out the door as well.

Isaac shook his head and set the poker back into place. Those two surely didn't hold much patience for each other. He winced at the sound of raised voices outside the smithy.

"How many times do I have to tell you? When I give you an order, you don't stop and do anythin' else along the way. You go straight there and come straight back."

Caleb mumbled something Isaac couldn't hear.

"What was that?" George's voice lowered dangerously.

"I said, 'Whatever you say, sergeant.'" Caleb's voice came clear enough that time—as did the insolence in it.

"I swear to you, boy—"

Isaac stepped out just as George's beefy hand collared his

son. At the sight of Isaac, the father let go. With a glance that could light a forge without any help, Caleb pushed past Isaac into the building, water sloshing from his bucket onto Isaac's boot as he went.

George Hoffman leaned his hand against the doorframe and blew out a sigh. "I apologize, McTavish, for you havin' to see that. I just can't seem to get through to the boy no matter how I try. We got a divide between us deep as that betwixt North and South."

"And that's somethin' of the problem, ain't it now?" Isaac wondered if he'd misspoken by the change on George's face.

But then the man nodded, his head seeming to hold the weight of an anvil. "You've heard about that, then. Reckon the whole town has."

"Reckon you might be right." Isaac tasted his next words before speaking them. "Not like your family's the only one. I had brothers in both blue and gray."

George met his eyes. "You on speakin' terms?"

Isaac swallowed. "Both gone." *And one my fault.* He didn't add that part.

"I'm sorry." George scrubbed his hand through his thick black hair. "I know I should be grateful—my son's alive when so many ain't. Tarnation, he didn't even see battle, was so young when he joined up the war was over before he could. I think he blames me for that somehow too."

"Why did he join up Confederate when you fought Union?" Isaac chewed the inside of his cheek. "If you don't mind my askin'."

But George's face closed as surely as a barn door in winter. "That's a story for another time." He squinted at the lowering sun. "Day's near done. You might as well call it so."

"You sure?" Isaac snuck a look at the silent smithy. What was Caleb doing in there? "I can stay a bit longer, help you fellas finish up."

But Hoffman shook his head, lines creasing his face. "However we're going to work this through, we're goin' to have to do it ourselves. Go on and get yourself some hot supper at the boardinghouse. I'd invite you to sup with us here, but I imagine the company'll be a sight more friendly over there."

His shoulders stooped, the blacksmith headed back into the barn, dragging his war-wounded leg behind him.

Isaac watched him go. *Lord, I don't know what the real trouble is here between father and son, nor yet the way out of it. But you do, so I ask that you help them.*

He took the long way back to the Nielsen House, stopping at the mercantile on the way. Might as well see if he'd finally gotten a letter from his cousin. He'd been expecting one for weeks now. It'd been a couple of months since Ambrose last wrote and confirmed he and his family did indeed want to leave Arkansas and come settle in Salton. Isaac wanted to be able to smooth the way for them, scout out land possibilities, make plans. Maybe even for himself. The thought of such put a right spring in his step.

"You comin' in here, McTavish?" Mr. Jorgensen paused on the doorstep of the general store, key in hand. "Was just about to close up."

Isaac set one foot up on the wooden sidewalk and leaned his hand on his knee. "I was, but I can come back on the morrow. Makes no never mind." What was one more day?

"What did you need?" The slight little man made to reopen the door.

"Just had a mind to see if any mail came for me."

"I believe I did see a letter with your name on it. One moment, I'll get it."

Isaac felt a grin begin in his middle and spread to his face. So Ambrose had written at last. No one else wrote to him, that was certain. He sobered. His ma, pa, and brothers had no way to write from the heavenly shores, rest their souls. And his sisters . . . if they still lived on this earth, he'd no notion where.

"Here you are." Mr. Jorgensen reappeared and handed the slim envelope over.

"I thank ye kindly." Isaac resisted the urge to rip it open immediately and touched his faded army cap instead. "Hope you and the missus are well?"

"Well as can be." The storekeeper locked the door and slid the key into his pocket. "Be glad when this mowing business is finished. This is the first year I've had my own machine, you know, and managing three teams to mow at different farms is a handful and a half. I don't know how Miss Larkspur does it."

Isaac chuckled. "She's some kind of woman, that's for sure." He checked his expression, not wanting to give his feelings away. He should go by the homestead tomorrow, though, see how the Nielsens fared with their haying. He'd only helped once or twice this year so far, smithing kept him so busy these days. And Larkspur might seem near able to handle anything, but he'd seen her a mite vulnerable too. Even if she tried to hide it.

"Well, I'd best home to supper before the wife has my hide. A good evenin' to you, Mr. McTavish."

"And to you, sir. And to you."

Strolling back down Main Street in the late summer evening light, Isaac studied the envelope. On second look, the writing didn't quite look like Ambrose's. Maybe his wife had written— though why would that be? Frowning, he ripped the seal and pulled out the letter.

Dear Cousin Isaac,

I am writing to you with news so grave I can scarcely hold the pen. Ambrose, your cousin—my beloved husband—is dead, killed by that horrible James-Younger Gang in a bank holdup in town. You know our financial straits. He had gone in to beg the bank for enough credit to get us through harvest, when we hoped to be able to move to Nebraska. And there was a robbery—a stickup—

whatever folks call it. Ambrose tried to stop it, brave, foolish man as he ~~is~~ was. I still can't grip my mind around it. I am half distracted, trying to care for the children and farm when all I seem able to do is weep on my bed.

Please, Isaac, come to us. I beg of you. Our farm is failing, my beloved Ambrose is gone, and I am at my wit's end.

In grief,
Matilda McTavish

Isaac folded the letter and methodically returned it to the envelope, his head pounding. His cousin, with whom he'd grown up only a farm's length away—gone? Hands shoved in his pockets and a knot in his gut, he continued down the street, unseeing.

Never mind that hot meal at the boardinghouse . . . tonight he just needed to walk. And pray. *Lord, can a feller ask what you're doing here? I thought you were leading me to stay in Salton, maybe build a future here—and now this?* Another family member gone. Nigh unto the last of his blood kin. Grief smote deep in his gut and choked his throat.

He'd thought his path was finally starting to clear of the murky fog that had clouded his way ahead these last three years—no, nigh on four. Ever since that November day in the prison camp, when everything had changed . . .

Isaac shook off the dark memories with a shudder. He needed to focus on the here, the now. Get a ticket to Arkansas to begin with. The sooner, the better.

Whatever hopes had dared to start sprouting in his heart for a life here in Salton . . . never mind the tender, unspoken dream of a life with Larkspur . . . would have to wait. He wasn't about to turn his back on one of his kin.

Not again.

Sunday morning, Isaac slipped into his customary back pew and bent forward, elbows on knees and head in his hands.

Tomorrow morning, he would leave. Hopefully not for long, but only God knew when he'd be back again.

Lord . . . too much swirled in his mind and heart to find words to pray just now. Good thing the Almighty didn't require them.

Since they lacked a preacher, Mr. Caldwell led the call to worship, then the congregation rose to sing, the Nielsen sisters joining their instruments to Mrs. Caldwell's accompaniment on the piano.

> "Jesus, lover of my soul,
> Let me to thy bosom fly,
> While the nearer waters roll,
> While the tempest still is high . . ."

The familiar words eased the tension in his chest and loosened his tongue, and Isaac joined the hearty chorus of the congregation, albeit with a faltering voice. But somethin' about music never failed to stir his soul.

> "Thou of life the fountain art;
> Freely let me take of thee;
> Spring thou up within my heart,
> Rise to all eternity."

The musicians shifted to "Blest Be the Tie That Binds," and Isaac found himself watching Larkspur again, the confident tilt of her shoulders and sure strum of her fingers on the guitar. The smooth waves of her dark hair, wound back in a simple bun, the spirited features of her face as she sang.

Had she any notion the pull she held on his heart? Not that he'd ever told her.

Rustling around him hinted the congregation was sitting, and he sat too. Now the good doctor would be due to share, if Isaac didn't misremember.

Dr. Brownsville stepped to the front, looking more self-conscious than was his wont. He glanced at Mr. Caldwell, who motioned him toward the pulpit.

Adam stepped up toward it, then hesitated. "I think I'd rather just speak to everyone from right here. If you don't mind."

Mr. Caldwell spread his hands and nodded.

The doctor turned toward the congregation. "Forgive me, friends. I'm afraid I'm far more comfortable in a surgery than a pulpit. Or before a group of people at all." He drew a breath and blew it out. "I'm reminded today of the first time I stood before you all, the citizens of Salton. Perhaps some of you remember that town meeting the summer of '65, shortly after I first began practice in this town. I believe I was even more nervous then than I am now."

People shifted on benches. Mrs. Jorgensen coughed in the front row.

"I stood before you then to defend myself as a conscientious practitioner of medicine, unlike the charlatan who came before me. And since then, we have built many relationships of mutual trust and respect, I'm thankful to say. I continue to consider the position of physician in Salton a great honor and privilege. But what many of you may not know is my story before coming to Salton."

Isaac leaned forward, listening. He'd heard some but not all.

"After running my own private practice in Illinois for six years, my first wife, Elizabeth, and I decided to head west on the Oregon trail, along with my nephew, Jesse, whom you all now know and love." Adam glanced over at Jesse and Climie with a smile. "I hoped for a place to practice where doctors were in shorter supply than in Illinois, and most of all, for a healthier place for my wife. Elizabeth's lungs had been weak since childhood, and we thought a different climate might help. But before we even reached the jumping-off point in Independence, she took ill once again. And this time, despite my best efforts, she did not recover." Adam paused and swallowed. "I remember thinking, 'God, what are you doing? I thought you'd laid this new path out before me clearly—and now this?' I truly did not know what to do. I considered going back east, but without Elizabeth, and my practice already turned over to another doctor, there was little for me there. I can remember simply weeping on my bed in the hotel room there in Independence, the night after I buried Elizabeth. I felt so alone, abandoned without her beside me. I wondered if my life was over. But Jesse . . ." The doctor stopped to clear his throat. "Jesse heard me and came in. He didn't say much, just sat beside me. I don't know if I've ever told you this, nephew, but you were the presence of Christ to me that night." Adam cleared his throat again, and sniffs scattered through the congregation. Forsythia wiped her eyes.

"At any rate, the next morning, Jesse and I decided to press on. What I never could have imagined was that within a matter of months, God would take the ashes of my grief and bring joy and beauty springing from them, beginning when I met the Nielsen sisters. Well, at first, I thought they were three sisters and a brother."

Chuckles rippled through the church. Most knew of Lark's charade as "Clark" for the protection of her younger sisters on the trail. Isaac smiled, remembering.

"Most particularly, things changed when I met my beloved Forsythia. Not to mention three children I had no idea would someday be mine, and now a fourth." The doctor smiled at his family, his eyes tender on his wife cradling their infant son. "And rather than continuing all the way to the western coast of this land, I ended up settling in Nebraska." He quirked a brow. "I guess you know that part." Adam slid his hands into his jacket pockets, his posture easing now. "I know my story is not particularly unusual. Many a man has lost a wife, many have had to start anew, for better or worse. I suppose all I really want to share with you today is not to lose heart if the path you thought lay clear before you seems suddenly murky."

Isaac leaned back and swallowed hard. Might have thought the good doctor was preaching straight-wise at his own heart.

"Our God is faithful, and He can be trusted. That doesn't mean we won't know heartache—I'm afraid Jesus promised we would. But though the twists and turns of our lives may often not be what we plan or expect, that doesn't mean they aren't for good. Not if we trust them into God's hands, even though we can't see the way clear before us." Adam glanced at Mr. Caldwell and shrugged. "Did I talk long enough?"

Laughter rose in a gentle swell again, then applause. With a smile and nod to everyone, the doctor sat.

"Thank you, Dr. Brownsville, for your willingness to be the first to share in this way." Mr. Caldwell stepped forward again. "I think we can all see this will be quite a valuable season for our church as we get to know each other more deeply by learning one another's stories, perhaps in ways we haven't before. Now, Mr. O'Rourke, would you lead us in a closing prayer?"

Isaac waited outside the church for the Nielsens to finish talking with the Brownsvilles. He needed to tell Larkspur he was leaving, to say good-bye, though he prayed it wouldn't be for long. But who could tell what would come next down life's path, as the doctor had surely reminded them all?

Lord, I know he meant mostly to remind us to trust you, come what may. Wish I were doin' a better job of that just now.

Lark, Lilac, and Jonah started to head for their wagon, so Isaac quickened his steps to catch up.

"Miss Larkspur," he called.

She turned, her hand on the wagon side. A smile lit her face.

"Mr. McTavish. We were just reminiscing with Adam and For-sythia about those early days. How we first ran into you at our campsite even before we met Adam."

"And a most fortuitous meetin' that was." Isaac pulled off his worn army cap, the same he'd worn that long-ago night. Holes poked through the wool now—he little knew how much longer he could wear it. "Even if I was under the same impression as the good doctor that I'd made the acquaintance of a fine young *man* and his sisters." He quirked a brow.

Larkspur made a face. "I'm never going to live that down, am I? At least you seemed to take the news better than Adam did."

Warmth circled his middle, remembering their meeting at the Thanksgiving benefit when he'd realized she wasn't a new male friend whose company he enjoyed but rather a skirted and lovely *Miss* Nielsen.

"Perhaps because I found it a mighty fine surprise." Isaac eyed her and detected a faint flush in her cheeks, her dark eyes darting away from his gaze. Clenching his hands to keep from reaching for her, he drew a breath and pressed on. "But I'm afraid I've had some grave news from my kin."

"Oh?" She met his gaze again straight on, her dark brows pulling together. "From your cousin who is moving up here?"

"From his wife." Isaac's chest heavied once more. "Ambrose got himself killed in a bank robbery."

"Oh, Isaac." She caught her breath and reached to touch his arm. "I'm so sorry."

"As am I. He was about my only blood kin left." The compassion in her eyes set a lump to lodging in his throat. "I leave on the first train tomorrow to go see what I might do for his wife and young'uns."

"Of course." But the light in her eyes flattened and darkened. She withdrew her hand. "Of course you must. Is there anything we can do?"

"Not that comes to mind. But I surely do appreciate it. I'm sorry I won't be around to help finish hayin' and such."

"Don't even think about that. Though we'll miss you." She bit her lip. "You probably have no idea how long you'll be gone?"

He inhaled hard through his nose. "I wish I did." How he wanted to tell her that he wouldn't be long, that he'd hurry back as fast as train or horse or any manner of conveyance could carry him. But Isaac just shook his head. "Won't know much till I get there, see the state of things."

"I'm so sorry, Isaac." Lilac stepped near, linking her arm through Lark's. "I overheard. We'll be praying for you and your cousin's family."

"Of course we will." Lark gripped her sister's hand on her arm. "God be with you."

"I thank you kindly." He hesitated, but there seemed nothing more to say. With a slight bow, he turned away, slapping his hat back on his head.

All the way to the boardinghouse, his feet felt weighted as if with cannonballs, everything in him wanting to run back to her, to Larkspur, and tell her something of what was in his heart. But how could he? Not now, when he was going away and couldn't promise a thing. So he made himself climb up the stairs to the boardinghouse upper story, pack his few belongings in the well-worn satchel. Then laid himself down on his cot to wait for the dinner bell and closed his eyes.

Lord in heaven, let this leavin' not mean good-bye.

13

D rat it all." Lark huffed a breath and bent over the mower.
"What's wrong?" Jonah poked his head in the machine shed.

"The bolts are coming loose again, the ones that hold the blades in the sickle bar."

"Let me take a look."

"I've got it." She stepped in front of the machine, blocking his view.

"If you say so."

The doubt in her little brother's voice rankled further. Maybe he was better at machinery than she was, but she could handle this. Jonah wouldn't be here forever, and this was her mower. Her farm. She began tightening the bolts back into place. There were so many pieces of this machine to keep checked and in order—one thing overlooked and the mower could get seriously damaged in the field. Or worse, someone injured.

She reached between the blades to tug out a stuck tuft of dried grass, then yelped at a nick on her hand.

"Ouch." Lark yanked her hand back and grimaced. Sure enough, blood seeped from a fresh cut across two knuckles. How could she have been so clumsy? She knew better than to touch near the blades without gloves.

Jonah blew out frustration. "I told you so." He stepped closer to see.

"It's fine." She jerked her hand back. "I'll go wash it."

"What's going on with you today?"

"Nothing." Lark spun and headed toward the soddy, biting her lip against stubborn tears.

What *was* wrong with her?

She made herself breathe slowly as she washed the cut at the washtub outside the soddy, scouring to avoid infection, though it wasn't deep. She'd been off-kilter all morning, no, the whole last few days—she couldn't deny it to herself, even if she did to her family.

Well, actually, ever since Sunday after church.

Her hands slowed as she dabbed a clean cloth over the cut.

So Isaac McTavish had left. He had certainly left before, time and again since they'd come to Salton. They never knew when—or if—he would come back.

So why did this time cut deeper? *Because you let yourself start thinking thoughts you'd no right to.*

"You and Jonah about to leave?" Lilac appeared in the door of the soddy, wiping her hands on the dish towel. "Wait, what happened?"

"Nicked my hand on the mower."

Lilac darted out and grabbed Lark's hand to see.

Lark gritted her teeth. Why did everyone have to make such a fuss? "It's not bad, but can you grab me a bandage and some of Forsythia's salve?"

"Of course." Lilac cast her an odd look. "You sure you're all right?"

Lark ignored her and pressed harder to stop the bleeding.

Her hand adequately wrapped, Lark headed back to the machine shed, where she found Jonah tinkering with the mower.

"Think I've just about got it. Where are we mowing first today?"

"The Dwyers', I'm afraid." Lark sighed. Just one more thing wrong with this day.

"Wasn't it supposed to be the Webers next?"

"It was, but they've got some summer sickness. And when Ephraim Dwyer offered their team instead when I saw him at the mercantile yesterday afternoon, I couldn't say no." Even if she dearly wished the Dwyer family had joined the group using the Jorgensens' mower instead. *Lord, give me a charitable heart.*

"Guess we're ready to go, then." Jonah gave the mower a pat, then cast a glance at Lark's bandaged hand. "If you're sure you—" He shifted his gaze to her face and clamped his mouth shut.

Good choice.

They rolled the mower up into the wagon, then Lark hauled herself up on the seat to drive, ignoring Jonah's subtle attempt to sidle himself over to the driver's side. She took up the reins, waited for her brother to climb aboard, then clucked the team into motion. Biting the inside of her cheek at the throbbing in her knuckles when she gripped the reins, she forced herself not to wince.

"Have the Dwyers always been . . . difficult?" Jonah broke the silence.

"I don't know about that." Lark shifted the reins to ease the strain on her knuckles. "Del never complained about their son, Thomas, in school. And in the store yesterday, Mr. Dwyer acted right neighborly. But it does seem more often than not that both mister and missus wield pretty sharp tongues."

Jonah chuckled. "From the little I've seen at the church meetings here, that's putting it mildly."

The Dwyer homestead lay a full two miles away, so the sun was rising higher by the time they drove up to the cabin—a real wooden cabin, not a soddy. Ephraim Dwyer stood outside, arms folded.

"Thought you folks would be here some time ago. My team's been ready an hour, day's a-wastin'."

"I apologize." Lark climbed down stiffly. "I nicked my hand

while fixing up the mower blade. But we should still be able to make good time." She scanned the fields, drawing a breath of relief that the farm spanned less land than she'd feared. "We should be able to finish cutting here by the end of tomorrow."

Mr. Dwyer glared at her bandaged hand as if it had personally offended him. "Never did think a woman should be handling one of these machines. Man's work is in the fields, woman's in the house, I always say."

The base of Lark's scalp burned, but she managed a tight smile. "Shall we begin?"

"This here's Paint and Punch." The man nodded at his pinto team. "Can I drive them?"

"The mower is a bit tricky to handle at first, Mr. Dwyer. I think it's best if I drive. You can walk alongside your team to talk to them and set them at ease while they get used to the mower—that's what we've found to work best."

But Mr. Dwyer shook his head, chin jutting out. "I'm not letting no woman drive my team. No, ma'am."

Oh for the love of . . . Lark clamped her teeth so hard her jaw hurt. "Jonah, would you drive the mower, please?"

"Sure." Shooting her a meaningful glance, Jonah moved to roll the mower out from the wagon bed.

Lark followed. Together, they hitched up the Dwyer team and checked the tongue and sickle bar connections once more, the rhythm so familiar now they didn't need words. Then Jonah mounted the seat of the mower, took the reins, and waited.

"If you'd walk alongside your team, Mr. Dwyer, as my sister said, that would be appreciated."

Lark hid a smile at the polite pointedness in his tone.

With only a faint grumble, Mr. Dwyer moved into place beside his team.

"I'll walk ahead of you and watch for rocks." Lark strode into the field without waiting for an acknowledgment.

As soon as the mower moved forward behind her, the clanking of the metal set off the horses. Lark turned back to see Paint rolling his eyes and tossing his head. Punch stamped his feet and let out a whinny.

"Whoa, there." Jonah raised up from the seat, drawing on the reins.

Lark moved well to the side out of the way, her heart pounding. They hadn't had many teams act up like this, but that extending bar of blades to the side could wreak havoc if the team actually spooked and ran.

"They ain't used to this." Mr. Dwyer stepped back, shaking his head. "What do you do when teams act up?"

"Most of them have done pretty well." As the horses stilled since the machine had ceased, Jonah eased himself back onto the seat. "We've had a few need a little extra reassurance."

"He means talk to them, Mr. Dwyer." Lark forced the bite in her voice to soften. "They trust you, so tell them there's nothing to fear."

Mr. Dwyer cast her a grumbling glance, then stepped near his team and rubbed their noses. "It's all right, there, fellas. This old machine ain't going to hurt you. Just makes a peck of noise is all."

Paint tossed his head again while Punch's ears twitched back and forth, listening.

"Let's try again." Jonah lifted the reins. "I'll start slower this time."

Lark waited, watching. At the clatter and rattle of the blades, the horses snorted again, but Mr. Dwyer kept his hand on the near horse's bridle, soothing them with words Lark couldn't hear. They seemed to have their effect, though, because the team moved forward, pulling the mower smoothly behind them, the sickle bar skimming through the grass to the side.

"Good." Releasing a breath, Lark turned and strode back into the field, keeping a good distance behind her and the mower. The waist-high grass swished and tugged against her skirts, hindering yet somehow calming her. She wasn't used to this job.

Normally she drove the mower or sometimes followed behind with others—men, women, and children, belying Mr. Dwyer's proclamation that women belonged inside—to rake and stack the cut hay. But today she kept a sharp eye out for rocks in the mower's path, and had to hold up her hand frequently for Jonah to steer around a hidden boulder. Mr. Dwyer, so critical of everyone else, had failed to properly clear his field. Surprise, surprise. Lark winced at the spitefulness in her own thoughts. *Forgive me, Lord, my heart isn't very right before you today.*

"Lark!"

At her brother's shout, Lark flung up her head and her hand, warning of the rock Jonah was already skirting around. The bar missed hitting it by the width of a rabbit's foot. Jonah shook his head back at her.

Lark's head pounded. Her wandering mind could have cost them a mower blade or worse—never mind confirming female incompetence in Mr. Dwyer's mind forever. *Lord, help me keep my mind straight here.*

They managed to mow the next several hours without incident, switching to their own Prince and Nell at noon. By the time Anthony Armstead brought his team to spell theirs mid-afternoon, nearly half the field was cut.

"Looks like a good day's work." Anthony nodded and swiped his forehead against the still-hot August sun.

"I'm grateful your team is already broken to the mower," Lark said. "We had a bit of trouble with the Dwyer horses this time."

"After mowing last year and this, mine are old hands by now." Anthony frowned. "Glad to hear no one got injured if Dwyer's team spooked. I heard tell of a family whose boy lost an arm to a runaway mower."

Lark's spine prickled. "They didn't quite spook. But that's why we have to be so careful."

They finished the day without incident, then sent the Armstead horses home and drove Prince and Nell back themselves.

Lark let Jonah drive and slumped against the wagon seat, cradling her throbbing hand. Amazing a little scratch could hurt so much.

"You two look plumb beat." Lilac met them outside the barn, carrying a full milk pail. "Chores are done. I've been harvesting seeds and drawing all day. Del said supper at her house."

"Bless you both." Lark climbed down off the wagon, then helped Jonah roll the mower down. "Think we need to sharpen the blades again before tomorrow?"

"I think it's good for another day. But definitely before we move on to the next farm."

They stabled, brushed, and fed the horses, then Lark checked, cleaned, and rebandaged her hand before heading over to Del and RJ's.

"How did it go at the Dwyers' today?" RJ jiggled his baby daughter on his shoulder while Lilac helped Del spread the simple supper of fresh baked bread, green beans, and rabbit stew from Lilac's latest trapline.

Lark shrugged and set out bowls. "Well enough. Apart from antsy horses and Mr. Dwyer's opinions on what sort of work is and isn't appropriate for women."

RJ grimaced. "Opinions are one thing that man is generous with."

"That and rocks in his field." Jonah shook his head. "Nearly hit one of them."

Because she hadn't been alert enough. Lark mentally scolded herself again.

Lily Belle squalled on her father's shoulder, and RJ heightened his patting and bouncing.

"She's been so fussy this afternoon." Del sighed and reached for her daughter. "I hope she isn't going to be colicky."

"I remember that with Lilac." Lark slanted a glance at their younger sister. "Ma and Pa took turns walking the floor with her in the evenings for months."

Lilac grinned and lifted her hands. "Fifth child, I had to make sure you all knew I was there."

"Well, let's see if she'll let me eat." Del sat down, cradling Lily Belle in one arm.

RJ extended his arms, and they all joined hands.

"Our Father, we thank you for protecting Lark and Jonah through another day of mowing, for this family and the food you have provided for us. We ask for your peace over Lily Belle and your grace for all our hearts. In your Son's name we pray, amen."

Lark breathed the amen along with the others, peace seeping into her weary bones. *Thank you indeed, Father, for my family.*

Plates passed and laughter rose around the table with Lilac's description of the sheep's antics today. The six-month-old lambs were growing big and spunky.

"How many more farms do you have to mow still?" RJ dug his spoon into the stew.

"After the Dwyers we have the O'Rourkes, then the Webers. Oh, and the Caldwells have a small field. That should be about it." Lark shook her head. "Still a wonder to me how fast this machine makes it go. Remember that first year when we cut our entire field with scythes?"

Lilac shook her head. "My back and fingers certainly remember."

"How did your drawing go today?"

"I finished another set to send off to the *New York Weekly*. Also did a little more on that drawing I'm enlarging of our grandfather's. Which reminds me, RJ, did you ever ask Lars Olsen if he can read Norwegian?"

RJ shook his head. "I did, but he can't, only speaks it. He can barely even read English."

Lilac's shoulders slumped. "Oh well."

Jonah nudged her elbow. "We'll find someone. There are more and more immigrants coming to this area."

Lily Belle, who had been whimpering on her mother's shoulder while Del tried to bounce her and eat, let out a full-fledged shriek. Del winced and bent her ear away from her daughter's open mouth. "Shh, sweet one. What's wrong with you tonight, hmm?"

Lark pushed back her chair. "Let me take her so you can finish your stew. I'm through."

"You're sure?" Del held out the squirming, wailing infant, her little feet kicking under her long gown.

"Of course." Lark snuggled the baby against her chest, small head fitting warm under her chin. She walked into the sitting room to get Lily away from the noise and chatter.

"There, little one. Shh." Lily hiccupped against Lark's chest, head bobbing. Lark lifted her higher, so her shoulder could press against the baby's abdomen. She remembered Ma saying how that pressure could help ease colic, if that's what this was. "Your belly giving you trouble tonight?"

Lily whimpered, but at least she wasn't wailing. Lark walked and patted, keeping up a calming murmur, then eased into an old Norwegian lullaby her father used to sing them as children. She didn't understand all the words, but their soothing lilt trickled comfort through her limbs just as it seemed to through Lily Belle's. Pa must have heard it from his parents, whose journey lay chronicled in the journal Lilac had found. What other stories would they find hidden there once they could unlock the words?

Lily Bell sniffled and sighed, her head relaxing on Lark's shoulder. Lark eased her lower and pressed a kiss to her fuzzy head, inhaling the sweet baby smell.

"Thank you." Del appeared and reached for her daughter. "Looks like you nearly got her asleep. I'll nurse her and maybe she'll actually stay down awhile."

Lark relinquished her niece with one more kiss. Her arms strangely empty, she headed to help Lilac with the dishes.

"I'll wash, you dry, so you don't get your cut wet," Lilac directed.

Lark obeyed, glad for the mindless task. Tomorrow would

be another day of haying at the Dwyers. At least the horses had eased into the rhythm by the end of today, so tomorrow should be easier. She needed to spend time in the garden too, see how many flowers still needed to be harvested before the precious seeds were lost. Always so much to do.

"There." Lilac wrung out the dishrag and hung it.

"I'll dump the dishwater." Lark hefted the tub and headed through the sitting room toward the front door.

She passed Del in her rocking chair, head bowed over her nursing baby, one foot swaying them back and forth. RJ bent over them, hand cradling his daughter's head. He pressed a kiss to Del's hair.

Lark pushed the door open with her hip and slipped into the darkness outside, blinking hard. She dumped the dishwater on the lilac bush and breathed in the cool evening air, willing away the tightness in her chest.

She didn't want to be jealous of her sister, truly she didn't. Or of Forsythia, with her upstanding husband and regular brood of little ones—or even of Lilac and the stars in her eyes she tried to hide whenever someone brought up Sam Gubberud.

Lark glanced up at the glittering span of stars, dwarfing her with their vastness, and drew a long breath.

Maybe, as she'd said to Lilac after Jesse and Climie's wedding, Lark was just supposed to be the aunt who took care of everybody else. *And if so, Lord, I'll try to be content. You've blessed me with so much.*

Then why did her heart ache so?

Perhaps because, for less than a week, she'd dared to open her heart to a sliver of hope.

And now she knew she'd been a fool to let it in.

14

Is this the place? Isaac frowned as he reached the broken fence surrounding his cousin's farm. He scanned the small wheat field ripe for harvest, the scrawny chickens pecking in the yard. A cow bellowed from the barn, but no sign of human life did he see, though the sun told him it was nigh on noon.

"Matilda?" Carrying his army haversack slung over his shoulder and a bedroll, which had made the main sum of his belongings since the war, he stepped up his pace toward the farmhouse. It stood a lonely sentinel, windows blank, paint peeling. He mounted the steps and nearly fell through a rotten board. His gut tightening, he took care in crossing the porch and knocked on the weathered door.

"Matilda? It's Cousin Isaac."

Nothing. Isaac rubbed his bearded jaw and glanced around. Could she and the children be in the barn? Not with the way that cow kept bellowing. He rapped again, harder.

A squeak, and the door cracked open to show a small pale face. The barefoot boy staring up at him couldn't be more than eight.

"Ma's too sick to come to the door."

Sick? Lord above, what was he walking into? Isaac crouched

to the child's level. "Are you Earl? Your pa wrote me about you. I'm your cousin Isaac."

"Yessir, but my pa died." The boy bit his lower lip.

"I know. And I'm sorry as I can be about that." Isaac straightened. "Might I come in and speak to your ma, Earl?"

The boy stared up at him another moment, then creaked the door open about a foot. Isaac took that as an invitation and stepped inside the farmhouse.

A sour smell pinched his nostrils. He glanced about the cramped space, a kitchen on one side, sitting room on the other. He stepped into the kitchen, where flies buzzed about a few crusts of stale bread on the table and a pitcher of—he stepped over and sniffed—what used to be milk. There lay the source of the odor. Isaac grimaced. How long had it been since the children ate properly? Or since that poor cow got milked?

At a young child's cry, Isaac crossed over to the sitting room. Earl squatted on the rug to comfort a small girl. The toddler clung to him and looked over her brother's shoulder at Isaac with round eyes. Her shift was stained and her diaper in dire need of a change by the new odor wafting toward him.

"This here's Julia." Earl stood, lifting his sister in his arms. "Ma's upstairs."

"I'll head on up, then." Isaac smiled despite the renewed clench in his gut. How long had these children been living like this? And was their mother rightly ill or leaving everything at sixes and sevens from grief? "Earl, when I come down might be you and I could tend to the stock."

The boy nodded.

Isaac mounted the narrow stairs two at a time, though mindful of his footing. *Lord above, help me know how to handle whatever I find up here.*

He found Matilda in bed as Earl had said, her light brown hair matted on the pillow, but she turned her head when he came in.

"Oh, Isaac." Tears brimmed and spilled down her cheeks as

if ever present, waiting for an opportunity. "I'm so glad you've come."

He sat on the edge of the bed and took her outstretched hand, cold in his despite the warmth trapped upstairs. "Came as soon as I got your letter. Earl says you've taken ill?"

"I haven't any fever, if that's what you're thinkin'. I just . . . can't seem to get out of bed. Not since Ambrose . . ." She closed her eyes and sobbed, face puckering.

"I'm so sorry." Grief gripping his own chest, Isaac tightened his hold on her hand till she calmed some, then dug out his handkerchief and offered it.

She took it with a sigh. "Fool man. Always thinkin' he could save the world." Matilda swiped under her eyes, the shadows stark against her pale face. "I m-miss him s-so much."

Isaac cleared his throat. "What can I do?"

She shrugged her thin shoulders on the pillow. "I'm so weak, can't hardly think straight." She glanced about vacantly, voice trailing off. "Ambrose . . . he always knew what to do. Now he's gone, and I . . . haven't any idea."

Didn't sound like his cousin always knew what to do if their finances were in the straits Ambrose had written about. But Isaac kept his thoughts to himself, as matters more urgent lay to hand. "Do you have food in the house? Looks like the children could use a good meal."

"I—I don't know." At the look on his face, she had the grace to flinch, color rising in her pale cheeks. "I've been so weak, I hardly know one day from another."

"And the animals?"

"Earl has been caring for them, I think. He's a good boy."

But an eight-year-old couldn't carry the weight of a whole farm. Isaac pushed himself to his feet and blew out a breath. He made himself speak gently. "Matilda, you've gone through a heavy loss, no mistake. But your children need you. I'm here now, but you're going to have to ask the Lord for strength to pull yourself together. Best I can tell, there's barely a decent scrap of food in this place, nor rag of clean clothing on young Julia. Once I tend to your stock, I'm takin' the children into town with me for some vittles. And I hope to heaven by the time we get back, you'll be downstairs waitin' for us."

He turned away from the stricken look on Matilda's face and headed downstairs, guilt pricking. Perhaps he'd been too harsh, the woman had just lost her husband. But he couldn't abide children and creatures bein' neglected like this.

"Now then, young sir." Isaac bent his hands on his knees to meet Earl's gaze. "Might you show me how to tend to your stock? You bein' the man of the house now."

Was that a shine of relief in the boy's eyes?

Earl nodded. "I been tryin' to do the milkin' and all. But my hands aren't strong enough to get all the milk out." He stretched out his scrawny fingers. "Bessie's been bellowin' more each day."

"Well, we'll just go see about Bessie. What other animals do you keep?"

"We got three horses, used ta be four but one died. An' pigs an' chickens." Earl took his sister's hand and led them barefoot out the door. "I'll show you, Cousin Isaac."

Isaac followed the children to the barn, where he found the cow with an inflamed udder and sores on her teats. Setting his jaw, Isaac settled Julia in an empty stall with some clean straw to play in, then set Earl to tossing hay for the hungry animals. Meanwhile, Isaac scrounged up the cleanest rags he could find. With a bucket of fresh well water and some lye soap, he cleaned Bessie's udder and sores the best he could, murmuring reassurances all the while, then milked her gently and thoroughly.

"Take a gander at this, young Earl." He motioned the boy over and showed him the milk in the pail.

"It's been kinda stringy the last few days." Earl peered in, then looked up at him, small brow furrowed under the hanks of unwashed hair. "Is that bad?"

"Means she's got an infection in her udder. You shouldn't drink milk like this." No wonder the milk in the kitchen had smelled so foul. Isaac emptied the bucket into a pan for the chickens. Later he needed to muck out the entire barn. The stench made his eyes water. "Let's put the animals out to pasture, then we're goin' to town." At least the sunshine and fresh air would be good for the stock, especially Bessie.

Inside the farmhouse, Earl dug out a moderately unsoiled frock for Julia. Isaac cleaned and changed the little girl as best he could, the motions coming back clearer than he'd reckoned from his years of caring for and dressing his younger siblings— even if his fingers fumbled with the diaper pins.

"There you are, young lady." Isaac set her on her feet on the bed he'd used for changing her and straightened the calico shift. "Purty as a picture." He'd even managed to comb some of the snarls from her brown curls.

Julia gazed at him, blue eyes solemn, then flung her chubby arms around his neck so suddenly Isaac nearly lost his balance.

"There now. That's a good girl." He patted her back, feeling out of his element, yet something warmed and expanded in his chest. He hoisted Julia onto his shoulder and winked at Earl. "Right, then. What do you say we head into town for some dinner?"

The boy's eyes lit, then he whirled and dashed outside so fast Isaac's own stomach pinched. Just how hungry were these kids?

The wagon wasn't in the best repair but sound enough far as Isaac could tell. Earl told him which horses to hitch up, a chestnut gelding named Fall and a gray mare named Winter.

"The filly, Summer, ain't broke to harness yet. And Spring died." Earl's eyes blinked solemnly. "I named 'em."

Isaac nodded, grateful for the boy's insight once again. He hitched up the team and set the children beside him on the wagon seat so he could keep a close watch on them, Julia in between him and Earl. Thankful town was only a mile away, he fought to keep his mind on his task and not wrassling through all the how-nows and what-fors of his predicament.

Lord in heaven, how did I go from thinkin' on courting Larkspur in Salton to flounderin' about trying to rescue a widow and her young'uns in Arkansas? Sure am glad you know what you're doing, for I don't and that's the truth.

Something burned low in his gut when he thought of Matilda, lying abed these weeks while her children ran hungry and unwashed. Grief could knock a soul down at the knees, he knew that well. But how could a mother neglect her own son and daughter? She couldn't let one loss derail her whole life.

Like you let it derail yours? He flinched at the inner voice, which was growing more pointed of late for certain.

The little town didn't boast much in the way of eating establishments, but it did have a new boardinghouse, so Isaac pulled up in front of the roughhewn building and stopped the horses. While Earl tied the team, he lifted Julia down and soon had them seated beside him at a long table crowded with travelers and peddlers. Not the crowd he'd guess Matilda would cotton to around her children, but they needed to eat and eat now. And when he saw their eyes go round at the huge bowls of beef stew the hostess plunked down before them, he knew he'd done right.

Isaac opened his mouth to say a grace, but both children had already reached for spoons and dug in. He covered a chuckle and reached to help Julia before she splattered stew from here to kingdom come.

"We thank you, Lord, for this food and thy provision," he murmured, blowing on a spoonful of beef and carrots before feeding it into Julia's open mouth. Good thing he knew the Almighty cared a sight more for hungry children than meal niceties.

Isaac fed Julia half her bowlful before snatching a bite from his own. Not bad, though nothing like Climie's cookin' back in Salton. Now, that woman could cook, much like the Nielsen sisters. Even Miss Larkspur, as much as she held a yen for work in the good outdoors. He'd tasted her sourdough biscuits with raspberry jam and thought he'd flown straight up to heaven.

"Cousin Isaac, may I have some more?" Earl held up an empty bowl.

Isaac signaled the hostess, who bustled over with the pot.

"Got yourself a hungry boy here, sir. You from around these parts?"

"No, ma'am, came down from Nebraska. These are son and daughter to my cousin, Ambrose McTavish."

"Ah, I heard about that. Terrible thing. Someone's got to get a hold of this James-Younger Gang, is what I say." She shook her head and clucked her tongue. "So we'll be seein' more of you around here, then?"

A mercy she didn't stay to hear his reply. Since he had none.

With the children finally sated, Isaac herded them to the general store, where he loaded up enough provisions to last a couple of months easy. Dug deep into his last pay from George Hoffman to do it, but these were his kin, his responsibility.

He drove back to the farm through the falling dusk, the children nodding off on the wagon seat against him. Poor mites, their bellies full for the first time in who knew how long. He'd want to sleep too.

He pulled the team up to the front porch, then lifted the children down. Earl roused enough to climb down the steps, while Isaac carried Julia slumbering on his shoulder.

The door opened before they reached it. Matilda stood shadowed in lamplight, then stepped back to let them in.

"I was worried you were gone so long."

Isaac felt his brows lift as he looked at his cousin's wife. She had put on a plain black dress, twisted her hair back from her face. Despite his strong words before they left, he truly hadn't thought they'd hit home. Mayhap he'd been mistaken, and glad he was if so.

"Let me lay her down." He inclined his head at Julia, and her mother nodded.

Isaac made his way down the shadowy hallway to the children's room by feel and laid the little girl in her cot. Next he helped Earl pull off his boots before the boy fell onto his own bed, clothes and all. Isaac drew the quilt over him. It would need washin' soon, that and the children too. But for now, he let them sleep.

He found Matilda sitting at the kitchen table, hands folded in a circle of lamplight. He hesitated, then eased himself down in the chair across from her.

"I beg pardon for worryin' you." He rested his hands on his knees. "I fetched the children some dinner at the boardinghouse, then took the liberty of pickin' up provisions." Which he still needed to unload from the wagon, along with tending the stock. Were the animals out to pasture still? "I didn't intend so long an absence, but I give you my word I kept careful watch over them every minute."

"I wasn't worried about that." She glanced away, her eyes unreadable in the dim light. "Ambrose always said he'd trust you with his life, so I knew I could with my children. I was afraid that—that you might not bring them back." She drew a long, quavering breath. "And that you'd be right not to. That you thought me unfit t-to care for them. And that you were, again, right."

Isaac swallowed. She wasn't wrong, not entirely. But seeing how she'd pulled herself together this evening . . . maybe there was hope yet. The kitchen was even cleared, and cleaned, by the improved aroma of things.

"I'd never take them without a word and not bring them back, on my honor, ma'am. I'm truly sorry you thought so."

"No, I'm sorry." She drew another breath, a bit stronger this time. "And ashamed of how I let myself just . . . give up. I knew it was wrong, knew my children needed me. But I just couldn't get myself out of bed. Not until you came, Isaac." She looked at him then, clasping her hands tighter. "Will you stay with us? Please? You can turn this farm around for better. I know you can. You've made such a difference in merely a day. Please stay and help us, Isaac. For Ambrose's sake and the children's."

He met her gaze, then lowered his to the table. He rubbed a scratch in the wood with his thumb, as if he could smooth it out by sheer will like he wished he could the path of his life.

Lord, is this the way you have before me? And must I walk it with such a heavy heart?

He didn't give Matilda his answer that day, yet in effect he followed her request. He set to turning the farm around as best he could, clearing barn and fields alike, tending the stock back to health, and setting Earl to helping him harvest the family's wheat before it went to seed. Matilda slowly retook her duties, caring for Julia and the house a bit more day by day. She even smiled a bit at Earl's animated tales at suppertime.

More than once he thought of writing to Larkspur, letting her know the state of things. But what would he say, when so much remained unknown?

At the end of a week, Isaac took himself into town to see the banker, the man Ambrose had been fixing to see when the robbery happened. And his murder. Isaac still shuddered to climb the building's steps.

"So you're Ambrose's cousin." The thin-lipped banker shook his head as he sat down across from Isaac. "That man never could sit back when he should. Lie low and let the storm pass by, I always say. But, no, he had to jump in and try to be a hero."

"The way I hear it, weren't nobody else willin' to try and stop those thieves." The back of Isaac's neck heated.

The man looked at him over his spectacles. "That gang can't be stopped, Mr. McTavish. Everyone around here knows that. Excepting, that is, your cousin. And you, it seems."

Isaac inhaled through his nose and made himself sit back.

"I've come to see about my cousin's state of affairs. Or his wife's, as now may be."

The banker gave a dry laugh. "I do hope she isn't trying to hold on to that farm at this point."

"And why is that?" He kept his tone even.

"See for yourself." The man pushed a document across the table to Isaac.

He scanned the papers, but he'd never had a noggin for numbers. "And this means?"

An eyebrow lifted. "The farm is seriously in arrears—has been for some time. You may know that was Ambrose's reason for coming to the bank that day. Trying to plead for mercy yet again, no doubt."

"Which you hold out none too freely, I'll be bound. Nor provide any protection for your clients from murderin' gangs." Despite himself, Isaac felt his hands fist on his thighs.

The man sighed. "As I said, Mr. McTavish, there's no stopping that James-Younger gang. Not till we get some real law enforcement in these parts. So are you here to discuss Mrs. McTavish's sale of the farm?"

"I'm here to gather information. No more, no less."

"Well, I can tell you it would take near a miracle to save that farm. Perhaps if a man put his whole heart and soul into it, morning and night for a year or two. But only perhaps."

Isaac rubbed a hole budding in the worn trouser fabric over his knee. *His whole heart and soul.* "And if she did sell it?"

"She could get a tidy little sum. Not much after settling all their debts, mind. But enough to set her and her children up for a while."

Isaac gave the man a peremptory thanks and left, mind awhirl.

So there lay the choice before him. Throw himself into saving his cousin's farm and caring for his wife and children. Or convince Matilda to sell her home and start anew somewhere else—where? Back somewhere with her own kin? He thought he remembered she hailed from Kentucky. Or should he bring her and the children up to Salton as Ambrose had planned?

Though she'd asked him to stay, in her current state he'd a notion she'd bow to whatever way Isaac chose to lead her. Which made the burden on him all the heavier.

He untied the bridle of his borrowed horse from the bank's hitching post. *Lord, what do you want from me?*

What do you want?

The thought came so strong, Isaac's hands stilled. He lifted his head, staring at the street scattered with mud puddles and fallen leaves.

What did he want? 'Twasn't a question he'd given much thought to for some time. More like let himself be blown from one place to another, like those dried-up leaves skittering away from his boots, gusted by a wind hearkening toward autumn.

Isaac swung up on the gelding and turned him down the street. Sortin' out the muddle of his thoughts would take some time, might as well head toward home in the meanwhile.

No, not home. His heart rebelled against the thought with such ferocity he stayed his hand on the reins. Home wasn't Ambrose's farm, or Matilda and the children, dear as they were.

Home was . . .

And just like that, slick as a whistle, he knew what he wanted. He sure and certain, for the first time since having his whole heart carved out from the war, truly knew.

Home wasn't here in Arkansas. Nor hardly anywhere else he'd traipsed to these past lonely years. Home was in Salton, Nebraska. With Larkspur Nielsen.

A sudden grin tugging beneath his beard, Isaac nudged his cousin's horse into a lope.

15

His first day of school in Salton.

Sam Gubberud used his good hand to adjust the neat stack of books on his desk once more and glanced at the clock on the schoolroom wall. When had minutes ever ticked by so slowly? Now that he had everything ready, he wished the students would just arrive and end this interminable waiting. Less time to ponder all the ways he could mess things up.

Had he thought of everything? Two weeks of lesson plans laid out for primer class through eighth graders, books stacked on shelves, slates at the ready, water barrel filled. Even a stool in the corner to which he might send recalcitrant students, if need be. All in order.

Save the fact that he'd never taught a single lesson to a school full of children in his life. He fingered his empty sleeve and breathed a prayer.

The door squeaked, jerking his eyes open. Had he missed the time to ring the bell?

But, no, Lilac Nielsen slipped through, a small paper package in her hand.

"Miss Nielsen." He mentally scolded the leap of his pulse and stepped around his desk. "What a pleasant surprise."

"Is it?" Her dark brows lifted a little.

He frowned. "What do you mean?"

Her cheeks reddened. "Nothing, sorry. I just wanted to bring you a little something, wish you well this first day of school." She held out the parcel, her manner unusually awkward for her, yet her dark eyes shone sincerely.

Had he offended her by his reticence that day she and her brother so graciously welcomed him to her town? Kicking himself, Sam took the package. "How kind. Thank you." He laid it on his desk so as to unroll the brown paper. She hadn't tied it with twine—happenstance or had she realized how difficult knots were to wrangle with only one hand?

A small waterfall of colored pencils spilled out. Beneath them lay a stack of paper—a small one, yet what richness for a one-room school.

"The town doesn't provide art supplies, I know." Lilac stepped closer. "You're fortunate to have books and slates. But the children love being creative, so I thought this might brighten up your schooldays a bit."

"How thoughtful you are." Sam shook his head, a tightness in his throat. "Miss Nielsen—I believe I owe you an apology."

"Oh?" She cocked a delicate dark brow.

"The day I arrived, I'm afraid I may have been—that is, I hope you didn't find me uncivil." Heat crept up the back of his neck. This young woman certainly had a way of throwing him off-kilter.

"Not uncivil." She folded her arms across her waist. "But I did wonder if I'd offended you somehow."

"Offended?" He took a step toward her, guilt pinching his chest. "No, never. I'm terribly sorry. I merely—everything was so new, and your family has been so kind, assisting me with this new opportunity. I didn't want to pay that back by seeming forward with their—" He stopped and swallowed, but how else to say it? "With you, their precious youngest sister." Now his ears must be truly flaming.

"Oh." She lowered her arms, her own cheeks flushing. "I—I see."

"But I went about it all wrong. Can you forgive me, Miss Nielsen? And let me start again?"

"I suppose so." A smile tugged the curves of her lips. "If you'll call me Lilac as you used to."

He exhaled and smiled back. "I suppose I could manage that. We are old school chums, after all."

"Well then, welcome to Salton, Sam." She held out her hand.

He gave it a firm squeeze, careful not to hold on too long. "Thank you, Lilac."

She glanced about the schoolroom and drew a breath, giving them both a beat to steady themselves. "I need to let you welcome your students. They're a wonderful bunch on the whole. I think you'll love them."

"Have you worked with them before?"

She nodded. "When Del was the schoolmarm, I came in to teach art from time to time or help with special projects. If you ever want me to do the same this year, let me know."

"I will, indeed. And thank you." He folded the paper over the precious colored pencils again. "I confess I was feeling perilously close to panicking till you came in. Now I'm quite fortified."

"You'll do fine. If it helps when things get rough, Del always says her motto was, 'When in doubt, read aloud.'" Lilac glanced at the clock. "But I'd better go."

So it was time. His pulse thudding anew, Sam fought a sudden urge to grab Lilac's hand again and beg her not to leave him alone to face the veritable army of children out in the schoolyard. But no. He nodded a good-bye, waited till she slipped out the back door, then squared his shoulders and headed to the front. He could do this—he must do this.

Or prove his mother verifiably right.

Barely had he rung the bell when he had to jump back from the stampede of boots and bare feet as denim- and calico-clad youngsters crammed through the door, laughing and calling to one another. Sam stepped back from the fray and grimaced. He probably should have told them to line up first or something. Making a mental note for tomorrow, he let the students stream in as they would for today and made his way to the front of the classroom. He waited a moment to be sure all were in, then cleared his throat.

"Will you please be seated?"

Chattering, commotion. Children knocked over slates, boys compared rocks from their pockets. A little girl wailed that someone had pushed her.

Sam racked his brain. What was it Schoolmaster Muller had always said to call attention at the beginning of the day?

"School, come to order!" boomed from his mouth at a volume Sam hadn't known he possessed.

Thirty faces swiveled to look at him, the clamor settling to a hush. An older girl picked up a whimpering little one and set her on her seat.

"Thank you." Sam ran his hand through his hair and drew a breath. "Please take your seats, younger students in the front, older in the back." Surely they knew that, but with such a beginning, he decided to assume nothing. He'd already welcomed chaos by not giving them instruction before entering the building, and heaven knew how long he'd pay for it.

"Welcome. I am your new teacher, Mr. Gubberud." A giggle snorted through the back row. What did they think was funny—his name? "We will now begin with the Pledge of Allegiance." At least he could muddle his way through that. He also made it through roll without much incident, though several boys on the list were missing—not uncommon with farmwork to be done, he knew. Next, he planned to start the older ones on history and work with the little ones on their letters and numbers to try to assess their levels and readiness for reading.

Should have been simple enough, but an hour later, he felt his hair must be sticking straight on end. Far from sitting and studying their readers quietly, the middle children were whispering and passing notes, the little ones squirming on their seats or crawling under them.

A shriek spun Sam around from trying to sketch out a complicated equation on the board for the older students.

"A snake! He's got a snake!" A little girl danced on top of one of the benches, pointing at a stocky young boy.

"Only a little grass 'un." The boy held a squirming, twisting reptile by the tail, swinging it closer to the girl.

She screamed and scooted backward, right off the end of the bench. She landed with a crash atop several classmates, squeals and howls mingling with others' laughter.

Sam set his jaw and marched down the aisle to the culprit. "What is your name, young sir?"

"Thomas Dwyer." The boy glanced up and amended, "Sir."

"Thomas, I want you to throw that snake out in the yard. Right. Now. Then come back here and sit on the stool in the corner till lunchtime."

Thomas made a face, but at the look Sam gave him, he shuffled toward the door and flung the unfortunate little reptile outside. Then clomped his way back up to the front and followed Sam's pointing finger to the corner. He cast a woeful grin at the class before turning on the stool to face the wall, eliciting another wave of laughter.

"That's enough. From all of you." Sam rubbed his forehead and glanced at the clock. Still nearly an hour till noon—how ever would he fill the time? And he had planned this day out with such care. Clearly, lesson plans in theory and teaching in practice were proving two very different things. *Lord, help.*

"When in doubt, read aloud." Lilac's quote from Del this

morning flitted through his mind. He'd originally left no space in his lesson plans for stories, but now he snatched at the notion as a lifeline.

"If you've all quite finished . . ." He leveled a stare at the still-giggling rows. "Please finish whatever problem or page you were working on, then put your books and slates away for now."

The children quieted and obeyed, casting him wondering glances. Sam strode over to the bookshelves nailed under the window and scanned the small library for something familiar. *Ray's Arithmetic, Robinson Crusoe, Gulliver's Travels,* a volume of Greek myths . . . *Nicholas Nickleby.* Sam drew a breath as if meeting an old friend and withdrew the Dickens volume.

"If you will all sit quietly in your seats, I will read to you until the lunch hour. Not a move from you, Thomas," he added as the boy twisted around on his stool. "You can listen just as well facing the corner." He opened the book and began to read.

"'There once lived, in a sequestered part of the county of Devonshire, one Mr. Godfrey Nickleby: a worthy gentleman, who, taking it into his head rather late in life that he must get married, and not being young enough or rich enough to aspire to the hand of a lady of fortune, had wedded an old flame out of mere attachment . . .'"

He glanced up after a few pages and saw rows of attentive young faces, some students leaning their chins on their hands, all eyes fixed on him. *Thank you, Lilac.* Sam turned the page and increased his dramatic expression in recounting the saga of the Nickleby family.

Classes proceeded somewhat better after lunch. Sam made it through half the alphabet with the primer class, not to mention an entire arithmetic lesson with the middle grades. He stood at his desk trying to decide in what order to have the older students recite when the schoolroom door banged open at the back of the room.

Two older boys—no, young men—stood in the doorway, blocking its light with their broad shoulders.

Sam closed McGuffey's sixth reader. "May I help you?"

"Dunno, kin you?" The taller boy guffawed and stepped inside. "Our pa said we had to come t' school!"

"I see. Well, I'm afraid you've missed most of the day." Sam drew his roster forward and ran his finger down the lines to the names of the boys who had been missing that morning. "Would you be Abraham and Jedidiah Omstead?"

"I'm Abe. He's Jed." The older boy jerked a thumb at his brother and spit a stream of tobacco juice, narrowly missing the students' water barrel.

Sam pressed his lips together. "Well, you are most welcome. However, I must tell you that there will be no spitting in my schoolroom. Please take your seats quietly in the back, and I will be along to assess your grade level once I have a chance." He seriously doubted these young men were ready for the sixth reader.

"Didn't know they got a cripple to teach this year," Jed muttered, turning to follow his brother to a back seat.

A murmur rippled through the classroom.

Sam shifted his jaw. Should he respond? Ignore it? Deciding on the latter for now, he reopened the reader, finding it hard to focus on the printed words. A prickle ran along his shoulders, a sense that he'd best keep watch. For himself and for the other children. Senses honed by leading fellow troops into battle snapped to attention as they hadn't in years.

The Omstead brothers boded no good, or he was much mistaken.

The last hour of school dragged to a close at last, a shadow cloaking the classroom despite sunshine through the window. Abe and Jed caused no outright disruption, save scuffling their feet, whispering to each other, and tacitly refusing to read the chapters Sam assigned. But this late in the day and with a headache beginning to pound, he'd little energy left to face off in battle against them—though he'd a sneaking suspicion he'd regret it on the morrow.

Sam rang the bell for dismissal, watched the ebbing stampede of students out the door, then sank into his chair and leaned his head in his hand, wishing he had two to hold the weight of it.

Father in heaven, what have I gotten myself into? If a single day of teaching trounced him so, how would he survive a whole year?

"Mr. Gubberud?" piped a small voice near his bent head.

He straightened with a guilty start. He'd thought all the children had left.

"I forgot to give you this apple at lunch. My ma always gives me one to give my teacher on the first day." Robbie Brownsville held out the rosy fruit.

"Thank you, Robbie." Sam took the gift and rubbed his thumb over the shiny skin. "How thoughtful of you."

"Sorry we were—hmm, what does my ma say? A 'bit of a handful' today." Robbie scrunched up his face. "I tried telling the others to be quiet and listen to you, but it didn't work so good."

Sam chuckled, something unwinding in his chest. "It's not your fault, Robbie. But thank you. I appreciate your trying."

"Tomorrow is a new day. My ma says that too." Robbie glanced out the window. "Oh, my tante Lilac is here, I've gotta go. Bye, Mr. Gubberud!" Flapping his hand, the little boy spun and pelted out of the schoolroom.

Sam tried to ignore the stab of disappointment that Lilac wouldn't be coming into the schoolroom. He had more important things to worry about just now than catching sight of an intriguing young woman. Like doing this all over again tomorrow—and the next day and the next. He stifled a groan. Why had he ever thought he'd make a good teacher?

He reviewed his lesson plan notes for tomorrow—completely scrapping some ideas and adjusting others—then, unable to think anymore, stacked the papers and slid them into his satchel to take home. Perhaps his brain might decide to function again after some supper.

Walking down the street in the waning afternoon light, he breathed deeply of the prairie air, so fresh and clear even here in town. He had a flash of gratitude for the Nielsen House and Climie Brownsville's fine meals. He would have no stomach for cobbling something together for supper were he on his own tonight. While he'd managed to concoct simple fare over an open fire in the army when necessary, his mother had seen to it that he never needed to really learn to cook.

"Well, Mr. Gubberud. How was your first day?"

Sam blinked and focused on the man stepping before him on the wooden sidewalk by the mercantile. Dark hair threaded with silver, a kind smile as he leaned on his cane. The attorney who'd helped call him to this town, if he weren't mistaken. Mr. Cartwright? No, Caldwell. He would get the names of everyone in this town one of these days.

"It was . . . well . . ." Sam pressed his tongue to his teeth. How to be honest without making one of Salton's leaders feel they'd made a grave mistake in their choice of schoolmaster? "A few bumps in the road, but I trust tomorrow will be better." *Or I may be on the next train out of town by your choice, never mind mine.*

The older man chuckled. "Put you through the wringer, did they?"

Sam allowed himself a wry smile. "Is it that obvious?"

"My father was a schoolmaster." Caldwell shook his head. "Many's the time I remember him reminiscing about his early days of teaching. Said they gave him more gray hairs than anything in his life—except his own children, once we came along."

Sam joined in the chuckle, the knot in his middle easing. Perhaps the man wouldn't ride him out of town after all. "I thought I came prepared, but I'm afraid children in practice aren't quite the same as in theory."

"Real people seldom are. But I've an idea you aren't a man to give up easily." Caldwell cast a glance at Sam's empty sleeve.

Sam firmed his jaw. "No, sir."

They fell into step side by side, heading toward the boardinghouse as the sun edged near the horizon in glowing orange.

"I'll tell you something else my father often said. 'Success in teaching depends on two things: respect and relationship.' He called them two ends of the same ruler—can't have one without the other. Have to be firm and consistent, insist the students show nothing less than respect for you and each other. Yet you must also earn their trust, show them you'll be consistently fair, share yourself with them, and show them you genuinely care about their lives too. Otherwise, they'll have no reason to respect you to begin with."

Sam nodded slowly. "I'm afraid I didn't do either very well today—connect with them or establish much authority. I was just trying to survive."

Mr. Caldwell chuckled. "As I said, gray hairs."

The attorney walked him all the way to the boardinghouse, leaving him on the steps feeling lighter of heart than he'd imagined he could an hour ago. Heaviness settled again, though, as he watched the older man walk away, leaning on his cane. He'd completely forgotten to mention the problem of the Omstead brothers—but should he have? Wasn't that his own responsibility to wrestle out anyway?

Lord, give me wisdom.

He headed inside, the aroma of fried chicken and mashed potatoes making his stomach growl. After supper, he headed up to his room, grateful it was a private one. Apparently it hadn't been too long since the upstairs had been divided from one long room. He settled at the small desk with pen and paper, then bowed his head.

He needed some ideas for tomorrow.

16

I have to stop thinking about Isaac.

Lark stirred the rabbit gravy on the stove for a hearty breakfast before haying. Early morning sunlight brightened the soddy window, birds outside raising a twittering chorus.

"Lark, what is the matter with you?" Lilac asked, a bit of a bite in her words as she pulled the tray of biscuits out of the oven.

She looked up to see a puzzled look on her sister's face. "Why, what's wrong?"

"I spoke, and you never answered. Didn't you hear me?"

"Sorry, guess my mind was somewhere else." She heaved a sigh and set down the wooden spoon. "What do you need?"

"I just wanted to tell you I heard from Forsythia yesterday that Sam Gubberud can write, read, and speak Norwegian. He mentioned it to Adam."

Lark nodded. "How wonderful. So you're going to ask him to translate the journal?"

"I think I'll bring it with me the next time I go to town." She paused and popped the hot biscuits into a basket with quick fingers. "He sure is a good man."

"That he is. Hopefully he's a good teacher too. School started yesterday, right?"

Nodding, a slight smile made Lilac appear dreamy in the soddy's dimness. "I-I think I could come to care for him. Do you think it's too soon after Ethan?"

Lark smiled to herself. Sounded to her like her little sister had already come to care for the man. "As you said about Ethan and Sylvia, when it's right, it's right. Wait and see." *Thank you, Lord,* whispered through her mind, followed immediately by thoughts of Isaac off again taking care of his family. That was good, as it should be, but what about . . . ? She slapped plates on the table, cutting that thought off. "We better dish up. Jonah will be here soon."

"I'll wash up after breakfast."

"Thanks, but can't cut till the dew is off the grass anyway. Jonah greased the mower so all is ready."

"I ran the trapline early before chores." Another one of those things that had to be done daily before the meat went bad in the heat or some wild animal had a free breakfast.

Jonah showed up just as they sat down to breakfast on biscuits topped with rabbit gravy. He'd been sleeping at Del and RJ's since they had more room.

"We set you a place."

"I see that, but I ate at Del's. Mmm, biscuits and gravy."

"Surely you have room for one. After all, I made them specially for you." Lark pointed to his place.

Jonah grinned and shrugged. "Can't disappoint you, then."

Lark handed him her plate and returned to the stove to dish up another, then sat down again with a smile at her brother.

"So the Webers' today?" He spoke around a mouthful.

"Yes," Lark said. "They'll be almost the last, except for the Caldwells'. Good thing, our wheat's looking near ready for harvest. And we need to be picking apples and gathering more flower seeds too." She gathered the plates and set them in the steaming pan on the stove. "Let's use our team first, and then I'll bring them home."

"I'm going to hoe corn this morning and work on drawings this afternoon," Lilac said. "Del said there are still plenty of raspberries. Maybe I can find enough for raspberry shortcake for dessert this evening."

Lark nodded. "How about frying that rabbit and picking lettuce for a salad for dinner? I've a hankering for greens. Any peas left? New potatoes?"

Lilac shook her head, along with an eye roll. "I'll do what I can."

When Jonah called that he was ready, Lark grabbed her wide-brimmed straw hat off the rack and clapped it on her head, tying the strings under her chin before she climbed into the seat to drive while Jonah settled in behind her.

Meadowlarks chorused from the wheat field, and swallows dipped into a mud patch by the road as they trotted to the Weber farm, where two other teams waited under a shade tree, tails swishing at the flies.

"If you don't mind, I'll drive our team the first few hours, and then Jonah will drive."

"Our first cutting is already dry enough to turn, so the rest of us will be in that field," Robert Weber said. "Wife will have dinner ready for noon, Miss Nielsen, if you want to stay."

"Thanks, but Jonah will eat enough for both of us," Lark said with a smile.

Jonah led out, searching the grass for snakes or big rocks, although each farmer was supposed to have removed the big rocks from his fields. Several big rock piles on the edges of the Webers' fields attested they'd been more thorough than the Dwyers. When Jonah was about fifty yards ahead, he waved for Lark to start mowing. A flock of quail lifted in front of him. He paused, then waved her on. Her teams' ears twitched, and one of them snorted, but they kept on with their steady pace. After the third round of the field, Robert waved her over to have a drink. Seeing the sweat dripping off those turning hay, Lark appreciated sitting on the mower even more.

"You want to switch?" Jonah asked as he mopped his forehead with a bandanna he pulled from a back pocket.

"Not really." She grinned at him. After dismounting from the mower seat, she drank the dipper of water the Webers' oldest son, Aaron, held out. "Thank you."

"That mower is some invention."

"That it is. Makes haying easier for all of us."

"My pa said 'bout time someone invented a rake for the horses to pull."

Lark nodded and climbed back on the mower, then waited for Jonah to walk out again before lowering the blade. When Robert waved her in to change teams, she didn't argue. While she unhooked the traces, Jonah hooked the reins up on the rump, and Lark led her team to the shade. She turned to Robert. "You got a different horse on your team."

He nodded. "He's working well with old Belle here. My mare is heavy with foal, and I traded for this younger gelding. He's settled in well."

"You're sure he's safe?" Lark understood the practice of train-ing younger horses by hitching them with an older but . . .

"He's good and solid, Miss Larkspur, not seen him shy at nothing. But I'll be keeping a close eye on him."

Lark nodded.

Robert strode out, holding his stick and looking over his shoulder to signal Jonah, who hupped the team and lowered the blade. The younger horse's ears twitched back and forth, but the team worked as one, the way it should. Nell nudged her and hung her head over Lark's shoulder to be petted and scratched. Prince did the same.

"You two . . . If all the teams were as dependable as you." The trade she'd made of her two oxen for this team after they moved here was indeed a wise choice.

As the horses and mower turned the second corner and started back, she decided to head over and help those raking the cut hay for a while.

Striding toward the other side of the field and humming one of her favorite hymns, she heard screams from behind her. She turned to see Robert's team rearing and jerking the mower. *Jonah!* Where was Jonah? Throwing proper over her shoulder, she lifted her skirts and ran.

"Please, God, please, Father, Lord God," Lark could only mutter as she pounded into the field, dashing between the other workers heading for the accident.

Robert Weber had gotten hold of his terrified team, but as she got closer, she could see Jonah flat out on his back on the ground. His right leg lay at an odd angle. She fell to her knees at her brother's side. One of the others already knelt beside him.

"Jonah!" she called but no response.

"Someone go for Adam," Robert yelled.

"What happened?" Lark scanned her brother. Jonah was unconscious but breathing. Blood soaked into the dirt and grass under his head, his shredded shirt soaking blood from his back. She ripped off her apron and clamped it under his head. "Jonah, can you hear me? Just blink if you can." No response.

Robert tore off his shirt and handed it to her. "My wife is bringing some sheets so we can load him into a wagon. Can't depend on finding Adam. We can get him to town faster." He shook his head. "I'm so sorry. My gelding spooked at a rattlesnake. I thought for sure he was steady enough for this."

Anthony Armstead drove his wagon up even with them.

Aaron Weber ran up with his arms loaded with bedding.

Lark sucked in a deep breath. "We need to see how bad his back is. If someone can brace his leg and someone else clamp that shirt over my apron to stop the bleeding, someone else help me roll him . . ."

"Let's get a sheet under him at the same time. Two of you roll a sheet. Better we move him while he is unconscious."

Lord God, help us kept galloping through Lark's mind. *Help us do what is best.*

Robert's wife, Rebecca, ran up with a bottle of whiskey. "Can he drink this to help the pain?"

Lark shook her head. "Still out."

Between them all, they got the sheet under Jonah, and Lark saw that the skin on his back was all scraped up. *Oh, Lord.* She inhaled, feeling like a warm river flowed into her. She sucked in another breath. *Lord, please keep him unconscious. The pain will be horrendous.*

"Best thing we can do is get him to Adam."

She nodded. "Would you cut up his pant leg and see if bone is sticking out?"

Someone else jumped to do that. "No, ma'am," the man assured a moment later.

While several people helped with Jonah, others were padding the wagon. Four men picked up the corners of the sheet and two more got up in the wagon, then Lark climbed up, ready to cradle his head.

With Jonah lifted into place, they slammed and locked the wagon gate.

"Drive careful as you can."

"I will. You ready, Miss Lark?" Anthony asked from the driver's seat.

"Yes." At least the bleeding had stopped as long as she kept pressure on the apron and shirt. "Hang on, dearest Jonah. You're in God's arms, and He is holding us all." Tears blurred her vision. When the wagon hit a bump, she tried to take the jolt in her arms.

"Sorry!" called Anthony.

"I know." She sniffed and wished she could dry her tears. But holding Jonah's head was all she could do for him. They were just about to town when she heard a horse galloping up. Adam pulled up to ride alongside the wagon.

"We're almost there. You have the bleeding under control?"

"I think so. There was no bleeding on his leg but looks to be broken too."

"Has he regained consciousness at all?"

"No." She shook her head.

"I'm going to round up help and set up for him." He waved and galloped back to town.

By the time the wagon pulled up to Adam's new office on Main Street, four more men were ready to help carry him in feet first so Lark could continue to hold his head.

"Okay, we are going to try to lay him on his side on the examining table so I can assess the damages. Sythia, roll a sheet to prop his head up. Lark, keep holding his neck straight as you can in case he's broken a vertebra. Someone hold his leg, there, good."

Lark continued her litany of prayers, including thanks for getting Jonah to Adam and medical care.

Adam probed the back of Jonah's head. "Not feeling broken bones. We'll suture that cut. Next, we'll clean his back and see how bad that is. Broken leg will be last. At least it's not a compound fracture."

William and Jesse stopped at the doorway. "How can we help?" William asked.

"Can you bring me that cradle for his head that you've been working on so we can lay him on his stomach?"

"S-sure, we can do that." Jesse eyed the width of Jonah's shoulders, and the two headed for their shop.

Mr. Caldwell and his wife, Beatrice, came in next. "We told everyone to pray. How can we help?"

"Light all the lamps and set them around so we can see to clean him up. Someone get a stool for Lark. Her arms must be at their collapsing stage. You can prop your elbows on the table."

"Thank you." She leaned over and whispered in Jonah's ear. "If you can hear me, know everyone is doing the best they can. We are praying you stay unconscious for a while yet."

"Sythia, how about moving that lamp over here so I can see to the head injury. Lark, can you still hold his head?"

Lark nodded.

Adam cleaned the laceration, causing it to bleed again, the swelling growing. He rinsed the wound with iodine until he could no longer find bits of debris. "Head wounds bleed the worst of anything, but by God's grace, no major arteries are involved."

Forsythia held out a tray with sterilized needles, silk thread, and scissors. "You want me to cut the hair around that?"

"Please do. I'd prefer to shave it but cutting will do."

Jessie and William brought in the headrest to attach to the table. They had padded the curved piece, and Jesse held it in place while William screwed the arms into the table frame. "There, that should hold it."

"Good, now we will lift him forward to rest his forehead in that, and he can be on his stomach." Adam grinned at the two young men. "You are geniuses. Had this ready just in time."

"I saw one like this once at a hospital." William smiled at Jesse. "Give us a need, and we'll find a remedy if'n it can be made with wood. You know, we shoulda put this on your table when we made it for you to begin with."

Together, they all lifted the sheet Jonah was still lying on, and with Lark holding his head and the young men dealing with his leg, they settled him on his belly, forehead cushioned on the cradle.

"Lark, go sit in that chair before you collapse," Sythia ordered. "Jesse, help her over there, please."

"I-I'm fine." Lark blinked, but when she tried to stand, Jesse grabbed her just in time and half carried her to the chair.

"Put your head down between your knees," Sythia said. "We don't need another patient."

Once Jonah's head was taken care of, Forsythia and Adam started on his back, both of them wiping the perspiration from their faces. Between the people inside the room and the lighted lamps, the late afternoon breeze hadn't much chance of cooling things off.

"I need to get home to do the chores." Lark blew out a breath.

"RJ is taking care of that, and someone took your team home and let them out to pasture." Beatrice laid a gentle hand on her shoulder.

"Lilac is at our house taking care of the little ones," Sythia picked up before Lark could ask. "I have a feeling plenty of food has already been brought to our house. That's the way this town works."

Adam sluiced Jonah's lacerated back with alcohol again and again. "Far as I can tell we got it all, but tiny grains of dirt can hide most anywhere."

Lilac set a tray of swizzle-filled glasses on one of the tables. "Adam, have a drink."

"Ah, thank you." Adam took the glass and downed it halfway without pausing to breathe. With the back finally bandaged, he moved to Jonah's leg, cutting off the entire pantleg, shaking his head at the swelling. He gently probed with his fingertips.

Silence seeped into the room as some people left and those remaining seemed to hold their breath. Lark and Forsythia held hands, lips moving in silent prayer. A fly buzzed around Adam's head. The laughter of children playing outside in the street made Lark smile despite the circumstances. While Lark kept her gaze on Adam's hands, she leaned against her sister's side. *Please, Lord*, her litany of the day broke into her awareness again.

Adam heaved a sigh and looked around at those gathered. "We are going to snap those bones back into place, near as we can, and pray God makes it heal right."

"Are you saying Jonah might not walk again?" Lark asked.

"Might have to use a crutch or cane. If we get through all this without infection or him losing the use of his leg, my prayers will be answered."

"Then the rest of us have our jobs cut out for him—to pray both singly and together," Lark whispered.

"You are so right. Doctors can do amazing things these days, but ultimately it is God who does the healing." He looked to his wife and her older sister. "We will have someone with him round the clock, and this first night it will be neither of you. Thank the Lord we just got these hospital rooms finished. Our first prayer is that he regains consciousness—though hopefully not till we get this leg set. So now, Jesse."

The two men took hold of Jonah's leg, one at the foot, one at the knee, and on three, they pulled steadily.

A grating sound made Lark close her eyes and grit her teeth. She and Sythia clung to each other's hands. A slight click filled the room. And everyone released a held breath.

"Thank you, Lord." Adam sighed too. "Now I'll cast him."

Lark blinked hard as she watched her brother's still form. How could she ever go home and sleep this night?

17

Sam glanced at the schoolroom clock and, as if on cue, his heart started thumping again. Would it do that at eight o'clock in the morning every day for the foreseeable future, even on Sundays?

Shaking his head at himself, Sam grabbed the brass bell off his desk and strode to the schoolhouse door. In the doorway, however, he gripped the bell without ringing it, scanning the schoolyard of students. Most didn't see him standing there, their games of ball and crack-the-whip continuing unabated.

Sam sucked a lungful of air. *Help me, Lord.* "Students! Time for class."

Only a few stopped and looked up. Robbie Brownsville ran over to the steps.

"Aren't you going to ring the bell, Mr. Gubberud?"

He'd hoped to speak with the students first, but it seemed that wasn't working. "I suppose so. But we aren't going to go into the classroom just yet." He gave the bell a firm clang.

That did it. The children abandoned their games and charged toward the steps.

Tucking the bell under the stub of his missing arm, Sam held up his one hand firmly. The students skidded to a halt, glancing among themselves and up at their teacher.

"Before we go in, I'd like to establish a few rules. Or did Miss Linden and Miss Nielsen let you stampede inside like a herd of cattle?"

Heads dropped, feet scuffed.

"I thought not. And it is my mistake for allowing it yesterday, but we will mend matters now. When I ring the bell, you will line up at the steps single file, younger ones in the front, older in the back. I will wait till everyone is quiet and then, only then, will we march inside in a proper manner. I don't want any shouting, pushing, or trampling when entering my classroom. Is that clear?"

He looked out over the crowd of nodding heads and sobered faces.

Good. Sam drew a breath and allowed a smile. "Let's try this, then. You may line up now." He retrieved the bell from under his arm and rang it once more.

With comparatively little shoving and scuffling, the students formed a line.

Sam scanned it and nodded. "Well done. Now you may enter. Ah-ah!" The older ones in the back surged forward, threatening to topple the little ones. "Slowly. Keep an eye on those in front of you and keep pace with them. Soldiers marching into battle must do the same thing." As he well knew.

The children filed in, not without whispers and giggles, but Sam let that pass. Once everyone sat in their seats, eyes more or less on him, he strode to the front of the schoolroom and smiled out over the students.

"Thank you. That was much better. Now, shall we open our day with prayer?" Another thing he'd failed to incorporate yesterday—no wonder he'd had a rather abysmal start.

The rows of students bowed their heads, and Sam followed.

"Heavenly Father, thank you that we can gather together to

learn in this school today. Thank you for each student here, and for the privilege of teaching them. We ask your blessing on our families, our community, our country, and our world. Guide us through this day, and help us learn what you want to teach us this year about your creation and about one another. In your Son's name we pray, amen."

The hearty chorus of "Amens" warmed Sam's chest and brought a smile to his face.

"Excellent." Rows of faces fixed on his—what a welcome change. *Thank you already, Father.* He ran through roll, focusing on beginning to connect names with faces. "Now, before we begin our lessons today, I realized I've been a bit remiss. None of you know me, and I failed to truly introduce myself to you. I want to get to know each of you this year, and you to also know me. So, to begin—"

The door in the back slammed open, then shut. Abe and Jed slunk into the back row.

Sam blew out a breath, his gut tightening again. Just when things were going well. "Thank you for joining us, Abraham and Jedidiah." As they didn't respond, he raised his voice. "If you gentlemen are going to be perpetually tardy, I will need a note from your parents as to why, or it will go on your record."

"We got chores to do in the mornin's." Abe slouched lower in his seat till his knees bumped the desk in front of him.

"No doubt. However, I expect that is true for most students here. And again, a note from your parents is all I require." He pasted on a smile. "Now, if you will please sit up properly in your seats, we will continue."

He ignored the Omstead brothers' mutterings and focused on the front rows of students, the young faces lifted up to his. "As you know, my name is Mr. Gubberud—Samuel Jakob Gubberud, to be precise. Some of you might have found my name a bit challenging to pronounce yesterday."

A few scattered giggles and grins.

"As with yours, my name comes from my family heritage. Does anyone have a guess where my family might have come from?"

A young girl—Bethany Kinsley, if he recalled aright—raised her hand. "Germany?"

"Excellent guess, but no."

Thomas Dwyer wiggled his fingers in the air with as much enthusiasm as when he'd wrangled the grass snake. "Japan!"

A burst of laughter from the children. "It don't sound like a Japanese name, silly!"

Thomas slid down in his chair, face reddening.

"Quiet, class. Any guesses are welcome, and, Thomas, I'm glad you are so aware of different parts of the world." Sam smiled down at him, and Thomas sat straighter. "But actually, my family hails from Norway. My father came over from the old country as a young man and met my mother in a community of Norwegian immigrants here in America."

Robbie waved his hand. "Part of my ma's family came from Norway too!"

"So they did." Sam nodded at him. "It's good to know about our family's heritage, and I'd like to hear more about all of yours at some point. Perhaps that's an idea for an essay. But I was born here in America, though my father taught me to speak and read Norwegian."

Klaus Hoffman raised his hand. "Do you have brothers and sisters?"

"No, I don't. I've often wished I did. But I've always liked working with other people, so that's one reason I decided to become a teacher. That and it's a job I can do with only one arm." He gestured with his shoulder leading to the empty sleeve. He'd decided he might as well address it outright.

Thomas Dwyer waved wildly again. "Did you lose your arm in the war?"

He might have known all focus would now go here. "I did, yes. I was an officer with the First Cavalry of Ohio."

"Does that mean you rode horses into battle?"

"Did your arm get blown off?"

"Did it hurt a lot?"

"Did you kill anybody in the war?"

That last question brought him up short. Sam raised his hand. "That's enough, children." He felt a bit dizzy, though he'd asked for this. "My arm was injured by a minié ball, so the doctors had to amputate it. I appreciate your questions, but we do have lessons to accomplish. So perhaps we should move on for now."

The buzz lowered, but Sam spied Abe leaning over to whisper something to his brother. Jed guffawed, slapping his desk and nearly falling out of his chair.

Sam raised his voice. "Gentlemen, is there something you'd like to share with the class?"

Jed sobered, but Abe slouched back in his seat and met Sam's gaze, challenge in his eyes. "Nope."

Sam's jaw tightened. "That will be 'No, sir,' please."

A slow grin spread over the boy's broad face. "Think ye're still in the army, do ya?"

"No, I think I am in a schoolroom where we treat each other with respect." Sam met the boy's gaze head on, though the fine hairs rose on the back of his neck.

Abe's eyes finally flicked away. "Yes, *sir*, Mr. Guh-buh-rude." He drew the name out as if it were an insult.

Sam inhaled through his nose. "Thank you. And I must warn you, Abe and Jed." Might as well use the names they identified with for now. "If you continue to cause disruption in my classroom, I will move you to separate seats on opposite sides. And take whatever other disciplinary action might be necessary."

Abe mumbled something to his brother, making Jed choke with laughter again.

"What was that?" Sam's words cut sharp.

Abe raised his head and glared at Sam. "I *said* bet I could clobber a one-armed man with both hands tied behind my back."

A collective gasp swept across the classroom. Sam's ears tingled.

"Indeed." He stepped out from behind the desk and shrugged out of his coat. "Might I offer you a challenge, then?"

Abe laughed, then stopped. "You wanna fight me? Right here? Now?"

"Not fight. I've seen more than enough of that in my time, and it's nowhere near as glorious as you may think." He cast a glance over the schoolroom. The rest of the children sat hushed, eyes fixed on him. "But I would challenge you to an arm-wrestling match."

Both Omstead brothers exploded with mirth, Jed nearly falling off his seat again.

"Y-you don't want to do that, Teacher." Abe wiped his eyes.

Jed pointed a shaking finger at his brother. "I p-promise you don't. He can even beat our pa."

"Perhaps so. Nevertheless, my challenge stands." Sam stood at the front of the schoolroom, feet planted, holding Abe's gaze. *Lord, I sure hope this idea is from you, because if not . . .*

Abe's face hardened, the laughter falling away. "Fine." He lunged to his feet and stomped down the aisle to stand before Sam. The primer class in the front row shrank back. "But if'n I win, I ain't comin' back to this stupid school no more."

"Fine." Sam still met the young man's fiery eyes. "And if I win, you will show respect to me and every person in this room each time you walk through that door."

Abe grumbled something under his breath and glanced around. "So where are we doin' this?"

His palm dampening, Sam grabbed the stool from the corner and set it on the other side of his desk. He plunked into his teacher's chair and placed his elbow on the desk, hand extended up in the air. "Ready when you are."

With a growl and a glance back at his brother, Abe plopped himself on the stool. He grasped Sam's hand with a strength that rocked him at first, nearly forcing his arm to the desk straight off. But Sam pressed his feet to the floor and pushed back, unable to steady himself with his other hand as Abe did, yet keeping his gaze locked with the young man's. His muscles bulged beneath his shirtsleeve. His shoulders, back, and legs all strained to keep from being pushed down. Together, they wrestled, eyes and arms locked, breathing heavily.

Lord, help me see this boy as you see him. Sam kept his eyes on Abe's, seeing there the bravado, the rebellion. Yet there—a flash of fear?

Fraction by fraction, Sam pushed, edging his arm up. Now they were evenly matched at the top—now Sam gained the advantage, pushing Abe's arm down. Abe shoved back. Sam almost went down but rallied and forced his way back. Inch by inch, up, up, up—they struggled at the top—then the fight died in Abe's eyes, and Sam pressed the young man's burly arm flat onto his desk.

Cheers erupted, students leaping from their seats. Sam leaned on his desk, panting, muscles jelly.

Abe slumped on the stool, breathing hard. His broad hands rested on his knees, quivering.

Sam pushed himself to stand, though his arm nearly gave way. "Good match." He extended his hand.

Abe hesitated, gave it a quick shake, then stumbled back to his seat. His brother shoved him, nearly sending the older boy reeling.

"That will be quite enough. From you, Jed. And from all of you." Sam scanned the openmouthed class and drew several more still-shaky breaths. He'd fought in many a battle in his time, but this had been one for the books. Hopefully, victory would not carry casualties this time.

"How did you do that?" Thomas Dwyer's jaw seemed ready to drop from his skull.

"Just because I have only one arm doesn't mean it's a useless one." Sam rotated his shoulder, wincing at a pulled muscle. He'd feel that tomorrow. He shrugged back into his coat. "In fact, since my injury, I've paid special care to keep myself physically fit. I regularly lift weights and do calisthenics. And I've always loved baseball, we played it often during the war when we had time to unwind. Did you know you can play baseball with only one arm?"

Heads shook.

Sam cracked a grin. "Neither did I—till I tried. I've even learned to pull myself up on a bar with one arm. We can't let life's difficulties stop us from living. Or from fulfilling our responsibilities." He drew another breath, steadier now, and smiled out over the classroom. "On that note, why don't we begin arithmetic?"

The children groaned. Chuckling, Sam palmed a piece of chalk, never mind that his fingers still trembled, and turned toward the blackboard, sneaking a glance at the back row on the way.

Abe leaned over his desk, hands folded on top, head down. But beside him, Jed appeared actually to be listening.

One step at a time. Sam began writing out multiplication tables on the board.

At the end of the day, the classroom empty, Sam again sank into his chair. This time, however, his exhale came more from gratitude than exhaustion. *Thank you, Father.* Not that all would be smooth sailing from here—three years of the battlefield hadn't made him that naïve—but a new atmosphere of ease and calm had entered the classroom. As for the Omstead brothers, he'd barely heard a peep out of them the rest of the day.

He thought of that flash of vulnerability he'd seen on Abe's face just before he capitulated in their match. What was the story behind that young man's bravado? *Lord, let me have the chance this year to find out.* He winced at another twinge in his shoulder. The pain would be well worth it, though, if today was any indication.

"Mr. Gubberud?"

Sam looked up to see Robbie padding down the aisle, dinner pail in hand, a pinch on his forehead.

"What's wrong, Robbie?"

"I don't see my ma or pa here to pick me up." Robbie rubbed one foot atop the other. "They always come. Or one of my tantes does."

Sam stood. "How about if I take you by your father's office?" It wasn't like this family to forget one of their own. What could have happened?

"Okay." Robbie's face brightened, and he slid his hand into Sam's.

They walked side by side down Main Street, Robbie quieter than Sam had seen him yet. But before they reached the doctor's office, the little boy's head popped up.

"Tante Lilac!" Robbie pulled his hand away and ran along the wooden sidewalk, dinner pail swinging, to throw his arms around his aunt.

"Robbie." Lilac pressed her nephew close. "I'm so sorry. Onkel Jonah got hurt falling off the mower, and we forgot what time it was."

"Is he gonna be all right?" Robbie craned his head back to look at her.

"It's going to take a while, but your pa thinks so. It just may be some time before we know whether there'll be lingering effects on his leg." She looked up at Sam, blinking hard. "Thank you so much for bringing Robbie."

"Of course." Sam's chest tightened at the tears in her dark eyes. "What else can I do?"

"Pray, for now. We'll all be at the Brownsvilles' tonight so we can take turns with Jonah."

"Perhaps I could take a shift tomorrow, give you all some rest. Let me know."

"You're so kind. Thank you." Her trembly smile made him clench his hand to keep from reaching out to comfort her.

He was falling head over heels for this young woman, so help him. *Lord, carry her family through this.*

18

"He is healing."

Lilac blinked back tears as Adam straightened from beside Jonah's bed in the hospital room. Their brother lay on his stomach, as he had for the last week. Other farmers had finished the haying, using Mr. Jorgensen's mower.

Beside her, Lark blew out a breath. "Thanks be to God."

"Amen to that." Adam covered Jonah's back. "We should be past the main danger for infection in the lacerations. But he certainly won't be able to help with harvest."

"Maybe I can." Jonah pushed himself up from the pillows. "If you help me onto the mower seat." He flinched and grabbed at his bandaged side.

"Careful." Lilac reached to ease her brother back onto his stomach.

"I don't think so." Lark shook her head. "Adam, do you think he would recover better back home in Ohio?"

"Maybe." Adam hesitated, snapping his bag closed. "But he can't manage the train trip yet, and it'll be spring before he should be doing farmwork again."

"Spring?" Jonah flopped his head back on the pillow with a groan.

"You barely escaped with your life, young man. Count your blessings." Adam looked to Lark and Lilac. "You might send a telegram to Anders to see if they'd be able to nurse him. He might be able to travel in another two or three weeks. Depends on his leg mostly."

"Maybe I can send that drawing with you I've been enlarging for their home." Lilac patted her brother's shoulder. "If I can get it finished."

"Fine." Jonah closed his eyes. "Guess that's about all I'm good for right now."

Adam lifted a brow and tipped his head, so Lark and Lilac followed him back out into his office.

"You're sure danger of infection has passed?" Lark asked.

"Fairly. Still needs to be kept clean and the dressings changed regularly, of course. And his leg kept still, but those plastered bandages help with that."

"We can move him to the soddy and manage another couple of weeks. You really think he'll be fit to travel by then?"

"Time will tell. But you'll have your hands full with the wheat harvest. You don't need a patient on top of it. I know you've already lost income you were counting on from finishing mowing for others."

"We do what we have to. Family comes first." Lark opened the front door. "We'd better telegraph Anders and head home, then. Got to plan out harvest in light of this. Thanks, Adam. Give Forsythia our love."

Back at the soddy, Lilac let the stock out to pasture—they'd done chores early this morning before heading to town to see Jonah—and spent an hour in the garden. She came back into the soddy to find Lark slicing carrots.

"I did quite a bit of organizing with the seeds we've harvested so far, so thought I'd start a stew simmering for supper with the last rabbit you trapped. Can you get some potatoes and onions from the garden?"

"Of course." Lilac grabbed a basket.

"Then I'd like to check over the mower, make sure all the parts are working properly since it hasn't been used since the accident. Our wheat is more than ready now. Give me a hand with it in the shed this afternoon?"

Lilac nibbled her lip. "Actually, I was supposed to go back and help Sam at the school this afternoon. He asked me to lead a drawing lesson. But if you need me—"

"No, it's fine. Go ahead." Lark's knife thunked hard through a carrot.

Lilac twisted the basket's handle between her fingers. "Lark, are you all right?"

"I'm fine." Lark slid the carrots into the pot.

"Are you sure? Ever since Jonah got hurt, you seem . . . I don't know." Closed off? Burdened? She didn't know how to put it.

"Just trying to get done what needs to be done. Please get the vegetables. I'll work in the flower garden this afternoon instead. You can help when you get back."

Lilac's chest tightened, but she ducked out the door to the garden. *Lord, I don't know how to help my sister. Should I cancel my time at the school this afternoon? But I don't know how I'd get word to Sam.* She should have stopped by while they were in town this morning. She'd just have to make it back as soon as she could. Jonah was the expert on the mower, him and Lark, but Lilac would have to learn.

Harvest had to be brought in, one way or another. And their first year here, they had managed with only cradles and scythes, so certainly they would manage this year. Somehow. She sighed. Just when one worry got solved, life always seemed to crop up another.

She fetched the potatoes and onions, then chopped them into the stew with only the necessary words between her and her sister. With the stew simmering, she tucked a sandwich in her pocket and headed out the door toward town.

"Want to take Prince and the trap?" Lark asked from the machine shed, already bending over the mower.

"Did you even eat?"

"I had a bite."

Lilac shook her head but only said, "I'll walk."

The prairie wind sifted her mind clean, blowing crisp and scented with drying grass and September leaves. Lilac drew deep breaths of it, craning her neck to look at a V of geese migrating overhead. Tomorrow they'd be back to the clank and clatter of the mower. *Already the season of harvest again, Lord. How do the months fly by so fast?*

The brisk walk to town had warmed her limbs by the time she reached the school.

She found the students clustered in the schoolyard around Sam, though it was past the noon hour. Lilac squinted up at the sun. Nor recess, best she could tell of the time. So what? She hurried closer to see.

"All right, children." At the front of the group, Sam held up a small ball in his hand. "We've been learning lately about the laws of nature that govern much of how God's creation works. Who can tell me who discovered many of these laws?"

Hands shot up. Sam nodded to Elsie Weber.

"Sir Isaac Newton." The girl spoke clear and confident, her pinafored shoulders erect. Lilac smiled. Elsie would be a young woman before they knew it, and a fine one too.

He beamed. "Correct. Now, are we all ready to see some of these laws in action?"

The children clapped.

"Splendid." Sam scanned the group. "Abe, come up here."

The burly young man shuffled forward.

"Go stand near the edge of the schoolyard."

Abe hesitated a moment, then obeyed.

Sam held up the ball. "What is one of the first laws we learned? An object in motion will . . ."

"Continue in motion!" the children chorused.

"In a straight line until . . ."

"It is acted upon by—"

"Another force!"

"Excellent." Sam wound up as if playing baseball, then pitched the ball across the schoolyard. Abe caught it with a solid thwack.

"Thank you, Abe. Who can tell me what happened there, students?"

"Abe was the force that stopped the ball," hollered Thomas Dwyer.

Sam grinned. "He was indeed. Throw it back now, please, Abe." Sam caught the ball in an easy motion. "This time, Abe, please do not catch the ball. Let's see how far it goes in a straight line." Aiming toward a space between buildings out toward the open prairie behind the town, Sam hurled the ball again. It soared out in a smooth arc, then sailed to the ground.

"I'll get it!" Robbie dashed away, legs pumping.

"Thank you, Robbie." Sam accepted the ball back a moment later. "No one caught the ball, yet it still stopped and did not continue indefinitely in a straight line. Who can tell me why?"

"Gravity!" hollered several voices.

"Yes, gravity was the force that affected the ball. Well done. Abe, you may come back now."

The young man hurried to join the group, his steps a bit brisker this time.

Sam cleared his throat. "You all might remember another interaction Abe and I had just after school started when we competed at arm wrestling."

Abe ducked his head and flushed while a rustle of giggles and murmurs ran through the group. Lilac raised her brows. She'd definitely have to ask Sam about that later.

Sam held up his hand. "All else aside, can anyone think of one of Newton's laws that could be applied to an arm-wrestling match?"

"Force equals mass times acceleration!" a heavyset older boy shouted out.

Sam smiled at him. "Very good, Jed. You have been listening. Now, one more." Sam turned and sprang up the schoolhouse steps in one fluid motion. The children migrated after him like a flock of goslings to cluster around the school. Sam bounced the ball on the steps, catching its rebound in his hand each time. "Which of Newton's laws am I demonstrating here? John?"

John Jacob Kinsley scratched his ear. "For every action . . . there is an equal and . . . opposite reaction."

Lilac smiled. To think that boy had barely spoken at all the first year Del had him in class. Another of God's healing miracles.

"Excellent." Sam beamed at him. "I am throwing the ball down, but the steps are bouncing it back up in the opposite direction." He caught the ball once more and closed his hand around it. "I do believe you have all grasped the basic foundations of physics." Scanning the schoolyard, he caught Lilac's eye. His eyes lit as if the sun had peeked out from behind the clouds.

Lilac smiled back, the meeting of his gaze bringing a pleasant warmth to her middle.

"That will do for physics today. And now, children, it's time to head back inside. We have a special treat this afternoon: Miss Nielsen is here to lead us in an art lesson."

The children turned to look Lilac's way, faces bright. Robbie waved.

Lilac followed them inside, giving Robbie a squeeze on her way in.

"Thank you so much for coming. What do you need from me?" Sam asked as Lilac approached the front of the schoolroom.

"Just the paper and pencils, if you still have them."

"I do indeed." Sam produced the stash she'd given from his desk and set it in front of her, his arm brushing hers.

"Thank you." Feeling slightly off balance, Lilac drew a breath. "I want to start with still lifes today. Is it all right if we borrow some objects from your desk, as well as the bookshelves and such?"

He nodded. "You're welcome to anything you'd like."

"Thank you." Lilac scanned the classroom and smiled. "Good afternoon, children. It's wonderful to see so many of you again, and some new faces as well. I think I enjoyed that outdoor physics lesson as much as you did! If you will each come up to the desk, I will pass out pencils and paper. We are going to learn to draw anything you like today, using simple shapes."

The afternoon passed smoothly as Lilac fell back into the easy rhythm of how she used to help when Del was teaching, encouraging an intimidated little artist here, showing an enthusiastic one how to shade with pencil there. The smiles at the end when they all held up their drawings put a grin on her face, too, as Sam promised the children they would tack the drawings up on the schoolroom walls as decorations for the upcoming Thanksgiving program.

"Thank you again for coming today." After he dismissed the class, Sam stepped up beside her while she collected pencils from departing children at the door, the students spilling out into the autumn sunshine. "I've rarely seen them so engrossed. And if I, for one, had realized before that I could draw a cup of pencils from a basic cylinder, I might have been an artistic prodigy long ago." He produced a sketch from behind his back.

Lilac laughed. His cup of pencils looked suspiciously like an odd-shaped porcupine, but she applauded his effort. "Well, Samuel *Jakob* Gubberud, it seems you have been paying attention after all." His grin said her imitation of Schoolmaster Muller wasn't lost on him. "But I don't know what you mean—they were quite riveted by your physics demonstration this afternoon. What a splendid idea to take it outside."

"I suppose I'm finding my rhythm a bit more." Sam fingered

his pencil, then took the rest from Lilac to put away. "Does seem that the more practical and interactive I can make the lessons, the more we all enjoy them. And the better they learn."

"From what I saw, you're turning into a splendid teacher." Lilac met his gaze. "And it sounds like there's quite a story behind that arm-wrestling illustration."

"Thank you." He gave her a brief smile. "It's been an uphill climb at times, and for a bit, I truly thought perhaps my mor had been right. But that's another story." He hesitated, then nodded to the door. "May I walk you out?"

A little flutter jumped from her middle into her chest. "If you like."

Sam strolled beside her to the edge of the schoolyard, then stopped, leaning his hand on the gate. "I'd better stay. A few children are still here." He glanced at the yard, then back at Lilac. "I'll see you again soon?" Question bloomed in his eyes.

Lilac smiled. "Soon."

She hurried up the street toward the edge of town. Perhaps she could still get home in time to help Lark prepare for harvesting tomorrow before sundown. Guilt nipped at her insides for leaving her sister today . . . yet it was hard to regret the afternoon in the schoolroom with the children's eager faces. And the way Sam's hazel eyes lit up when he saw her.

Lilac hugged her arms around herself. Too soon to think too much of that . . . to consider what it might mean that her heart lifted and beat faster when Sam was near. That the reserve he'd worn around her when he first arrived now seemed discarded like a winter coat in springtime. That the way he smiled at her made her want to spin around and dance.

Too soon, after all that had happened with her and Ethan last year. She must be sure this time, very sure. And yet . . .

"Help! They'll kill each other!"

Lilac jerked her head up, scanning her surroundings for the source of the cry. She was near the train station now, on the outskirts of town near the smithy. And there, running from the blacksmith's shop, came Charlotte Hoffman, panting, clutching her skirts in her hands.

"Lilac," she gasped, reaching out. "Get help, please. George and Caleb—they're fighting in the forge."

"What happened?" Lilac grasped the woman's arms, steadying her.

"I don't know. One moment they were shoeing RJ's horses, the next I heard shouting, and they'd come to blows. Caleb knocked George down. I'm afraid . . ." She covered her mouth with a sob. "I'm afraid he's going to kill him."

Shouts came from the barn where the Hoffman forge stood, the raw rage singeing Lilac's scalp, though she couldn't discern the words. "You said RJ? Where is he?"

Charlotte pointed a shaking finger toward town, then turned to run back toward the barn.

Lilac took off sprinting, her skirt slapping against her legs. *Father, please, help the Hoffman family. Help me find RJ, show us what to do—* Where could her brother-in-law be? Surely he wouldn't have gone far, if he left his team to be shod.

The station. Del had said something about RJ picking up some supplies from the train today for finishing Adam's new office.

Lilac pivoted toward the station. She could see the platform from here and RJ's familiar lanky form in the distance. *Thank you, Lord.* "RJ!" she hollered.

He shaded his eyes, then started running toward her.

Lilac waved wildly. When he drew near, she panted out, "Trouble at the Hoffmans'."

His eyes widened, and he took off.

A scream spun Lilac around. Ahead of them, George and Caleb exploded out of the barn, fists swinging. Charlotte tried to push herself between them, and an errant blow knocked her to the ground.

Lilac caught her breath and dashed forward.

"Now see what you've done, you ungrateful—" George Hoffman swore and grabbed his son's collar with both hands.

Lilac bent to help Charlotte. Dazed, the woman sat up against her, an abrasion reddening the side of her face.

The blacksmith growled, beefy fists tightening as he lifted Caleb half off the ground by the shoulders. "Time I taught you a lesson you'll never forget."

Caleb wrenched free, then landed a punch straight in his father's face.

"Caleb!" RJ held up his hands. "George. Both of you, stop."

George let go and lurched back, a hand to his jaw. But Caleb kept coming, pummeling the blacksmith's shoulders and chest. George staggered, backing up toward the building.

"Never could—do anything—to please you." The boy gasped, sobbing. "Why should I—try—anymore?"

Stumbling against the barn, George stared up at Caleb, panting, his face purpling. "Once a rebel, always a rebel, eh?"

With a roar, Caleb picked up a rusty iron bar that lay by the side of the barn.

Lilac froze. Charlotte Hoffman reached out with a cry.

With a sob, Caleb raised the iron bar high.

"Caleb!" RJ ran out in front of him. "Stop. You don't want to do this."

"Yes, I do." The words choked out. Caleb lifted the bar again.

"Caleb, no. Caleb!"

The young man swung the rusty iron but was then sprawled flat, knocked out cold by a blow from RJ's fist to his temple.

Shakily, George pushed himself to his feet, rubbing his jaw, and regarded his unconscious son. "It's like I told you, Lottie. Ain't no use tryin' with him."

Lilac cradled the sobbing mother and met RJ's pained gaze.

They got the unconscious young man to Adam's office, where cold water and a whiff of ammonia soon brought Caleb to. He sat quietly on the examining table, holding a cold cloth to his purpling eye.

Adam tended his wounds, then stepped out to speak to Charlotte in the waiting area. RJ and Lilac stayed with Caleb.

"I'm leavin'," he said low, to no one in particular.

"Leaving for where?" RJ kept his tone even.

"Anywhere." Caleb drew a breath rough with hurt. "Anywhere he ain't."

"Listen." RJ drew a breath and touched his eye patch. "War leaves its scars on the best of us, never mind a family who fought on both sides. But surely you—"

Caleb laughed mirthlessly, shaking his bandaged head. "I didn't fight. I joined up too late—thanks to him. And he won't never let me forget it." He drew another breath.

"Well, if you're leaving, you need someplace to go." RJ tapped his hand on the boy's knee. "Why not come out to the Nielsen farm for a time? They need help with harvest with Jonah laid up, and you need a place to be. Works for everyone."

Caleb hesitated, then shook his head again. "I don't want him knowin' I'm anywhere around."

"He wouldn't have to. Not for a while." RJ shot a glance at Lilac, asking her.

She hesitated, then nodded. "Of course. For a time. But, Caleb . . . surely if you just talk to him. He's your father."

The young man kept his gaze on the floor. "No, he ain't. Never was."

19

Matilda, I can't stay." Isaac sat across from his cousin's widow at the farmhouse table, the kerosene lamp a flickering circle of light between them against the evening shadows. The children already slumbered in their room down the hall.

Matilda's eyes welled, and she lifted a trembling hand to brush the tears. "I know I had no right to expect it. . . . I'm sorry."

"You had every right to ask." He reached to cover her other hand, her fingers still so thin and cold his gut squeezed with guilt again, but he pressed on. "And for a time I thought might be I could, or at least should. But after a powerful lot of thinkin' and prayin', I don't believe that'd be best. For any of us."

"Why?" She lifted her gaze, eyes dark pools of sorrow.

"You need a new start." He spoke gently, though he saw her flinch and knew his words pricked. "Here on the farm, this place you and Ambrose built together—every board and blade of grass reminds you of him. Keeps you from bein' able to move on."

"I don't want to move on," she choked.

"I know. But is that truly best for Earl and Julia?"

She withdrew her hand and twined her fingers together, staring at them in the lamplit shadows.

"With your permission, I'd like to write to your folks—back in Kentucky, ain't that so? Now, there's a green and pleasant place. Or if you'd rather, you can write yourself. From what you've said, they'd like nothin' better than to welcome you and your young'uns in. Give you a place to rest and heal until you're ready for whatever the Lord has for you next."

"And you?" Matilda's words whispered.

Isaac swallowed. "I'll own I'm feelin' in need of a new start myself . . . but I've a mighty strong sense that tryin' to fill Ambrose's place, save his farm, isn't the life I'm meant for. I'll stay by your side till you and your children are well settled and provided for, I give you my word on that. But then I need to go back to Salton."

"What if we came with you?"

He shifted his jaw. "If that's what you want to do, I'll make you welcome. But do you truly want to start all over without Ambrose? In a place where you don't know a soul, save me? It's a harsher land than this, I'll make no bones about it."

She sighed and shook her head. "I suppose not." Then she cocked her head, a sudden spark in her eyes. "If it's such a harsh place, what do you want to go back for? Or should I say . . . who?"

"I . . ." Isaac rubbed the back of his neck, suddenly warm under his hair. "I'll confess there is, a, well, a certain lady friend. . . ." Confound it, his face must be redder than a turkey's wattle. He felt a surge of gratitude for the room's darkness.

Matilda's soft laughter warmed the air, making Isaac stop and stare. "Cousin Isaac, I never did see you so flummoxed before. Well, that's all you need to say. I understand." She reached across the table and gripped his hand. "I've some notion what a sacrifice it's been for you, staying with us for weeks. And I'll never forget it." Her voice caught. "I hope she knows what a treasure she has in you, this lady friend of yours."

A treasure? Isaac shook his head. He surely didn't think so. But he had to swallow hard before he could answer. "I thank you, ma'am."

"I'll write to my parents." Her voice steadier now, Matilda pushed back her chair and rose. "Good night, Cousin Isaac."

Isaac turned down the lamp and sat in the darkness long after Matilda went up to bed, leaning his head on his hands.

Been a long time since he'd spoken so open-like with anyone, let alone a woman. Could he find that same courage with Lark?

"I don't want you ta go, Cousin Isaac."

Isaac ruffled his nephew's hair as they stood on the front porch of the boy's grandparents' Kentucky home. "Now, don't be frettin' yourself, young Earl. You'll have a fine new life here with your papaw and mamaw, just you wait and see."

"But not with you." Earl looked up, tightening his arms around Isaac's waist.

Eyes burning, Isaac hugged the boy's head against his side. *Lord in heaven, am I doing the right thing?*

But he'd been over all that. Two weeks ago now, he'd finished selling off Matilda's land and stock—with her full blessing—and loaded up his cousin's wife, young Earl, and little Julia on that dilapidated wagon. They'd creaked their way to the nearest train line, then chugged all the way back to Kentucky. He'd stayed a week to see them well settled with Matilda's folks, but now it was time.

Time for him to go home. To Salton. And Larkspur?

He was ready to find out.

"Come now, son. Let Cousin Isaac go." Matilda stepped out from the doorway and held out her arm to her son. Julia poked her head out from inside, wearing a clean pinafore and with a cookie in hand. The little girl had blossomed into a tiny chatterbox this last week under her grandmother's doting care.

Earl gazed from his mother back to Isaac, then his mouth drooped. Dropping his arms from Isaac's sides, he stepped to his mother.

"Go with God, Isaac." Matilda met his eyes, face still pale but steady now above her high-necked black frock. "And thank you for everything."

Isaac swallowed and nodded.

"I want you to take Winter." She wrapped her arm around Earl's shoulders.

"Beg pardon?" Isaac cocked his head.

"Winter, our mare. Her saddle too. We don't need three horses now, not when my parents have their own team. You don't have a horse of your own, and I've seen how she's taken to you, and you to her."

"I—I couldn't."

"It's the least we can do, Isaac. Please."

He blinked back a powerful stinging in his eyes. "Then I thank you."

"If you hadn't come and found us when you did . . ." She drew a trembling breath. "I don't know if we would have survived. So Godspeed." A faint smile tipped the corners of her mouth. "And I hope your Larkspur has the good sense you credit her with."

Unable to think of more to say, Isaac held out his hand, and she gripped it. Then with a brief kiss for each of the children, he hurried off the porch toward the barn.

Early morning sunlight splayed across the small farm, warming the damp chill from the air. Sparrows fluttered and chirped from the spreading trees sheltering the yard, so different from the treeless expanses of Nebraska. Isaac opened the barn door and felt his way through the dimness to the stall he sought.

"Hey there, girl." He held out his hand, and Winter snuffled it, eager for the carrot stubs he usually brought her. Isaac chuckled, and he rubbed her gray nose. "Appears you're goin' to be comin' along with me." His throat tightened, closing off further words. *My own horse, Lord. Never would have thought it. But thank you.*

He'd have to pay for space in a cattle car now, but she was well worth the extra cost. If they'd let him ride along with the mare, he could at least save the price of a passenger ticket.

He brushed, saddled, and bridled Winter, then saw to it that she'd drunk from the trough. Finally, he swung up on her dappled back and headed out of the barnyard, sending one glance back at the comfortable farmhouse, smoke wafting from the chimney, autumn-cloaked trees spreading sheltering arms overhead. Matilda and the children had already gone back inside, as well they should. They were safe here, loved. Cared for. Would have a chance to heal and grow, and someday walk into a brighter future, please God.

Isaac turned Winter's head toward the lane lined with trees turning copper, russet, and gold. Now for parts north and west.

And whatever awaited him there.

He arrived back in Salton on the late afternoon train a few days later and led Winter out of the cattle car while the hiss and screech of the brakes still filled their ears. The mare tossed her head and snorted.

"I know, girl, you didn't like that clacketing locomotive any more than I did. But here we are, back in wide open spaces again." He stepped away from the platform, leaving the choking clouds of smoke and soot behind to fill his lungs with pure prairie air.

"We're home, Winter, my girl." A grin crept its way up from his chest to stretch beneath his beard. "Home. Been a long while since I knew that word friendly-like. But maybe that time is comin.'"

His heart tugged to head toward the Nielsen homestead right off, but reason and the smoke-stink of his clothes turned him toward the boardinghouse instead.

He stabled and fed Winter, popped into the workshop for a hearty welcome from William Thacker, then climbed the back steps of the Nielsen House. The familiar warmth embraced him, thawing the stiffness from his face and hands, filling his lungs with the scent of baking bread and venison stew. He found Jesse Brownsville laying plates in the dining room. The young man's eyes lit when he saw Isaac.

"We've b-been wondering when you'd t-turn up again. Everything okay with your family?"

"They'll be all right, now. Good to see you, my friend. Your wife in the kitchen?"

"No, up-s-stairs, havin' a lie-down."

Isaac frowned. Right before the supper hour? Climie? "Is she ill?"

"N-not exactly." Jesse's grin shone brighter than the just-lit lamps. "But looks l-like we're gonna have us a little one, come spring."

Isaac gripped the young man's shoulder, grinning too. "Now, that's the best news I've heard in a coon's age."

Jesse nodded. "Me too. Since Climie agreed to m-marry me, anyhow." He shrugged toward the table. "Mrs. Hoffman and Mrs. Wells will have s-supper on soon, if you want to take up your things and wash. Your usual cot is free, I think. Guess you w-won't have heard about what happened with the Hoffmans yet, either, or— "

"Afraid I'm behind on all the news." Isaac glanced at the stairs. "I'll head up to wash but don't wait on supper for me tonight."

"You s-sure?"

Though his belly growled empty, his insides were wound too tight for vittles. "I got somethin' I aim to do first." Isaac slung his pack on his shoulder and headed up the steps two at a time.

If he timed it right, he might make it just in time to help Larkspur with her evening chores.

He rode up to the Nielsen homestead as the sun slipped away in a quiet glory of gray clouds edged with fire. He swung off Winter just when Lilac stepped out of the barn, carrying milk pails.

"Isaac." She stared at him. "You got a horse."

His mouth quirked. Leave it to Lilac to focus on the mare first. "I did. Her name is Winter."

"She's lovely." Lilac stepped near to stroke the dappled gray neck. "Did you bring your family back to Salton?"

"I did not. They're home with her kin in Kentucky." Isaac scanned the homestead. "Where's your sister?"

"Which one?" But Lilac smiled at him, a knowing in her eyes. "She's in the machine shed." Her face sobered. "It's been a rough few weeks, Isaac. Tread gently with her."

His gut tightened. "What happened?"

"There was an accident with the mower during haying. Jonah was hurt bad. He'll be all right, but we had to send him back home to Ohio, put him on the train last week. Caleb Hoffman came out to help us with harvest, which is a secret and whole story in itself, but Lark—she hasn't been sleeping much. She seems to eat and breathe work right now."

"When doesn't she?" But Isaac's chest ached as he thought of the burden on Larkspur's shoulders. All while he'd been gone. "I can help now. I'm here."

"If she'll let you." Lilac tipped her head. "I'd best get the milk in."

He tied Winter to the pasture fence rail and settled his army cap. Then, squaring his shoulders, he headed for the machine shed.

Curious how facing a woman could beat staring down a whole line of Confederate artillery when it came to weakening a man's knees.

Isaac smoothed back his beard and breathed a prayer. She

must be powerful intent on her work to have not even heard him and Lilac talking. Of course, the pounding and tapping he'd heard from the shed might have somethin' to do with it.

Enough of your lollygaggin'. He could hear his mother's voice. He cleared his throat, then peeked around the open edge of the three-sided shed.

By lanternlight, Lark bent over the mowing machine, tinkering with a part on the sickle bar. Her hair caught the light with a mahogany gleam, tied back with her typical leather string and falling in a loose, dark rope over her shoulder. She held the hammer with quick, light taps, arms precise and steady as ever she was. The hem of her woolen skirt brushed the dirt floor.

Every strong, feminine line of her caught him in the chest and made swallowing near to impossible.

His knees suddenly weakened, and he reached for the side of the shed to steady himself. Lord above, what exactly was he going to say? And should he have had a ring?

Lark bent closer to set the blade back in place on the sickle bar with quick, gentle taps of her hammer. Just one more day of wheat harvest tomorrow, since they'd had to take breaks some days to shock the wheat, not to mention spend time in the flower garden to save precious seeds before they were lost.

Thank you, Lord. I wasn't sure how we'd make it through this year, after Jonah's accident, but you helped us. Like you always do.

Now they only had the threshing, and the corn harvest, and gathering from the rest of the late-seeding flowers, and getting in the rest of the vegetables from the garden before a hard freeze, and finishing the designs for the seed catalogs, and . . . there went her shoulders scrunching tight up toward her ears again. Lark forced them down and breathed a prayer, bending over the machine. Just one more blade to set back in place. *I trust you, Lord. I trust you, I trust you. . . .*

"Miss Larkspur?"

She jolted upright, sending her hammer clattering against the bar, then to the floor. "Land sakes." Straightening, she stared at the travel-worn man standing before her. "Isaac McTavish, don't you know better than to startle someone working on machinery?"

He had the grace to flinch and pull off his army cap. "I did make a noise."

"Well, I didn't hear you." She blew out a breath, her heart still pounding—both from the scare and from his nearness. So many weeks without a word, and now there he stood, real and alive, his breath forming puffs of steam in the frosty evening air. She folded her arms against the urge to reach out for him. "Don't you know these mowers can cut off someone's limb?"

He rubbed the back of his neck. "I'm truly sorry, ma'am. Lilac told me about Jonah. Is he doin' all right?"

She sighed and lowered her arms. "He will be. He's back in Ohio now, should be more comfortable there—we couldn't even let him have a room to himself once we moved him to the soddy. But we don't know yet if he'll fully regain the use of his leg."

Isaac shook his head. "Must have been right terrible for you."

Silence hung a moment. Lark met Isaac's eyes for a beat, then caught her breath and glanced away from what she saw there. "When did you get back? I thought you were still in Arkansas."

"I was, then Kentucky. Ended up sellin' my cousin's farm and takin' his wife and children to her kin back there."

"No wonder you were gone so long." Lark bit her tongue. She hadn't meant the words to slip out quite like that.

Isaac shifted his feet. "I meant to write to you, but . . ."

"But what?" But she knew the answer, didn't she? Isaac meant to write, and he didn't. What did that say about, well, whatever he felt toward her? The reminder settled heavily in her chest, and Lark bent back to her work.

He cleared his throat. "Can I help you?"

"I can do it. Thank you." Silence fell but for the ring of hammer on steel.

"Miss Larkspur, please." Isaac's threadbare army boots moved closer, till they stopped just by the mower wheel. "I meant to write, I should have done. But you haven't left my mind a day I've been gone, nor yet an hour."

The hammer stilled in her hands. Lark twisted the handle, her fingers stiff and chilled in the cold. "Oh?" She couldn't find voice to say anything else. Her heart beat hot in her throat.

The straw on the floor shifted as Isaac knelt down to her level. "May I talk to you, ma'am?"

She looked up, meeting his maddening gray gaze. "I'm right here."

"I mean . . . proper like."

With a sudden burst, Lark threw down her hammer and sat herself on the mower seat. This man could try her last nerve. "What is it, Isaac?"

He stood. "I'm sorry. Maybe I should come back another time."

"Well, you can't expect people to just drop what they're doing every time you happen to come around." She crossed her arms. "Whenever under heaven that might be." She bit her tongue, fighting sudden hot tears.

"What do you mean by that?"

She sniffed hard. "Never mind. You want to say something, say it."

He shifted his feet. "I've been doin' a lot of thinkin' while I've been away."

"And?"

"And I—tarnation, Miss Larkspur, you ain't makin' this easy." He crumpled his cap in one hand, then switched it to the other.

"Making *what* easy?"

"Askin' you to marry me." The explosive words hung in the air between them like floating sparks.

Lark stared at him, her ears tingling. "What did you say?" Her whisper scratched her throat.

"I didn't mean to ask you like that, but there it is." Isaac sucked in a breath, hesitated, then stepped near enough for her to smell the travel soot on his clothes. He took her cold hands in his work-roughened ones and smoothed his thumbs over her knuckles. "That's why I couldn't stay in Arkansas. My home is here. With you. If you'll have me."

Lark stared at him a moment, caught by those heavy-browed gray eyes. Was he really asking . . . ? *Oh, Isaac . . .*

"No." She jerked her hands from his and paced away, as far as she could in the cramped shed, then turned to face him, gripping her elbows. "What are you thinking?"

Isaac stood still, silent.

"Why would you ask me that, right now? *Why?*" She wanted to pound her fists on his chest.

"Because I love you, Miss Larkspur."

The words sent a shiver down her arms. Then she clenched her jaw, shook her head hard. "No. No, no."

"Why?"

She flung her arms wide. "You say you love me. But what if—when—something bad happens and you leave again? You always just leave, Isaac. You've been gone nearly two months. I never heard a word from you, meanwhile my brother nearly died, I've been trying to manage harvest by myself, and where were you? Not here."

Isaac scrubbed a hand through his hair. "I told you I had to go tend to my kin."

She pressed her fingers to her temples. "And it's right you should. I'm sorry. But I never know when you'll leave nor when you'll pop up again." Lark strode back to the mower and shoved the sickle bar down. "I don't hold it against you, Isaac, you've no obligation to us or certainly to me. But for you to come waltzing in here and think you can just—that you can . . ."

She gripped the wheel rim of the mower, hard, but her hand still shook.

He reached out to her. "Lark—"

"Don't touch me." She stepped away from him, avoiding his gaze. Pain stabbed behind her eyes.

"Fine." He eased back, hands raised. "But can't we talk this out?"

She shook her head.

Isaac lowered his hands to his sides and stood gazing at her a moment longer. "You want me to just leave?"

Her chest heaved, then she nodded in a quick jerk.

Not till she was sure he was gone did Lark let herself crumple to the shed floor and bury her head in her shawl to stifle her sobs. She didn't want Lilac to hear.

Of course Isaac left. She'd practically sent him away.

And as likely as not, broken both their hearts.

20

"You did what?" Lilac stared at her sister.

Lark slammed her flail down on the threshing floor harder than seemed necessary, sending up flurries of chaff. "You heard me." She sneezed.

"But he actually proposed?" Lilac reached for another bundle of wheat stalks, mind awhirl. "I knew he liked you, but I never dreamed that was why he came by the other night."

"What do you mean, you knew he liked me?" Lark pulled a handkerchief from her sleeve and blew her nose.

"Well, it's fairly obvious." Lilac cocked her head at her sister. Was Lark really that oblivious? Or willfully so? "Didn't you see how he looked at you during that dance?"

"Have you been talking to Climie?" Lark set back to beating the wheat again.

"Not lately, why?"

"Nothing."

Lilac bit her lip and set back into the rhythm of threshing. "So . . . why did you?"

"Why did I what?"

"You know. Refuse Isaac."

"Why shouldn't I?"

"Lark."

Her sister sighed and straightened, wiping her nose again. "Lilac, we never know when he'll be here or not. He comes and goes fickle as the prairie wind. How could I count on a man like that?"

"You didn't say whether you love him."

Lark bent back to her threshing, mumbling something that might have been "What does that matter?"

Oh, Lark. Lilac's chest squeezed for her sister. She drew a breath to say something else, then glanced out at the October sunshine slanting lower across the yard. "Uh-oh. Sam agreed to take a look at Farfar Nielsen's journal, and I was supposed to drop it off by the school during recess. Want me to pick up anything from the mercantile?"

Lark blew her nose and shook her head. "I don't think so."

Lilac frowned. "Are you getting sick?"

"I don't have time to be sick." Lark shoved her handkerchief back into her sleeve. "And it's just the chaff. How are things between you and Sam?"

Lilac blinked, her face warming. "Meaning?"

Even with straw sticking in her hair, Lark had that big-sister look perfected. "You want to know all the details of my affairs of the heart—or lack thereof. Don't hold back yours."

Caleb Hoffman appeared in the doorway, arms full of more wheat shocks he'd been hauling in by wagon from the fields.

Ears burning, Lilac set down her flail and turned to clear a space. She waited till Caleb had left before answering her sister. "I don't know. Sam and I are friends. We've always been."

"Uh-huh. Well, Ethan was more than a friend for a while, and he never made your eyes go all starry like they do around Sam."

Lilac's heart beat hard. Did they really? She drew a steadying breath. "Well, I'd better go. You take care of yourself and don't push too hard. I'll do the chores when I get back."

She drove the trap with Nell today, the lowering sun still

warming her shoulders as they clipped along the prairie, despite the early October nip in the air. She tied the mare at the school's hitching post, then checked to be sure the journal still sat tucked safely in her coat pocket and walked toward the school, her heartbeat picking up in anticipation. Of learning more about the journal, or seeing Sam?

The schoolyard brimmed with children's laughter and shouts, boys tossing a ball, girls building tiny houses from sticks and fallen leaves.

"Tante Lilac!" Robbie ran to throw his arms around her waist.

"Hey there, Robbie boy." She hugged him tightly.

"Are you here to see Mr. Gubberud?" He craned back to give her a knowing look.

Was everyone beginning to suspect something? Lilac ignored the heat creeping up her neck. "Yes, I need to give him something."

"All right, children, that's it for afternoon recess. Back inside now." Sam clanged the bell from the top of the steps, then smiled down at her as the children tramped past him. "Hello there."

"Hello, yourself." Lilac smiled up at him and climbed the steps herself. "Or should I say, *god dag*?"

"We'll make a Norwegian speaker of you yet." He held the door for her, his eyes warm.

"I'm sorry I missed your break. I can just leave the book and go."

"No matter. Most of the older students are out right now for threshing and finishing harvest anyway, so our days are a bit more relaxed. Let me start the younger ones on their next reading, and then we can talk for a bit."

Lilac nodded and stepped inside, a happy bubble rising in her chest that she didn't have to leave right away.

Sam spoke quietly to the children, settled them to work on their readers with the older helping the younger, then came to join Lilac at two of the empty desks in the back.

"Now then, I'm eager to see this family treasure."

Lilac withdrew the worn little volume from her pocket. "I found it this summer when I went home to Ohio for the store's grand reopening."

"I remember." His eyes met hers.

Did he remember that first long talk of theirs as well as she did? Lilac fought to bring her focus back to the journal. "I'm not sure why we've never seen it before—our father must have known about it. But at any rate, we'd love to know what it says."

"May I?" Sam held out his hand, and Lilac placed the book in it, her fingers brushing the warmth of his palm.

Withdrawing her hand, she pressed it to her lap.

Sam turned the fragile pages, holding the book steady on the desk with his thumb while his other fingers maneuvered the leaves. She marveled at his dexterity with only one hand— gained by much practice, of course.

"It does look like an account of their journey on the *Restaurasjonen*. Did I tell you my grandparents came over on that ship too?"

"Really?" Lilac stared at him. "I mean, I suppose that makes sense. Did you know them well?"

"They lived long enough for me to hear some of their stories. But I've never read a firsthand account like this. I can hardly wait to delve into it." He glanced over a few more pages, then closed the journal. "May I take it back to the boardinghouse with me for a few days? Perhaps I can even begin writing out a translation, though that will take some time."

"Oh, that would be wonderful. But that's asking a great deal. Can we pay you?"

"Please don't. It would be a privilege. You mean—that is, your family means a great deal to me." His ears reddened under his neatly combed shock of wheat-colored hair.

Oh, Sam. Lilac's heart swelled toward him, and she restrained herself from reaching to touch his hand, his arm. He lifted his gaze to meet hers, and for a moment she could neither look away nor breathe.

Was this what it was, then, to truly come to love a man? To know rest in his presence, to be at ease with who you were. To think of him every day and to feel most yourself when he was nearby. To muse at night on his steady hazel eyes, the winsome humor of his grin, and dream of running her fingers through his hair—

"Mr. Gubberud?"

They both jumped, Sam slamming his knees into the desk.

"Ouch." He winced and slid out to stand. "Yes, Thomas, are you finished?"

"The primer class done finished their lesson. Ain't it 'most time for class dismissed?"

"I'll come." Sam drew a breath and picked up the journal, glancing once more at Lilac. "So I can keep this?"

"Yes. And thank you." Willing her pulse to calm, Lilac slipped out from the desk, waved at the children, and headed out the door.

"Lilac!"

Just at the bottom of the steps, she turned back to see Sam hurrying down toward her.

"I thought you had to dismiss class." She shaded her eyes to look up at him, the sunshine bright.

"I did—do. But if I don't ask you this soon—well, I don't know what's to—" He sucked a breath and ran his hand through his hair. "Before I become a stammering schoolboy altogether, I was wondering, would you like to go for a walk after church this Sunday?"

Her heart skipped. "You mean, with you?"

"Yes, with me." He stepped near and held out his hand, question in his eyes.

She laid her hand in his, and the gentle rub of his thumb over her knuckles sent shivers down her limbs.

"I'd dearly like to get to know you better, Lilac Nielsen. And perhaps . . . more, if the Lord so leads us. Might I hope that could be something you'd like as well?"

She smiled up at him, the sunshine filtering through the gold-leafed cottonwood branches above them. "You might. And, yes, I would love to go walking with you on Sunday, Sam."

"Wonderful." His grin rivaled the brightness of the leaves. "I mean, good. Excellent. Well." He released her hand and glanced back toward the schoolhouse. "I'd best go before the teacher gets reported for playing hooky. Till soon, then?"

"Soon." Lilac watched him leap up the steps and disappear into the schoolroom, then headed back up the street, autumn breeze kissing her face, hugging her arms about herself.

Lord, thank you for keeping me from marrying Ethan last spring popped unexpectedly into her head. *I would have missed . . . this.*

But what about Lark? Was she to leave her sister all alone?

He surely had made a mess of things.

Isaac pounded and clamped the last nail into a new shoe on Winter's hoof and gently lowered her foot to the ground within the blacksmith's forge. "There you are, girl." He ran his hand down her foreleg, checking for any hint of heat or swelling, then moved on to the next.

What had he been thinkin'? That Lark would throw herself into his arms, when she'd heard nary a word of him for months? No wonder she thought leavin' was what he did best. Isaac flinched at the memory of her words.

Now what lay ahead for him and Winter? He had a horse but still no home. Not as he'd hoped, not as he'd left behind the last of his known kin in search of. Not after throwing himself at Larkspur Nielsen like a fool, thereby ruining any chance he might ever have known with her. Should he ride the rails for parts west, seek work again on the railroad as the Union Pacific continued its march to join with the Central Pacific? Or spend the winter in Salton, where he'd see Larkspur at every turn?

Winter nosed the front of his army coat, where he'd resewn two more buttons last night. Tried to mend the worst of the holes again too. "Sorry there, girl." He rubbed her velvety gray muzzle. "No sugar for you today."

"If you've finished with your horse, give me a hand with these plowshares?"

Isaac turned to help George Hoffman. He hefted the heavy metal blades up to the forge to heat till the edges glowed red, then brought them to the smith at the anvil, where he held them steady with tongs and pounded the shares sharp once more. Isaac took a turn on the next, the ringing blows of the hammer bringing a certain relief.

If idle hands were the devil's workshop, as his ma always said, certainly hard labor had a way of making room for God's peace.

"You've got a steady hand, a strong arm." George crossed his burly arms, watching. "Have any interest in learning more of the trade? Could use another skilled smith to bring along, since . . . well, since I don't know when or if I'll have other help again." His bushy brows drew together.

Meaning Caleb. Isaac lowered his hammer. "Reckon I never thought on it."

"Well, think on it. Folks always need a blacksmith."

Isaac turned the tool in his hands, the words on the tip of his tongue to say no. But would that only prove what Lark had said? Keeping to his pattern of never committin' to anything, never takin' the time to put down roots enough to stick with and learn an actual job that might, heaven forbid, keep him someplace long-term?

Isaac rubbed his ear beneath his army cap. "I'd be obliged if you'd show me a bit, sir."

"Right, then." George nodded. "I've an order of coat hooks

to make, that's one of the simplest to start on when it comes to makin' things from scrap. Watch and then try is usually best."

"Yes, sir." Isaac hesitated. "Haven't heard from your boy, then?"

"No." George thrust an iron into the fire, lines deeper on his face than Isaac had ever seen.

"I'm sorry."

"So'm I." George pulled the iron out, red hot. "But seems plain that sorry won't let me fix the past, nor yet change the future." He held the glowing tip on the anvil. "Here. First you flatten out the plate." He struck with his hammer in quick, precise blows. Sparks flew.

Isaac watched as the man bored a hole, then heated the steel again and began scrolling the metal and bending it over the anvil into a hook. He weighed his thoughts, debating whether to speak. "Family ain't never easy, sir, and that's the truth. But now that mine's gone, I'd give about anythin' to go that extra mile and make things right. If I could." He hesitated, then pressed on. "At least your son is still alive. It's not too late, not yet. If you don't mind my speakin' so frank-like."

George turned the hook, examining the scroll. "I don't."

The blacksmith handed him the hammer and let Isaac try making the next hook. At first his hands fumbled, the precise strikes so different from the heavy blows for shoeing a horse or reshaping a hoe. But slowly, the rhythm of the task, how to shift the angle and adjust the force as needed, crept into his hands. His first hook broke when he tried twisting the scroll too hard, but his second looked worthy to bear the weight of a respectable coat.

"There ye are." George clapped him on the shoulder with a beefy hand. "We'll make a smithy out of you yet."

Isaac grinned, a burn of satisfaction in his aching muscles. He rubbed a sore spot near his shoulder. "Think I held the hammer a mite too tight."

"Have to hold things loose-like, for most of these jobs." George rubbed his beard. "And in life, I s'pose."

"Sounds like you might could share next in church."

George stared at him. "Caldwell did ask me. I told him no, didn't feel fit for it."

"Well, that's up to you, sir. But could be that's when we're most fit—when we're most knowin' we're not." So what did that mean for him? Isaac shook off the thought. "Now what?"

"Jorgensen's mower needs mendin', took some damage at the end of harvest. That's our next big job. It's out back, give me a hand rollin' it in?"

Together, they maneuvered the machine inside. Isaac ran his hand over the seat.

"I was right sorry to miss helpin' with harvest this year. Family obligations and all."

"Miss Larkspur sure takes the helm on fieldwork around here, least till her brother had that accident." George shook his head. "I'm sure you heard about that."

"I did." Isaac bent to examine the damaged blades, a rock sinking in his gut.

"You ever . . ." The older man trailed off.

"What's that?"

"Nothin'. My wife can talk too much at times, that's all."

"What about?"

"Oh, she and some of the womenfolk, guess they've set to wonderin' if there might be somethin' between you and Miss Larkspur." George waved his hand and climbed over the sickle bar to Isaac's side. "But you know how women talk."

Isaac rubbed the back of his neck, feeling it afire. "I, uh."

The blacksmith glanced up. "So there's an 'I, uh,' is there?" He chuckled. "No wonder you didn't stay in Arkansas."

"She . . . she won't have me." His throat closed after the words. What was he doing, spilling such to this man? He didn't do that.

It wasn't his way, not since Andersonville. He blinked against crowding memories.

"Ah. Well, no tellin' a woman's mind, now, is there? She got her cap set on someone else?"

"Not far as I know." Isaac sat back on his heels out of George's way and held the bar steady as the blacksmith hammered the blades back into place.

"What then?" The older man huffed a chuckle. "Sorry, no need to answer. Guess it's nice to hear about someone else's problems for once."

"No matter." Isaac blew out a breath. "I don't tend to speak of such things to folks, not anymore."

"You don't speak much period, son."

"Granted. Don't mean that's the best way to live, though. Accordin' to Miss Larkspur, I've got a good deal to set in order in my life 'fore I'd be ready for a family. Namely, stayin' put."

"She don't like all your comin' and goin'."

Was it that obvious to everyone but him? "'Fraid not."

"But that's good." The man straightened and clapped Isaac's shoulder.

"Good?"

"If she's upset about you leavin', that means she wants you stayin'." George leveled a look at him. "Don't tell me you still haven't got that straight."

Isaac stared back, his brain slower than late winter slush. Lark . . . didn't want him gone? She *wanted* him to stay? He clenched his fists with the sudden urge to thump his own thick head. "So what do I do?"

"What do you plan to do?"

"Well." Isaac hesitated and scratched his beard, face suddenly burning. "Till now, I'd been thinkin' I might . . . leave town."

"Well, I don't know that I'm any man to give advice, fool that I am." George tipped his head. "But if you want that woman, you're going to have to do better'n that. Show her you're serious, and you're not goin' to leave when the wind blows foul. Prove yourself to her, man. Stay."

Isaac stared at the blacksmith, the word pounding in his head. *Stay.*

He drew a breath, feeling somehow as if he were about to step off the edge of a mountain overlook back in Appalachia. But if he were to fall—better it come from stepping by faith than running away. "Well then, sir, I believe I'd like to take up your offer to learn blacksmithery."

A grin broke over George's sober, black-bearded face. He clapped Isaac's shoulder again. "Good."

The mower mended, Isaac fetched an iron for another hook and thrust it into the fire. The heat warmed his face, flames flickering in time with the fear wavering around the edges of his heart.

So he'd stay, but what if that made no difference to Larkspur? What if he did his best to prove himself to her—and failed? Was he to dance around her forever in this town, waiting on a woman he'd never have?

Let me worry about that.

Isaac half-chuckled, the message simple and straight to his heart as the bellows' wind to the flames. He pulled out the glowing rod and set to shaping his next hook, peace chasing out the fear with every new blow of his hammer.

All right, Father. Here I am.

21

Would Lilac really want to be seen with him?

Sam ducked a glance at his reflection in the small mirror above his washbasin at the Nielsen House. He straightened his shoulders, his collar. Dipped his fingers in the basin to slick back a few stubborn hairs that kept springing from the crown of his head.

His mother used to vex herself over that sprout of hair. Comb it back with water endlessly.

What would Mor think of him today? Walking out with a young lady after church?

She'd like Lilac, of that he felt certain. What wasn't there to like? And Lilac's winsome liveliness would soothe some of his mother's overprotectiveness, perhaps. But would Mor think him ready for this? To be out from under her wing, going a-courting.

At least her letters had spread out to twice a month now, rather than twice a week. And she sounded more resigned in them overall, even asking after his students and classes. He needed to write to her again—it had been a couple of weeks. But he'd had a lot on his mind.

Against his will, Sam's gaze pulled to his empty sleeve. The stub of his amputated arm itched, and he reached to rub it, wishing he could will it once more whole. Lilac didn't seem to mind, and yet . . . if their relationship progressed as he hoped it would . . . would she ever have regrets? Wish she had a man fully whole, with two arms to protect her, provide for her, love and keep her?

A couple of blocks away, the church bell clanged, and Sam grabbed for his coat. *Get ahold of yourself, man. One step at a time.*

He hurried along the street, turning his collar against the crisp breeze. They'd had a hard frost again last night. The sun beamed in a deep blue sky, though, promising well for their walk this afternoon.

He climbed the church steps, nodding to many congregants and greeting others. Several of his students offered smiles and waves. It felt good to know and be known more and more in this town.

He found a spot not far behind the Nielsens' usual pew, where he could watch Lilac without being too obvious. Now she stood up front by the piano, violin balanced under her chin, accompanying Larkspur on guitar and Mrs. Caldwell on piano. But he only saw Lilac, the slender lines of her figure in her berry-hued woolen dress, the graceful dance of her fingers on the strings as if playing silently as she waited. The way the morning sun beamed through the church window, catching glints from her dark curls, painting her as a minstrel angel in a stained-glass window.

"Good morning, everyone." Mr. Caldwell rose to begin the service with a smile. "This is the day the Lord has made. . . ."

"Let us rejoice and be glad in it," chorused the congregation.

"Excellent. Let us all rise for our opening hymn, 'Savior, Like a Shepherd Lead Us.'"

Sam rose and joined in the chorus of song, the familiar words seeping peace into the questioning corners of his soul.

"Savior, like a shepherd lead us,
Much we need thy tender care;
In thy pleasant pastures feed us,
For our use thy folds prepare:
Blessed Jesus, blessed Jesus,
Thou hast bought us, thine we are . . ."

Strange how much belonging he felt in this little church, even without a pastor since he'd arrived. Surely the Lord had indeed shepherded him to this place and would lead whatever came next too.

What had gotten into that man?

Lark stood at the front of the church, accompanying "Abide with Me" on guitar along with Lilac on fiddle and Mrs. Caldwell at the piano. But though her fingers strummed the chords of Ma's favorite hymn automatically, what happened last week kept circling her mind like a trapped insect.

What had possessed Isaac to show up out of nowhere and propose like that? She'd sensed something between them this summer, she couldn't deny it anymore. But to walk into their machine shed and ask her to marry him, after two months of silence . . . that she hadn't seen coming. She hadn't even known he was back in town.

Lark's throat ached. Why did the one man to ever show any interest in her have to be the one she couldn't depend upon?

Though she kept her gaze away from him, she stood acutely aware of Isaac's presence in his usual spot in the back pew. His shoulder-length sandy hair and beard, broad shoulders, worn army uniform . . . every masculine line of him blazed in her mind's eye.

Lilac nudged her elbow, and Lark realized the congregation was rustling back into their seats, the hymn ended. Face heating,

Lark slipped the guitar strap over her head, set the instrument aside, and hurried after her sister to sit by Del and RJ. Lily Belle cooed and waved her arms, and Lark took the baby onto her lap, glad to bow her head over the little face till her breathing came steady again.

"Oh, it's Mr. Caldwell's turn to share," Lilac whispered. "I'd forgotten."

Lark lifted Lily to her shoulder and patted her back, watching the attorney make his way to the front of the church.

Leaning on his cane, Mr. Caldwell smiled out over the congregation.

"Good morning, friends. Thank you for the privilege of sharing a bit with you today.

"I want to begin with a story. When I was in the war . . ." He paused and scanned the gathering. "I want to acknowledge for a moment how easy those words are to speak and yet how much weight they hold. We can easily forget how immense a trial we have so recently weathered as a nation, and the impact on so many of our lives and those of our family, friends, and neighbors. Let us be mindful."

Lark blinked against a sudden burning in her eyes. She glanced down the row at RJ with his eye patch, Sam Gubberud with his empty sleeve. William, whose early life had been trapped in the terrible system that finally ripped their country in two, and who still didn't know where his little brother was. Then behind them, the Hoffman family, still torn apart just as their nation had been riven. Even Anders back home still bore the scars of his time in a Confederate prison camp. And Isaac . . .

How like Mr. Caldwell to give them all pause to remember.

"At any rate." He cleared his throat. "I was an officer, and I led my company at Bull Run. Some of you know too well how the stench of gun smoke and blood never leaves your memory. I was wounded in that battle, a slash across my chest and a bullet in my knee." He tapped his lame leg. "Many held worse wounds than I, but as I lay in that hospital tent, awaiting the surgeon, I've never known such terror. I was older than most soldiers, so one might think I'd carry more courage—but no. All I could think of was my beloved wife, Beatrice, and that I might never see her sweet face again."

He glanced at Mrs. Caldwell, who sniffed and dug for a hand-kerchief. "I wasn't afraid of death itself. I know the hope of Christ and heaven. But I knew my human frailty so deeply in that moment, and, I'm ashamed to say, wept like a child." He paused to steady his voice. "And I cried out to God—nothing particularly faith-filled or saintly. I merely said, 'Lord, help. I'm frightened, and I don't know what to do.' And, friends, I will never forget what followed. In an instant—a twinkling of an eye, as the apostle Paul says—that fear was gone. And in its place, the peace Christ Jesus promised His disciples when they too huddled in fear washed over me like a warm blanket. And I lay there, truly no longer afraid."

He cleared his throat. "I didn't quite intend this to be so sober. At any rate, I did live to see my Beatrice again and recovered most of the use of my leg. But I've never forgotten that encounter with the presence of God in that hospital tent. I wish I could say I've never known fear again, but that wouldn't be true. I've known fear, pain, and tears many times—we all have. Home-steading here in Nebraska, helping establish this town, coming to grips with our inability to have children . . ." He glanced at his wife again. "Our struggles have been many. But so have our joys. We've been blessed by beautiful friendships with so many of you, some of whom have come to feel like sons and daughters to us."

Beatrice sent a tremulous smile across the aisle to the Nielsen sisters, and Lark smiled back, a lump in her throat.

"So I suppose what I wish to tell you, friends, in all my ram-bling, would be simply this: the Lord is near. He is here, when-ever we might call upon Him, even if it's simply a childish cry from our hearts like mine on that battlefield cot. His path for us may not be what we would choose or expect, but He can be trusted. We need not be afraid."

He sat down to a gentle swell of applause, holding up his hand to shush the crowd.

Lark handed Lily back to Del and followed Lilac up to the front of the church to accompany the closing hymn. She strummed the chords to "Fairest Lord Jesus," the words so familiar her thoughts wandered even as she sang.

Mr. Caldwell's words had mirrored Adam's words in some ways—God's path may be different from what we imagine and whatnot. Was the Lord trying to tell her something? That she needed to accept the path God had laid before her, staying single and running the farm, rather than having a husband and children as she'd always dreamed? And He'd give her the grace to find joy in the midst of it?

She swallowed hard. *I trust you, Lord.* But her chest weighed heavily.

Out in the churchyard after the service, the women clustered around Charlotte Hoffman, autumn breezes sending a shower of golden cottonwood leaves raining around them.

"So you don't know where Caleb has gone?" Rebecca Weber asked.

Charlotte shook her head, her face pale and shadowed. "He didn't tell us. I pray he's not sleeping in a ditch somewhere."

Lark bit her lip. Should she tell Charlotte that Caleb was out with them? RJ had promised the young man they wouldn't tell his father, and perhaps that held as the wiser course for now, but his mother would rest so much easier if she knew.

"Our home feels like someone died." Charlotte swiped a finger under one eye. "The other children tiptoe around, their sad faces break my heart. And George . . . he hardly says a word."

Forsythia shifted Nils on her hip to hug Charlotte. "We should have a gathering of just us women, a sewing circle or some such as we've often talked about. We need to support each other, especially you just now."

"That'd be nice." Charlotte sniffled and tried a smile.

"What about this Wednesday afternoon?" Beatrice Caldwell nodded. "We could meet right here at the church."

"True, and no need for worryin' we might disturb the pastor, since we haven't any as yet." Bridget O'Rourke smiled and ran a hand over her daughter's red braids.

"How is the search going, do you know, Beatrice?" put in quiet Margaret Kinsley.

"They've exchanged letters with a few candidates but nothing definite yet."

"Well, I surely appreciated Mr. Caldwell's sharing today." Forsythia patted Nils's back. "To be not afraid and to trust . . . that's a lesson we all need repeated over and over, it seems. At least I do."

"I see George lookin' for me, so I'd best go." Charlotte glanced around at the women. "Till Wednesday, then?"

Lark looked around for Lilac and saw her standing near the wagons. Seeing the light on her sister's face when she saw Sam Gubberud brought a smile to Lark's. That's right, Sam had asked Lilac to walk with him today.

And she needed to speak to Charlotte. Lark turned and hurried to catch up with her friend.

"Charlotte." Lark touched her elbow. "May I speak with you just a moment?"

The older woman turned, a furrow between her brows.

Lark glanced around. "Caleb is with us."

Charlotte clutched at Lark's arm with a gasp.

"Shh, we thought it best not to tell George, in fact Caleb insisted we not, but I couldn't stand to see you worrying so." Lark winced. *Lord, I hope I'm doing the right thing.* "I hope you can forgive me for not speaking sooner. He's helping us on the farm with harvest and threshing, which we sorely need just now."

"Of course. Oh, thank heaven he's safe." Charlotte pressed her hand to her calico bodice. "And he's all right?"

Lark tipped her head. "He's still angry. But safe and well."

Charlotte's face shadowed. "I wish I could . . ." She glanced to her wagon, where her husband waved an impatient arm. "I must go. But thank you, Lark, thank you."

Lark nodded and watched her go. At least Charlotte would leave with a lighter heart today.

She glanced about the churchyard and caught Isaac watching her. She felt a flush start in her toes and work its way up to overheat her face.

22

Lilac was waiting for him.

Sam greeted the Caldwells, Webers, and Dwyers before he was finally able to make his way across the churchyard to Lilac, who stood under the cottonwood tree watching the small children play while her sisters visited nearby.

He returned her smile, noting the way simply seeing her face brought a grin to his own, bidden or not.

"You look to be enjoying the sunshine." He took off his hat.

"I am. We'll have blizzards soon enough. Mikael, no." She crouched to take away a rock the little boy was digging into the tree trunk, then glanced back up at Sam, cheeks suddenly rosy. "Did you, uh, still want to walk?"

"Of course." The words burst out so quickly, he felt his own neck heat. "That is, uh, if you do."

"I do." She smiled and straightened, even if her eyes shone shy. "I just need to let Forsythia know so she can watch the little ones."

A few moments later, they headed out of the churchyard, side by side. Was it only Sam's imagination that the majority of the congregation's eyes followed them? He rubbed the back of his neck with his good hand.

"Perhaps setting off on our first outing from such a public place wasn't the best idea." He glanced at her. "Sorry."

She laughed and shook her head. "It's all right. Goodness knows the Nielsen sisters should have learned by now not to care too much what people think."

Sam smiled. "A good lesson for us all. Where would you like to go?"

"What about over behind the school? I love the big old cotton-wood there, and that stretch of prairie is a bit more sheltered."

Sam held out his arm. "Lead on, my lady."

They walked down the main street of town, still abandoned with most folks at church. Perhaps in that way, his timing hadn't been so bad. They chatted of this and that, her nieces and nephews, mutual acquaintances back home. Of the schoolchildren and his plans for a Christmas program this year.

"I love your idea of an original play." Lilac's dark eyes sparkled. "Last year was a simple nativity production the children did on Christmas Eve. But it was lovely."

Sam nodded. "I heard about that, sounded wonderful. I'd like to do something similar but perhaps have a slightly different story each year, all centered around the same holy narrative, of course. I've an idea buzzing around in my brain, something about a shepherd boy with a lost lamb. And then he finds it waiting for him at the manger next to the Lamb of God." He glanced at Lilac to see her staring at him with tears in her eyes. "Are you all right?"

"That's beautiful." She swiped her knuckle under her eyes. "Makes me want to illustrate it. Have you written stories before?"

"I've scribbled now and then since I was a boy, when I could fit it in between baseball and studies and other shenanigans." He chuckled, then quieted. "I've done a bit more writing since, well." He shrugged the shoulder of his missing arm.

Lilac followed his gaze. "Was it your writing hand you lost?"

His throat tightened with gratitude for how she said that simply and directly, without any awkward side glances or ahems like most people did. "No, thankfully. I can write as well as ever—as long as I don't send my paper flying with a particularly enthusiastic stroke of the pen. Then grab for it with the hand holding that same pen and send my inkwell spilling over desk, floor, and newly destroyed story alike." He pulled a serious face. "Not that *that* has ever happened."

She burst into laughter that reminded him of Christmas bells. "Oh dear. Well, perhaps it served you right after all the braids you dunked in ink."

Sam sighed. "As I'm reminded each time my students pull a trick that mirrors one of mine from our schooldays. 'Whatsoever a man soweth, that shall he also reap,' as my mother might remind me."

"How is your mother? And your father? It must be difficult for them, having you so far away."

"For my mother, certainly." Sam blew out a breath. "I nearly changed my mind many times about coming out here because Mor was so distressed. But the truth is, I think she needed to let me go. She's been wrapped up in me since my injury, more than was good for either of us. From her letters, she hasn't stopped worrying, but I think it's lessened a little. Thank the Lord for my father. He's her steady rock, and he never stopped encouraging me to go, if that's what I wanted to do."

"And are you glad that you did?" She searched his face.

He gazed down at her, a smile warming up from his chest to his face. "Very glad."

She held his gaze a moment longer, her breath coming quickly, then glanced away, the color in her cheeks matching the deep rose of her dress. "Oh, look."

Behind the shelter of schoolhouse and cottonwood tree, a patch of wild sunflowers bloomed as if sunshine had gotten trapped there.

"How lovely." Lilac hurried among them, caressing the golden-beamed, black-centered blooms. "I should pick some to take Lark." She snapped stems here and there, gathering a slender bouquet in her arms.

Sam watched her, wishing he could capture the picture she made.

"There's some yarrow still too." Lilac bent to pick a few sprays of the white-clumped blooms.

"How is your flower seed business coming along? That is the focus of Leah's Garden, correct?"

"Yes, though we may sell vegetable seeds at some point too. We plan to send out our first catalog this winter. Anders has a printer in Ohio who will help us. I just need to finish a few last drawings."

"That must be exciting, your dream this close to coming true."

"It is. Hard to believe after three years." Lilac straightened, her arms full of yellow and white, her dark curls springing loose beneath the falling golden leaves of the cottonwood tree.

"You'd make a mighty fine picture for the catalog cover, just now." Sam flushed at the words that jumped out. "Forgive me. That was brazen."

Lilac laughed. "I think our current cover of the Leah's Garden sign surrounded by flowers is much better. But thank you."

"I just . . ." He stepped near her, swallowing. "I'm very thankful to be here with you today, Lilac. That you would be willing to walk with me. Be with me. Even with . . ." He shrugged his empty sleeve again.

"You think I care about that?" She stared at him. "I don't, not one bit. Except to be sorry for the pain you've endured and grateful for your sacrifice—and that you're still here. Sam, being with you is . . ." She nibbled her lip and looked away. "It's very different than with Ethan."

The former pastor. She'd told him a bit in their conversation at the store reopening about their courtship and broken engagement last year. Sam tamped down an irrational surge of jealousy. After all, the man was moved and married. "How so?"

"I don't fully know yet, it's just . . ." She looked up with a shy smile that weakened his knees. "I feel like . . . me when I'm with you."

And she hadn't with Ethan? Sam tucked that thought away for now and instead nodded, knowing her words fit a puzzle piece into place in his mind also, the reason he'd been drawn to Lilac from that June day in Ohio. "And so do I."

Lark threshed the next day till the early darkness made it too hard to see, then she was back at it the next morning. Wednesday they started harvesting the corn, then after a cold dinner, Lilac washed up while Lark headed back to the threshing floor Jesse had built them. Together with Caleb, she continued beating the stalks of wheat till the grain fell through the wooden slats to the canvas beneath. The dusty chaff made her sneeze till she had to step aside to blow her nose on her handkerchief—also covered with wheat dust.

"You all right?" Caleb paused his flail.

Lark sniffed hard and nodded, tucking her handkerchief in her pocket. Hopefully the cold she'd beaten back last week wasn't rearing its head again.

Lilac popped in a short while later. "Lark, it's almost time to go. I've got our sewing things."

"Drat. I forgot about the women's gathering." Lark straightened, glanced at the piles yet to be threshed. "Lilac, you go on without me. There's too much to do." They needed this wheat as their one cash crop, not to mention their own bread for the year.

"There's always too much to do, but you're the one who's been saying we need to get the women together more, almost since we moved here. You have to come."

"If I had time to do all the things I *have* to do . . ." Lark muttered, then sighed. "You all right to work awhile on your own, Caleb?"

"Sure." The young man nodded.

"Oh, very well." Lark set her flail aside and blew her nose again. "Let's go, then. Maybe we can still be back before sundown and do a bit more. We're almost finished." She sneezed once more. *Please, let it just be from the chaff.*

By the time they arrived, Climie and Harriet Wells had a fire going in the potbellied stove in the church, though the corners of the building still held autumn's chill.

"Feels good in here." Lark shed her coat and rubbed her hands, her heart lifting despite herself to see so many friendly faces. Beatrice Caldwell, Rachel Armstead, Rebecca Weber. Margaret Kinsley, with her toddling little boy. Forsythia and Del, babies in arms. Tilda Hoffman gathered the little ones old enough to play in a corner spread with quilts, bringing out a basket of blocks and dolls. Her usually lively face drooped pale, though. Even her thick dark braid hung limp over her shoulder.

Beatrice Caldwell spread her hands and glanced around the women circling their chairs around the stove. "I know we all brought our own sewing today, but would we want to start something together at some point? Perhaps some project for those less fortunate?"

Forsythia stood swaying from one foot to the other, patting Nils's back to try to settle him to sleep. "I hear the Indian reservation is in need of warm quilts and blankets. Perhaps we could help there."

Beatrice nodded, her brow pinching. "There's a good deal of need, according to a Pawnee friend Henry sees on occasion. You know the northern part of Indian Territory was taken from them with the Kansas-Nebraska Act and given to settlers, and now they're being forced on smaller and smaller reservations, and our friend says they don't get nearly the amount of provisions the government promised them."

Lark's gut pinched. She didn't often think about the suffering brought to others by people like them settling this prairie . . . didn't like to think about it, to be frank. But there it lay, an uncomfortable truth. "Can you ask your friend how we might help?"

Beatrice gave a firm nod. "I will. But I think knitting blankets and perhaps making a quilt or two would be well appreciated."

Del rocked Lily Belle in her arms. "That we can do."

"Is Tilda all right?" Lilac drew her chair near Charlotte Hoffman's. "I've never seen her look so sad."

Charlotte sighed. "My poor girl. I don't know if you'd noticed, but I believe she was startin' to moon after your brother Jonah."

Lark and Lilac swapped wide-eyed glances. How had they missed that? And had Jonah known? Reciprocated?

"Between him going back to Ohio and now Caleb gone, I've caught her weepin' in her room more than once of late. And she used to be my sunshine girl." Charlotte pressed her lips together and sighed.

Lark shook her head. Sounded like another letter home was due—and not just to Anders, their usual correspondent. She bit the inside of her cheek. Her own first proposal she'd definitely leave *out* of said letter.

"How is Jonah doing?" Climie's voice came gentle as ever, if with more confidence. She sat near the warmth of the stove, knitting something small and yellow.

Lark smiled to see the tiny garment in her friend's hands. So much this dear one had been through. . . . God willing, this baby would be one she'd get to keep.

"Anders telegraphed that he made it safely," Lilac answered. "That's all we know."

"Terrible it was, that accident." Bridget O'Rourke shook her head. "Thank the good Lord 'tweren't even worse."

"Amen to that."

"Seems one crisis after another these days." Charlotte Hoffman pushed her needle through a patch on a pair of small trousers. "I've little hope things will ever mend between my Caleb and George." Her voice wobbled.

Forsythia stepped back from laying a sleeping Nils on a folded quilt and sat down. "How did it happen that Caleb joined up Confederate? If you don't mind my asking."

Charlotte sighed and laid her mending in her lap. "No use trying to hide our family's troubles now."

"It's all right if you'd rather not share."

Mrs. Jorgensen, silent thus far, nodded. "Many a family with both blue and gray."

"No, I want to. You all are the closest to family we've got out here, and goodness knows we're going to need help if we're to weather this storm." Charlotte drew a breath and lifted her chin. "To begin with, George isn't Caleb's father."

A murmur rippled around the circle. Lark shot a glance at Lilac. Her sister had told her what Caleb said at the doctor's office that day, but they'd thought perhaps he spoke only in anger.

Charlotte's face reddened. "Not that there was anythin' improper. My first husband, Caleb's namesake, was George's brother. He went off to the Mexican War soon after we married, when I was carrying Caleb. George looked out for us while he was away, and when my husband got himself killed, George married me. Mostly out of duty, at least at first—I hadn't any other family around. But soon, he did come to love me, and I him." She sighed and stared across the room. "But the baby . . . when Caleb came, George couldn't seem to forget he was his brother's child—and there was little love lost between them. Something about an old rivalry. I suppose my namin' Caleb for his father didn't help matters either, but it seemed right at the time. At any rate, it wasn't that George treated him cruel, but Caleb . . . as he grew into a little boy, he wanted nothin' so much as to win George's approval, to please him. But it seemed he never could. Then the other children came, our girls and the little boys. George gave them the attention, the affection even, that Caleb never got." She exhaled a shaky breath. "I think Caleb just gave up. He started rebelling any way he could—little ways, just whatever his stepfather did, he wanted the opposite. So when George joined up with the Forty-Fourth Ohio, and expected Caleb to stay home and be the man of the family during the war . . ."

"He rebelled in the furthest way he could." Lark nodded, the pieces clicking into place.

"He did." Charlotte sighed. "Too young and too late to see action, but he made his point. And his father—I mean, George—can't forgive him for it. Nor does Caleb think he'll ever understand, I do believe."

Lark reached to squeeze Charlotte's hand. "I'm so sorry, friend."

"In his own way, I think George does care for Caleb, but he just . . . doesn't know how to show it. And now I'm afraid it's too late." She wiped her eyes with a handkerchief Beatrice Caldwell passed over and glanced around. "You all are so kind. I'm sorry to burden our time together like this."

"Nonsense. What is a community for?" Beatrice squeezed her shoulder. "And it's never too late for God. Don't you forget that, my dear."

"I'm grateful George at least has Isaac McTavish to help him in the forge with Caleb gone." Charlotte picked up her sewing again. "He's the kindest man, always doin' little things for us and trying not to be noticed."

Lark stared at her own needle and thread, a pinch in her heart. That sounded like Isaac.

They sat and sewed awhile longer, talk drifting to colicky babies and plans for this year's Thanksgiving program at school. At last Lark glanced out the window to see the sun had nearly set.

Drat. She'd lost track of time. She rolled her sewing and

tipped her head at Lilac. They'd make good time getting home with only Prince and the trap but not much daylight left for threshing.

The sun slipped near the horizon as they pulled up by the barn, days cutting so much shorter now. Frustration clamped Lark's middle as they hurried to do chores. She sat fuming at Clover's side, hands squeezing mechanically. She should have just stayed home. If they didn't get the wheat threshed and safely stored, they might run short on their chief cash crop, not to mention grain for flour and seed for next year. And they were already late harvesting the corn, and finishing getting in the garden, and . . .

Lark sneezed over her shoulder again, hard.

"Want me to do Buttercup?" Lilac stepped over after feeding the animals.

"Fine," Lark snapped, sniffing back the running in her nose.

Lilac raised a brow that said *You sure are grumpy* and headed to milk the other cow without a word.

But Caleb had made good progress, little knowing he'd been the topic of much conversation this afternoon. The tension in Lark's chest eased a little, seeing the bags of wheat he showed her. Till she started coughing.

"I don't care what you say." Lilac steered her toward the soddy. "It's supper and bed for you, and no nonsense."

While Caleb headed to Del and RJ's, where he was sleeping in the unfinished Leah's Garden addition for now, Lilac reheated rabbit stew. She set a bowl before Lark, and she managed to eat most of it, sneezing all the way.

"I can't be sick." She leaned her elbows on the table and groaned, head in the heels of her hands. "There isn't time."

"Go sleep, then." Lilac cleared the dishes from the table. "Maybe you'll be better tomorrow."

But the next morning, Lark woke with head pounding and nose streaming.

Lilac took one look at her and shook her head. "You'd best get back to bed. I'll bring you some tea."

"Tea, fine." Voice croaking, Lark held up her hand. "But Caleb can't do it all."

"I'll help him."

"It's too much for two people. I'll be fine. It's just a cold."

She drank the tea, shaking her head at Lilac's offer of fried cornmeal mush. The thought made her stomach roil.

"I'll do the chores," Lilac said firmly. "At least I can spare you that."

Lark waved in acknowledgment and stumbled her way outside, squinting in the sunlight, head on fire. The barnyard and fences undulated oddly, but she made her way to the threshing floor and stood staring stupidly at the piled sacks of wheat.

"Mornin', Miss Larkspur." Caleb strode up, arms swinging, and clapped his gloved hands before him. "What do you want me to start on today?"

Lark blinked hard and moistened her lips. She couldn't . . . couldn't think. A coughing fit sent her stumbling to the fence to hold on.

"Miss Larkspur?" Caleb's voice seemed to come from far away.

Lark lifted her hand to wave vaguely in the direction of the threshing floor. Took two steps forward on ground that shifted under her feet. Pitched forward, hardly feeling the impact of her body on the rough ground.

Then everything went black.

23

"You sure you're all right with me leaving for a while?" Lilac stoked the small stove in the bedroom.

Lark tried to answer, then lifted off her pillow with coughing.

Lilac stepped near to hand Lark her cup of tea. "I don't like the sound of that."

Her sister sipped, sputtered, then drank some more and kept it down. "I'm fine. I keep telling you it's only another case of the catarrh." She sank back on her pillows with a sigh. "Just hate being laid up like this."

"You've been pushing too hard again, no wonder you're sick. Caleb and I have things in hand, so you just rest and stop worrying that head of yours." Lilac shook her head at her sister. "I don't want any repeat of finding you sprawled on the ground yesterday. Scared me half to death."

"I'm better after resting, so quit your worrying, little mother hen. Caleb is finishing the threshing?"

"Yes, and I'll help him once I get back from town. We need a few things from the mercantile, and I'll get something from Adam for your cough. Then I told Sam I'd eat with him on his lunch break at school."

"Not very romantic to meet in a noisy schoolyard, is it?" Lark said, her voice raspy. "Ouch, my throat hurts."

"We don't mind." Lilac smiled, her heart doing a little skip. "I'll just wrap up a sandwich to take with me."

Lark sighed and smiled back from her pillow. "I'm happy for you, little sister. Truly."

"I know you are. I just wish I could make that same happiness happen for you." She stepped near to kiss Lark's forehead, then straightened. "You've got a fever."

"Sure hope I can sleep this off in a day or so." Lark closed her eyes.

Lilac studied her a moment, then went to stir the chicken soup she had simmering on the stove before heading out the door, slipping on her coat as she did. A light frost had crunched beneath her feet this morning when she did chores. At least Lark had finally acquiesced to staying in bed, however long that lasted. Lilac shivered at the memory of finding her sprawled unconscious, Caleb hollering for help. Lark still bore the evidence in an abrasion on her face.

Thank you, Father, that it wasn't worse.

She'd meant to stop first at the mercantile in town, but by the time she reached Main Street, the clang of the school bell let her know she'd arrived later than she meant. She'd have to do her errand after or miss her chance to see Sam. Lilac clucked and turned the trap toward the schoolhouse. She'd hitched Starbright today, and her mare's ears flicked and responded to every hint she gave.

"Such a good girl you are."

She pulled up at the schoolyard and climbed out of the trap to wrap the reins around a fence post.

"There you are." Sam approached the fence, a brown paper package in his hand. "I was afraid you'd forgotten."

"Sorry I'm late." Lilac smiled up at him, the bright October sunshine making her squint a bit. Overhead arched a sky so blue it caught her breath. Or maybe that was just the man standing before her. "But, no, I wouldn't forget."

He smiled down at her, sending warmth trickling clear to her booted toes. Sam tipped his head toward the schoolhouse. "Shall we?"

Lilac fell into step beside him, her sandwich snug in her coat pocket. "How did classes go this morning?"

"Well, I think. We've started working on the Thanksgiving program, and it's coming together nicely. I wondered if I could get your opinion on the students' ideas for decorations before you go."

"I'd love to see."

They perched side by side at the top of the school steps, a vantage where they could see the whole schoolyard yet be a bit removed from the sea of schoolchildren running, laughing, or sitting in clumps eating their dinners.

"Shall we pray?" Sam laid his paper parcel beside him and held out his hand, then hesitated. "I'm sorry, if you'd rather not—"

Lilac laid her palm on his warm one, her heart skittering at the squeeze of his fingers on her own.

Sam's Adam's apple bobbed, and he closed his eyes. "Father, thank you for the beauty of this day, for this food you've provided for us. Thank you for the privilege of the company of this wonderful woman. Bless us and guide us, we pray in the name of Jesus, amen."

"Amen." Lilac pressed his fingers once more, then withdrew her hand. She wasn't sure either of their hearts could take it for much longer, at least not with an audience.

Sam blew out a breath and unwrapped his paper package, clearing his throat. "Mmm, roast beef. Climie does spoil me, packing delectable sandwiches like this. I'll have quite an adjustment once I get my own place."

"Is that something you're thinking about?" Glad for the

distraction, Lilac unwrapped her own parcel of Del's thick home-made bread sliced with cheese, plus an apple she'd tucked along-side. She crunched into the crisp fruit, one of the first harvested from their very own trees this year.

"I am. Salton agrees with me—and I hope the feeling is mu-tual." Sam gave a quick smile. "And I've heard the house Rev-erend Pritchard used to live in might be available."

"Really?" Lilac licked up a stray drop of juice from her thumb, then winced to think what her ma would say. "I thought some-one else would have rented it by now."

"Not according to Banker Young. Anyway, I'm supposed to meet with him about it next week." Sam brushed crumbs from his mustache and eyed her. "Would it be strange for you, me living where he did?"

Lilac scrunched up her face. "A little. I mean, that was the house he rented for us when we were engaged. But not strange in a bad way. Just . . . ironic, I guess." She shook her head with a slight laugh. The Lord did have a sense of humor. "What would your family think if you stayed permanently in Salton?" The thought made her want to dance, but she remembered Sam had a doting mother back home.

Sure enough, his eyebrows pulled together a bit. "My mother seems to have resigned herself to my establishment here, at least for now. But by her last letter, she dearly wants me to come home for Christmas."

"Will you?"

"I haven't decided, but I'd rather not. I don't feel ready to spend the money for the train trip back after only being here a few months. And I . . . well, I don't really want to leave you." His hazel eyes met hers till Lilac had to glance down to catch her breath.

"Maybe you could visit in the summer."

"I'd prefer that. But she's worried about the blizzards out here—doesn't seem to realize going home for Christmas won't mean I escape them. Or maybe she hopes I won't return." He sighed and rubbed his forehead. "Sorry, my mother can be a bit of a handful, as I've heard Robbie say."

"Family can be, can't they? I've been worried about Lark lately."

"Is she ill?"

"Just a case of the catarrh, though she gave me a scare yesterday. She just works so hard. Sometimes I think she feels she has to be the one to hold everything together. Like if she drops one thing, all we've built out here will fall apart. And she won't even think about imagining a personal future for herself." Lilac rubbed the crumbs from her fingers. "Sorry, maybe I shouldn't be saying all this to you."

"Are you thinking of Isaac McTavish?"

Lilac slanted a glance up at him. "You do notice a lot."

Sam shrugged. "Suppose I have to as a schoolmaster." He folded his brown paper and tucked it into his pocket, then rose and extended his hand to Lilac. "It's hard not to worry over those dearest to us, isn't it? Even if they try us at times."

"It is." She let him help her up. "Thanks for listening, though."

"I'd listen to you anytime you'd let me, Lilac Nielsen." He gave her hand a gentle squeeze, then let her go and scanned the schoolyard. "But I'm afraid I've already given these youngsters a longer dinner hour than I ought, not that they'll complain."

"Do you still want me to look at the Thanksgiving decoration ideas?"

He snapped his fingers. "That's right. I nearly forgot." Sam rang the bell to call the students back in, then once they sat quietly at their afternoon lessons, he beckoned Lilac up to his teacher's desk.

"Here are a few sketches the older ones composed this morning. They had an idea of making garlands from fall leaves, but I don't know how we'd keep them that long. I know the leaves will be long gone before Thanksgiving."

"Not if you dip them in paraffin wax. That preserves them nicely."

"Really?" Sam glanced up. "I never would have thought of that."

"I'd be happy to help. We should do it soon before the leaves all fall. Let me know when might be a good time. We'll have to melt wax on the stove, so you'll need to be careful with the little ones. Any other ideas?"

He showed her a few other plans, then the drawings he and the students had posted on the walls from Lilac's last art lesson. She walked the length of the school building, admiring them, while Sam moved to help the primer class with their spelling.

At last she glanced at the clock and caught her breath. "Goodness, I didn't realize how late it was. I must go, Lark will be wondering."

"Forgive me." Sam glanced up from correcting a small slate. He stood, his hazel eyes finding hers with a quickness she was coming to know. "I hope I haven't caused you trouble. I'll see you Sunday?"

"See you Sunday." Lilac smiled into his eyes, then held herself back from skipping all the way to the door, waiting till she climbed into the trap behind Starbright to hug herself and draw a long breath.

If only Sunday weren't two whole days away.

She urged Starbright down the street to the mercantile and picked up more lard, coffee, sugar, and salt, along with a can of peaches to tempt Lark's appetite. Then on to Adam's office where he supplied her with a small bottle of cough syrup.

"Got whiskey in it, so careful on the dosage. But it should calm her cough and help her sleep." Adam leaned his hand on the doorframe of his new office, still smelling of fresh wood and paint. "Make sure you get enough sleep too, Lilac, so you don't catch it."

"I will."

The sun had slid well toward the west by the time she pulled Starbright beside the barn at home. Scolding herself for not planning the time better, Lilac hurried to unhitch her mare and met Caleb coming out of the machine shed.

"Sorry I was gone so long. Did you have dinner at Del and RJ's?"

"I did. Del said she'd come check on Lark."

"It's all right. I'm here now. She shouldn't come over with the baby. I'll be back out to help you with chores soon."

Caleb took Starbright's halter, and with a nod of thanks, Lilac hurried inside.

The clatter of a stove lid greeted her. She stared to see Lark standing at the stove stirring the soup pot, a shawl draped over her nightgown, long dark braid hanging down her back.

"What are you doing?"

"Getting us some supper. What took you so long?"

"I was at the school with Sam. I'm so sorry I lost track of time. You shouldn't be up." Lilac set her bundles on the table and hurried to her sister's side. She tried to take the wooden spoon from Lark's hand, but Lark shrugged her away.

"I'm better after sleeping most of the day. You go do chores. I can finish this." Her voice still croaked but did sound a little stronger.

"You are more obstinate than a mule, you know that?" Lilac reached up to feel her sister's forehead. "You do feel cooler."

"Told you."

Lilac shook her head but put away the groceries, then headed out to do chores with Caleb, coming back to find Lark ladling the soup into bowls, coughing over her shoulder as she did. She pulled out a chair to sit down, but Lilac waved her finger.

"Ah-ah. You are eating in bed, and no arguments. I'll get you a tray."

Lark opened her mouth to protest, then groaned a sigh. "Fine. I suppose you are right."

She grumbled only a little as Lilac tucked her back in bed, setting a tray with a bowl of soup, fresh bread, and a cup of tea across her knees.

"Thank you."

"You are welcome."

"How is Caleb coming with the threshing?"

"Nearing finished, I think. He's a good worker."

"We should be finishing the corn harvest already. I should be well enough to help by Monday."

"Lark . . ." Lilac puffed out a breath and shook her head. *Lord, what am I going to do with my stubborn sister?*

Lark snapped another drying corncob from its pale brown stalk and tossed it into the wagon Lilac drove through the field, Caleb picking on the other side. It felt good to be out in the fields again.

Lilac had wanted her to drive, but Lark insisted on walking and picking, relishing the stretch of her legs as she gathered the corn. Once the wagon was filled, they'd deliver the cobs to the corncrib, where they would finish drying.

Lark dumped another armload into the back of the wagon, then arched her back against the aches. They could use the mower to cut the drying stalks once the harvesting was done, then bundle them for animal feed over the winter.

She sneezed into her shoulder. The dust from drying cornstalks didn't help the remnants of her congestion. Harvest hadn't come easily this year—first Jonah's accident, then her getting sick the end of last week. Thankfully, the last couple of days she'd felt much better.

Thank you, Father, that it all wasn't worse. Please help Jonah to heal fully. They'd had another letter from Anders saying Jonah was much improved and starting to walk on his leg, though it might be months before he'd reach full strength again.

She sneezed again, dumped another armload of corncobs, then dug her handkerchief out of her sleeve.

Lilac stopped the horses and climbed down. "Come on. You're driving now."

"I'm fine." Lark blew her nose.

"I'm not driving anymore, so you'd better."

Lark eyed her. "And you call me stubborn." With a sigh, she climbed onto the driver's seat and hupped the team into a slow walk through the corn rows. It did feel good to sit for a while.

The sun slanted low, and a breeze nipped by the time they stopped for the day, still over half the cornfield left to harvest. Legs aching with weariness, Lark took off her leather gloves and washed up outside the soddy, then examined the scratches on her arms from the cornstalks. A cough shook her hard, and she leaned against the soddy doorframe. *Wish I could just go to bed.* The thought caught her off guard.

"You all right?" Lilac spoke at her shoulder.

"Think so. Just got a lot of dust in my throat." Lark tried to clear it.

"Want Caleb and me to do chores?"

"No, I'll help. Quicker with three of us." The words set her to coughing again, but she ignored Lilac's look and grabbed the milk pails from inside. Stubborn malady. But she was stubborner. *Larkspur Grace Nielsen, since when is that a word?* Ma's voice in her head made her smile.

After chores, Caleb stayed for supper since Lily Belle was colicky, then headed back to Del and RJ's for the night.

"He certainly has been a godsend." Lilac cleared the plates and filled the dishpan with hot water from the stove reservoir.

"Not sure his folks would put their situation that way. But God works all things together for good. I trust He will for their family too. I sure am grateful for his help." Lark set to wiping the dishes while Lilac washed them. "I'm going to get the business books out once we're finished. Need to go over our expenses for the catalogs one more time, not to mention everything else. Do you have those last drawings finished?"

"Almost."

"Lilac, we should have sent them all off already. Who knows how long it will take this printer Anders has found, then we have to receive them, and get them ready to mail out . . ."

"I know, I know. But first Jonah was injured, then you were sick, and . . ."

Lark sighed. "Can you finish tonight or tomorrow? I'd really like to get it all in the mail to Anders by the end of the week."

"I think so."

They sat together at the table, kerosene lamp pooling light between them. Lilac bent her dark head over her drawing pad, pencil flying, a shawl around her shoulders. Lark looked over the copy for the seed catalog once more, then added figures and balanced columns, rubbing at the headache pressing behind her eyes. Usually numbers marched in neat order for her, but tonight she was so tired.

"Want some tea?" Lilac pushed her chair back.

"Sure, thanks." The steaming cup Lilac brought soothed her still-raspy throat. "That's good."

They worked some time longer, Scamp sleeping on Lark's feet, a canine footwarmer. At last Lilac sat back with a sigh and pushed her sketchpad toward Lark.

"There. What do you think?"

The last page of seed packet labels stamped the paper like quilt squares, four to a page. Tansy, salvia, marigolds, and larkspur. Lark smiled to see her namesake. "Finally got to mine, huh?"

"Best for last, you know." Lilac squeezed her shoulders. "Will they do?"

"More than do. They're beautiful, little sister." She reached up to press Lilac's hand. "Can you believe Ma's dream is this close to coming true?"

"I hope she knows, somehow. From heaven."

"If it's right she should, the Lord will see to it."

Lilac yawned and closed her sketchpad. "I'm off to bed. You coming?"

"Close. Still got this month's expenses to balance. You know we have one more payment due on the boardinghouse the first of November." Lark covered a cough that hurt her chest.

"Lark, you really should go to bed."

"I will, soon. I promise."

Lilac sighed and headed to the bedroom.

Lark kept on, bending close to the lamp and working till the figures danced before her eyes in beat with the pounding in her head. Finally, she put out the lamp and pushed to her feet, closing her eyes against a wave of dizziness in the darkness. Scamp stood too with a whine and padded after her to the bedroom. Lark stumbled, catching herself on the doorframe.

Lord, what's wrong with me? She felt her forehead and cheeks. *Do I have a fever again? Please, God, no. I don't have time for this.*

Shivering, she fell into bed and let quilts and darkness swallow her whole.

24

P neumonia?"

"That's what I'm thinking by the sound of her breathing. But we can't be sure till Adam comes."

Lark fought to swim up through the fog that held her under. Voices . . . her sisters. Lilac and Forsythia. She tried to open her mouth, her eyes, but her body wouldn't obey. Was Scamp lying on her chest? Hard to breathe. The quilts too heavy, too hot—she hadn't the strength to throw them off.

"I knew she was pushing herself too hard, that she wasn't well yet. But when does she ever listen?" Heat tinged Lilac's words. She was angry. Or afraid.

"I know."

"Where is Adam?"

"He got called to a birthing before dawn. I sent Jesse after him. He'll be here as soon as he can. Tilda stayed with the children so I could come. In the meantime, let's get that water boiling with herbs on the stove."

Steam . . . that sounded good. Lark tried to breathe deeply, then choked with the stabbing in her lungs.

"Lark, we're here. Easy now." Forsythia's hand came gentle and cool on her forehead. "Just rest."

Lark tried to say she couldn't do much else, but the words wouldn't come. She managed to flutter her eyes open enough to see her sisters' faces, then heaviness claimed her again, and she slept.

The rumble of Adam's voice roused her sometime later.

"Sorry I couldn't make it sooner. Twins."

"Is all well?"

"The second baby was breech, but yes, all is well now. How is she?"

"She's pretty sick." Lilac's voice held a tremble. Lark wanted to reach for her little sister's hand, reassure her. But she couldn't manage to move.

She shivered as cold metal touched her chest through her nightgown, the instrument moving to different spots to pause and listen.

"What do you think?" Forsythia's voice moved closer.

"You're right, sounds like pneumonia. She's got that telltale crackle in her lungs."

"But she just had a cold. And she said she was better."

"It can start that way. Then, especially with how run-down she's been, pneumonia can seize the opening."

"What can we do?"

"Rest, warm liquids. Bloodletting was the old approach, but I don't like it, weakens patients more than it helps them. I don't like using mercury either, but might be worth trying a touch as a purgative. I'd like to move her to one of the hospital rooms in town."

"Is that wise?"

"It has its risks, but this afternoon is fairly warm. Things can change quickly with pneumonia. I'd rather have her where I can be nearby and monitor her closely."

"Then that is what we will do. Lilac, have Caleb go tell RJ and Del, then get as many extra quilts and blankets as you have. We'll wrap her up and make a bed in the wagon. RJ will need to help Adam lift her in."

Lark worked her jaw, mustering all her strength. *Come on.* She forced her eyes open, blinking in the bright light from the window.

"Don't I . . . get a say?"

The three turned to stare at her. Adam chuckled.

Lilac sat on the bed and pressed her hand. "Not today, sister mine." She smiled, though her lips trembled a bit. "Today we take care of you."

Lark floated in and out through the bustle of preparations, the rumble of a wagon pulling up outside, hushed voices. At last, bundled in quilts and blankets, RJ and Adam lifted her between them, armchair fashion, and carried her out the door to lie in the wagon bed.

"I feel like . . . a trussed turkey." The words set Lark coughing till she clutched at her chest, half expecting to find knives there.

"Lilac, you'll drive?" Adam's doctor voice came in full force.

"Of course."

"I'll help Caleb with the chores." That was RJ. "Don't worry about anything here."

"H-harvest," Lark croaked out. The corn wasn't half gathered—did no one realize but her? No one seemed to hear.

Lord, why are you taking everything out of my hands?

A long jolting ride. Fitful sleep, snatches of dreams. Coughing. Then she was lifted again, up steps this time. Another set of strong arms joining Adam's, a different voice, gentle and halting. Jesse.

Lark tossed her head back and forth as they laid her on a bed. "Jesse . . . shouldn't be here. Climie, the baby—" Coughing claimed her again.

"It's all right, Lark." Adam's hand steadied her shoulder. "Pneumonia isn't usually passed from one person to another. Stop worrying about everyone else."

Lark opened her eyes and looked up at him, the dimmer

light inside easing her eyes. Forsythia and Lilac stood at the side of her bed.

"Th-that's right." Jesse nodded. "For once let everybody else w-worry about you."

How was she supposed to do that?

But she lacked breath for any more words.

"What can I get for you today, Mr. McTavish?"

Isaac stepped up to the counter of the mercantile and drummed his fingers on it, glancing from Mrs. Jorgensen to the shelves behind her. "I'm wondering what you might recommend for, uh." He fingered his beard. How to go about this? "In the way of yard goods."

The proprietress smoothed her apron over her ample middle. "Yard goods? You mean cloth?"

"Yes, ma'am. I aim to make myself some new clothes."

"Well." She eyed his ragged uniform, one sleeve near to falling off. "You're overdue for that, if you don't mind my sayin' so. What did you have in mind?"

"I, uh." He rubbed the back of his neck, feeling the skin heat. "What would you say?"

"Well." A businesslike gleam came into her eyes. "I've got some nice new gray wool in. That'd do up a handsome winter jacket and trousers for you. You'll want some flannel for a couple of shirts, can choose from the unbleached plain or we've got gray, red, blue, and plaid."

Isaac blew out a breath. "I'll trust your judgment, ma'am."

Beaming, she bustled toward the bolts of cloth. Isaac fingered the coins in his restitched coat pocket, hoping he had enough from his last payment from George Hoffman. The man had graciously increased his wages, with Isaac now aiming to learn the trade and taking on more difficult tasks in the forge. He'd been working sunup to sundown, even taken to sleeping nights in the Hoffmans' barn, further saving from his modest board at the Nielsen House. This was his first trip into town proper in a week.

Thank heaven for Mrs. Jorgensen. Him in the dry goods section felt about as natural as a buffalo might be in his West Virginia mountains. But if he wanted to prove to Larkspur Nielsen that he truly wasn't going anywhere, might as well start by looking respectable.

"Here we are." The mercantile proprietress laid several bolts of cloth on the counter and unfolded the first in a river of charcoal gray wool. "Shall I cut the yardage you'll be needin'?"

"If you would please." Isaac stared at the amount she unfurled and sheared. "That much?"

She clucked at him. "You don't know the first thing about this, do you? Who's going to make it up for you?"

"Well, uh." He swallowed. "I aim to try my hand at it myself. My ma taught me to sew a seam."

"Mmhmm." She shook her head and began cutting the blue flannel he'd nodded at for a shirt. "There's a sight of difference between runnin' stitches and cuttin' and fittin' a suit. You wouldn't know which end went up, or I'm much mistaken." She sighed. "I'd suggest you ask one of the Nielsen girls to sew it up for you, bein' as you're such a good friend of the family, but they've got enough to worry about just now."

He nodded, guilt pinching again. "With harvest and their brother gone back east."

Mrs. Jorgensen's hands stilled amid folding the fabric. "Then you haven't heard."

"Heard what?"

She clucked her tongue. "Hate to be the bearer of bad news, but Miss Larkspur's sick bad. Doctor's got her in one of his new hospital rooms here in town, says it's pneumonia. She's young and strong, oughta be able to fight it off, but . . . I don't know. Folks say she's been terrible run-down these last months."

Everything around Isaac seemed to have gone still, save his heart, thudding till it hurt in his chest. "How . . ." He moistened his lips. "How long's she been ailin'?"

"Not sure about that, but they brought her into town—let's see, would have been three days ago now. Her sisters have been taking shifts at her bedside ever since, from what I hear." She finished folding the yardage and wrapped it in brown paper, naming her price. "Maybe Climie at the boardinghouse could sew it up for you."

Numb, Isaac dug the coins from his pocket. "She's got enough on her hands. I'll figure somethin'." What would a fancy suit of clothes matter if . . . if Lark . . . No, he couldn't think that way. He wouldn't.

Mrs. Jorgensen clinked the coins into her cashbox. She started to hand the brown paper parcel to him, then stopped. "See here, Mr. McTavish. For another dollar, I'll make the suit and shirts up for you myself. And you don't need to pay me till you see it and are satisfied."

He stared at her, his mind struggling to function. "You would do that?"

She pursed her lips. "Don't have much to keep me busy in the evenings these days."

He rubbed his forehead, then nodded. Didn't seem he had many other options. "Then I thank you."

"Glad to do it. And Mr. McTavish . . ." She hesitated till he met her eyes. He saw a wet gleam there. "Don't give up on Miss Larkspur. She's a fighter. We all know that."

Isaac had to try twice before words could work past the roughness in his throat. "Thank ye."

He turned and fumbled his way out of the store, then down the street, hardly seeing where he stepped nor whom he passed till he stood in front of Adam's new office.

He might not be welcome inside, nor helpful just now. But he had to see her.

Had to see Lark. His Lark. Even if she never would be.

He lifted his hand to knock and saw it was shaking. He rapped once, twice.

Adam opened the door. His weary face relaxed when he saw Isaac.

"Isaac, come in. I hope you're well?"

"I heard about Miss Larkspur." Isaac stepped inside the office, pulling off his army cap. He scanned the small waiting area with its desk, potbelly stove, and wooden bench. An examining table was visible through an open door to one side—and a second door was closed off to the other.

Adam followed his gaze and nodded. "She's in there. We finished these rooms just in time, I guess. Between Jonah's accident and now . . ."

"How is she?" He scrunched his cap till his knuckles ached.

The doctor sighed and rubbed his hand across his eyes. "I won't lie to you, Isaac. She's quite ill. I've seen worse—but not by much."

A harsh coughing, almost a choking, came from the next room, making Isaac's own chest clench. Then a murmur of voices.

"Lilac and Del are with her now. The sisters have been taking turns. Lilac's bedding down on a cot in the room at night."

"Can—can I see her?" The words near to choked him.

Adam glanced at him, then his face softened. "Of course."

Isaac followed on wooden feet as Adam opened the door, whispered something inside, then held it for Isaac.

Del and Lilac, easing Lark back onto the pillow, barely looked up when Isaac came in. Lilac dabbed her sister's perspiring forehead with a cloth, then folded it over and hurried past Isaac and out the door, her face pale and strained.

"Adam, she coughed up blood that time. See?" The words came low from outside the door.

"That's not unusual."

"What else can we do?"

"Everything we've been doing. And pray."

Del straightened from the bedside and attempted a smile. "Isaac, it's good to see you. Thank you for coming by."

He nodded.

"I need to head back to feed Lily Belle. Forsythia's keeping her at her house. Would you like to sit with Lark awhile?"

His throat tightened at the understanding in Del's eyes. Did she know? Did they all know? He nodded again, mute.

Del slipped out, leaving the door slightly ajar.

Isaac stepped near the bed, drawing close the chair Del had left. Seeing Lark like this made his chest ache. He'd never seen her so still. Always working—planting, hoeing, mending, mowing. So alive, so strong, so busy . . . so beautiful.

Now she lay motionless, save an occasional tossing of her head on the pillow, the rapid, shallow rise and fall of her chest. The struggling wheeze of her breathing.

"Lark." He hesitated, then reached for her hand and covered it with his, her skin hot and dry against his palm. "It's Isaac."

He gave a half chuckle, though it stuck in his throat. "I reckon if you could, you might throw me out this minute, but you don't have much of a say just now. Reckon that's a mighty big change for you, ma'am." He ran his thumb over the back of her hand. Did her hand shift closer within his, or was it only a feverish twitch?

He traced her face with his eyes . . . her strong brows, the bold but delicate lines of her nose and cheekbones. Her shuttered eyes, dark lashes fluttering now and then against her cheeks. Parched lips that everything in him wanted to cover with his own. His grip tightened on her hand without his meaning to, and she flinched. "Beg pardon, Miss Larkspur." He loosened his grip and stroked the back of her hand with one finger.

He jumped when the door opened, and Lilac slipped back inside.

"Adam said to try and get more broth down her."

"Of course." He stood and slipped out of the way, watching as Lilac gently spooned broth between her sister's lips. Lark took a few spoonfuls, then set to hacking, spilling and spitting out the rest. She coughed near to choking, her whole body spasming on the bed. Adam hurried in to help Lilac support her and hold a basin to catch the phlegm. Isaac caught a glimpse of the red tinge himself this time. At last they laid Lark back on the bed, sweating and shaking, eyes closed and face so pale she nearly looked blue.

Jaw set, Adam carried out the basin.

Lilac wiped her sister's face again, then sat on the edge of her bed, stroking her hair.

"I don't know what to do." Her words came so softly Isaac barely heard them.

"You're doin' all you can, Miss Lilac." He firmed his voice. This wasn't about him now, not at all. "You're bein' here with her."

"Like she always is for us." Lilac's voice caught, and a tear slid down her cheek. She bent to kiss Lark's hand on the coverlet, then laid her head down on the bed beside her sister.

Isaac slipped out and found Adam sitting at his desk, supporting his head with one hand, flipping the pages of a heavy medical book with the other.

"What can I do?" Isaac fisted his hands at his sides. He had to do something.

Adam looked up. "Not much you can do here, I'm afraid."

"Out at the farm, then? Anything?"

The doctor rubbed the bridge of his nose. "Well, I believe they still have much of the corn harvest to get in. Caleb Hoffman's staying out there, he'll care for the animals and such, but harvest is a lot for one man."

"I'll go." He seized on the task as a drowning man on a raft. "Might I come back this evenin'?"

Adam hesitated, then nodded. "You can try."

Isaac rode Winter out to the Nielsen homestead, grateful for the horse's quiet knowing, her lack of need for conversation. Caleb wasn't a man of many words either, but the young man seemed grateful for the help. Together they gathered ears from the drying cornstalks in the field till twilight fell, then mucked out stalls, milked the cows, and fed the stock. The rhythm of farm labor, as familiar to his blood as Appalachian air, weighted his muscles with a certain comfort. Even as his chest tightened to think of Larkspur lying on that bed so still, her breathing so strained.

"Thank ye, sir." Caleb strained the milk inside the soddy, the building dark and close with emptiness.

Isaac lit the kerosene lamp on the table. "You beddin' down here?"

"I am, since the ladies left. Keep an eye on the place. And this feller." Caleb rubbed Scamp's head, the dog attached to his side like a burr.

"Could you use some comp'ny?"

Caleb stared, then nodded. "If'n you don't mind. And if . . ." He hesitated. "You won't tell my pa, will you?"

"Haven't yet. Don't aim to start now." Isaac pressed his tongue to his cheek. "But you should, son. One of these days."

Caleb sighed. "I know."

"I'll be seein' you, then." Isaac headed back out the door.

"Don't you want some supper? There's smoked venison, bread, and cheese."

"Not tonight."

He rode back to town, shivering in the wind. Be frost again tonight, maybe a hard freeze. That new coat would cut the wind this winter . . . not that he cared about that just now.

He found Lilac and Forsythia both with Lark in the hospital room, Del and RJ caring for the children at the Brownsville home tonight. Adam was giving Lark a purgative, which set off a wrenching round of vomiting. Isaac tucked himself into a corner, refusing even a chair, and prayed, sitting on the floor, arms hanging between his knees. Sometimes his head slipped to rest on his knees, then he'd jerk it up at the sound of Lark's tortured hacking.

After nodding off more fully, he roused sometime later to see all three of Larkspur's sisters kneeling at her bedside.

Lamplight flickered, lighting the sisters' anxious faces and braided hair, shawls about their shoulders, hands folded on the bedcovers around their sister, facing each other.

"Adam says the turning point will probably come by morning." Forsythia reached to smooth Lark's matted hair. "For better or worse."

"Should we have telegraphed Anders?" Del whispered.

"I did." Lilac's whisper now. "At the train station yesterday. I'm sorry, I should have asked first—"

"No, you were right." Forsythia squeezed her shoulder.

"But what's the use? Even if he comes, he might not be in time if . . . if . . ." Lilac's voice broke, and she buried her face in the quilt, her hand reaching to clasp Lark's still one.

Del and Forsythia moved to huddle around her, arms enfolding and tears mingling.

"Father in heaven, we cry out to you for our sister's life."

"Please, Lord, please spare her."

"Yet if it be not thy will . . ." Words broken, halting.

"Thy will be done."

The lamplit scene blurred before Isaac's eyes, and he covered his face with his hands, sniffing back a great burning. *Abba, Father. Have mercy. Don't take her from these good women, please. Or from me . . . little as I deserve to ask it.*

The night dragged on endlessly. Forsythia and Del had to leave to tend to their babies back at the house. Adam and Lilac kept vigil, Isaac in his corner. Toward dawn Lilac slipped into sleep on the cot near Lark's bed. Adam dozed in a chair.

LAURAINE SNELLING

Isaac pushed to his feet. Knees stiff, he padded to the empty chair by the bed and eased himself into it. The lamp burned low, yet enough to gently highlight Lark's face. She rested quieter just now, not coughing, just a whistling wheeze with each breath. Whether that boded good or ill, Isaac didn't know.

He laid his hand over her hot one once more, then sat quietly a moment.

"It's me again, Miss Larkspur," he whispered at last. "You're givin' everyone a good fright, you know that? I wonder what you'd think to see us all round you, if you were in your rightful mind. Send us all packin', might well be. Like you tried to send me." He aimed for a chuckle that only managed to be a sigh. "But here I am. I didn't leave this time. I want you to know that. When I said I'd stick around for you, I meant it."

He paused, watching to be sure she was still breathing. "You were right. I've been on the move these last years, never stoppin' any place for too long. Reckon I hadn't even rightly thought about it till you made me. And you made me think all right, Miss Larkspur. You always do." He drew a long breath. "Figure I owe you somethin' of an explanation. I've been runnin' ever since the war. Believe I told you, way back when we met—remember that fireside where you drew me in with your music?—I told you then I'd been in a prison camp like your brother. What I didn't say was I was there with my brother. I told you my brothers both died in battle. Which weren't quite true, and I'm sorry." He sighed. "It's my fault my Union-clad brother died. I didn't mean for it to happen, but I made a poor call of judgment and got him killed." Isaac sniffed hard and passed his wrist over his eyes. "Guess I've been on the move ever since. Never felt I deserved to settle down anywhere, have a real life. Not after that was taken from my brother because of me."

He stared at her nightgowned arm, ran his thumb gently over the fluttering pulse in her wrist. "Now I reckon I can see it weren't entirely my fault. I'll tell you the whole story sometime.

261

But I think I was afraid to put down roots, make attachments. Since I knew how easy they could get snatched away from me." He swallowed. "Till you."

"You made me want to live again, Miss Larkspur. Really live, not just exist from place to place. Like I've been doin' till I've near forgotten any other way. The way you care for your family, for anyone who comes near—it puts me to shame. You've cared for me and welcomed me in ever since I showed up a homeless drifter to your campfire, made me feel I belonged. And that's the truth." He slid to his knees by her bed, gripping her feverish hand with both of his.

"So I'm here to tell you, Miss Lark." His voice caught, but he kept going. "I will never leave you again, you hear me, ma'am? Not unless you flat out order me to. We can have a life together, a good life, you and me, if you're just willin' to see it. And I'll give all that I am and have to build it with you. So don't you dare go dyin' on me, you hear?" A tear fell on his hand, others sliding hot into his beard, but he paid them no mind. "I love you, Larkspur Nielsen. And I'm not leaving you, not now nor ever, so help me, God."

The clock ticked. Isaac sat back on his heels with a long shuddering breath, drained as if coming in from battle.

Lark wheezed and coughed, though not into paroxysms. Isaac stood, stepping back as Adam roused from his chair and bent over her with his stethoscope.

Just outside the lightening window, a meadowlark announced the morning with his familiar aria.

25

"Are you really getting better, Tante Lark?"

Lark opened her eyes and met her nephew's dark-eyed stare beside her bed. She smiled and reached for Robbie's hand, hoping to bring a smile to those eyes. She hadn't seen him so sober in a long time.

"I really am, Robbie boy." Her voice rasped, but the terrible pain in her chest was gone. "Your pa says so, and he's a pretty smart man, isn't he?"

Robbie heaved a sigh. "He sure is. And he's a real good doctor."

"That's for sure." Lark squeezed his hand, then released it to sink her arm back onto the covers. Even that much effort and she felt as feeble as an old sheep.

"How long till I get over this blasted weakness?" she'd asked Adam yesterday.

He'd leveled a glare at her. "As long as it takes. And if any of us catch you doing any more than you should, we'll hogtie you in bed and station a guard. One brush with death is quite enough for a lifetime as far as your family is concerned."

Fair enough. Seemed she'd given everyone the scare of the century to hear her sisters talk.

And Isaac. But surely she'd imagined him sitting at her bedside, sometime in that fevered haze of days and nights?

"There you are, Robbie." Forsythia came in, chubby Nils riding on her hip. "Are you letting your Tante Lark rest?"

"She likes to talk to me." Robbie clasped his hands behind his back and tipped his head toward his ma.

"Indeed I do." Lark smiled at her sister, hating the new lines on Sythia's gentle face. Knowing she was the cause.

"I know she does. But she also needs to rest. Come home with me and play with Sofie and Mikael for a bit. I need to put Nils down for his nap."

"Okay." Robbie leaned to hug Lark, then bounded out of the room.

Lark met Forsythia's eyes. "You think all this brought some memories back for him of losing his ma and pa?"

She nodded, her eyes damp. "I do."

Guilt squeezed Lark's chest again. So much she'd put them all through, at least partly because of her own stubbornness, her insistence she had to do everything herself. She tried to say something else but coughed instead, bringing up brown phlegm.

Forsythia handed her another handkerchief. "It's good you're getting the rest of that out. I'll send Lilac to check on you. She's supposed to be along shortly. She was meeting Sam at the school for a bit. Something about Farfar Nielsen's journal."

"How are those two getting on?" Lark lay back on her pillows.

"Very well, from the look of things. Sure is a different feeling than with Reverend Pritchard, isn't it?"

Lark nodded. "I'm so glad."

Nils fussed and grabbed at Forsythia's bodice. She shifted and bounced him in her arms. "You need anything else before I go?"

"I don't think so." Lark hesitated. "Sythia . . . Isaac wasn't here at all while I was ill, was he?"

"He was, actually." Forsythia's eyes softened. "That night we thought we might lose you. I don't think he left that corner all night, wouldn't even take a chair."

Mingled wonder and disappointment pricked tears into Lark's eyes. So he had been here, bless him . . . but not sitting by her bed, holding her hand. That—and the words she'd imagined murmured into her feverish ears—had been merely a figment of her sickness and imagination.

"That was kind of him."

"Kind? Lark . . ." Forsythia blew out a breath, then glanced out the window at a call from her children. "I've got to go. But sometime . . . we've got to talk about that man."

Lark avoided her sister's look till the door shut behind her.

With Forsythia gone, Lark glanced about the room, seeing it now as she hadn't while so ill. The new timber walls still smelled of fresh wood, covering the lingering odor of sickness, and sunshine beamed through a window near her bed. Another cot tucked into the corner, where Lilac still slept at night for now. Perhaps someday, Adam could hire a nurse to watch patients here. A small table with a basin stood near, also a little tin pitcher of goldenrod blooms—Forsythia's touch. Warmth from the potbellied stove in Adam's office radiated through the wall next to her bed.

After the dark valley she'd struggled through, this place seemed pure heaven.

She dozed till a soft rap at her closed door roused her. Must be Lilac. "Come in." Her throat croaked like a bullfrog. She cleared it and reached for the glass of water by her bed. "Come in."

The door creaked open, but a broad-shouldered male frame stepped through instead of her sister's slender one.

For an instant, Lark could only stare. "Anders?"

Her older brother pulled off his hat and grinned at her. "When a man gets news his sister's on her deathbed, there's only one road to take. And that'd be a railroad."

"But didn't they tell you I was better?" Her voice was muffled by his hug, enveloping her in his woolen coat and scent of train soot.

"They telegraphed, but I was already at the train station, ticket bought, when it came through. Wasn't going to turn back then." He pulled back and frowned at her. "What have you been doing to yourself? Thinking you have to shoulder the weight of the world or something?"

She winced. "Not you too."

"Sounds like you're in need of a good old-fashioned elder-brother lecture. We need our Larkspur around, not working herself into an early grave."

"There's just always so much to do—the farm, Leah's Garden, the boardinghouse—and the other girls are all getting busy with their own lives. I can't ask—"

He held up a gloved hand. "And there's your problem. You have to ask for help when you need it. We all do. That's called being a family, not to mention the body of Christ."

She pressed her lips together and nodded. She was getting a bit weary of everyone's sermonizing, not to mention being stuck here in bed.

"Anders?" Lilac slipped in and threw herself into their big brother's arms. "Where did you come from?"

"The train, where do you think?" Anders lifted her off her feet with his hug.

"I was over at the school, Sam has been helping me translate Farfar Nielsen's journal. We hope to share it with the whole family soon—how perfect you are here. How long can you stay?"

"As long as needed, or at least till snowfall. Jonah's recovered enough to run the store, along with Josephine of course. I figured you'd need help out on the farm while Lark's recuperating."

"What a good brother you are. But actually, Caleb Hoffman and Isaac McTavish have things well in hand at the farm."

"Isaac?" Lark burst out. Her siblings turned to stare at her.

Lilac beamed. "I didn't know either, but I rode out this morning to check on things. Isaac has been staying out there with Caleb, bunking down in the barn, though I told him he could sleep in the soddy. They've gotten all the rest of the corn harvest in, nearly finished gathering all the dry stalks too. Caring for the animals, milking, mucking stalls. They even asked my advice on getting in the rest of the flower seeds."

"Well." Anders shook his head. "There's a man to count on."

Lark lay still, her pulse thumping in her ears. Isaac was doing all that . . . for her?

No, not just for her. For *them*. He held a remarkable loyalty to their family, for whatever reason.

You know what reason.

Maybe so. But it was too late . . . she had rejected Isaac outright. Barely even listened to him that day he surprised her in the machine shed. She shivered slightly to think of it.

"Lark, I'll bring you some soup, then take Anders out to the farm. Maybe we can all gather at Forsythia's for supper in a few days, once Adam says you're strong enough."

"That would be good." Lark sniffed hard and kissed Anders's bristled cheek when he bent over her to say good-bye. "Thanks for coming, brother mine."

"Of course."

With her siblings gone, Lark left the steaming soup on the tray before her and closed her eyes, hot tears spilling down.

Isaac. A man to count on, Anders had said. Had she been so blind to that? If so, it was surely too late now. For if he still cared in . . . in that way, wouldn't he have come to see her while she'd been recuperating? But she'd not seen hide nor hair of Isaac McTavish, save that night she'd imagined him by her bed, his broken whispers, hand so tight on hers she could still feel his work-roughened grip.

"I will never leave you. . . . I love you."

She squeezed her burning eyes against the words. They weren't real—Forsythia had said Isaac never left that corner all night.

Lark sniffed back the tears, opened her eyes, and reached for the spoon. Breathing a prayer, she set into her soup bowl with the determination of her ancestors crossing the Atlantic.

All she could do now was make it up to her family for the scare she'd given them. Get herself well, then figure out a more sustainable way forward to manage all the Nielsen enterprises.

And trust time and the Lord to heal her newly tender heart.

Barely November, yet tonight felt like Thanksgiving.

Lilac bent to open Forsythia's oven, the scent of roast pork with apples—a barter from one of Adam's patients—steaming her face as she drew out a tray of biscuits. At the counter, Forsythia mashed potatoes and added butter and salt, while Del sat at the table nearby, nursing Lily Belle. In the dining room, Climie was setting the table with Jesse's help.

Best of all, Lark lay on the sofa in the Brownsville sitting room, watching the children play. Not well enough yet to help in the kitchen, but better, so much better. After she lay so close to death only a couple of weeks ago . . .

Thank you, Father. Thank you, thank you.

All would be perfect, if only Sam were here. Lilac glanced at the clock and set to washing the mixing bowls. He'd said he would be by now. It was Sunday, but perhaps a student's family had wanted to talk to him this afternoon or something.

Del buttoned her bodice and lifted Lily to her shoulder to burp her. "This little lady eats like a pig." Lily beat her chubby fists on her mother's shoulder and squealed.

"That's what I used to say about Nils. And now he's already starting to reach for table food as well. I might let him try these mashed potatoes tonight." Forsythia smiled and sighed. "Where does the time fly to?"

Boots stamped, and voices rumbled on the front porch.

"Sounds like Sam and Anders." Forsythia set her wooden spoon down.

"I'll get it." Lilac wiped her hands and flew from the room, her sisters' chuckles trailing behind her.

She opened the door to Sam and her brother, both of them scarved, coated, and red-cheeked from the wind.

"Feels like snow out there." Anders hung his hat on the rack and unbuttoned his coat. "Good thing I'm heading home on the train tomorrow."

"Your family will be glad to have you back before Thanksgiving. This feels like an early celebration for all of us." Lilac reached to take Sam's coat, giving the slightest tug on the sleeve to ease his shedding of the garment over his missing arm.

He turned and smiled down at her, gratitude in his hazel eyes. And a light that sent swirling warmth through her middle.

He reached his hand to lightly brush her fingers, and she gave them a quick squeeze before turning to hang his coat. *This man.* How was it he could both make her giddy and ease peace into her heart at the same time?

Because he loved her. The thought gave her pause, and she smoothed her hand over the collar of his brown wool coat, straightening a fold. And she loved him. She knew that now, knew it with a certainty she'd always lacked with Ethan.

She wasn't in a rush this time for things to move forward. But whenever they did, she knew she wanted her place to be at Sam Gubberud's side. As long as the Lord would allow.

"Supper's ready," Del announced from the doorway. "Sam, Anders, you're just in time. Isaac didn't come with you?"

Anders glanced into the sitting room, where Lark lay watching the children play on the rug. William sat near, showing them the new carved animals he'd brought tonight to add to their menagerie. "Isaac said he had too much to do tonight at the blacksmith shop. He's been spending so much time helping at our farm, you know. Sent his thanks, though."

Del nodded, though her brows pinched. "Well, let's gather in the sitting room to pray, so Lark can join us. Then we'll go sit at the table. Forsythia is fixing Lark a tray."

They all crowded around the sofa, RJ and Adam holding Lily and Nils, the older children extending hands to the adults around them. Lark looked up from the middle of the circle and cocked her brows.

"I feel like a strange sort of lying-down maypole."

Everyone laughed. Adam shifted his babbling son in his arms and nodded to Anders. "Would you give the blessing?"

Their brother bowed his head, then had to clear his throat before he could speak. "Our Father, we thank you."

Thank you, Father, Lilac's heart echoed. She squeezed Sam's hand beside her, feeling his steady grip.

"Thank you that we can be gathered together tonight—and that Lark is with us, something we do not take for granted. Thank you for our family, for Sam's presence here, for William and Jesse and Climie. Thank you for this good food, and the little ones among us and to come." He drew a long breath. "In Jesus' name we pray, amen."

"A-men!" Mikael shouted, sparking chuckles again.

Supper passed in a warm hum of pork roast and potatoes, laughter and stories. Afterward, they carried plates of dried-peach pie into the sitting room and perched on chairs and stools so Lark wouldn't be alone, the children cross-legged on the rug once more.

"I can't remember food ever tasting so good," Lark said, handing her empty plate to Robbie, who carried it carefully to the kitchen. "Thank you, everyone."

Lilac helped Robbie clear the rest of the dishes, William and Jesse jumping in to help and shooing the young mothers back to their seats, including Climie, her middle now gently rounded. Lilac rinsed and stacked the plates, then slipped into the pantry where she'd tucked her surprise.

Holding the large folder behind her back, she stepped back into the sitting room and paused a moment to drink in the scene of firelight and family. Another picture her fingers itched to draw.

"I'm so grateful we made that last mortgage payment," Lark was saying. "Now the boardinghouse is well and truly ours." She craned her neck to look around at everyone. "We couldn't have done it without all of you, Climie, Jesse, William. And your help, too, Anders."

"That's for sure. And, Anders"—Lilac stepped in front of her brother—"since we won't see you at Christmas, I wanted to give you your present early." She drew the folder from behind her back and handed the large sheet of paper to Anders, who held it low for Lark to see.

A collective gasp rose from her sisters, and Del and Forsythia rose to peer over Anders's shoulder.

"Oh, Lilac."

"It's beautiful."

Tears pricked her eyes as she stepped behind them to see the drawing once again too. Enlarged from their grandfather's own sketches, she'd chosen the picture of their father as a child, kneeling in the garden beside one of his sisters, her towheaded pigtails springing from her small head as she held out a pea pod to her brother. A simple log cabin rose in the background against a wooded hill. The tenderness in the bend of their father's young head toward his sister, the lines of their rounded limbs and innocent concentration on their little faces—truly Farfar had been an artist, whether he'd realized it or not. She hoped she'd captured the essence of the original in her rendition.

"Lilac, I love it." Anders tapped his finger on the signature she'd copied at the bottom. "But you should sign it too, alongside Grandfather Nielsen's name. I only feel badly to take this away from everyone here."

"It belongs in the family home, where we found the journal.

And we have the original here." Lilac squeezed next to Sam on the small upholstered settee and nodded at him. "We thought Sam could read aloud from the translation he's been working on. If you all would like to hear."

"Oh yes, please." Lark pushed herself up straighter on the sofa, her eyes bright.

Sam cleared his throat and pulled the small worn volume from beside him. He leaned forward and opened the fragile pages, withdrawing several closely written sheets of paper. "My translation isn't perfect, certainly. But I hope it gives you at least a bit of insight into your grandfather's life. He sounds like a wonderful man. This is an excerpt from his account of the voyage across on the *Restaurasjonen*."

Lilac leaned back and listened to Sam's rich voice begin to read.

5 July 1825. Today our ship the Restaurasjonen departed from Stavanger, our number being fifty-two persons, most of them Quakers. While I cannot count myself a member of their particular faith, my heart admires their courage to stand for their convictions in how they worship the Lord, even against persecution from the government and official Lutheran church in our homeland. For myself, I seek a new chapter in life, though I know not what it will hold. With my parents gone and few prospects here in Norway, I set sail with these Friends and trust the Lord of us all to guide my steps as we journey to the New World.

They listened, even Robbie in rapt attention, as Farfar's words reached across years and miles to tell the adventures and misadventures of this brave little ship—from nearly getting fired upon by cannons at Funchal Harbor, Portugal, because they neglected to raise their flag to accidentally breaking the Passenger Act when they arrived in New York, having been unaware of the limits America placed on number of passengers for their ship size.

At last Sam lowered the papers in his hand. "Sorry, that's as far as I've translated."

"Oh, Sam, thank you. That was wonderful." Forsythia rocked a sleepy Nils, her face shining in the firelight.

"What a lot of trouble they had." Anders shook his head. "But they persevered and saw the Lord's faithfulness, even when they made mistakes."

"A lesson to all of us." RJ patted the back of his baby daughter, drifting off on his shoulder.

"Thank you indeed, my friend." Anders nodded to Sam.

"It was a privilege." Sam folded the translated sheets and tucked them carefully inside the journal once more. "I want to finish, as I have time. It's been an honor to get to know your family better these last months, both through the journal and in person." He set the journal aside and clasped his knee with his hand.

Lilac noticed his fingers trembling and raised her gaze questioningly to his face.

"And I'm hoping you might, well, allow me to become a more permanent member." He turned to meet Lilac's eyes, and what she saw there sent her heart winging upward, then dipping into her stomach.

"I've already spoken to Anders about this, but it seems only right to ask in front of the rest of your family as well." Sam slipped from the settee to one knee before her, holding Lilac's hand fast in his one good, strong one. "Lilac Nielsen, you have become so much to me in these last months. So much more than the lively little girl whose pigtails I used to dip in ink."

Teary chuckles sounded around the room from her sisters. Lilac held Sam's hand tightly, looking into his hazel eyes, so earnest just now. Eyes of the man she loved with all her being.

"Your wit makes me smile, your heart gives me courage, your

presence sets my feet steady. I wish I had two arms to shield you from the storms this life will doubtless bring, but I will offer all I am and have to walk alongside you for the rest of my life, if you'll have me." He drew a shaky breath. "So, Lilac Patience Nielsen. Will you marry me?"

"Yes." She nodded so hard a tear flew out of her eye. "Yes, I'll marry you, Samuel *Jakob* Gubberud."

A grin broke out from beneath his mustache like sun from behind a cloud. He pressed a kiss to her hand, warm and full of promise, then Lilac pulled him to his feet amid the applause of her family, both of them dizzy and beaming.

"Is that why you and Anders were so late?" she whispered, pulling him into the entryway a few moments later, away from the buzz of congratulations.

"Had to seize the chance to ask for his little sister's hand." Sam brought her hand to his chest, and she added the other. His eyes damp, he covered both her hands with his one. "Are you sure you'll be content with . . . me?"

"With you?" Lilac reached to trace the lines of his beloved jaw, as she'd never dared do before. "I love you, Sam Gubberud. I can hardly wait to walk beside you all the days of my life." And she rose on her toes to kiss him soundly enough to leave no doubt.

26

I never saw a soddy before we moved out here," Caleb said. Isaac worked beside the young man to mend a corner of the Nielsen soddy just below the roofline. Three winters of rain and snow had done their worst.

"Not much call for them in the country I hail from either." Isaac hefted a fresh chunk of sod into place, breathing hard with its weight. "But then, so many trees in those West Virginia mountains you couldn't even see your neighbors, most times."

"Think the Nielsen sisters will ever build a real house?"

"Reckon so. They've just had a passel of other things on their mind. Never saw such a bunch of enterprisin' women." Especially Larkspur. The thought of her tugged his chest with an ache.

If this fall had gone like he hoped, he might have been working on a house for her and himself by now. A right pretty farmhouse, front porch and all. He'd laid it all out in his mind when he couldn't sleep.

But at least she was alive. He needed little remindin' to be grateful for that.

Caleb helped tamp the sod brick in, then sealed the gaps as Isaac had showed him.

Isaac glanced at the young man, his face serious beneath the shock of dark hair sticking from under his woolen cap. Boy could use a haircut . . . over two months away from his mother were showing their wear. Isaac stifled a chuckle. As if he were one to talk. But his own rough-cut hair and beard helped keep his neck warm at least.

They moved the stool Isaac had borrowed from the barn to another corner where the sod was crumbling and set to clearing space for a fresh block.

"So are you thinkin' of goin' home for Christmas, son?"

"I don't know."

Isaac chewed the inside of his cheek. "I know what your ma would say."

"She ain't the problem." The young man's words came so low Isaac could barely hear.

"I never did ask you why the Confederacy. Any special reason?" Isaac kept his gaze on his work, his tone casual.

Caleb's mittened hands scraped hard at the crumbling sod and roots. "Just wanted to go where my pa wasn't."

"He weren't at home, though, was he?"

"Should have been. He was too old to take off to war, leavin' us. Expectin' me to do his job."

"So you decided to leave too."

The young man had the grace to flush. "He never cared what I did before. Unless to tell me I was doin' it wrong."

"Sometimes that's how folks show they care. Even if it ain't the best way. So you were tryin' to get him to notice you by runnin' off?"

Caleb stared at him. "You sure ask a lot of questions."

"Beg pardon. Just conversin' to pass the time."

Silence hung as they lifted in the next sod brick and tamped it tight.

Isaac stepped down and nodded. "That should hold. Just one more corner needs our attention, I'm thinkin'."

"I did feel bad later." Caleb finally spoke while handing the sod brick up to Isaac. "When I found out how worried my ma was. And about joinin' the South. I didn't really think it through, but after gettin' to know William, out here . . . I was kinda glad I didn't see action. Missin' out had made me so mad before."

Isaac nodded. Meeting someone who'd been trapped in that awful system of slavery, learning to see him as an equal and a friend . . . that would certainly give a man pause about signin' up for the Confederacy.

Isaac tapped his gloved hand on his thigh. "Now that I think on it, I do believe I heard your pa's to be speakin' in church this Sunday. Might be a time you could hear what's been on his mind, without havin' it be just the two of you, if you take my meanin'."

Caleb shook his head at the ground. "I don't know about that."

At the clop of horse's hooves, they both turned to look. A lone rider came up the lane to the homestead, a man in hat and coat. When he swung off near the barn, Isaac recognized Anders.

"Everythin' all right?" Isaac hurried toward him, his pulse galloping irrationally. But after what they'd all just been through . . .

"Fine, everyone's fine. Didn't mean to worry you. Just thought I'd stop by before I head out of town. My train leaves this evening."

"Ah." His heart thudding back into place, Isaac extended his hand. "Been good to see you again. And I reckon even more so for your family."

"Thank you for all you've done, McTavish." Anders gripped his hand firmly, looking into his eyes. "I don't take it for granted, nor do my sisters. Same to you, Caleb."

The younger man ducked his head. "They've helped me out too." He climbed up on the stool and started back to working on the sod.

"Well, I may be out in these parts again come spring." Anders tucked his hands into his coat pockets with a grin. "Lilac and Sam got engaged last night."

A smile spread over Isaac's face. "Well, ain't that plumb wonderful."

"Not sure Sam was planning to pop the question this soon, but with me in town, he didn't want to wait to ask for her hand. And happy as they are, there wasn't any need to wait longer." He cocked his head. "I'll confess I almost wondered if you'd be approaching me with a similar question, McTavish. If for a different sister."

Isaac sucked a breath with a wry smile. "Well, I won't lie to you, sir. I'd like to do that. But considering how I seem to have offended the lady in question, I don't reckon it'd be of much use just now." Not till he figured some way to win that woman's heart. If he hadn't already messed things up beyond repair.

"I see." Anders eyed him. "Well, if something were to change . . . you'd have my blessing, for what it's worth."

Isaac glanced at the man's eyes and saw he meant it. "Thanks."

He and Caleb kept working after Anders left, packing the sod in good and tight till the air turned dark gray with dusk, their breath puffing white in it. At last Isaac stepped back and scanned the soddy, rubbing his hands together, numb despite his worn woolen gloves.

"That oughta hold her through the winter. Least better than before."

"Seems like." Caleb blew on his hands. "Guess it's time for chores. You comin' to the Eastons' for supper?"

"Not tonight. The Nielsen ladies'll be movin' back tomorrow, from what I hear. Time I head back to your folks' place." He let out a long breath, clouded in the frosty air. "And figure out what's next for me."

Caleb headed toward the barn, and Isaac surveyed the farm a moment. The fields lay brown and fallow, sleeping till the spring, even the cornfield. They'd gathered the last of the drying shocks into the barn for winter feed.

He'd done all he could for Larkspur for now. At least there lay a certain peace in that.

"Show her you're serious, and you're not goin' to leave when the wind blows foul. Prove yourself to her, man. Stay."

Thinking of George Hoffman's words, Isaac ran his fingers through the thick hair covering the back of his neck. *I'm stayin', Lord. But what else can I do to show her how much I care?*

After helping Caleb milk and feed the stock one more time, Isaac rode Winter back to the Hoffmans'. Grateful George and Charlotte asked few questions, save to confirm Lark was recovering, he set his belongings in the Hoffman barn, brushed and fed Winter, and left her nosing hay in a stall. Supper passed in a pleasant blur of children's chatter, thankfully requiring little from Isaac.

That night, by his bedroll in the hayloft, Isaac dug under the straw in the corner and felt with relief the hard iron shape of the object he'd tucked there before he learned Larkspur was ill. Lying back on his thin pillow, he held the iron piece up in the moonlight seeping through a crack, ran his thumb over the still clumsy edges.

He'd work more on it tomorrow. Even if he never gave it to her . . . it was something he wanted to do.

He tucked it into his haversack, then rolled over and slept deep and dreamless.

Sunday morning, George met Isaac outside the barn after milking. He wore a starched shirt, jacket, and pained expression.

"Don't know why I ever agreed to Caldwell's fool notion of me speakin' in church. I ain't no preacher, and there surely ain't nothin' I have to share that anyone'd care to hear."

"I'm sure you're wrong about that." Isaac tipped his head. "I for one been mighty lookin' forward to hearin' what you have to say."

"Well, you may change your mind." George grumbled, trying to get the buttons on his jacket to meet in the middle. "Should have had Charlotte let this out . . . never mind. Charlotte! Young'uns!" His bellow reminded Isaac of the slam of the blacksmith's hammer. "Into the wagon, we're gonna be late."

Hiding a smile, Isaac turned to saddle Winter. 'Twould seem George Hoffman did not relish speakin' in front of a crowd. Truth be told, who did? Preachers and politicians, that might be the whole of it.

He arrived at church ahead of the Hoffman family, thanks to Winter's easy gait, and slipped into his customary spot in the back. Ahead he saw folks takin' their seats . . . the Caldwells, O'Rourkes, Webers, Kinsleys. Climie and Jesse with the doctor's family. Mr. and Mrs. Jorgensen stopped beside him in the aisle.

"I've got your suit near to finished, Mr. McTavish." Mrs. Jorgensen cocked her brows. "When might you have time to stop by and try it on?"

All business, that woman was. He'd near forgotten about the blasted clothes. "Might tomorrow afternoon work, ma'am?"

She nodded and bustled ahead to her pew. Just ahead of the storekeeper and his wife, Del and RJ took their seats, followed by Lilac and . . . Lark.

Isaac straightened in the pew, pulse pounding. First he'd seen her since that awful night, lyin' so still, her dark hair spread and matted on the pillow. She was still paler than her usual hearty color and thinner. But she held herself erect, her dark eyes sparkling as she nodded and greeted the welcoming friends around her.

Isaac sat back. He'd not spoil her first day back in church. Better she didn't even see him.

But she did see him. He knew the very instant her eyes landed on him, their gazes darting together, then just as quickly apart, like partridges startled from the prairie. A flush suffused her face, and Lark turned away and sat in the pew, facing straight ahead.

Isaac's heart pounded. Did it cause her such pain just to see him? Or did he dare hope for something else?

Mr. Caldwell rose to give the call to worship, and Isaac sat back, trying his best to listen.

Father, I sensed you tell me to stay. I even promised her I would, not that she recollects it. But what else can I do to prove myself to her? I can't just keep skirtin' round her forever, 'twould torment us both.

They were rising for the first hymn. Isaac followed, though his tongue stumbled on the words at first.

> "Nearer, my God, to thee, nearer to thee!
> E'en though it be a cross that raiseth me,
> Still all my song shall be,
> Nearer, my God, to thee,
> Nearer, my God, to thee, nearer to thee!"

Isaac cleared his throat and tried to sing heartier on the next verse. Mrs. Caldwell played alone today, without the Nielsen sisters. Somehow the piano alone threaded the plaintive melody straight to his heart.

> "Though like the wanderer, the sun gone down,
> Darkness be over me, my rest a stone . . ."

That was him all right . . . the wanderer. Always searching, never resting. And now that he was tryin' to stay in one place, his feet and soul itched till he could hardly stand it.

> "There let the way appear, steps unto heav'n;
> All that thou sendest me, in mercy giv'n . . ."

His throat suddenly thick, Isaac tried to swallow. Wasn't this what mattered all along? That in all the twists and trials of his way, all he'd shouldered that wasn't his burden to carry, and all he'd shirked that should have been . . . It all came down to whether he'd let it draw him nearer to his Savior. The One who held all history in His hands and also somehow cared about the life of paltry Isaac McTavish.

Could he believe all the Lord sent him truly was "in mercy given"?

Blinking hard, he mouthed the final words of the chorus.

"Nearer, my God, to thee, nearer to thee!"

Another hymn, then everyone sat. Caldwell spoke, then George rose. But Isaac struggled to focus. He kept looking from the back of Lark's dark head, to the ray of sunlight falling over the simple wooden cross at the front of the church.

Surrender. The word fairly burned into his soul, hot and cleansing as the smithy's coals.

He covered his eyes with his hand. *Father, help me. How can I let her go?*

"I didn't want to let him go."

Isaac's eyes snapped open, and he sat up straight. Hoffman was speaking.

"He was my brother, you understand. A year younger'n me, and I thought I should be the one to sign up, not him. We always had this fool rivalry, and then he had a new wife and a baby on the way to boot." His nerves seeming forgotten, George warmed to his task. He leaned on the pulpit stand, coat open, easing into the storytelling as he often did around the table or fireside with friends and family.

Isaac smiled and sat back to listen. The man had worried over nothin'.

"But he was bound and determined. Stubborn, as younger brothers often are."

"Like me!" Klaus shouted from the congregation. Folks chuckled, and Charlotte hushed her youngest son.

"'Tany rate, off he went, into the Mexican War. And got hisself killed, not three months after."

A hush fell over the congregation. George glanced at his wife. "He left a widow in the family way. So I took it as my duty to marry that woman and raise her child." He nodded. "That was Charlotte right there."

Soft gasps and murmurs scattered. Isaac saw Charlotte shift in her seat and wondered if she'd known George planned to share all this.

"I already cared for her—didn't take long for me to love her." A wistful smile touched the blacksmith's face. "But that baby—you all know him as Caleb—well, seemed we was made to butt heads from the very start. I distinctly recollect havin' a full-on argument with him when he was only six months old." Chuckles spread, but George sighed. "I'm ashamed to say I didn't take that well. He was my brother's child, but I was determined he'd know I was boss. So I took that little boy to task every way I could. I meant well, least I hope I did. Wanted to teach him respect, shape him to be a man. But mostly, I pushed him away."

Charlotte put her arm around Klaus and bowed her head.

George shrugged. "Ain't no secret to any of you that my family's known some trouble these last months. Much of it from my failures over the years. Toward Caleb . . . my son. For he is my son, my flesh and blood, truly as if I'd sired him. And I'm proud of him." The man's mouth worked a moment under his beard. "Sure wish I'd get another chance to tell him so."

Silence hung a moment, then the blacksmith blew out a long whistling breath. "Well, suppose that's what I want to tell you folks. That I hope you won't wait till it's too late to tell your families you love 'em, even if they might drive you wild some days. Remember the gift they are before you lose it forever. Don't be stubborn—stiff-necked the Bible calls it. Let the good Lord tenderize your heart." He swiped his wrist across his eyes and gave a half laugh. "Guess He's been workin' on me."

George sniffed hard and rubbed his beard. "There's a verse Charlotte and me been learnin' by heart with our young'uns. It's from the fourth chapter of Paul's letter to the Ephesians. 'Be ye kind one to another, tenderhearted, forgiving one another, even as God for Christ's sake hath forgiven you.'" He patted the podium and stepped away. "Thanks for listenin', folks."

"Pa?"

A murmur again rustled through the gathering. Caleb Hoffman stood near the side entrance to the church by the corner of the front pew. Eyes fixed on his father.

"Caleb." George stared. "Where have you—I haven't known where you were."

"I've been at the Nielsens', Pa. Helpin' out on their farm." Caleb cast a glance at the sisters' pew. "I'm sorry, but I wouldn't stay unless they promised not to tell you."

George frowned, then rubbed his beard and sighed. "Reckon I deserved that. But, boy, I've been worried sick."

Caleb hesitated. "I'm sorry."

"Caleb." His father took a step toward him, then stopped. "These folks already know, but I'm the one who's sorry. Sorry for so much. I've done a terrible job as your pa. If you coulda heard what I said a few minutes ago . . ."

"Pa." Caleb stepped near and laid his hand on his father's shoulder. "I heard."

George tensed, then his shoulders slumped. "You did?"

"I did. I heard you were goin' to speak this week, and I heard what you said now. And I—I'm sorry too."

Then father and son were in each other's arms, gripping shoulders as if they might never let go again.

Hopefully they wouldn't. Isaac smiled, a lump in his throat, as the congregation broke into applause.

"I think that's the finest conclusion to any sermon I've ever seen." Mr. Caldwell stood, beaming. "And I do believe it's starting to snow outside, so let's close our service and all get home while we can."

Chattering and laughing, families rose and hurried outside, children squealing and reaching to catch the first flakes of drifting snow.

Lord, thank you. Looks like you've taken care of the Hoffmans— and as only you could. Isaac clattered down the church steps and squinted up at the floating flurries. *Now, beg pardon to keep botherin' you like this, but what am I to do about Miss Larkspur?*

Let me take care of that too.

Really? Isaac hushed a chuckle. Well, reckon he didn't have much choice.

All right, Father. Have it your way.

27

"Any mail for me, Mrs. Jorgensen?"

Lark waited for the proprietress to check, breathing deeply of the spiced scent from the apple turnovers on the mercantile counter. So wonderful to be up and about again.

"Here you are. One from your brother Anders."

"Thank you." Lark took the envelope with a smile. "Maybe he'll have news on when we can expect our seed catalogs to come in."

Mrs. Jorgensen tallied Lark's purchases. "Well, let us know. I've already had folks ask about your seeds."

"Really? That's good to hear." Their Leah's Garden dream was drawing so close she could nearly taste it—yet still so much to do before they would know if their business could really fly as they hoped. Getting the catalogs, sending them out, waiting to see if orders came in . . . Lark shook her head at herself and paid her tab. She wound her scarf tighter and carried her bundles to the wagon, squinting against the wind's bite on her eyes and nose. They'd only had intermittent snow since Thanksgiving, but today's thick gray cloud blanket promised more.

She tucked the letter from Anders inside her coat and hupped to the horses. Prince and Nell stepped smartly, as eager to get to warmth and home as she was. The sky gradually darkened as she drove across the prairie, the first flakes falling as she pulled into the machine shed and unhitched the team. She stabled and fed them, grateful to see Lilac had already done the rest of the chores. Bless her.

Hurrying into the soddy, she found Lilac straining the milk.

"How much did we get tonight?" Lark shed her coat and shivered in the warmth beaming from the stove.

"Not much, Buttercup's about ready to go dry again. You didn't get yourself too chilled, did you?"

"I'm fine. I promise. Quit worrying." Lark gave her a side hug, then dipped hot water from the stove reservoir to wash up. "We got a letter from Anders." She laid it on the table as they sat down to eat. "Think it's all right for us to go ahead and read it without the other girls?"

Lilac scrunched up her face, then shrugged. "Seems harder and harder to get all four of us together in one place these days. We can pass it on to Del and Forsythia when we see them." She extended her hands for grace.

After the prayer, they dug into their bowls of beans flavored with salt pork.

"Mmm." Lark savored her bite. "Just right for a snowy night. Thanks for finishing supper off, sister."

"Anytime." Lilac passed the still-steaming corn bread. "Enjoy the butter and make it last. We won't be able to make much more."

Lark finished her piece and wiped the butter from her fingers before slitting open the envelope. "Let's see if our big brother has any news on the catalogs." She withdrew two letters folded separately and examined the names scrawled on each. "Interesting. One for all of us, one just for me."

Lilac cocked a brow. "You aren't secretly sending off submissions to newspapers now, are you?" Last year Lilac and Anders had held a private correspondence as she tried to find a market for her drawings—and eventually did.

"Certainly not. I'll see what that's about later." Lark set hers aside, then unfolded the letter for all of them.

Dear sisters,

We are well and trust you are too. Praying Lark has made a full recovery. Jonah tries to walk farther each day, though Josephine begs him to be careful on the icy streets. He has made it up to a mile and a half each way, showing his leg strength is indeed returning. So much to be thankful for.

I wanted to let you know I was informed that the catalog shipment will be delayed till after Christmas, but hopefully you will receive them by mid-January, still in time to send out for spring orders. I have requested two hundred as you asked. Let me know right away if you want that adjusted.

We missed you at Thanksgiving as always but had a nice time with Josephine's family. One bit of news from us is we are expecting another little one, Josephine thinks around May or so. She tires easily but is doing well and sends her love, as do Marcella and Greta, and Jonah, of course.

Ever your brother,
Anders

Lark and Lilac exchanged grins.

"Another baby on the way." Lark shook her head and folded the letter. "This next Nielsen generation sure is growing by leaps and bounds."

"Maybe Anders will get a boy this time."

"And maybe the next baby in our clan will be yours."

Lilac's cheeks pinked, and she ducked her head. "Maybe."

Lark chuckled, then stifled a sigh. If she hadn't been so stubborn over Isaac, would she have had a chance at being a mother one of these days? But that possibility seemed past. She'd barely seen Isaac for weeks, let alone spoken. RJ said he'd been spending long days working at the Hoffmans', and at church he slipped in late and left early. As was his wont.

"I will never leave you."

Lark blinked the words away. They only hurt, knowing they were not memory but her own wishful thinking.

They did the dishes, then sat around the lamplit table for a while, Lilac sketching her next installment for the *New York Weekly*, Lark working on a list of places to mail their catalogs. The fire crackled in the stove, Scamp lying at Lilac's feet.

At a quarter to nine, Lilac yawned. "Think I'd better turn in, or I'm going to mess up this drawing. You coming?"

"Soon."

Lilac gave her a look.

"Really soon, I promise. Goodness, how long are you going to hover over me?"

"Till I'm sure you're not going to nearly work yourself into an early grave again."

"I really am almost finished."

"Fine." Lilac came behind her and hugged her shoulders. "Night."

"Night."

Lark added a couple more addresses, then closed her books. She reached to turn down the kerosene lamp, then hesitated, seeing Anders's letter to her lying near. It would only take a few minutes. Drawing her shawl more tightly about her shoulders, she leaned closer to the flickering light and opened the single, closely written page.

Dear Lark,

Ever since my visit this fall, I can't get something off my mind. So I'm writing to you, though you may think I'm interfering. If so, then what are older brothers for?

It's Isaac McTavish. Lark, that man cares for you—I'd be willing to wager he loves you. You'll wonder how I know. Well, I talked with him a bit. Not much, and he said even less. But it was enough to see how he feels and that he's convinced you want nothing to do with him.

Trouble is, I'm not sure that's the case, just that you're too stubborn to admit it. I know you're used to doing things yourself, Lark, carrying the weight of the family on your shoulders—even more than I do, for all I'm the eldest. But I wish for once you'd have the humility to listen to others and even to your own heart.

You've got a good man there, and he cares for you. Heaven knows he showed it enough taking over the farm while you were ill. And if I were a betting man I'd wager you care for him too. So you're throwing all that away because of what? Pride? Fear? Neither one's worth beans in this life or the next.

At least think about it, little sister. (I'm the only one who can call you that, you know.) Even better, pray about it.

> *With love from your brother,*
> *Anders*

Lark folded the letter, then sat rubbing the folds between her fingers for some time. Her heart ached. *Anders, you don't know the whole. Yes, I was a fool, but it's too late. I told Isaac no, and now I don't think he wants me anymore. If he did . . . why would he hardly even speak to me?*

Have you tried talking to him?

Was that the Lord's voice or her brother's? Or merely her own continuous inner debate? Snorting at herself, Lark blew out the lamp.

The snow set in for good over the next few weeks. Caleb Hoffman, now living back with his family again, came out to help them finish winterizing the barn and string a rope between the barn and soddy for safe passage in case of blizzards. And before Lark knew it, it was almost Christmas.

After snowfall all week, Christmas Eve dawned clear, and they drove the wagon, with sled runners attached, over a snowy white world crusted like a sugar loaf. The sky blazed with evening gold and rose as they headed into the church for the Christmas Eve program.

Lark squeezed Lilac's hand beside her in the pew as several lamps lit up the "stage" at the front of the church. Robbie, cast as the lead role in Sam's new play, stood garbed in a shepherd's robe, a gangly-legged lamb in his arms.

"Someone had an early lambing," Lark whispered to her sister.

"The Webers, surprised them too. Sam says they've been keeping it in the house and hand-feeding," Lilac whispered back.

Bethany Kinsley, also dressed in shepherd's garb, entered the stage and glared at Robbie.

"Joel, when are you going to stop coddling that lamb? It's got to learn to join the flock."

"But it's mine. He trusts me." Robbie held the lamb tighter and lifted his chin, determination in his eyes.

Lark's heart swelled as the little play unfolded, catching her up in the story and bringing tears to her eyes and laughter to her lips. Sam had a gift with words as surely as Lilac did with a pencil, and the children threw themselves into their parts wholeheartedly.

She pressed her knuckles to her mouth to stem the tears when Robbie knelt on the stage near the end, mourning for his little lost lamb.

"Please, Lord," he cried. "I know you probably don't care about one little lamb . . . but you're the only one who knows where he is. Please, help me find him."

And just then came the flooding light of the heavenly chorus—or more correctly, a bright lantern and a half dozen children in white robes, including a beaming Sofie. But teary laughter rose in Lark's throat as she watched the young shepherd be lifted out of his troubles by the news of a Messiah born that day in the city of David, a Savior, Christ the Lord. And when he hurried along with the other shepherds to the manger, he found not only his lost lamb lying there, warm and safe, but the Lamb of God bringing good news for all people.

Lilac jumped to her feet at the conclusion to start the applause, and Lark followed suit to stand along with most of the congregation, clapping till her palms stung.

"Robbie, you were wonderful." She clasped him close amid the milling chatter afterward. "You made me cry."

"I did?" He craned back, brows drawing together. "I didn't mean to, Tante Lark."

"I just mean you touched my heart, Robbie boy." She smoothed his hair. "The play was beautiful."

"Oh." He beamed. "I'm glad you liked it. Oops, I need to go get Mikael." And he ran off after his busy little brother.

Lark hugged Sofie next, assuring her she'd been a beautiful angel. Then Jesse and Climie came over, and she embraced Climie, smiling to see her friend's blooming face and figure.

"We need to have a sewing circle for some baby clothes for you."

"That'd be nice." Climie glanced up at her husband, who hovered at her side, his gentle face wreathed in a smile. "Jesse's already near finished with the cradle."

"I'm sure it's a beautiful one." Jesse had such a gift with wood.

The young couple headed over to see Del and baby Lily, and Lark glanced around at the various happy knots of conversation. There were Lilac and Sam talking with some of the students, their faces animated. The Caldwells visiting with Forsythia and Adam. And William deep in some discussion with Isaac.

Lark drew a steadying breath. Would her heart always catch so at the sight of him? Though something did seem different about him tonight. But she needed to get over this—they lived in the same small town, after all. And at this point, it would seem Isaac had every intention of staying.

A fine time for him to decide on that.

Well, she couldn't avoid him forever. She'd been raised better. And best to confront a problem straight on. When William moved on toward Jesse, Lark strode up to Isaac, never mind that her insides wouldn't stop trembling.

"Merry Christmas, Isaac." She ordered her lips to smile.

He quirked a brow, then gave a courtly nod. "Merry Christmas to you, Miss Larkspur."

A dreadful silence hung then, despite the merry hum around them.

Say something, Lark. "You and William looked deep in conversation."

He nodded. "He was tellin' me about his progress with tryin' to locate his brother."

"Oh." Lark's heart lifted. "He's made progress?" It had been too long since she asked.

Isaac tipped his head. "Well, might be I overstated a touch. But he's at least learned through the Freedmen's Bureau where his brother was before the war's end. Now he's writin' more letters, seein' if he can track down where he headed after."

Lark bit her lip. "I can't imagine. If I didn't know where one of my sisters was for years on end . . ."

"Hard to figure, ain't it? Though come down to it, I don't know where my sisters are either. Best I can learn, they married and moved elsewhere. That's a sight different than not knowing whether they're dead or alive after bein' enslaved."

Lark swallowed. So much she took for granted. And so much she still didn't know of Isaac's story, let alone William's. Regret pinched her throat. "Isaac . . ." Suddenly it struck her what was so different. "You got a new suit." She nearly clapped her hand over her mouth, so abruptly did the words blurt out.

Isaac chuckled. "So I did. Courtesy of Mrs. Jorgensen."

"I beg your pardon." Her ears burned. "I didn't mean to . . . I've just never seen you in . . . except for that suit you wore at the Valentine party last winter." Where he'd first danced with her, setting her heart to winging in a way she'd refused to process at the time. Lark averted her eyes, the heat traveling to her cheeks at the memory of their second dance at the celebration last summer. A mercy he couldn't read her mind.

"Ah yes, borrowed that 'un off one of RJ's crew to look halfway decent for the occasion." Isaac shrugged. "I liked my old uniform well enough, but seems it didn't feel the same way. 'Twas fallin' to pieces from my shoulders."

"Well, I'm glad Mrs. Jorgensen was able to assist." Lark drew a breath. "Isaac . . . would you join us for Christmas dinner tomorrow? We're meeting at Forsythia's again since they have the most room."

He cocked his head, brows raised. "You want me there?"

"I do." She pressed on a smile she hoped he could see was sincere. "Why, you've been with us every Christmas since our first in Salton. It wouldn't seem like Christmas without you."

An answering smile glimmered beneath his beard. "Then I'll come. And thank ye."

Christmas dinner passed the next day with less awkwardness than Lark had dared hope, thanks in large part to the children's welcome distraction. Their glee over Jesse and William's gift of a wooden barn with real working doors, stalls, and even milking stanchions for their carved animals kept smiles on everyone's faces through the evening. Lilac's gifts also brought oohs and ahs as she handed out enlarged drawings from Farfar Nielsen's journal: families crowding the ship's rail to sail into the New York harbor for Forsythia and Adam, the log cabin being built for Del and RJ, the brave little sloop sailing the Atlantic for Lark.

"These are treasures, Lilac." Lark hugged her hard. "Thank you."

The only tricky part came when Isaac left. He asked her to follow him to the door, then held out a slender package, simply wrapped in brown paper and twine.

"'Fraid I don't have anythin' for your sisters." He clasped his hands behind his back. "But I hoped you might could find a use for this."

She unwrapped the package, her fingers suddenly clumsy. And swallowed hard at the graceful curve of the cast-iron ladle in her hand. It had even, delicate scrollwork on the handle, and her initials were stamped on the underside, *LGN*. How had he known her middle name?

"Thank you. I love it." She glanced up to see a look in Isaac's eyes that stole her breath as quickly as an icy wind.

"Merry Christmas, Larkspur." His voice husky, he made a hasty bow and hurried out before even buttoning his coat, the door banging behind him.

Lark pressed the cool handle of the ladle to her chin, her eyes blurring. *Oh, Lord . . . is Anders right? Does he truly still care? But if so, what am I supposed to do about it?*

She barely saw Isaac over the next weeks, a January blizzard hunkering everyone down and even stopping the trains for a few days. At last a milder spell cleared the tracks—and brought the Leah's Garden seed catalogs.

"They're beautiful." Del smoothed her hands over the covers again, as they all sat gathered at her table to pore over the catalogs. "Lilac, you outdid yourself."

"So did the printer Anders found. I didn't know he was going to do the cover in color." Lilac shook her head. "Anders must have paid the extra himself, bless him."

"And I love the logo you designed." Forsythia let a wriggling Nils slide off her lap and crawl over to the rug to play with Sofie.

"All our namesake flowers entwined under Ma's name . . . it's perfect."

"All that remains is to mail them out." Lark glanced around the table and held up her list. "I've got the addresses here. If we all work together, we should be able to get them out soon. We're already running a bit behind for when people start to order seeds."

"Well, let's have at it, then." Lilac extended her hands.

All that week they packaged and addressed, readying the catalogs to arrive at every mercantile and general store within the surrounding territory, and a number back east as well. At last, on a sunny morning the first week of February, Lark laid the last labeled catalog atop the stack with a sigh.

"There. I think that's all of them."

"Let's pray over them, shall we?" Forsythia extended her hands to her sisters.

Leave it to Sythia. Lark bowed her head, a sudden pricking in her eyes.

"Father, we thank you for our beloved mother and her dream of a flower seed company to bless others with the beauty and joy of your creation. Thank you for taking us this far in bringing Leah's Garden to life. Bless each catalog as it goes out and guide them into the hands of each person you want them to reach. Make our seeds a blessing, Lord, and sow them as far and wide as you will. In Christ's name we ask it, amen."

"Amens" echoed with hands squeezed around the circle.

Lark headed into town, the stacks of catalogs beside her in the trap. The bell jingled on the mercantile door as she pushed through, arms piled high.

"Land sakes, Miss Lark." Mrs. Jorgensen clucked. "Would those be your catalogs at last?"

"They are." Peeking around her load, Lark made her way to the counter and set them down with a sigh of relief. "Do you have time to help me post them here, or shall I take them to the station?"

"Just give me a moment."

The bell jangled behind them again, bringing in a gust of cold air. Lark turned to see Mr. Owens, the telegraph operator, hurry in.

The wiry little man's eyes sparked when he saw her. "Thank goodness. I was just coming in to ask if Mrs. Jorgensen might know where to find you." He held out the unmistakable slip of yellow paper. "Telegram for you, Miss Nielsen. From your brother."

Her heart quickening, Lark took the paper and read.

Slate Ringwald reported to be on his way west STOP Folks say still talking about revenge STOP Don't know details please be careful STOP Praying STOP

28

W hat should we do?"
Lilac pressed her mittened hands together, her
insides all wound tight. Her sisters stood with her
in a huddle outside the church Sunday morning, heads bent
together against the February chill.

Del snuggled Lily closer in her layers of bundling. "I wish
we had a sheriff in Salton."

"What would we even tell him? It's not like we have an actual
threat."

"Or do we? Anders said he didn't know any details."

Lark shook her head. "I can't believe Ringwald would come
all the way out here just because I beat him at cards over three
years ago. Maybe it's still just rumors." A thread of doubt un-
dercut the firmness in her words.

"And surely he doesn't know where we are, anyway," Forsythia
added.

Lilac shivered. "But what if he does? What if he saw me in the
saloon last summer and figured something out? Or somehow
saw one of our seed catalogs and put two and two together?"

"Those haven't even had time to arrive anywhere yet. Certainly not before Anders's telegram."

"Seems the best we can do is be watchful and tell our close friends in town so they can keep an eye out also. RJ keeps his gun by the door. You girls do too, right?" Del shifted Lily and scanned Lark's and Lilac's faces.

They nodded.

"Morning, ladies." Sam stopped beside them, his breath puffing in the frosty air. "Folks are going in. Lilac, are you ready?"

She nodded and slipped her hand through his arm. He pressed it as they headed up the church steps and into the relative warmth of the building.

"You're awfully quiet. Everything all right?"

"I don't know." Sighing, she followed him into her family's pew, where he'd begun joining them since their engagement. "I'll tell you about it after the service."

Lark beckoned to her from the side aisle, and Lilac jumped up again, having forgotten she was to play today. She took her fiddle from her sister, then hurried to her place up front by the piano.

Mr. Caldwell stood to welcome the congregation, leaning a bit harder on his cane than usual—his war wound must be acting up with the cold. His smile came as warm as ever, though. "Welcome, friends. This is the day the Lord has made."

"Let us rejoice and be glad in it!" came the hearty response.

Lilac's lips formed the words, but gladness escaped her today. Her middle still knotted with worry. She closed her eyes for an instant. *Lord, help me trust you. I'm afraid.*

"Before we begin the service, I wanted to share with you all some wonderful news," Mr. Caldwell said. "The committee we formed over the summer to search for a new pastor has successfully chosen a candidate. The Reverend Paul Fordham, an experienced minister with a wife and grown children, will be coming to visit our congregation in March. After he gives a candidate sermon, all our members will have the chance to vote to confirm him as our new pastor—a position he will then assume if approved by the congregation."

Applause broke out, grins spreading from one pew to another.

The attorney beamed out over the congregation. "I see you share my enthusiasm. I am exceedingly grateful for how the Lord has led us in this search, and I look forward to us all having a chance to meet Reverend Fordham. Now, let us rise for our first hymn, 'Guide Me, O Thou Great Jehovah.'"

Lilac lifted her fiddle to her chin to play, the words coming as automatically to her lips as the tune to her fingers.

> "Guide me, O thou great Jehovah,
> Pilgrim through this barren land.
> I am weak, but thou art mighty;
> Hold me with thy powerful hand."

Her throat tightened. What a hymn for them this morning. They were indeed weak, but God was mighty.

> "Open now the crystal fountain,
> Whence the healing stream doth flow;
> Let the fire and cloudy pillar
> Lead me all my journey through.
> Strong Deliverer, strong Deliverer,
> Be thou still my Strength and Shield."

The hymn ended, and Lilac followed Lark to sit back down, the knots loosening in her middle. She slid her hand into Sam's beside her, the warm pressure of his fingers on hers calming her further, as he always seemed to. The Nielsen sisters had been through many a trial since that sudden scramble to leave Ohio nearly four years ago, yet the Lord had indeed led them all their journey through. Surely He wasn't about to stop now.

Mr. Caldwell rose to speak again. "On this day of announcing our pastoral candidate, it seems fitting to have share with us the man who started us on this idea in the first place—that is, to use this interim time in our church to hear from various members of this body. And hasn't it been a worthwhile endeavor?"

Nods and murmurs through the rows.

"I heartily agree. So please join me in welcoming Isaac Mc-Tavish to share with us today."

With a flicker of surprise, Lilac joined in the clapping. She snuck a glance at Lark beside her. By the look on her sister's face, she hadn't had an inkling this was coming either.

Oh, Lark. When will you ever let your guard down? Lilac wound her fingers in her lap. Everybody else could see how Lark and Isaac felt about each other. Were they just trying to see who could out stubborn the other? *Lord, help them too. There's so much we need your help with . . . but isn't that always the case?* Lilac blew out a breath as Isaac walked up the aisle. *Thanks for being with us in all of it anyway. And please help my sister be brave enough to open her heart.*

Isaac turned at the front of the church to face the congregation, sliding his hands into the pockets of his old, threadbare army coat. Funny he wasn't wearing the new suit they'd seen on him of late, but he must have a reason.

"Mornin', folks." Isaac propped one foot on the rung of the chair Caldwell had set near. "I thank y'all for the privilege of sharin' with you today. Don't feel worthy of it, to be sure, but I reckon that's true for all of us. And I know I've been blessed by hearin' testimonies of the Lord's faithfulness from those who've shared this year, and been humbled by your willin'ness to take my little idea and go with it. So I reckoned I'd just share a bit of my own story here today." He drew a breath and passed a hand over his beard. "Some of which I've never told another soul, truth be told, so I thank you for bearin' with me."

Lilac cocked her head and sat up straighter. Would Isaac really bring some of his mysterious past to light?

"Reckon y'all know I was in the war." He spread his hands to lift the corners of his army jacket, bringing chuckles. "Ain't been somethin' I've tried to hide, nohow. But other things . . . other things I have been hidin' from, ever since the fightin' ended, I'll confess. I remember the first night I met any of you. It was the Nielsen sisters on their journey west." He glanced at their pew, and Lark's arm tensed by Lilac's. "I told them then I'd fought for the Union and had kin on both sides, mayhap like some of you." He glanced at the Hoffman pew. "Even said I'd been in a Confederate prison camp, as had their brother Anders. But I didn't tell them it was Andersonville."

A murmur swept through the gathering. Isaac nodded. "Yep, the one where they hanged Captain Wirz, the prison commandant, for war crimes after the war. I won't tell y'all much. You don't need me dredgin' up all the horrors. But what I do want to tell today is that I was there with my brother." Isaac inhaled hard through his nose. "I told the Nielsens back then my brothers both died in battle. Well, that weren't quite true, and I'm sorry."

Lilac met his eyes, hoping he could tell she bore no malice. Isaac glanced from her to Lark, held his gaze there a moment, then shifted to the rest of the congregation.

"Truth is, I still hadn't quite faced it myself. But it's my fault my brother died at that awful place. See, we were plannin' to escape. We and another prisoner had been diggin' a tunnel for months, a bit at a time, all the way under the prison walls and to the outside yonder. Some had done the like before and been shot, but a few had gotten out. We thought we had a chance, and we'd reached where we could tell we'd only a few feet to go. The next night was goin' to be it. Then that night, I come down with the runs." He winced. "Sorry, ladies. Believe they call it dysentery. Anyways, I weren't fit to move. I told my brother and our friend to go ahead, leave me behind. Take their best chance and not worry about me." He rubbed his knee and drew a long breath. "They didn't want to, but I convinced them to go. And they were caught—and shot. No trial, just dropped where they stood, seconds after climbing out of our tunnel to freedom." Isaac paused, his jaw working.

Silence hung, as if the entire gathering held their breath. At last he cleared his throat. "Few weeks later, most of us got moved to other camps. Next spring, after the war ended, I went home, found my parents gone and our farm ravaged. So I took to the road with nothin' but my army bag and bedroll and the uniform on my back. And I never rightly stopped . . . not till I landed in a little town called Salton."

"Didn't really stop here either at first," someone called out behind them.

Lilac frowned over her shoulder.

But Isaac merely rubbed his beard and nodded. "True. I still couldn't bring myself to stay in one place for too long. But I kept comin' back here. This little town grabbed hold of my heart in a way I couldn't rightly figure for a while. Then I realized it weren't the town. It was the people in it. Closest I'd known to kin since I lost my own." His gaze rested on the Nielsen pew again. "These last months, I've realized a lot of things. One, that it ain't no use tryin' to outrun the past. The past is behind us, but its mold shapes us, and denyin' that . . . well, we neither can nor should. Two, that it can be a heap harder to stay than to leave. But sometimes that might just be why the Lord asks us to do it—because He's still at work shapin' all of us, surely as the blacksmith does the iron, if we let Him. And three . . ." He paused again. "Three, that love is a whole lot more powerful than regret. And even if it ain't returned, letting God's love have His way in our hearts is mighty worth it."

Isaac blew out a long breath and lowered his foot from the chair, straightening. "Well, folks, I reckon that's about all I have to say. Let me leave you with a Scripture my ma quoted so often I can't recollect a time when I didn't have it put to memory. 'Trust in the Lord with all thine heart; and lean not unto thine own understanding. In all thy ways acknowledge him, and he shall direct thy paths.'" He dipped his head once more. "Might we all take that to heart."

Lilac couldn't restrain herself from reaching to squeeze Lark's hand as Isaac stepped quickly back down the aisle. She wanted to shake her sister and whisper, *"See? He's talking about you!"* But Lark sat staring straight ahead, lips pressed together, though her color rose high and her breath came quickly.

Lilac sighed and slumped back against the pew. At this point, she wasn't sure if even Isaac shouting from the housetops would make much difference.

Sam walked her out after service, and they greeted Jesse and Climie, William, and the Brownsvilles.

"So what's going on?" Sam drew her aside near the corner of the church building. "You and Lark both seem jumpy today."

Lilac blew out a breath. "Lots is going on. But the most pressing thing is that we got a telegram from Anders." She explained as briefly as she could, and Sam's brows drew together.

"Have you contacted a sheriff?"

"The nearest one is in Lincoln, and right now we don't really have anything to tell him. Lawmen don't put much stock in rumors and hearsay."

"But there must be something we can do." Sam laid his hand on her shoulder, face flushing. "I'd offer to come sleep out at the farm, except I'm afraid that wouldn't be proper just now."

Lilac smiled up at him. "You're a true knight in shining armor, but I think we'll be all right. RJ is within shouting distance, and Lark and I are both crack shots."

Sam raised a brow and sighed. "Are you now? Well, I suppose all I can do is pray. But you'll let me know if there's anything else, anything at all?"

"I will." She patted his arm. "Did you still want to go over wedding plans tomorrow?"

"I do. But should you leave Lark just now?"

"I have to come into town tomorrow to mail some more drawings anyway, but I won't stay late."

"I'll see you at the school right after dismissal, then." He glanced about, then, since no one near looked on, bent to kiss her.

Lilac hurried to find her sisters, schooling away her smile since such serious matters lay afoot. The smile faded of its own accord when she saw Lark standing by the wagon, watching Isaac visit with a cluster of men. The loneliness and longing on her sister's face made Lilac's chest clench.

Lark, will you just admit that he loves you? And you love him?

Had Isaac really been talking about her in church?

Lark sat at the kitchen table Monday after their simple midday meal, packaging seeds and trying to keep from labeling marigolds as zinnias or any other tomfoolery. If only Isaac's words from yesterday would stop circling through her mind like a persistent fly.

"Love is a whole lot more powerful than regret . . . even if it ain't returned."

Lark grabbed for another can of seeds and knocked over a different one, sending phlox seeds scattering all over the table and onto the floor.

"Of all the . . ." She smacked her hand on the table, then dove beneath to start gathering up the seeds. They couldn't afford to lose even a few.

"You all right?" Lilac hurried in, buttoning her coat.

"Fine." Lark winced at the bite in her own voice. "Going to town?"

"If you're sure you don't mind." Lilac hesitated. "I can wait another day or two if you think that would be safer."

"Go ahead." Lark pinched up the last of the seeds she could see in the light from the window, she'd have to get a broom for the rest. The packed earth floor made it even harder to see them. She pushed to her feet. "RJ is working on the Leah's Garden addition to their place, so I'll be fine. We can't live every day waiting for a man who might never show up."

Lilac eyed her, as if wondering if she meant Ringwald or someone else. "All right, then. I'm supposed to meet Sam at the school afterward to talk about the wedding, so I might not be home till chores."

"It's fine." *Just go already.* Lark flinched at even thinking that.

Lilac pressed her lips together, then picked up her folder of drawings and hurried out the door.

Alone at last, Lark sorted and packaged till the ticking silence made her want to scream. She was a regular crotchety old woman today, cross with company, cross without. Whatever happened to her trusting the Lord with all things, as she prided herself on doing? She finished the tins of seeds she'd set on the table for today and wrapped a shawl over her sweater. Maybe some fresh air would help. She'd go hunting, but her sisters would have her head for setting out on her own, especially right now. Maybe Lilac and Jesse or William would go with her later in the week. Her mouth watered at the thought of fresh venison. They'd been living off rabbit and squirrel from Lilac's traps l ately.

She tramped through the patchy snow to the barn. Inside Starbright's Rose stuck her head over a stall and nickered, and Lark rubbed her velvety nose, breathing in the balm of hay and horses. "You all sure are a lot less complicated than people."

"Lark?" RJ's call came from the door.

"Here." She sighed and ducked outside.

"I need some more nails, didn't realize I was running so low. You have any in the machine shed? I don't want to go so far as town just now."

Lark nodded. "There should be a can on a shelf toward the back."

RJ turned, then spun back around and leaned his hand on the side of the barn. "May I ask you a question?"

"Sure."

"How long do you intend to make that man wait?"

She stared at him. "What man?"

"Isaac McTavish, who do you think?"

Lark huffed a laugh. "I don't believe this. Are you and Anders conspiring against me?"

"Anders?"

"He sent a letter . . . never mind." Her eyes suddenly burned. "But I honestly don't see why it's any of your business, either of you."

"Because we care about you, Lark." RJ puffed a breath and took a step closer. "I know a thing or two about being stubborn myself, and I sure am glad I finally let you folks here in Salton get through to me. So I'm asking what's it going to take to get through to you?"

"About what?" Lark spread her arms. "What on earth is it you want me to do?"

RJ opened his mouth, then closed it and shook his head. "The man loves you, Lark. It's plain to everyone else around but you. But you're so determined to live life alone you're missing the gift God's put right in front of you." He clapped his hat on his head. "I just hope you open your eyes before it's too late."

Lark stared after him till he disappeared into the machine shed. Then with a whirl, she stormed into the barn, shutting the door so hard Rose startled back in her stall.

"Sorry, girl." Shoulders slumping, Lark headed over and rubbed the filly's forehead, then leaned her own against it. And the tears came, hot and spotting Rose's winter coat. Lark swiped the backs of her hands across her eyes, then gave up, buried her face in her arms atop the stall door, and sobbed, the filly gently nosing the elbow of her sweater.

At last she mopped her eyes with her shawl and climbed up

into the hayloft, sinking onto a clean pile of hay and sniffing back the clogging in her nose. She hugged her knees close and laid her head on them, wishing she could just be a little girl at her mother's knee again. Before life got hard and she had to be the grown-up and make decisions for everyone, never being sure if they were right or wrong.

I'm so tired, Lord. Of course I don't want to go through life alone. Why do they all think I'm so set on that? Of course I'd rather have a strong and good man by my side. Of course I love Isaac. Her eyes filled with hot tears again. *I love him, Lord, I do. But I thought . . . I thought a solitary life was what you were calling me to. And I've been afraid he'd just leave again, afraid his saying he loved me was too good to be true. Afraid to believe you might actually give me such a gift.* She leaned her weary head on the heels of her hands and let all the weight seep out of her in one long shuddering breath. *I'm sorry.*

She sat there awhile, resting her head on her knees. Heard RJ come out of the machine shed and head off. Let the dozy comfort of the barn loft wrap around her like a hug till she nearly fell asleep.

What is it you would have me do, Lord?

Scamp barked outside, a sharp, shrill bark.

Lark jerked her head up, then scrambled to her feet, senses on high alert. That wasn't a greeting for RJ or Lilac. That was Scamp's danger bark. Coyotes again? Or, worse, wolves? She stepped to the loft window and looked out below.

All seemed quiet, the sheep in the corral, no fuss from the henhouse. A gentle curl of smoke from the chimney of the soddy.

Then she heard it: distant hoofbeats. And saw a lone rider coming up the lane.

Scamp barked again, running toward the lane, then planting himself. He growled, a rumbled threat she could hear clear up in the loft.

The rider, clad in a long black coat, drew near. He brought his horse to a stop and sat there, scanning the land. Scamp barked again, and Lark reached for the pitchfork beside her, her heartbeat coming in painful thuds.

Ringwald. She knew it even before the gambler threw back his head and hollered her name.

"Lark! Larkspur Nielsen!"

She shuddered, gripping the pitchfork handle. He had actually come. All their worries, all their carefulness over these years—somehow, he had found them. Oh, why did she have to be up here away from her gun?

Perhaps she could just hide till he went away. *Thank you, Father, that Lilac is in town.* But Del and RJ and baby Lily were only a short ways away at the other house. *Lord, please, keep Ringwald's focus here. Or bring RJ back alone.* She'd scream for RJ, but then the gambler would know where she was.

"Larkspur Nielsen! You come out of there, woman, or I'm comin' in after you." He doubled over with a fit of coughing, nearly falling off his horse. Then righted himself and dug under his coat, pulling a revolver from his hip.

Her breath came fast, pulse pounding in her ears.

"Make a fool of me, will you?" Shakily, he raised the gun and nudged his horse toward the soddy. "Humiliate me, in front of everyone? Beaten by a woman, they said. No one took me serious after that. Career went downhill from that very day. Debts pilin' high. And now I'm dying, they tell me. Well, I'm not leavin' this earth till I've a chance to get even with the person who ruined my life."

Scamp darted in front of him, barking till his whole body shook with it. Cursing, Ringwald lowered the gun to point at the young cattle dog.

"No!" Lark dropped the pitchfork and scrambled for the ladder. She dashed out of the barn, halting a few yards from the gambler. "Ringwald, wait. I'm here."

He veered his horse toward her, swinging the gun away from Scamp. A slow smile spread over his haggard face, revealing the glint of a gold tooth she remembered. His clothes were less fine, though. They'd seen several seasons of wear and hung on his frame.

"You." His voice laced the word with venom.

"I'm here, Ringwald." Lark raised her hands. "Please don't shoot. We can talk this out."

"Thought you'd gotten away from me, didn't you?" He coughed again, then waved his revolver at the surrounding farm, his finger dangerously near the trigger.

"How did you find us?" Lark managed to keep her voice steady.

"Luck, you might say." He rasped a laugh. "Finally found my luck again after all these years. Fittin', all things considered."

"How?"

"You don't think I'd leave that town without a friend or two stayin' behind to be my eyes and ears, do you? Feller of mine saw a parcel layin' in the post office there in Linksburg. Big package addressed to the Nielsens in Salton, Nebraska. Figured that made a lead worth followin' up on."

Lark tightened her grip on the pitchfork. The seed catalogs. After they'd been so careful for so long . . . It must have been the size of the package that got it left sitting out like that.

"Homesteading and a seed business, eh?" He narrowed his gaze. "Tall order for a bunch of women. But you seem to like pastimes not befittin' a young lady."

"I regret some of my behavior that evening those years ago." Lark tried to swallow. "But I was only trying to help my brother. And I beat you fair and square, sir. You have nothing to charge me with. Please, put the gun down, and let's put this behind us once and for all."

He barked a laugh, then bent over coughing again, his gun dangling against the side of his leg.

Could she lunge at him, grab the gun before he set it off? Lark measured the distance and angle with her eyes, calculating the odds.

"Behind us?" He wheezed a breath and met her eyes, the emptiness there stunning her soul. "My whole life is behind me. At least let me leave it with some satisfaction." He raised the revolver and cocked it in one motion.

With a snarl, Scamp launched himself at Ringwald's foot, hanging on to his boot. The gambler swore and lunged forward toward the dog, falling off his horse with his foot caught in the stirrup. His gun exploded in a puff of smoke as the horse bolted.

Something zinged Lark's scalp before she even heard the shot. She seemed to fall slowly, hearing Ringwald's yell, seeing him dragged along the ground by the stirrup. She was glad she was alone, that her sisters weren't here to see this, that they were safe. Her head slammed the ground, and all went dark.

29

M r. McTavish? You ain't seen RJ around, have you?"
Isaac looked up from shaping nails on the anvil to
see Mr. Jorgensen's worried face peeking in the door.
"No, sir, I haven't. Somethin' amiss?"

"I hope not." The wiry little storekeeper hesitated. "Just that
this feller came into the mercantile little while ago, askin' about
the Nielsen sisters and the whereabouts of their farm. Somethin'
didn't set right about him."

"What did you tell him?" Isaac dropped his hammer and
reached the doorway in two strides.

"Nothing—I'm no fool." Jorgensen hesitated. "But I'm not
sure where he went next, and I got to worrying. Plenty of other
people he could talk to in this town. So I thought if you'd seen
RJ, I'd tell him—"

His voice faded as Isaac ran for the stable.

His fingers fumbled with Winter's saddle straps. *Come on.*
Maybe he shouldn't even bother with the saddle. He'd talked to
Adam at church yesterday and learned from him about Anders's
telegram regarding the gambler Lark had bested long ago. This
stranger had to be him—or if not, Isaac wasn't going to take
the time to find out.

Hurry, hurry. His gut urged him forward. He trotted Winter out of the stable and swung onto her back, gripping with his knees.

"Tell Dr. Brownsville," he hollered at Mr. Jorgensen, who still stood by the forge, now with George Hoffman. Wheeling Winter away from their staring faces, Isaac bent forward and kicked her into a gallop.

Dear God, please, protect Lark and her family, please. His prayers kept time with the beat of Winter's hooves and thump of his heart. He couldn't form more words than that. The good Lord would have to take care of the rest.

A gunshot pierced the air as he turned into the Nielsens' lane. Isaac urged Winter still faster. Reaching the Nielsen barnyard, he slid from his horse before she even stopped and took in the scene at a glance. A stranger lying on the ground near the corral, foot tangled in his snorting horse's stirrup, a gun in his motionless hand. And a few yards away, sprawled just in front of the barn . . . Lark.

Dear God, no. He crashed to his knees at her side, pushing aside the whining young cattle dog. "Good boy." Blood pooled beneath her head from a wound on her scalp.

"Lark?" He yanked the scarf from his neck to press to her wound, then cradled her head onto his lap. "Lark, darlin', it's Isaac. Can you hear me?"

She moaned and turned her head slightly.

Oh, God, thank you. Praise your mighty name. "I'm here, Larkspur. You're gonna be fine. Lie easy now." He wound his scarf about her head tight as he could, binding the blood-matted hair close, then shed his coat to wrap around her. If only he had his gloves to cover her hands, purpling with the cold, but he'd left in too much of a hurry.

No, not hurry enough. His chest clamped with rage at the man lying by the corral. *She's alive. Focus on that.*

A pounding of footsteps and RJ came dashing toward them. "I heard the shot, is she—?"

"She's alive but bleedin' bad." Isaac hoisted Lark into his arms and stood. "I'm takin' her to Adam. Help me."

RJ supported Lark's weight while Isaac swung onto Winter, then helped prop her against him. Lark moaned, her eyelashes fluttering.

"Easy there, darlin'." Isaac leaned his cheek against her head to steady her, wrapping his arms around her to grip the reins. "I've got you."

"I'll see about this lowlife here, then be right behind you." RJ slapped Winter's rump to start her off.

Holding Lark firm against him, Isaac glanced back to see RJ bending over the gambler's motionless body.

A wave of hate rocked him, so searing he sucked a breath and closed his eyes against it. *Lord, vengeance is thine, and I trust you have repaid. Now protect this precious child of yours. Help me get her safely to Adam. Help her to live.*

The two miles pounded away with his prayers. Soon and not soon enough, they clattered to a stop in front of the hospital, Adam and Forsythia already out front.

"Jorgensen told us you took off. What happened?"

"Ringwald. Her head. I think a bullet just grazed her, but—"

Arms reached out, easing Lark down. Jesse appeared from nowhere to help carry her inside. Isaac dropped to his feet beside Winter and patted her heaving sides, his legs quaking like a newborn foal's. He shook himself, looped Winter's reins to the hitching post, and leaped up the steps to follow inside.

Lark lay on the doctor's table, Adam unwinding the bloodied scarf from her head. Forsythia brought a bowl of warm water and a cloth, her hands trembling.

"She's still bleeding." Adam applied pressure to the wound. "Get the suturing supplies. I'll need to shave her also."

"Did the bullet get the bone?"

"I think her skull's intact. But it's a bad graze." Adam lifted the cloth, trying to wipe enough to see. Lark moaned and turned her head. "She's coming to. Laudanum."

Forsythia had the bottle in hand before he finished speaking and carefully dosed a few drops into her sister's mouth.

"What can I do?" Isaac's hands clenched and unclenched.

"Hold her head still, if you would."

Isaac stepped forward, throat filling with gratitude that he could do something. He stood by her, hands on either side of her beautiful head, holding her steady while Adam's hands wielded razor and needle, shaving away the matted hair, then stitching the edges of torn skin together as best he could. Forsythia brought lamps to light his work in the falling dusk.

At last Adam heaved a sigh and swiped the sweat from his brow with the back of his wrist. "There. Looks like that's mostly stopped the bleeding." He sponged away a few drops of blood that had seeped between the stitches.

Lark lay still, face ashen, a grayish bald patch across one side of her head in place of her flowing dark hair, the stitched gash stark across it. But she was alive. Isaac swallowed hard. That was all that mattered.

"What now?" Forsythia brought fresh warm water and began cleaning her sister's face and hands, smudged with dirt and blood.

Isaac stepped back to give her space, though he kept his hand resting on Lark's shoulder.

"We'll put her in a hospital bed and let her rest. She'll have a powerful headache when she comes to."

"But she will?" Isaac's fingers tightened on Lark's arm.

Adam hesitated, then nodded. "She's nearly roused twice, so I think so. God willing."

The door flung open, and RJ and Del burst in, followed by Lilac and Sam.

"How is she?"

"What happened?"

"Mr. Jorgensen just found me at the school. I came right away—oh, dear God." Seeing her sister lying on the table with a shaven head and bloodied dress, Lilac clapped her hands to her mouth and nearly sank. Sam caught her.

"She's alive." Forsythia hurried to take her into her arms. "Adam thinks she's going to be all right."

"It was Ringwald, wasn't it?" Lilac's voice clogged with tears. "I never should have left her. This is all my fault."

"No." RJ's voice cut through firmly. "The only person at fault here is that low-down skunk who chose to carry a grudge all these years. And you're never going to have to worry about him again. He's dead."

Isaac jerked his head to look at RJ. The man nodded.

"Did Lark kill him?" Del shifted Lily Belle in her arms, the baby looking around wide-eyed.

"We'll have to get the whole story from her, but I don't think so, didn't see her gun anywhere. Way he was lying, I'm thinking his gun went off when he fell off his horse, and with his foot caught in the stirrup, the fall broke his neck. We still need to go back out and get the body. I let his horse out in the pasture."

Del shuddered. "When I heard that gunshot from our house, my heart just stopped. I didn't know what to do: run to check on Lark or stay with Lily."

"Isaac got there first," RJ spoke up. "He already had Lark's head bound by the time I arrived. You must have rode like the wind, man."

Everyone turned to stare at Isaac. His neck heated.

"It's a mercy you did." Adam shook his head, washing his hands at the basin. "With a head wound like that, she would have been losing a lot of blood."

Lilac slipped up behind him and gave his hand a quick squeeze. "Thank you for saving my sister."

Isaac shrugged. Tried to say something but couldn't. He lowered his gaze to Lark and ran his fingers gently down her arm.

Someone was holding her hand, the pressure warm and comforting.

Lark struggled to open her eyes. A kerosene lamp burned low on a table nearby—but she wasn't in the soddy bedroom. The hospital?

"What . . . happened?" She tried to lift her head, then gasped at the pounding pain.

"Easy there, darlin'." A gentle hand pressed her shoulder. "Lie still."

Lark blinked at the face that bent over her. "Isaac?"

"I'm here." He slid to his knees by the bed, still holding her hand. "I'm not goin' anywhere."

"Did I get hit in the head with a hammer?" She raised her free hand to the throbbing place, felt a bandage.

"A bullet."

Lark stared. *Ringwald.* It all came crashing back, and she struggled to sit up despite the blinding stab in her skull. "Where are my sisters? Ringwald—"

"Ain't never gonna trouble you again." Isaac's voice came soft but firm. "Please, Miss Larkspur, you've got to lie still. Shall I call the doctor?"

Breathless from the pain, Lark let him ease her back onto the pillow, barely breathing till the pounding eased a touch. She released a long breath and closed her eyes. "Did you say Ringwald is . . . ?"

"Yes. Fell off his horse and broke his neck."

Shuddering, Lark exhaled. Relief mingled with guilt that she'd be glad at another's passing into eternity—and not a pleasant one, by her best guess. But to finally have that weight of dread lifted after carrying it all these years . . . "My family?"

"They're all just fine, exceptin' yourself. But you'll be all right too."

She lay a moment, soaking in the stillness, knowing the warm pressure of his hand still on hers, not wanting him to let go. "Where is everyone?"

"Adam's in the next room. I made him try to get some sleep. It's near on midnight now. Your sisters are at Forsythia's. I promised I'd call someone when you roused. Shall I?"

Warmth curled through her middle that he was here—that he wanted to be here. "No need yet. Let them rest. But you must need sleep too."

"I couldn't, not just now." His thumb brushed the top of her knuckles. "Though I must say, Miss Larkspur, I've had quite enough of this business of watchin' by your sickbed. Enough for a good long while." His voice came huskily, though she could tell he was trying for levity.

She turned her head a touch and blinked at him. "Forsythia said you stayed in the corner all night when I was so sick last fall. I never thanked you."

"I stayed all right." Isaac shifted on his knees.

She closed her eyes. "I dreamt then that you were by my bed . . . holding my hand, like when I woke just now. Or am I dreaming again?" What was she saying? Seemed a bullet to the head loosened her tongue, here in this midnight haze of lamplight and pain with Isaac beside her. And she wanted him to stay for always. How had it taken her so long to see that? Did it really require two near brushes with death to open her eyes? She risked a peek at Isaac to see if he found her altogether brazen.

He lifted his other hand to ever so lightly trace her jaw with his fingertip. "You weren't dreamin'. I did come sit by you a spell, but didn't think anyone knew, you least of all."

Lark reached up to press his hand to her cheek. "So you were there." Tears spilled over, wetting his hand. "I'm sorry. I just—I thought I heard you say . . ."

"That I wasn't going nowhere unless you plain ordered me

to? That I love you?" Isaac's hand tightened on hers. "I told you that before when I asked you to marry me, if you recollect, ma'am."

"You did. But I didn't believe you. At least I didn't believe you'd stay."

He nodded and inhaled through his nose. "And I deserved that, I've come to realize. The Lord's been workin' on me these last months, no mistake. But . . . what do you think now?"

Laughter bubbled up through her tears, making Lark snort in a most unladylike manner. "I think I can't get rid of you, you maddening man."

He smiled, though his gray eyes flickered. "Do you still want to?"

"Isaac McTavish." Lark sniffed hard. "I surely don't deserve you, stubborn as I am. But if you still want me . . ." Her insides trembled, but she wouldn't turn back now. Not when she'd already been given more chances than anyone had reason to expect. Not when today had brought one more reminder not to take life's gifts for granted. "I'd like to amend my previous reply to your question. If—if I may."

He stared at her. "Might be you should wait a bit, think this through. Doctor gave you some laudanum, maybe—"

"It's not the laudanum. Or the blow to the head, unless it finally knocked some sense into me to stop pushing away love when it's offered." She held his gaze. "So, please, Mr. McTavish. While we have this rare moment to ourselves, ask me again."

His fingers tightened on hers till they ached. "Larkspur Grace Nielsen, will you marry me?"

"Yes."

A short breath escaped him, something between a sigh and a sob. He bent his head, resting his forehead on her coverlet. His shoulders quivered.

"Dear man." Her own eyes full, Lark reached to lift his bearded chin, then slid her hand to the back of his neck and gently drew his head near.

He cradled her face with his hand, the warmth of his palm against her cheek.

At long last, Larkspur kissed her Isaac.

Epilogue

S ometimes it's hard to believe this is real," Lilac said.

Lark smothered the chuckle as she watched her dreamy-eyed baby sister doodling on the drawing pad in front of her. The doodle comprised of her new name-to-be, *Mrs. Samuel Gubberud*, repeated in various styles and shading.

The light from the kerosene lamp threw shadows of its own, including on Lilac's face, where happiness glowed like the lamp on the table.

Lark closed the damper on the stove and hung the dishcloth on the back of the stove. "About time we turn in for the night."

A contented sigh. "How can you always be so . . . so . . . ?" Lilac shrugged and gathered her art supplies into the bag that went everywhere she went. At least it seemed that way. "I've been thinking."

Lark paused with her hand on the doorframe. She felt her eyebrows arch and kept herself from saying, *"And what's new about that?"* At that same moment, the peeper frogs pipped up a song of spring. "Listen." The world around them seemed to be listening too, including Scamp, who waited to join them in the sleeping room.

"Ahhh." Lilac closed her eyes, the better to hear. "Now we know spring is really here, and I have an idea or more of a suggestion really. . . ."

"Well, I'm waiting with bated breath."

"I think we should have a double wedding," Lilac said in a rush. "That way we only have to prepare one giant celebration and—"

"Oh my, what a grand idea. Lilac, you're a genius."

Scamp yipped at her tone of excitement and jumped off the step.

Lark returned to the table and sat down, her smile widening. "You're sure?"

"Sure what?"

"Well, I mean some brides want their own wedding. This isn't just a financial thing, is it?"

Lilac rolled her eyes. "Lark, you're my sister. We've shared everything else. To me this makes perfect sense. After all, you're the most sensible one. I'm thinking the beginning of June, after school is out and the gardens and fields are all planted."

"Fieldwork depends on the weather, but if we're still planting, we'll take some time off. I always pictured you getting married when the lilacs are blooming. The church filled with lilacs."

Lilac stared at her sister. "You surprise me sometimes. What about your own wedding?"

Shrugging, Lark studied her hands clasped on the table. "I don't remember ever dreaming about a wedding. I thought I would be the spinster aunt and available for however I was needed." *And now there is Isaac. Thank you, Lord, I found the plan you had for me. In spite of me.* She could feel the heat coursing up to bloom on her face.

She looked up to find Lilac smiling her gentle smile. She reached over and covered Lark's hands with her own.

"We will each talk with our future husband and see what he thinks of this idea. And then the four of us can sit down with

Reverend Fordham and tell him our plan. I know Samuel's folks will want to come and . . ."

"And Isaac really has no one. We have Anders, who could give us both away." Lark thought a moment. "But who will mind the store?"

"Jonah has a friend who has helped at times. I'd hope both our brothers could be here, and Jonah might come out for haying anyway, now that he's well enough."

"True." Lark put her hand up to cover a wide yawn. "And I'm going to bed. Morning will be here before we know it."

"How can I help you today?" Isaac looked to Lark, leaning on the rail beside him. They'd been watching Robbie and Scamp out herding sheep, the lambs racing and jumping.

She turned her head to look at him, aware clear to her toes of the shoulder pressed against hers. *Help* . . . What was she going to do today again? The warmth of his shoulder drove out all rational thinking. She'd been planning on dragging the plowed fields. That's right. But the ground was too wet after two days of rain. She inhaled and puffed out a breath. "I need to sharpen the plowshare, and the team needs shoeing."

He nodded. "Let's load the plow on the wagon, and I can rightly take care of both at the smithy."

"That would be a big help. The gardens need to be dragged as soon as we can." *Ask him, ask him* kept dinging in her mind. She sucked in another breath. "Lilac had a marvelous idea the other night." She turned so she could watch his face. "She suggested we have a double wedding, and I think it's a grand idea." The words poured out like a tumbleweed driven before the wind.

"Yes."

"And we would have one big celebration instead of two and—" She braked to a stop. "Yes?"

"I think it's a fine notion. Has she mentioned it to Samuel yet?"

"You like the idea?"

"I do. And the sooner we can say I do, the happier I will be. Did you ladies decide on a day?"

"First Saturday in June." His grimace made her catch her breath. "Too soon?"

"No, not soon enough." He took her hand. "Next week would be mighty fine with me."

She blew out a breath. "We have dresses to sew, and this way Samuel will be out of school, and we should have a pastor by then."

"According to Caldwell, Reverend Paul Fordham will be arrivin' in these parts in about two weeks. His wife will come later. RJ and crew are workin' on his house right now. They had to wait to dig the cellar till after the frost left the ground."

Lark nodded, grateful her heart had settled back to where it belonged. "So for today let's push the plow and extra shares up in the wagon and hitch up Nell and Prince. If you want to take care of that, I have so much else to do here. Robbie and I will divide up cleaning out the chicken coop and spreading last year's aged manure out on the garden."

Isaac left with the wagon, and Robbie skidded to a stop beside her. "Doing the chicken coop now?"

"Which would you rather do, that or the garden?"

"I'd rather be outside."

Lark nodded. That was where she would rather be too, but she'd let him choose.

By the time Del clanged the dinner bell, they were both ready for a break. *Good thing Isaac made me another wheelbarrow,* Lark thought as she stopped at the bench to wash. The brisk spring breeze dried the sweat she'd worked up in the chicken coop, making her shiver.

"Fried bread!" Robbie shouted as they sat down at the table. "You are the very best."

Del set bowls of venison soup on the table and held her finger to her mouth, but it was too late. A wail came from the crib in the bedroom.

Robbie flinched. "I'm sorry."

Del rolled her eyes. "I should have warned you. You both go ahead and eat. I'll see if I can get her back to sleep."

Lark and Robbie finished and headed out the door to keep shoveling and forking. With the chicken coop cleaned out, Lark helped Robbie to spread another load on the garden when Scamp announced family was coming. He had a special bark for them.

Isaac, Lilac, and Samuel shared the wagon seat, with RJ trotting beside them on Captain.

I hope Del has plenty for supper because I've not been in the house long enough to even think about food. Lark waved and fetched the milking pails out of the well house. Together, she and Isaac finished all the chores, including skimming the cream off the pans in the well house, and filling the churn to carry to the soddy, while Lilac and Sam helped Del with supper. What a gift to have this man to work alongside.

After supper and the dishes were done, Del shooed them to the parlor. "RJ and I will bring in dessert in a bit."

Lark raised an eyebrow at Lilac, and she answered with a nod and a grin. Time to discuss their plans. The four of them sat down and silence stretched. "So . . ."

"Lilac asked me what I thought of a double wedding," Sam started, "and the only question I have is, Why do we have to wait so long?"

Isaac snorted a laugh, and Lark shook her head. "So we all agree? June fifth. Reverend Fordham will be here, and—"

"And I will design our wedding dresses, and we'll sew them in our spare time."

Del brought gingerbread cake in, Robbie carried the applesauce, and RJ filled the coffee cups. As they discussed the wedding plans, Lark snuck her hand around Isaac's arm, reveling in the tingles that ran up her own. *Thank you, Father God* filled her mind. She and Isaac were going to be married. He cupped his other hand over hers, and the smile he sent her made her warm all over.

The last Sunday in April marked the Rev. Paul Fordham's first official service as Salton's pastor, after the unanimous vote of approval last month.

"Thank you." A gentle smile on the older man's face brought return smiles as the congregation settled down. "I thought today instead of a sermon, I would tell you about myself. First of all, I am so grateful you wanted me to come. My wife and I look at this as our Western adventure. We were wondering what God had planned for us now that our children are grown and out on their own, and He brought your letter to me. I was impressed when I visited here, partly because you made me feel so at home and partly by what you did in your time with no pastor. Such a creative idea, honoring each other and the lives He has given you."

He went on to share his story and closed the service with his arm raised in benediction. A spring breeze wafted in as he stood at the door, greeting everyone. Lark and Lilac waited till the last. Isaac and Samuel came to stand beside them.

"Have you ever officiated at a double wedding?" Lark asked.

Rev. Fordham smiled at each of them. "Funny you should ask. I have indeed. A pair of identical twin sisters marrying two men who were cousins. Ah, the stories I could tell. I take it the four of you would like one wedding?"

They all nodded.

"And have you set a date?"

"June fifth."

"Ah, just five weeks away. Well, we know my calendar is clear. I'm not sure if my wife will be here yet." He smiled and tipped his shiny-topped head slightly to the side. "I would like to have a meeting with each couple sometime before then, and the night before the wedding we would have supper together and go through a practice run." He looked each of them in the eyes. "Any questions?"

"Where would you like to meet?" Samuel asked.

"Right here in church would be fine."

"You are going with us to dinner at Adam and Forsythia's house now, aren't you?" Lark asked.

He nodded. "If you'll bank the stove, I'll get my coat. I take it we don't lock the building since no one has given me keys?"

While the men closed things up, Lark and Lilac smiled at each other. "I really like him," Lark said softly.

"Me too, me too."

May flew by with the gardening and fieldwork and sewing dresses, which Del did the most of so she could be indoors with Lily. Del put the final stitches in the hem of Lark's gown the night before the wedding.

When the rooster crowed on Saturday morning, both Lilac and Lark sat straight up in bed.

"Today's the day." Wonderment made Lark's words sparkle.

Lilac giggled. "I thought I'd be awake all night." She yawned and stretched both arms straight above her head before wrapping them around herself in a hug. She paused. "Who's out there?"

"I imagine Robbie and RJ are doing the chores. They said they would, and only one cow to milk instead of two makes it easier."

"Lark, Lilac, come see!" Robbie shouted from outside.

"Coming!" They threw shawls around their nightdresses, shoved their feet into boots, and charged out the door. "Where are you?"

"In the barn. Hurry!"

"Oh, Lord, now what?" They ran to the barn and puffed their way inside.

"Over here." RJ leaned on the half wall of the stall. They joined him, and Lark chuckled.

"Well, Clover, thank you for the wedding present."

Robbie grinned at them in the dimness. "We got a heifer, and she stood up just a few minutes ago."

"Looks to be a pretty smart little girl since she is already nursing."

The calf's tail switched from side to side, metronome style.

"I better let the others in." RJ went to open the rear door where Buttercup was mooing her impatience.

Lark and Lilac locked arms and returned to the house to get dressed. "What a wonderful way to start our wedding day. A double wedding is such a grand idea, Lilac. Thank you for thinking of it."

They had breakfast at Del's with Anders and Jonah, since they were staying there, while RJ and Robbie finished the chores.

"Let's take our coffee outside," Del suggested, jiggling Lily on her hip. "Such a perfect June morning. A perfect day for a wedding, er, two weddings."

"One wedding, two marriages." Lark took a sip of her coffee. "Thank you, Anders and Jonah, for making that long trip again. Whoever dreamed this is why you'd be doing it?"

"My privilege. It's hard to believe all that has gone on. God most certainly has been taking care of all of us. And Jonah is now the only single one." He elbowed their younger brother.

"I have a feeling that Tilda would like to change that situation." Lark grinned as Jonah's ears turned red behind his coffee cup. "You should have seen the joy on her face when she told me you'd written to her. Are you still serious about wanting to homestead?"

Jonah nodded. "I'm afraid there's nothing left around here though. I have to keep reminding myself to trust that God will provide."

"I hate to break up this time together, but one o'clock will be here before we know it." RJ looked to his wife. "Everything ready from here?"

"Just need to load up the wagons. The food can go in one, the brides in our buggy, and everything else in the other. Robbie, you need to scrub up from doing chores."

"I'll check on our new baby first." He ran the path to the sod house and the barn, Scamp barking along with him.

"Oh, to have his energy." Lark paused. "Oh, listen." She smiled at Lilac. "Your favorite music, the songs of the meadowlarks."

"Giving us an extra blessing on today. You know, I'm just sorry for one thing, that Samuel's parents couldn't come after all."

"But the two of you are going back to see them."

"I know, but he really wanted them to see what his new life is like." Lilac rose from her chair. "Let's get moving."

The brides dressed at Forsythia's house. While the design was the same, one dress was the purple of lilacs and the other the blue of a spring sky. White lace edged the scooped necklines, the cuffs of the three-quarter length sleeves, and the front of the bodices.

Forsythia carefully pinned Lark's hair in swirls to cover the area where her hair was still growing in after being shaved.

"You both look so beautiful." Climie watched from the side, swaying with a new mother's rhythm as her baby boy squirmed against her shoulder.

"Only a year since we were gathered for your wedding. And look at you now." Lilac hugged their friend and brushed a kiss onto the baby's tiny head. Little William Jesse Brownsville, Willie for short, had made his appearance three weeks ago after a long labor that ended in much joy. Climie's arms were empty no longer.

They walked the short distance to the church, carefully holding their skirts up to keep the hems from dragging in the dirt. Anders accompanied them and assisted them up the three wide front steps. They both inhaled lilac perfume when their brother held the right side of the double doors open. The sisters grinned at each other. Most of the lilacs were done blooming, so where had Sythia and the others found these?

"Oooh." Lilac stopped in the doorway to the sanctuary. Bouquets of lilacs graced the altar, and on a table to the side waited two small bouquets for the brides with bows made from the leftover fabric of their dresses.

"You better go into that room." Anders motioned to the small room off to the side. "I hear people coming."

In a few minutes, a knock on the door announced Rev. Fordham. "May I come in?"

"Of course."

"You both look lovely. Sure can tell you are sisters."

"Thank you." The two spoke as one, making them laugh again.

"I came to pray with you, then I'll do the same for the men." At their nods, he clasped hands with them. "Our gracious and loving Father in heaven, bless this day with your love and joy as these young people unite in holy matrimony. Fill our hearts so your love washes over all who come to celebrate with them. Guide and guard their hearts as we all draw closer to you. In the precious name of Jesus, amen." He squeezed their hands. "See you at the altar."

Mrs. Caldwell at the piano, Forsythia with her violin, and Bridget O'Rourke on her dulcimer welcomed the guests with music that rippled like a stream over rocks. Another knock and Del stuck her head in the door. "Do you need anything?"

"For this to get started before we get any shakier?"

"Well, there is a crowd. Already standing room only."

Lark sucked in a deep breath. Why was she getting nervous? These weren't strangers but relatives and friends. She shared a look with Lilac. "How come I'm shaking and you're not?"

"I am inside."

The music softened, and Rev. Fordham greeted the guests. Anders opened the door and stepped inside. "Are you ready?"

They both nodded. "Then here we go." He ushered them out the door, and with a sister on each arm, they waited. Mrs. Caldwell nodded. The music changed, and everyone stood.

Floating on lilac perfume, the three of them paced down the aisle to join the waiting men.

Isaac shimmered through Lark's tears. He took her hand, and they turned to face the altar.

"Dearly beloved, we are gathered here together to share in the joining of Isaac Joseph McTavish with Larkspur Grace Nielsen and Samuel Jakob Gubberud with Lilac Patience Nielsen. Let us pray. Heavenly Father, thank you that you are right here with us and for your blessings shining down on all of us, but especially these four young people. We praise you and thank you for this privilege, amen."

A loud "Amen!" came from the Brownsville chairs.

"Sofie, come back." Robbie had his older brother voice on.

Trying not to laugh, Lark felt a small hand tug on her skirt. She glanced down to see Sofie with one hand on each of the brides' skirts, her smile beaming up.

As they took turns with the vows, Lark felt herself drowning in the love shining in Isaac's eyes. To think she'd doubted for so long. When Forsythia sang "Come Thou Fount of Every Blessing" accompanied by Del, her joy leaked down her cheek. *Oh, Lord, thank you for this man and your plan for us.*

When Rev. Fordham declared them husbands and wives, the kiss she and Isaac shared filled her heart with promise. Robbie fetched his sister, and they turned to face the congregation as Rev. Fordham pronounced the benediction. Lark and Lilac both hugged Sofie, and Robbie gravely shook hands with both the grooms.

Mr. and Mrs. Sam Gubberud joined Mr. and Mrs. Isaac McTavish at the door, where they greeted all the guests as they filed past.

"'Bout time." George Hoffman looked Isaac in the eye. "Two of the most stubborn people I ever knowed."

"Really? Hmm." Isaac's grin with an arched eyebrow made them all laugh.

William stepped up to give his congratulations, his arm around a slender boy who looked about twelve.

Lark's jaw dropped. "William, is this . . . ?"

The grin on William's face spoke volumes. "Meet my brother, Ben."

Isaac offered his hand. "We're mighty proud to meet you, son."

Lark hugged the lad. Tears in her eyes matched those shining in William's. *Finally*. What an extra beautiful gift for this day.

As the sun sank toward the horizon, those with chores headed out, and Lark and Lilac made sure to thank them all.

"You sure have a mighty big family here," Samuel said, his arm around Lilac's shoulders. "If someone had tried to describe this to me, I wouldn't have believed them."

"We are indeed blessed beyond measure, as Rev. Fordham said." Isaac tucked Lark's arm through his.

She leaned her head against his shoulder. Whoever dreamed when they fled from Ohio and landed here in Salton that all this could have happened in four years. Land of their own, a budding business to fulfill their mother's dream, five growing families, a railroad that made contact easier between them . . . It would take pages to write all their blessings down. Just this week a woman had shown up in Jorgensens' store inquiring about "those Leah's Garden seeds," one of their catalogs in hand.

Her mother's advice echoed as if she stood right beside them. *"Remember to thank Him for everything."* To think all this had been in His plan for them.

Remember. Remember. Remember.

Lauraine Snelling is the award-winning author of nearly one hundred books, fiction and nonfiction, for adults and young adults. Her books have sold more than five million copies. Besides writing books and articles, she teaches at writers' conferences across the country. She and her husband make their home in Tehachapi, California. Learn more at laurainesnelling.com.

Kiersti Giron grew up loving Lauraine's books and had the blessing of being mentored by her as a young writer. Now it is her joy and honor to collaborate with Lauraine on this new series. Kiersti has a passion for history and storytelling and loves writing about reconciliation, healing, and God's story weaving into ours. She lives in California with her husband and their lively young son. Learn more at kierstigiron.com.

Sign Up for Lauraine's Newsletter

Keep up to date with Lauraine's latest news on book releases and events by signing up for her email list at the link below.

FOLLOW LAURAINE ON SOCIAL MEDIA

Lauraine Snelling Author

LauraineSnelling.com

More from Lauraine Snelling

After turning the tables on a crooked gambler, Larkspur Nielsen flees her home with her sisters on a wagon train bound for Oregon. Knowing four women will draw unwanted attention, she dons a disguise as a man. But maintaining the ruse is harder than she imagined, as is protecting her sisters from difficult circumstances and eligible young men.

The Seeds of Change
LEAH'S GARDEN #1

Del Nielsen's teaching job in town offers hope, not only to support her three sisters but also to better her students' lives. When their brother visits with his war-wounded friend RJ, Del finds RJ barely polite and wants nothing to do with him. But despite the sisters' best-laid plans, the future—and RJ—might surprise them all.

A Time to Bloom
LEAH'S GARDEN #2

Lilac Nielsen must learn to balance her new courtship with the young reverend and her pursuit of another dream—the publication of her artwork in a New York newspaper. But when a family crisis back in Ohio shakes the Nielsen sisters, can they continue the new life they've begun in Nebraska? And will Lilac be prepared for what God has in store for her future?

Fields of Bounty
LEAH'S GARDEN #3

BETHANYHOUSE